'Sinfully delicious - completely unputdownable. Be prepared to stay up late!'

Louise Bagshawe, author of *Venus Envy*

'A savvy romance with an unforgettable heroine, *Only My Dreams* is a story that kickstarts the heart. Anna Blundy has written a touching, often humorous novel with contemporary characters and a plot that moves between England and Russia with ease and perception. Reading it is a dream in itself.'

Cindy Blake, author of *It's My Party*



Anna Blundy was born in 1970 and went to City of London School for Girls and Westminster School before reading Russian at University College, Oxford. She has lived in Russia three times – as a translator, a blues singer and then as Moscow correspondent for *The Times*. *Every Time We Say Goodbye*, Anna's memoir of her father, the foreign correspondent David Blundy, was published in 1998 to great critical acclaim. *Only My Dreams* is her first novel.

She now lives in London with her husband, Horatio, and their two children, Lev and Hope.

*Also by Anna Blundy*

Every Time We Say Goodbye

# ONLY MY DREAMS

Anna Blundy

ARROW

Published in the United Kingdom in 2000 by
Arrow Books

3 5 7 9 10 8 6 4 2



Arrow Books Limited
The Random House Group Ltd
20 Vauxhall Bridge Road, London SW1V 2SA

Random House Australia (Pty) Limited
20 Alfred Street, Milsons Point, Sydney,
New South Wales 2061, Australia

Random House New Zealand Limited
18 Poland Road, Glenfield
Auckland 10, New Zealand

Random House (Pty) Limited
Endulini, 5a Jubilee Road, Parktown 2193, South Africa

The Random House Group Ltd Reg. No. 954009

www.randomhouse.co.uk

A CIP catalogue record for this book
is available from the British Library

Papers used by Random House UK are natural,
recyclable products made from wood grown in
sustainable forests. The manufacturing processes conform to
the environmental regulations of the country of origin

Typeset by SX Composing DTP, Rayleigh, Essex
Printed and bound in Great Britain by
Bookmarque, Croydon, Surrey

ISBN 0 09 941527 5

For Grace

And with love and thanks to
Olga Shevtsova

# ONE

At first she tried to pretend she couldn't find it. The light was yellowing to darkness outside and the snow was coming in fat lazy flakes. She beetled about her tiny flat, slippers flapping at the soles of her feet and dangly earrings bobbing by her powdery cheeks.

I was desperate to get back to the hotel. I wanted to call Zander, and by now even a plate of smoked fish on stale bread and a shot of vodka seemed vaguely inviting.

'So it was a present to your grandmother, was it?' I asked for the fourteenth time, unwrapping the disgusting sweet she had forced upon me as slowly as I could in the hope that I could abandon the thing in awe when she produced the egg.

'From her lover. He was one of the soldiers who had to pack up the stuff from the Anichkov Palace and haul it off to the Kremlin in 1917. He couldn't resist!' Mrs Shevtsova laughed. She coughed some gravel back down her throat and stubbed out her evil-smelling Belamor Canal cigarette. 'Aha,' she croaked.

Thank God, I thought, swivelling my rings and looking out at the snow. I could see her dragging a tatty cardboard box from the bottom of her bedroom wardrobe. She carried it back into the living room with two hands, as though it were very heavy, and put it down on the smoked-glass coffee table. She drew out a scuffed leather ice skate with a rusting blade, leaving its pair nestled inside the box. Shoving her hand into the toe, she at last produced a perfect Fabergé egg, glittering white and gold in the dim light, its thousands of diamonds seeming to illuminate the whole dismal apartment. I smiled, more at it than at her and reached out. Tears streaming down her old face now, she kissed the egg and handed it over, glancing only briefly at the fat envelope on the table next to her skate box.

'It was a great honour to meet you, Mrs Shevtsova,' I said, pulling my fur hat on and pushing my hands down into my pockets. 'Thank you.'

Mrs Shevtsova nodded in acknowledgement and raised a hand to me as I stepped into the dark lift, the buttons all melted by a teenager's lighter, and the bulb flickering grey in the metal gloom. I shut my eyes and clasped my fingers round the perfect shape of Zander's new egg.

The driver was waiting where I had left him, slumped in his ancient Zhiguli, reading the small ads and smoking, oblivious to the overwhelming stench of cheap petrol and the fact that his windscreen was now covered by three inches of snow. The wipers making visibility ever so slightly worse, we skidded in the dark up the long path that would lead us out of the soulless grey estate of tower blocks that seemed to surround Simbirsk – known for the last sixty or so years as Ulyanovsk, Lenin's birth town. Although the place is an uninspiring Soviet thing on the Volga river, it is actually a bit less of a scum hole than other similar places, purely thanks to Lenin's cult of personality. For seventy years Ulyanovsk has been a site of pilgrimage for all Soviet people and is therefore relatively clean and well kept. Though now, of course, its museums and monuments to Vladimir Ilyich are completely deserted apart from the crones who tend them.

Back at my empty twenty-nine-storey hotel the woman who spied on all the guests on our floor gave me a glass of tea out of the electric silver samovar and pulled a plate of ageing fish and bread out of the chugging fridge. Obviously her vigilance was by now entirely redundant but she was used to it and couldn't think what else to do. I bought a bottle of vodka from her (although as a matter of course she denied having any until I got five dollars out of my wallet) and went back to my room to wait for the call from Zander to come through.

I put the egg down on the empty smaller-than-single bed and sat myself creakily on the other one to eat, drink and look at my prize. I swigged the vodka and chased it with tea and fish until I was warm. The phone rang.

'Call to England. Please speak now.'

'Hello? Hello? Fizzy?' I could hear Zander saying over the operator's voice. The way Zander said Fizzy never failed to remind me what an idiot I was. I wished I had chosen a more mature-sounding label. Or, ideally, that I had been secure enough to keep my name just as it was. Zander managed to inject it with more ludicrousness than anyone else ever had. Fizzy.

'Hi. Hi. It's me. I'm in Simbirsk.'

'Yeah, and?' he asked.

'And I'm fine, my only darling. You mustn't worry,' I laughed. Two years into our relationship, if that's what it was, and he still cared more about the job than about me.

'Come on, sweetheart. Not funny. Yes or no?'

'Yes.'

'I love you. You're gorgeous. Me and you Fizz – we wouldn't be alive without each other. You're my princess. I could fuck you senseless.'

'Promise?'

'As soon as you get back.'

'My train to Moscow's at midnight so I'll see you in London tomorrow. OK?'

'Got a hard-on just thinking about it. Far left-hand customs queue. Sergei will be waiting,' said Zander, and hung up.

Well, I wasn't terribly keen on the way he talked, but the way he did other things more than made up for it. At least I thought it did. It used to. Though lately it had all been taking a turn for the uncomfortable. I was beginning to suspect that his tone was not, in fact, quite as irony-laden as I had always hoped.

I whiled away the rest of my time in Simbirsk in

the hotel restaurant, drinking beer and watching a man in an old shiny black suit and frilly nylon shirt playing Lionel Ritchie covers on a battered synthesiser in front of red, orange and blue disco lights. The restaurant could have seated three hundred, but it was just me, a few middle-aged and over-made-up waitresses, and a table full of local gangsters, two of whom had passed out with their shaven and scarred heads slumped on to the table, their mobile phones still clutched in their fat hands.

The only thing available from the menu was 'julienne', which is mushrooms baked in cheese, sour cream and cheap oil. I ate it with some stale-ish black bread and stared out through the smoked glass at the snow. I had done it.

Standing on the station platform at eleven thirty, blinded by a blizzard and almost paralysed by cold, I grinned to myself at my success. So often they didn't have what they said they had, or by the time I got to them they had sold it elsewhere for less, not believing I would come. And this was our first Fabergé egg. The Alexander III.

It disappeared along with seven others when the Communists looted all the Imperial palaces and took everything of value to Moscow, where most of it is now displayed in the Armoury. But things had been uncertain in those days. Life was precarious, the people were poor and all respect for the law belonged to the past and future. Basically, a lot of stuff went missing.

Fabergé himself presented his eggs to the

Imperial ladies every year on Good Friday, in later life enlisting the help of his son to give an egg to the Dowager Empress while he was busy with the Tsar.

It was the last Tsar, Nicholas II, who passed the Alexander III egg on to his mother, Maria Fedorovna on 28 March 1909 – Easter Sunday. It was kept at the Anichkov Palace outside St Petersburg along with the other nine she received before the Revolution came and swept away all thought of eggs and empresses. But after the royals had been murdered and the palaces sealed by the Communists the egg was never seen again, and it never appeared on any of the inventories of Imperial wealth.

I had seen it, though. It was in my pocket. Nothing obscure about why it might have been stolen – just a glance at it was enough to make you feel that whoever had it in their possession was, on parting with it, going to have a pretty good life. Most of it was in a kind of white enamel with gold stripes and strings of leaf-shaped rose-cut diamonds set in platinum.

When I had called the Archduke Dr Lupus von Freisburg, the world's leading Fabergé expert, from London to ask lots of disingenuous questions about what the egg should look like (I pretended I was writing a thesis), he told me there were 3,467 rose-cut diamonds on it in total.

There were huge diamonds at both ends of it as well, making me feel conspicuous and guilty, and it was supported on a kind of upside-down heart-shaped frame. When I had opened the egg back at the hotel I saw a tiny gold bust of Alexander III, the Dowager Empress's father, on a deep blue lapis lazuli stand.

The egg might only have cost 11,200 roubles to make at the time (actually that was a lot then), but it was worth millions now.

Irritatingly, the two Chechen blokes standing next to me on the platform seemed to think I was smiling at them. Dark eyes flashing and cigarette ends glowing in swarthy ungloved fingers, one of them leered and asked me my name.

'Svyeta,' I lied, not wanting to be obviously foreign. I was always nervous at this stage – the victory almost mine, but the precarious journey home still to come. For this, really, was the dangerous bit, the bit that required a large element of risk.

I was saved from certain lechery by the carriage lady appearing from within the orange warmth behind her heavy dark green door to say we could now board the big comforting Moscow train. It smelt of tea and clean linen and I had both beds of a first-class cabin to myself. I have always loved moving through the Russian countryside, imagining the cold and the wolves and the endless forests outside, while I lie comfortable and hot, reading, drinking tea and being rocked to sleep by the train. I put my wet boots under the bed, took off my snowy clothes and slumped down in jeans, T-shirt and socks for the sixteen-hour trundle back to civilisation.

I was dying for tea and irritated that the woman had taken so long, so I was relieved by the eventual knock at my compartment door. I twisted open the big steel lock and was punched hard in the face by one of the Chechens from the platform. I felt a tooth crack at the back of my mouth. Hideously, there was something about this that did not surprise me as much as it should have done. I had not hidden the egg well, and in any case it was clear that the Chechens weren't too shy to torture it out of me. Both men bundled themselves through the door, slid it shut and locked it behind them.

I had been knocked backwards and was half lying on one of the beds wishing I could scream. I had read about the kind of fear that obliterates every aspect of a person apart from a blind and speechless, deaf and motionless will to survive. This was it. The thug with the greater number of gold teeth and the breath that smelt of vodka and cheap salami drew a knife out of the pocket of his black leather jacket and leapt on top of me, straddling me, the knife to my throat, his groin pressing on mine. He didn't speak. I couldn't breathe. I thought my heart would give out. I couldn't understand why no noise was coming from my mouth and no movement from my body.

'So. You are Zander Sinclair's?' said the one standing up, in his heavily accented Russian. 'Are you?' The bloke kneeling over me drew the knife away and hit me round the head. I didn't feel it.

'Do you know Zander Sinclair?' asked the first one again.

I tried to nod without getting cut by the blade back at my neck.

'He murdered our sister. Tell him hi from us,' he said, and unlocked the door to leave. His brother climbed off me and followed him out.

What fucking sister? Didn't they even want the bloody egg?

Gasping and choking now I tried to stand up but fell backwards again at the sight, in the mirror opposite, of the blood that was pouring out of my face. I had been slashed from the corner of my eye to my mouth. I fell down again in shock as the pain began to sear through me. I held a pillow to my cheek and crouched shivering in my compartment.

Pathetically, I did what I always did when something went wrong. And something had, undeniably, gone horribly wrong. I thought of Cassian Vinci and what my life might have been like. Cassian, who could have softened me, who could have taken me into his world of cricket whites and Pimm's, and made me safe. I only needed to say his name to myself and I could slip back into the body of a fifteen-year-old, smoking a joint in the overgrown grass of an English lawn, tanned from an idle summer in a perfect garden under buzzing bees and a sweltering sun. I could feel his breathing next to mine, the casual stroke of his arm as he turned his page, a squinting smile as he threw me a lighter, a mischievous grin as he wriggled his hands under my top.

Eight or nine hours later, when a yellowy-grey

dawn rose over the industrial countryside, the people we passed, standing grimly in their fur hats on the snowy platforms, could see me through the window and I felt forced to regain active consciousness.

The awful thing wasn't my face, which, when the bleeding stopped, looked more like a long scratch than a gash, but that I sort of believed the brothers. Before the Chechens or the egg, I had thought of Zander as a kind of comedy villain, a nice guy with a nasty streak. His simmering brutality made him exciting, dangerous. When he first touched me in the shadows of the party from hell the force of him had thrilled me. But now I realised I had always slightly suspected him of more. That I believed these thugs so readily – not just believed them but knew that they were telling the truth – showed me the extent to which I had been deceiving myself. The violence that had seemed in some way compelling had lately been creeping out of the theoretical and into the actual. He hadn't hit me or anything, but the rough sex that had once been playful and exhausting was beginning to slip over into something that was almost frightening.

I wasn't proud of my relationship with Zander. I knew it was a terrible low-life thing to be doing. I also knew that at some stage I was going to have to tell Tara I was sleeping with her father.

The feeling of the egg against my stomach gave me no comfort as I made my way now through the steaming crowds, out to the slush, the noise and the taxis, glancing constantly over my shoulder for the

Chechens, flinching in horror at every dark head that rushed past me, my hand to my stinging cheek. I needed to decide who to talk to first when I got home. Speeding through the Moscow traffic, looking out at the dim streetlights blurring into one another in the snow, I thought of Hermione.

# Two

I had known Zander for seventeen years – since before I was Fizz to anyone but my mum, since before I had ever been to a stately home or to Russia. When I first saw him I was Alice Reynolds. But I had plans to be someone else.

Me and my Mum lived above a record shop on Clapham High Street, behind dirty net curtains that did little to conceal the suburban gloom of the decaying high street outside. We were next to the chip shop and opposite the pub. The pub jukebox played late into the night and Blondie songs entangled themselves in my dreams.

I think Mum was depressed. She used to say she was going to be a famous sculptor. Dad was always taking her off for weekends in Marxist communes, where they would sculpt and write poetry and Dad would do his own translations of Vladimir Mayakovsky's verse. But when he died she lost all the hope and sparkle she had once had. The sparkle that seemed to me to characterise my childhood – the idyll before the abyss.

One Christmas morning Dad crept in and laid a pink crepe-covered wand on my pillow. It had silver foil stars hanging off it on streamers of pink ribbon.When I woke up he was sitting on the edge of my bed and he told me he would like to have given me the world. 'But I, being poor, have only my dreams,' he grinned apologetically. The wand, he promised, would make all his dreams for me come true. When they took him away in the ambulance I worried I hadn't wished hard enough.

Nowadays Mum seemed to have resigned herself to being a supply pottery teacher at St Joseph's. The kids had twice pissed in her handbag when she wasn't looking, and almost every week the contents of the kiln got smashed up and Mum came home red-faced and snivelling. I hated those evenings. She would slump in front of the telly and wait for Martin to come round with some cans of beer or for Lorry to come round with hash. I preferred Lorry. He made Mum laugh and he brought me sugar cane and called me Princess.

Ideally, I liked to be addressed as 'Your Royal Highness'. I was born determined to get out of there. I refused to drink out of anything other than a tall sundae glass – my princess cup – and I made my room a haven of gentility and grace. Everything was pink. My curtains, duvet, wallpaper and lampshade. I had a big dressing-up box of pink clothes I made Mum buy from jumble sales and I dressed all my dolls and teddies in outfits appropriate to my station.

The walls were covered with pictures that showed what I thought the world should be like, wished the world would be like. There were fairies with butterfly wings resting gently on rose petals, girls in pink taffeta ballgowns flushed with innocence and excitement stepping out of horse-drawn carriages. There were brides in explosions of white lace and daisies standing serene with their bridesmaids, and princesses in long gloves, diamonds and stiff petticoats making their way on to sparkling dance floors.

This, of course, was in glaring contrast to the scene in the sitting room. I seemed to spend my whole time emptying overflowing ashtrays, sponging over hash burns in the carpet and listening to Mum going on about how her next piece was going to make her famous. She would loll there on the cushions, smoking giggling spliffs with Lorry and trying to get me to join in their spastic conversations.

'Once, right, we were at Glastonbury and Hamish was so stoned that he went out for a wazz and lost our tent,' Lorry would say (quite often). 'He was like naked and covered in mud . . .' he managed to croak before they were both laughing so much they choked.

'Imagine that, Fizzy,' Mum coughed, cackling into her beer glass.

I remained on the sofa, feeding myself dripping slices of pizza by holding them high above my head like grapes to a Roman emperor, and I smiled superciliously over at them.

I didn't care. I was at Whyteleafe, swinging my hockey stick, skipping across the cobblestones in the dappled light of a summer evening, eating midnight feasts with my chums, laughing with twinkly-eyed rosy-cheeked boys in cricket whites and essentially preparing myself for the day when a prince would fall in love with me at a ball and waltz me away to his castle. There, his strong arms clasped about me, he would propose and I would be happy for ever. 'Stephie, Stephie, remember that time when we had those Thai buds, man?' I could hear Lorry saying through the fog of my fantasies.

Mum seemed to have parties every weekend. I loathed the parties. Now I can see she was lonely – a single mother and starting to feel old. Margaret Thatcher was about to get elected and everything Mum stood for would be over for twenty years; she was making the best of the time remaining to her. Then, however, I just wished they would all die. I wanted my dad back. I wanted to wave my magic wand and make them disappear.

So Mum would hang up pieces of tie-dyed material, purple, orange and red, over the windows and put heavy pyramid-shaped candles all over the place with joss sticks poked into the sides of them. The Rolling Stones crackled from ancient speakers and people drank beer, sweet warm wine and gin out of plastic party cups. Men who were five years too old to have long hair or wear tight trousers leant thinly against the kitchen table rolling joints and scratching at their sparse blond beards. Women in wraparound skirts and wooden beads, their unsupported breasts sagging against their shabby

T-shirts, sat cross-legged on the floor, talking about the genius of Bob Dylan and how they were just about to move to a caravan in Devon to make jewellery out of horseshoe nails.

Now, of course, all those evenings have merged into one for me. The one when everything changed.

I was ten, and I was lying on my bed wrapped up in a huge piece of pink satin. Underneath I was wearing dungarees and a Brotherhood of Man T-shirt and I was reading *Jane Eyre*. One day, I thought, someone will recognise me, just as Mr Rochester recognised Jane. I believed it too.

But suddenly, to my horror, I needed to go to the loo. On party nights I tried not to drink any liquids at all after midday in order to avoid situations of this kind. I put chairs up against my door in case anyone thought of rolling in, and briefed all my toys on what to do if they tried.

Peering round into the reddish light I could see a few people slouching languorously against the corridor walls. 'I mean, who's to say what is a dream and what's real?' asked a bloke in a ganga-leaf T-shirt. It seemed safe enough. I crept along unnoticed to the loo and listened at the door. Once I had walked in on Martin being sick. This time there were muffled squeals seeping through the wood at me and I set off back to my room, wriggling to stave off the need to wee. That was when I got caught.

'Fizzy! Fizzy darling, how the hell is school?' asked my mum's oldest friend from art college, Kris with the big earrings.

'Tolerable, thank you,' I replied, waddling away.

'Oh, good for you, good for you, sweetie,' she dribbled drunkenly. 'God knows mine wasn't. Bloody hockey every Tuesday, lax every Wednesday, stupid fucking uniform. I thought I was going to die in there without a shag . . .' she told the smiley yellow face in a 'Nuclear Power No Thanks' poster – I span back round to face her, Barbie in hand, frozen with expectation. Kris had forgotten about me, but she had my full attention.

This was my first inkling that the books I loved might not be the wild flight of someone else's fantasy, but instead gritty documentary fact. What she had said, so idly, so drunkenly, made me hope for the first time that the life I longed for was available to be lived.

'Kris, Kris! Did you, did you really play lacrosse?' I screeched, my stomach fluttering with delight.

Focusing on me with difficulty, Kris stared through the smoke and pulled at the pendulous fish in her ear. 'Mmm. Yeah. Awful. Daddy said he'd horsewhip me if I didn't go to Queensbury. Bastard would have, as well. Got a scholarship in the end so he didn't have to pay a penny . . . Fat lot of good it did me . . . Queensbury Fucking School for Bloody Girls . . . prisoner in that place, I was. Seven years . . . bloody balls, bloody chapel . . .'

By now Kris was sobbing. I, on the other hand, was grinning with ecstatic realisation – until Kris collapsed unconscious on the floor in front of me and I had to pick up her joint. I didn't even care about the new hole in the carpet and I put the roach in the dregs of an abandoned cup of beer. I hoped someone would drink out of it.

In the end though Kris lent me a white shirt to wear to the interview, and she even drove me and Mum up there in her old blue Morris Minor van. The event was the result of six months of sustained whining and pleading on my part. I promised to look up from my book every time anyone addressed me directly. I swore I wouldn't sneer at Mum's friends. I vowed I would always do well and never be in trouble and that I would go to university and get a well-paid job and support Mum in her old age. I lied on every count.

I wrote off to the school myself, asking, in a ten-year-old's fat circular writing, for information about Queensbury. Within days I got the second most exciting letter of my life – a huge envelope containing a breathtakingly glossy brochure full of pictures of happy girls in green skirts peering into microscopes and holding glass test tubes over Bunsen burners, their thick protective glasses distorting their faces. They leapt through the air towards netball hoops, glided impressively through turquoise water in goggles and red rubber hats and sat studiously in libraries, poring over ancient tomes, pencils in hands. I longed to be one of them.

I immediately filled in the application form and slapped it in front of Mum to sign the moment she got home, her hair straggly, her bag hanging wearily from her shoulder. She thumbed through the brochure, flipping straight to the price list at the back and snorted in horror.

'Sorry, sweetie,' she said with a sigh, ambling over to the fridge to see if there were any beers.

In the end, though, I persuaded her to let me try for the scholarship. If I got it – no skin off her nose. If I didn't – I would shut up about it for ever. I knew perfectly well I had to get it. This was my one chance to get out of Clapham and away from the flat of hippie death.

I stood by her when she phoned the admissions people to ask for the scholarship application forms and I barely slept until they came. I practised filling the boxes in on rough paper so I didn't have to use any Tippex on the thick cream card, shiny enough to make your pen slip (Mum wouldn't have anything more to do with it than absolutely necessary – she was against private education).

On the morning of the exams I was sick with fear. I had hardly eaten for days and I sploshed the spoon around in my Puffa Puffa Rice, stirring until they were soggy in the hope that my butterflies would go away. Mum said I should have tea with sugar in to calm my nerves, but the thought of the sweetness sent me off to the loo to pace about and fail to throw up. I clung hysterically to my wand, getting dressed without letting it out of my clammy hand, dragging it through the sleeves of Kris's white school shirt.

Kris wouldn't even come through the Queensbury gates, so Mum sat on the lawn on her own by the lake, smoking rollies, while I worried about who Potiphar was and how many apples were left in the barrel after two-thirds of them had rotted away. Seven. Or was it eight?

I was the only girl in there without a) a pair of pearl earrings b) a pair of smart leather loafers and c) a transparent pencil case covered in little pink hearts with matching fountain pen. I sat at my desk – a real wooden desk with an inkwell like the sort you see in museums – daydreaming, looking at all the portraits in the great hall and watching the sunlight stream through the stained-glass windows to make fairy dust above the girls' heads. That is, until a tweed-skirted teacher shouted, 'Fountain pens only, girls' above the high-pitched twittering. I raised my hand, terrified and blushing. The posh girls, who all knew each other and had tans, stared at me. Their successful entrance must have been a foregone conclusion. The woman got larger and larger as she made her way up the aisle to humiliate me, to tell me this life would never be mine, to send me back to South London and St Joseph's and the world I had already pushed to the back of my mind. She was coming towards me in her sensible shoes to crush my hopes as if they were eggshells.

'Don't worry, dear. Biro will do for now, but make sure you buy one before September,' the tweedy lady winked. 'I've never been wrong about a girl yet.' Miss Tarlton. My Russian teacher.

I walked slowly out down the steps to meet Mum at the lake, my pencil case clutched tightly to me. I heard the girls jeering at the hippie on the grass. 'Look! It's bloody Janice Joplin!' somebody shouted – Flossy as it happened. 'Pass us a joss stick, Tara!' giggled another. I pursed my lips and looked straight ahead.

Two weeks later a stiff cream envelope fell on to the grimy doormat of our flat. Mum and someone who snored very loudly and smoked Piccadilly were still asleep in the next room when I waded through last night's debris to retrieve the portentous thing. I knew what it was though it was addressed to Mrs Stephanie Reynolds. Sliding my finger under the heavy flap I opened it – a thick page headed with the school crest and entitled, in big green letters: 'Queensbury School for Girls'. It began:

> Dear Madam,
>
> We are pleased to offer your daughter, Alice, an unconditional scholarship to Queensbury.

Back in my room, still in my pink-ribboned nightie, I sat down in front of the mirror and put on my tiara. From now on things were going to go right. I beamed. 'You shall go to the ball,' I told my already altered reflection, and waved my wand.

# Three

And that was how I met Zander. Or at least, that's how I began to be posh enough to move in Zander's world. Crawl around on the periphery of Zander's world. Be hated by Zander's daughter.

Tara Sinclair was the last to arrive on the first day of term. I tried to stop Mum coming along to embarrass me but I failed. I made her park Kris's van in the village and then we lugged my suitcases through the rain to Queensbury where we joined the throng of parents around the entrance to the new girls' house. Everybody else had brought their things in large leather trunks with metal corners.

Parents were heaving them out of the backs of Range Rovers, pearls swinging over soft sweaters, and rain dripping on to conker-coloured brogues. I, of course, was the only one with my sports stuff in a carrier bag from Budgens. Mum had sold Dad's books to pay for my uniform and my hockey stick so I was not supposed to complain. I packed her off as soon as I could, though, and shoved my things under my bed so nobody would see them. The other girls not only had trunks, they also had mini trunks with padlocks on, which, it transpired, were treasure chests of home-made cakes, packets of biscuits, jars of Nutella and bars of chocolate. I was hungry. I would insist on having one for next term. For now I would just have to pretend I had a brother who had stolen mine when he went off to Eton.

But as soon as I saw all the pretty girls from the exam chatting so easily and laughing as though nothing was new, the last shreds of my childish self-confidence began to ebb away. I was a poor girl present on the sufferance of charity at a posh school and that was the end of it. I would never fit in here.

I curled up on my bed to read, hiding from the real world of dormitories, tuck boxes and lacrosse sticks, in the imaginary one that I had so longed for. In that life I was naughty and popular.

I didn't get to read for long.

Shaking a wild mane of blonde curls out of the confines of a ponytail, a slim, golden-brown girl with gleaming teeth and cornflower-blue eyes exploded into the room. '*Salve Amici!*' she shouted, victorious. The others crowded round her adoringly and, noticing that I hadn't joined them, she flashed me a disdainful glance before making her way over to the bed next to mine marked – 'The Hon. Tara Sinclair'.

And then it happened. In the shuffle of an expensive shoe the room was full to bursting with the presence of a man who commanded attention without seeming to request it. He wore a three-piece pinstriped suit with a red silk handkerchief in the breast pocket. The chain of a gold watch was visible in his waistcoat and his shoes shone as though servants had been spitting and polishing since dawn. He was big rather than fat, his black eyes betraying his grandmother's Asian origin, and his skin was the colour of toasted almonds. He was accompanied by the pungent smell of spicy Trumper's aftershave and a very young woman with blancmange breasts that poured out over the top of her boob tube.

'Don't forget the money, honey,' he boomed, mimicking the Sugar Puffs advert of the time and holding out a fan of twenty-pound notes. The girl giggled and Tara approached them meekly, pale and refusing to meet their eyes. She snatched the money from her father's hand and walked away, smiling a little at her friends and lavishly ignoring me as she sat down, chastened, on her bed. I could have sworn then that Zander looked at me oddly, his face losing its arrogant composure for a millionth of a second. But perhaps not.

'Be good,' the man twinkled to Tara's back, and, patting his escort on the bum, he left the room. The girl's titters and Zander's presumably lewd comments echoed back up to the dorm as they made their way down the stairs. The beamed hall felt quiet and empty when he had gone.

Actually, I felt a bit sorry for the Hon. Tara Sinclair. She had obviously been mortified by this intrusion into the world in which she was Queen.

'Don't worry,' I whispered across from my lair. 'My mum's really embarrassing too.'

Tara's face hardened to a tight grimace. 'That

was not my mother,' she hissed, speaking directly to me for the first and last time in a gruelling four years.

This was the inauspicious start of my relationship with Tara Sinclair and it was to get much worse.

It began the very next day. I woke up first and was sitting on the end of my bed in my green skirt, white knee socks, crisp white shirt and green jumper by the time the others opened their eyes. I had studied the timetable meticulously and all the books I would need for the day were piled neatly beside me in the order in which I would need them. My unused ink pen contained a new cartridge and my pencils were all sharpened to exactly the same length as each other. I had written 'Alice Reynolds, Queensbury School for Girls, First Form' on the blank white first page of my hymn book and I was anxious for my new life to start. It did.

Tara was singing at me even before she had slipped out of her Laura Ashley pyjamas, dribbling toothpaste down her front as she did so, rolling her head around in a Joplinesque manner. I tried to keep my eyes down. Florence, whom I soon recognised as almost Tara's equal, certainly not one of her slaves, hit her on the bum to shut her up, but playfully, in a way that plainly wouldn't have any effect. Especially since she giggled at the same time.

In chapel I stood in a line of newcomers, chin up to the eaves, eyes on the altar, but I was completely alone. The others kicked each other in the shins, sniggered behind their hands and passed scrumpling sweets down the row, deliberately omitting me.

Trundling from lesson to lesson that first day, my books pressed to my chest as I walked across cobbled courtyards and exquisitely trimmed lawns, I was aware that I was not one of the girls in the brochure. If the photographers arrived now they would make sure to leave me out, the sullen lonely-looking one in the background – 'Couldn't we crop her off? Too depressing.'

The horror really began on the first own-clothes day, a term into my first year. We had to donate a pound to charity in return for not having to wear school uniform. Naively I was mildly looking forward to it that first year. I felt a bit constrained in uniform seven days a week. We were allowed to change in the evenings but I never bothered because I mostly stayed in the dorm. The others put on tight jeans and sweatshirts from American universities and then ran off to rehearse their plays, practise their instruments, run their races. I was never selected for sports and would not have dreamt of daring to audition. So on own-clothes day I wanted to wear something really special.

Before I came up to Queensbury Mum gave me her mirrored waistcoat. Dad had brought it back from India for her years before and I had loved it since I was little. It was black but embroidered a million different colours with elephants and exotic birds. The hundreds of tiny mirrors sewn into the cloth twinkled when you looked at it and I used to think it must be magic. It was the most precious thing I owned, but I realised how wrong it was when I saw all the others dressed up in ra-ra skirts and puffed-sleeved blouses.

At lunchtime in the refectory Tara bustled her way up behind me, jamming her tray accidentally on purpose into my back. 'Nice jacket Janice's got,' she said loudly to her posse. I smiled to myself, thinking, God knows why, that she might be sincere. I heard her exaggerated 'Oops!' before I realised what had happened. I could feel the slime going down my back but it was not until I had walked, with as much dignity as I could, back to the dorm across the courtyard that I could assess the full extent of the damage. She had emptied the whole bowl of ketchup over the back of my waistcoat. It is still stained today, with bits of congealed sauce stuck round the edges of some of the mirrors.

I was too stunned to cry. I even remember wondering whether it might not have been a genuine accident. I sat ostentatiously near her in prep that night in the vague, though entirely vain, hope that she might deign to apologise. She didn't, but she did flick a rubber at me and then ask Flo, at whose feet it eventually bounced to a halt, to pass it back to her.

Flo was somehow less offensive than the others in Tara's gang. She had a power of her own but didn't use it to be a bully. Tara treated her with a certain amount of deference though Flo was never a ringleader, and she did tend to participate in whatever Tara had cooked up.

It was people like Ursula who were really dangerous. She had long mousy hair in plaits and a plump freckly face. She might have been a candidate for automatic victim herself had she not served Tara so diligently. She wore white ankle socks with hearts round the top and had a photo of her horse in her locket.

At school she worked much harder than Tara, diligently underlining her essay titles in red with a ruler, and drawing her diagrams on blank paper which she then glued in with a gunge-free Pritt Stick from her pretty pencil case. She did her best to pretend to be stupid though, perhaps for Tara's sake. She is a criminal barrister now with a predilection for defending armed robbers. I can imagine her sweeping about chambers in her gown and wig, taken seriously at last.

Occasionally she took pity on me. That first year, when I was still awed by the cakes and crisps in the refectory at four o'clock and the fact that cleaners emptied the bins on the dorms, the girls were planning a summer midnight feast down by the lake and they had talked about nothing else for ages. I couldn't help hearing them and I suppose Ursula noticed and just felt sorry for me.

'You should come too,' she said one day, after they'd all been plotting on Tara's bed, right next to me. I imagine none of the others heard, but it didn't cross my mind at the time that I should just bloody well ignore her. I saved my pocket money for a week and bought Curly-Wurlys, Rolos and a whole chocolate orange to bring along.

On the night in question I was pathetically excited. I didn't have to fight to stay awake, reading by torchlight under my covers, much too hot in my pink pyjamas. I heard the signal – an enormous fart proudly produced by Tara – and I leapt up like the others, grabbing my contribution from its hiding place in my knicker drawer. We were running, giggling, even me, out of the dorm door when Tara spotted me. She stopped dead, staring at me in the dark.

'You must be fucking joking,' she shouted. 'Who invited Janice?' Ursula ducked behind someone else so I couldn't see her, but she didn't say a word.

'I'm going to the loo, actually,' I said defiantly to the crowd at large, and marched past them across the polished parquet carrying my sweets out to the toilets.

'Thank God,' Tara laughed, and they went on their way.

At the end of every term the girls all made arrangements to stay at each other's houses, to go on holiday with each other's families. They came back talking about tennis, riding, the South of France and Italy. I always went home to Clapham and read next term's reading list more thoroughly, I'm sure, than any student in the history of the school. Mum was distraught.

The memory of it cows me still. I only have to see

an old school book on the shelf and my toes curl in my shoes, my palms sweat and a blush begins to spread into my neck.

I think Tara must have known what she was going to do for Valentine's Day of my second year, months in advance. Must have taken some planning. As I stood alone in physics, not paired with anyone as usual, refracting light through different coloured lenses, they must have known. As I read the part of Cordelia to Ursula and Minty's Regan and Goneril, the plan must have been underway. As I bit my nails to the quick in the lunch queue, missed the ball in rounders and carefully shaded in my still life of oranges and plums in art, they must have already thought it up.

Never before could I have imagined what a big deal Valentine's Day was going to be. Every year everyone got together to send joke cards to the teachers and Tara drew a huge heart on the blackboard in maths to tell Mr Morton that we all loved him. Every year he blushed and seemed to sweat a tiny bit more even than usual. It wasn't just that I hadn't got any cards last year. I mean, of course I didn't get any cards. And it wasn't really that everybody else seemed to have at least five, proudly displayed pink and red, and happy and loved on their dressers, although clearly these things were terrible. It was the fact that nobody else expected me to get any. It was as though in this regard I just didn't exist. I couldn't possibly be an object of desire.

But I hoped, of course. I hoped that maybe somebody, anybody – Mum even – might send me something. Or, better still, a secret admirer I had never even imagined. A boy who had seen me on Clapham High Street, or on the train down to school. Or anywhere. I pictured it being handed out to me by Matron to everyone's astonishment, a big pink envelope. The writing inside would be in shy blue Biro.

And then, in February 1983, as I sat on my bed squirming and blushing, twelve and a half years old, Matron handed me the very card. It wasn't as big as I had imagined and the envelope was white. But it was stiff, it was a card, and it was addressed to me in the very blue Biro I had envisaged. I almost cried.

'Hey, nice one, Alice,' said Ursula. I smiled at her joyfully, disbelievingly and began to peel back the flap while the others squealed and shouted and groaned over their own messages. 'Oh he's such a loooooser,' Tara was saying.

I pulled my card out. The hope and the excitement coupled with the crushing hurt and disappointment that made my stomach leap from its place were too much for me. They had won this time. I did burst into tears. I did run sobbing from the dorm.

I locked myself in the loo and missed first lesson, rocking backwards and forwards in the cubicle, waiting until I could stop crying. It had been a photo of some shit on a piece of newspaper. Whose? Tara's? A dog's? No, it looked human. Had she got poor Ursula to perform the act? They had written 'I'd rather kiss this' on the back.

All the rest of the day people kept coming up to me to ask if I'd got any Valentines. Then they laughed and ran away. Tara didn't dare ask me herself, of course.

You would have thought that the only advantage to all this would be that I was teacher's pet, adored by the Establishment and taken under the wing of all the old spinsters dying for a protégée. But my entanglement with Tara, my place in her twisted heart, meant that I was alienated even from them, my potential soul mates. Tara managed to see to it that I was rarely out of trouble even though my marks were flawless. She always stole my hockey stick when she had lost her own, so I got shouted at. 'Reynolds – we are going to have to do something about that memory of yours,' Miss Bacon would say, and I bit my lip and looked down at my shabby plimsolls. Tara took my pens and pencils, threw her chocolate wrappers across the thickly varnished parquet towards my bed and she took my finished essays out of my hands in the library to copy into her squat hand with hearts dotting the i's, often telling the teachers that I had plagiarised her masterpieces. 'Miss, I can't help it if they're the same. She's always looking over my shoulder,' she'd whine.

The summer before the world changed Tara and the cabal had a picnic on the high grass – a lawn over a mile away from the school buildings, occasionally used for nature walks but basically overgrown and deserted. For ages they were secreting bottles of Bacardi, Baileys and Cointreau under their beds and into their drawers, wrapping packets of menthol Consulate cigarettes in socks and shoving them down into the bottoms of their trunks, whispering loudly. They'd all got their mums to send them cakes by pretending it was someone's fifteenth birthday and Minty had stolen some hash from her brother in the Easter holidays. He had known it was her and had cracked all her Japan albums in two (she loved David Sylvian) but he hadn't found the gear.

On the big day Ursula came to find me in the library and told me that Tara had specifically requested my presence. I traipsed up to the high grass, hot, sweating, the brambles scratching my legs, knowing perfectly well that the experience was not likely to be a pleasant one. They were already pissed, swigging the sweet drinks straight out of the bottle under the hot sun, smoking feverishly and puffing on a very loose and badly rolled joint in the hope of some interesting results.

'Tell Janice to keep watch,' Tara called out when she saw me.

She was lying on her back in bra and knickers, stuffing a whole slice of chocolate cake into her mouth. When she had finished she washed it down with some Baileys and got Ursula to take her clothes off too and suck the cake crumbs off her fingers. I once heard someone say that Ursula had to pretend to be a boy and suck Tara's nipples some nights. Minty brought me over a cigarette and told me to smoke it while I 'manned the fort', so I stood, the sun beating down on my head, holding a burning cigarette and staring out towards the school.

I saw the deputy head as soon as she set off across the courtyard, purposeful and determined. 'Miss Bowles is coming up, I think,' I shouted immediately. Five minutes later I was sure and shouted some more. This time they took me seriously and gathered up their stuff in a drunken stumble. They put their fags out and pulled their uniforms on, running away chaotically, down the back way to school.

'Tell Janice to stay here and if she grasses us up I'll make her fucking life a living hell,' Tara screamed, dashing away in bare feet, dragging at the joint one last time before Latin.

The teachers must have known it had nothing to do with me, but I was much too scared to tell on Tara and the others, and it was me they found, standing amid the bottles and the smouldering butts. The matter was especially grave since Ursula and one other girl ended up in hospital overnight with sunstroke and alcohol poisoning.

'Alice, if you will just tell us who else was involved we may not have to send you home,' Miss Bowles coaxed, pacing up and down on a thick maroon carpet in her curtained office.

I cried a lot but I didn't speak and they packed me off back to Mum for a fortnight.

'Well, at least you had a good time. Made friends at last then?' Mum laughed. I glowered at her and locked myself in my room to read.

Nothing, though, could compare to the English lesson I endured not long before my metamorphosis. Agonisingly, we all had to learn and recite a poem that meant something to us. Tara spoke the words to a Duran Duran song – 'Rio' I think it was – and somebody else did a pop song about a wishing well and I . . .

I knew I would be embarrassed, I knew even the teacher would ache with pity for me and I knew people would hate me even more, but there was only one poem that meant something to me and I was going to recite it whether they liked it or not. I ignored my burning cheeks and neck. I buried my clenched fists in the sleeves of my regulation jumper. I stared at the clock on the back wall and, stinging with anticipated shame, I began.

> Had I the heavens' embroidered cloths,
> Enwrought with golden and silver light,
> The blue and the dim and the dark cloths
> Of night and light and the half-light,
> I would spread the cloths under your feet:
> But I, being poor, have only my dreams;
> I have spread my dreams under your feet;
> Tread softly because you tread on my dreams.

As I wiped the tears off my hot cheeks, Tara and her friends did their best not to actually die laughing, and my fate as the school's most pathetic outcast would have been sealed then if it hadn't already been sealed for years. Until, that is, the Russia trip.

# FOUR

It was not going to be easy to find Hermione. I knew she was in some kind of home. Rehab or a mental institution. I knew it would be the most expensive one available. Everyone knew she was an addict of pretty much everything, and there was a time I dimly remembered, just before I went to Queensbury, when the tabloids were full of photos of her falling over at parties given by the Queen, throwing up in gutters and getting done for drink driving. In the end I called Alcoholics Anonymous, Narcotics Anonymous and the Samaritans and asked for the best private treatment centres they knew of. I tried to sound convincing – a bit forlorn. Well, I was a bit forlorn.

Zander had had his driver meet me at Heathrow and deliver me to his London flat on Hyde Park Gate. Climbing out of the black Mercedes I looked up to the window and saw him, a sinister silhouette now, not a reassuring bulk, waiting like a spider for my arrival and the arrival of his egg.

'Fuck me, Fizzy, what happened to your face?' he asked, unconcerned, when he pulled back the door. Peter was behind me with my bags, but Zander ignored him and kissed me in a way that was more an invitation to immediate sex than a welcome. I shivered, but I was drawn in already. 'I know you better than you will ever know yourself,' he used to say to me, kissing the palms of my hands. The moment I was with him it felt true. We couldn't do without each other Zander and me – an island of brutal emotional honesty in our separate seas of lies.

'I was attacked,' I said, plunging myself into a colossal red sofa and pulling a cushion on to my lap to knead as I spoke. I stared at the Repin above the fireplace – stolen from the Russian Museum in Petersburg ten years ago and bought by Zander on the black market six months previously – a moody-looking Cossack.

Zander muttered some instructions to Peter and sent him away, moving into the immense space of his golden glowing living room and pouring himself a whisky.

'Drink?' he asked, tipping ice into his own from an old pewter bucket.

I nodded and he slopped some warm vodka into a glass for me. The smell of him made my stomach lurch with desire as he sat down next to me and rested his hand proprietorially on my upper thigh. I despised myself, but I could feel my cheeks flushing and my breath quickening. The fear that was drying my throat and clenching my fists was not, for some reason, quelling my desire. I was not going to let him see this, though.

'They didn't get it . . . did they?' he wanted to know.

'They didn't get it, no. I was, however, nearly

raped on the sodding train though actually,' I lied.

'Darling thing! You are the sexiest girl alive . . . who wouldn't want to fuck you?' smiled Zander, taking a breast in his hand and kissing my cheek in an unpleasantly familiar gesture of control. 'So, where is it?'

'Jesus Christ, Zander,' I spat, wrenching the egg from my handbag and shoving it into his face. 'It's here. I could have been killed.'

'But you weren't,' he beamed, unwrapping his egg, transfixed by joy and greed. 'Oh God, that's beautiful,' he moaned, holding it in cupped hands. It seemed to produce a light of its own. 'Just need the Danish Jubilee egg now and we're laughing,' he sniggered – another lost treasure sent to Denmark in 1903 with a little note from Nicholas II to his mother and not seen since. 'No trouble at customs?'

'No. Sergei was perfect. You know I know him? Met him on a school trip with Tara years ago,' I told him, knowing he would be livid that I had mentioned Tara, and saying it in such a way as to suggest that I might have had some kind of sexual relationship with Sergei. I hadn't, and in fact he hadn't even recognised me as I slipped through with my prize. 'Don't worry. I didn't go and see her,' I promised.

Tara had used her Russian too and was now the Moscow correspondent for the *Chronicle*. She loved it – imagining herself important because she met important people, crowing daily to a foreign editor no brighter (but more self-serious) than herself about a situation that the people working in London resolutely refused to understand. I used to quite like listening to her talk about it though, and she had a lovely flat on the river right opposite the White House. She social-climbed at all times and had important people she thought were her friends over to dinner a lot. They laughed at the standard of her Russian and at how stupid Westerners were but she didn't notice. The thing is, we had, despite our past, been quite friendly until things escalated between me and Zander.

Zander was always terrified I would start seeing her again. He did have some scruples. They didn't involve not going out with your daughter's friends but they did involve making sure your daughter doesn't find out.

'Guy's an arsehole, Fizz,' said Zander, seething about Sergei, blackening now. Well, that was true.

I got up for some ice, knowing the routine, already years old but never stale. Fearing him. Desperate for him. I braced myself for the assault, closing my hand round the ridges on my glass and breathing slowly out in an effort to maintain an acceptable level of sanity. The thought that this was all a bit sick was one that arose only in Zander's absence.

He grabbed me from behind, one hand round my waist, the other twisting my arm up behind my back so that it nearly hurt. 'I know how much you want it,' he said, with a challenging edge of irony, but I didn't rise.

My legs collapsed under me as I leant back into him, falling into the power of him rooted unflinching behind me, feeling the heat of him warm the chill of Russia out of my bones, ready to give myself up to him whatever the consequences. He dragged his hands through my hair, holding my head and pulling it towards him like something he could easily crush between his palms. I closed my eyes and fell into him, spinning in the darkness as I felt him pull my skirt up, enjoying the vulnerability of my progressive nudity while he remained clothed and controlled.

Throwing me on to the sofa he tore at my clothes, held my head back with a handful of my hair and brought me close to a shuddering climax, pausing and standing back to look at me dishevelled, gasping and naked before he finished me off quickly, making me scream as he jammed himself into me with such savage hardness that I forgot everything but his violent lust – and my own.

Afterwards, when he had vented his rage and calmed mine, he became tender and gentle as he always did. Somehow, while I was still breathless and quivering, he was already composed again, his voice even and quiet. He asked about the attack and he believed my lies, stroking my hair, kissing me gently in the very places he had just bitten me. He called me his princess.

This time, though, this millionth time, it was different. This time his softness seemed fake, as the rage that had proceeded it had lately begun to seem real. When had it stopped being a game? I couldn't remember. There was a time, I thought, not more than a few months ago, when I believed I was instigating the rape fantasies myself, playing the defeated victim, encouraging him to take me and do with me what he willed. Now I knew the power was all his and probably always had been. I began to feel cold and I edged away from him, goose pimples rising along my arms. Zander leant heavily off the bed to look at his watch – discarded in perpetual motion on the floor.

'They'll be here any second,' he announced suddenly, leaping up to get the door.

Jolted out of my post-ecstatic fog I swore and gathered up my shreds of clothes, running into the bedroom, still dizzy with sex. I heard Zander barking instructions to a caterer as I turned on the shower and I realised that I was about to be subjected to one of his antiquey drinks parties. The shower cubicle was enormous, and the water came flooding out of the brass power-shower head on to the black and white marble like thousands of burning needles searing my skin. The soap was big, one of those slabs from L'Occitane, the shampoo was in a heavy glass bottle from Trumper's and the thick white towels reached to the floor when I wrapped them twice around me. Most of the clothes I kept at Zander's needed to go to the dry cleaners and the only vaguely suitable thing I had was my red silk dress from Shang Hai Tang in New York. It was on the revealing side but Zander was always saying how he liked my hair tumbling down a bare back. He also liked me in red. 'Blondes think they can wear red but they can't,' he said. 'Only beautiful brunettes look good in it.'

By the time I came out, canapés were being passed around by Filipino ladies in black and white frilly uniforms, and the Russian art and artefacts world was milling expensively about the place, sipping glasses of champagne from lily-shaped flutes. There was a fire roaring lavishly in the vast hearth and the women's jewellery glittered with overt genuineness in the light of the flames. People's brand-new shoes sank into thick rugs and the smoke from the men's cigars swirled up to the ceiling, making a blue halo over the room.

Princess Yevdokhia Galitsina, a woman who had been on the receiving end of an awful lot of expertly held knives, was having a pinched conversation with a fat bald icon dealer about her society for Russian aristocrats abroad. She was heavily involved every year in the War and Peace ball, an opulent affair usually held at a London hotel, and had set up an organisation arranging social events for those as lofty as herself.

'The thing is, these societies for the aristocracy in Russia are getting completely out of hand. All sorts of people crawling out of the woodwork. They simply cannot all be genuine. Let's face it, you can't make a silk purse out of a sow's ear,' she smiled. Or at least she tried to but her skin was too tight so it came out as a grimace. I happened to know that she had married her title and I wondered what exactly her status had been before the happy day.

The icon dealer snorted in a way that suggested he might well have been a bit of a sow's ear himself. If so, he was certainly not alone. Among the immaculately turned-out crowd were a fair few of Zander's best buyers.

Although smuggling things out of Russia used to be all the rage, the foreign market was now virtually dead, since Moscow prices for the most exclusive items were far better at the moment than international ones.

Sotheby's and Christies might once have struck the big deals but nowadays you could make more selling privately within Russia and avoiding the large cut the auction houses end up taking. However, the most sensible Russians of the kind who can afford to buy a Fabergé egg or an Orlov diamond have residences in London and, not unreasonably, they prefer to keep their best pieces in the relative safety of a host country. This means that the deal usually takes place in the UK and the pieces must be extremely illegally smuggled out for them – by me. The ten per cent of the overall value that you end up using to bribe the customs chief (he, of course, must distribute his bribe a bit among the minions, like Sergei, who help him out) is nothing compared to what the auction houses might snaffle.

And here they were – Savile Row suits, sweet-smelling aftershave, perfectly coiffed hair and moustaches, shiny shoes and soft hands, smiling and chatting for all the world as if they hadn't embezzled billions of roubles from government coffers, ordered dozens of contract killings, helped rig countless elections and indirectly deprived millions of their pensions and wages. My job was to flirt with them. We liked to make it clear that we could procure whatever piece might interest them. They loved collecting – it made them feel established. You needed underworld contacts to get the stuff but selling it, owning it, was and is highly prestigious.

While I tried to wheedle some information on her family's lost wealth out of an aged Yusupov aunt who had managed to flee with only a few brooches and bracelets after the Revolution, Zander was making a shameless pass at one of his most valuable clients. Unfortunately my crone was telling me something about a tree at her brother's country estate and a buried box beside it, so I couldn't eavesdrop to much advantage.

This Cara woman, to whom Zander was standing provocatively close, was a procurer of antiques for American interior designers. She was old enough to be my mother, and plainly a bit younger than Zander. I sighed inwardly, but hauled myself up when he raised his head to wink at me reassuringly. At least, he meant it to be reassuring. Since the train, though, I felt more as though he was showing me that I was his. Flirting or no flirting, there was no escape.

Cara often managed to persuade her people to go for a Russian piece just for the exoticism. She made

Zander a lot of money, what with all the Park Avenue palaces she kitted out, and he liked to make her feel that she was a mere whisper away from an incredible screw.

'Good to see you've put on a bit of weight,' he murmured into her ear, using this vantage point to look down at her enormous breasts. Cara giggled excitedly and undid another button on her lilac cashmere cardigan. A wave of nausea swept over me.

But at two o'clock in the morning I crawled, hot and sated, out of Zander's enormous bed and padded about the thick carpet trying to collect my things without waking him. Muttering in his sleep like he always did, I thought in the eerie shadows that I heard him say, 'Don't kill her.' Perhaps I was going mad.

Creeping back over to the heat of the bed I leant close enough to smell his sweat and Armani aftershave and I tried to listen. The mumbling was incoherent now but somehow more disturbing than usual.

I was lifting my head away from him when he flashed his eyes open in the dark and grabbed hold of my wrist. 'Please. Please don't leave me, Fizzy,' he almost shouted. 'Say you won't leave me.'

When he was like this I got butterflies of love and pity in my stomach. My throat closed up with sorrow for him and I forgave him everything. He always did it when I least expected it. He seemed to sense when I was backing away from him and at those times his nightmares would begin to plague him. In the couple of years that we had been together properly it had happened at least ten times. 'Read to me, Fizz. Read me the one about the stars.'

I pulled the book of poems out from under the bed and read Yeats to him. 'When you are old and grey and full of sleep and nodding by the fire,' I began, 'take down this book,

And slowly read and dream of the soft look

Your eyes had once, and of their shadows deep;' but by the time I got to 'And paced upon the mountains overhead,

And hid his face amid a crowd of stars,' he was asleep. This thing he did always made me think that somewhere under his swagger he was as lonely as me, as sad and as desperate, as vulnerable and as bruised.

Stroking his forehead until he shut his eyes and until his grip on my wrist loosened I promised him I wouldn't go. I crawled back into bed and wrapped myself round his back, kissing the nape of his neck and pressing my cheek into his shoulder blade until his breathing slowed down and the horrible muttering stopped. Then, when I heard the milk van clatter on to Zander's cobbled side street I lightly slipped my shoes on again. He wouldn't care by morning. He might not even remember.

I turned away from the photograph of Tara on her horse that rested on the bedside table and that he so persistently refused to move, and I crept out into the night, hauling my suitcase and hoping to find a taxi to take me back to my little flat in Hampstead – a present from Zander in the guise of a bonus for all my good work.

Home, still dry and metallic from the Moscow plane, I flicked the lights on and made myself some coffee. Mr Ali at Mag One was already dragging his bound piles of newspapers in through the door as my cab chugged to a halt behind the bread van outside the deli. Huge trays of croissants, bales of baguettes and boxes of still hot loaves were being hoisted on to white-aproned shoulders in the half-light.

Leaning on my elbows, the coffee brewing on the stove, I heard the horses. I love the horses. At the crack of dawn every morning hundreds of horses ride up Hampstead High Street, perhaps to some barracks somewhere – I don't know. Someone in green khaki rides one horse leading two others on either side in a long and chaotic parade that takes minutes to snort and clop and steam past my windows.

It was a tiny flat but I adored it. The bedroom was only just bigger than my super-king size mattress but it had high ceilings and big windows looking out over green Hampstead gardens, church spires and gnarled trees. I had sanded the floors and they always gleamed golden under their Caucasian rugs in the sunlight that forever flooded the place. I had overflowing bookshelves up to the ceilings and a cooker and fridge crammed against the back wall in a little alcove. The table was one Zander had given me, probably very valuable but covered now in mug rings, pan burns and wine stains. This was where I hid.

Sipping at the hot coffee in my Bill Clinton a Cure for the Blues mug (an airport purchase) I wondered how I was going to track Hermione down. I needed to know about Zander. I needed to get him into perspective and I knew that only she could help me. It was not going to be spectacularly easy though. Our relationship had changed a lot since that first meeting at the end of the Russia trip. The one that had changed my life. The one that had led me to Cassian. The moment of my initiation into the class I had always intended to be a member of. It was all thanks to dear Flossy, but also, indirectly, to the Hon. Tara Sinclair herself.

# Five

Strapped into the seat of the Aeroflot jet growling its eagerness for take-off, I could feel Tara in the seat behind me, hating me. I crossed my feet, self-conscious even now about the bare legs Mum wouldn't let me shave. 'Why should we be slaves to male oppression?' she said. I didn't know any males and the only oppression I was aware of was Tara's. She had, at least I think she had, put a razor and some shaving foam in my locker as a friendly hint. I wished I had put my snow boots on for the journey.

Glancing out at the grey tarmac under the vast white wing I practised the Russian phrases I had learnt, closing my eyes to hear the sounds better. 'Oh Lord, wooon't you buy me a Merceeeyyydeeez Beynz,' Tara sang in a whisper at the back of the seat. The other girls, boisterous and squealing, compared the Aeroflot plane to those that had taken them to Italy, Barbados, Miami and Nice. Unfavourably.

Flo (apparently named after the city of her conception) had noticed a cupboard at the front of the plane marked 'Oxygen'. 'What are we supposed to do? All rush in there when the air runs out?' she screeched.

Miss Tarlton could barely keep control and the

other passengers were beginning to look a bit tetchy. 'Let's all have a read of our Pushkin, shall we?' she suggested pleadingly, but only I got out my copy of *The Bronze Horseman*.

I didn't really want to read it – of course I didn't. But I liked Miss Tarlton and I felt I owed her my place at the school, my better-than-average Russian and my inclusion on the Russia trip, paid for by a bursary effectively invented for me. Perhaps she had been like me once, or maybe it was just my enthusiasm for her subject.

She was a spinster of fiftyish with bright ginger hair and a powerful jaw. She loved the Soviet Union more than anything and was always telling us about the time she had spent there as a student in the late 1950s. She had been amazed to get a visa, she said, but on application from Oxford had been packed off to Kiev University, all accommodation and everything taken care of. She stayed with a family in a large crumbling apartment near the centre of town and, since no provision had yet been made for foreign language students, was enrolled on a history course with ordinary Soviets. Few of her contemporaries spoke to her and she realised later that the family with whom she lodged had almost certainly been KGB. Her favourite story was about being stopped on the street carrying a string bag of oranges. 'Hey, redhead, where'd you get the oranges?' someone had asked her. Her moment of acceptance. More than I had ever managed in my own country.

I had, however, managed to endure four years at Queensbury. Four years of Tara's taunts, four years of Mum's pale-faced chain-smoking concern and four years of my own defiant silence. The Russia trip, I was determined, was going to be different. I was going for Dad. This was the holiday he had always wanted to take and I was going to have it for him.

It was March, and as the plane swooped in to land at Moscow's Sheremetievo airport I saw a landscape of snow stretching out to the white horizon. Lurching to a halt in the bleak grey of a winter's evening, we were immediately surrounded by khaki Jeeps bearing serious-faced armed soldiers, their hammers and sickles proud on their grey fur hats. They stood to attention as the cabin doors were switched to manual and kept their gaze to the middle distance while the foreigners tumbled awe-stricken from their cocoon into the iron twilight. Snow began to fall in thick flakes and even Tara was silenced by the air of menace and the stark grey of the scene around us.

Hustled into the sudden and sweltering heat of the dimly lit airport building, we made our way to passport control through the smoky yellow light given out by what looked like a million cheap saucepans hanging from the ceiling. We stood there for three hours. We were each inspected by the steely eyes and imposing hat of an otherwise invisible official and not a word was spoken as the eyes stared at each shuffling capitalist, one of them me, for upwards of ten minutes. Their gaze would occasionally shift to the mirror above our heads – designed to check for wigs and the other cunning disguises that an Imperialist spy might dream up.

Eventually we emerged, exhausted and irritable, into the snowy night, led by a young tour guide in high-heeled boots and a faceful of make-up to a rickety orange and white bus with grimy curtains in its windows and a heating system that seemed to pump heat and petrol fumes directly from the exhaust pipe into the passengers' faces. We were all given a greasy plastic bag containing a boiled egg, a slice of black bread and piece of sweaty cheese. Tara immediately dropped hers on the floor in disgust but probably regretted it later when it transpired that this was the only food we would be getting before bed. I, on the other hand, was in heaven.

The others slept on the bus, but I stared out of the window in amazement. The snow was thick on the pavements and the streets were only barely lit by the weakest of lamps. A few old ladies, wrapped up in coats, fur hats, scarves and thick boots trundled along the anonymous streets in the dark holding large string bags of shopping. There were no billboards, no neon lights, litter or graffiti. Just impossibly wide and empty roads, faceless buildings, each indistinguishable from the next, and signs above the shop windows reading 'Bread', 'Milk', 'Chemist', 'Meat'.

When we pulled up at our vast hotel, a monstrous modern thing called the Kosmos, stretching up and out into the night, I saw a silver statue of a spaceship shooting towards the sky. The power of it all sent a shiver down my spine.

Checking in involved the confiscation of everyone's passport and a great deal of arguing. Some English drunks started harassing our guide, asking if she would like to see the ceiling of a Moscow bedroom, and Flo said she was going to faint.

When the rooms were allocated she nearly did. She was sharing with me. Tara was already paired with Ursula, easier to boss around and patronise than the others, and what with her fainting escapade and prolonged whinging Flo had missed out on the whole process and ended up with the shortest of straws. She rolled her eyes dramatically at Tara while I stood, hard, oblivious and determined as ever not to let them break me. '"Take another liddle piece of my heart now, baybeeeee!"' Tara crooned.

We were given our room keys by a fat, dough-faced woman on the sixteenth floor who snapped rudely at us and made it clear by her manner that she would be watching. Certainly she didn't seem to have anything else to do. Miss Tarlton called out helplessly to all of us to have an early night and sighed as she watched the other girls screaming and screeching, hurtling off down the long corridors. Russia!

I suppose I was a bit less appalled than Flo by the brown nylon curtains, the smoked glass in the windows that made the thick falling snow itself look brown, and the stench coming from the bathroom. I started unpacking, pulling all the clothes the others so despised out of my cheap suitcase. Flo's was old and leather, with her grandfather's initials on a brass panel near the lock. She was lying on the bed staring at the ceiling.

'God, what a fucking nightmare,' she moaned, lighting a cigarette.

I shoved my bedraggled wand into my pillowcase and decided to go outside to escape the smoke. 'I thought I might explore,' I said quickly, and left.

This was easier said than done. The lard woman asked where I was going and took my key off me before making what looked like an urgent call. The policeman guarding the inside of the huge revolving hotel doors insisted on seeing my hotel pass (a piece of official cardboard) and looked dubious as to its authenticity when I produced it. I was on the point of giving up and facing Flo's room full of nicotine, when, with an unexpected whoosh of the doors, I was out.

It must have been minus fifteen, and my wool jacket and shortish skirt were not doing much to help me. No sooner had I taken my first sliding step on to the icy slope towards the tram lines than a crowd of little boys pounced on me, offering to trade badges of Lenin for chewing gum. '*Dyevushka! Dyevushka!*' they called after me as I walked away, bemused. Leaning against the railing behind the mini blackmarketeers were some older boys in heavy coats, smoking and affecting the air of foreigners without much success. Every now and then they would approach the hotel door and wave a pass at the guards, who turned them away without speaking or altering their facial expressions.

Near the statue a few stragglers emerged, bundled up and steaming, from the pale glowing arch of the metro. I slipped down towards them, naively fascinated by the fact that these people, in the snow, in Russia, were going about their nightly routines, coming home with a loaf of bread and some sausage. The man with the trilby who had just become their leader had yet to make a serious impact on their lives.

Shivering and suddenly afraid, I began to lose my nerve. I wanted to talk to Miss Tarlton, be teased by Tara, ignored by Flo. At home, I thought, we dress everything up to make life seem less bleak. Here they didn't seem to have bothered. I scurried straight back up to the gloomy hulk of the hotel and met with a scuffle by the door.

Flo was shouting, crying, flapping her arms about near the entrance. 'I am staying here. I am English. Stop it!' she squeaked. The street guards were ignoring her protests and would not let her past them to the revolving door. Behind her the little boys were tugging at her coat and the bigger boys were laughing and waving worn bits of paper at her, trying to get her to take one. She seemed to think they were mocking her and had burst into tears of fear and frustration.

Her face lit up when she saw me. 'Oh my God! Tell him! Tell this moron Russky that I'm staying here. I haven't got my bloody pass. I think I dropped it in the lift.' I explained the situation to the guard, who declined to move a muscle. Flo stood pale and tearful, wishing she had paid more attention in Russian conversation classes. 'What the fuck are we going to do?' she whined.

Blinking the snowflakes off my lashes I gave Flo my own hotel pass and turned to the older boys. I inspected each of their shabby pieces of card and chose the best one, smiling up into the eyes of eighteen-year-old Sergei Borisov.

'Thank you,' I said in Russian. 'Wait here. I will bring you something.' Actually I think I told him I would drive him into something, but he laughed kindly and seemed to understand.

Back inside we were elated and hysterical with relief. Our view of Russia was still dominated by the evils of the KGB and the terrors of the prison camps, and we were proud to have overcome a small piece of Soviet bureaucracy all on our own. Compounding our glee, our adventure had also involved a blackmarketeer – people Miss Tarlton had warned us not to associate with on pain of . . . well, a half-hearted reprimand from her but ten years in a Siberian gulag from somebody else.

'Oh God. Oh God. What are we going to give him?' Flo complained back in our room. We! She was throwing her clothes off her bed, riffling through her wash bag, hopefully holding up packets of cigarettes and her Frankie Says Relax T-shirt for my inspection. I shook my head, laughing, and we both slumped down into the brown armchairs in desperation.

'My Walkman!' Flo suddenly announced, tapping her temple and raising her eyebrows at me, delighted by her own brilliance. The headphones trailing like ribbons in our wake, we ran back out towards the lift, to the bemusement of the watchful ball of dough, and back through the revolving doors to a surprised Sergei. We ran into him in our haste, slipping on the ice and shivering without our coats.

'To you,' I said proudly in Russian.

'*Spasibo,*' Sergei smiled, turning the machine over in his hands.

Flo held out a tape to him. '"Kissing to be Clever". Culture Club,' she said eagerly. Sergei bent forward and kissed her on the cheek. Flo blushed and wiped the snow from her hair, mumbling about how she hadn't meant him to . . . it was just the title of the . . .

'Oh fuck. Tell him, Alice,' she begged.

Sergei turned round to consult his friends and then stepped forward, bowing slightly, as though to ask for the last waltz. 'Come. Nightclub?' he asked in a whisper. We both fluttered at this, chirping our excitement, and with great difficulty an arrangement was made to meet back by the entrance at midnight.

With only two and a half hours in which to get ready, our preparations took on an air of great seriousness.

'Well, you obviously can't wear anything *you* own,' Flo told me straight away, and began flinging scrumpled bits of material at me to try on.

'Why can't I?' I wanted to know, giggling, knowing, though, that Flo wanted to help me, not to demean me.

'Do you want to look like something out of the Carpenters or do you want to look like Madonna?' she asked.

'Madonna,' I confessed meekly.

'Right,' said Flo, offering a black lacy top and some Lycra leggings.

We smeared red lipstick across our mouths and lay down flat for the painting on of liquid liner. I discovered I had quite a talent for this. I had never been so happy in my life. We backcombed our fringes and put our hair up in fluorescent green and pink elastic bands.

'I look awful in make-up,' I sighed, looking at my coloured face in the dim mirror.

Flo stuck her tongue out at me and lit a cigarette. 'Fuck off, will you? If I looked like you I wouldn't wear make-up either. You know that's why Tara hates you so much, don't you? Potential style-cramper you are,' she said, blowing smoke rings above her head. I stared again into my own green eyes and clouds moved aside in front of my face. I saw myself suddenly in that instant as a snapshot of somebody else. Somebody I would be jealous of, somebody who would think the old me repulsive, poor, hippyish, bookish. Nobody had said it since

Dad died but I saw it then. I was beautiful.

'Hey, get off! Stop it, you spasmoid!' Flo snapped, as I put a huge red lipsticky kiss on her right cheek. '"I made it throoooo the wiiiiiilder-ness! Yeah I made it throoo-oooo-ooooo!"' I sang, leaping up on to the bed, feeling my old self of years and years before surge back into me, feeling my dad's admiring eyes on me from the heavens. I was in Moscow and I was beautiful.

'"Never knew how lost I was until I found yoooo-oooooooo."' Flo answered, jumping up to join me in some lycric writhing.

It was all very well in the privacy of our own room, but sneaking down the corridor at five to twelve, dreading the appearance of either Tara or Miss Tarlton, we began to realise that we looked like underage prostitutes. The men we passed in the lobby gazed longingly at our barely concealed breasts, spilling over the tops of the tiny lacy vests we wore, and the receptionists glowered with entirely unconcealed envy at the delicious youth and brazenness of the teenaged foreigners.

Sergei's verdict lacked the subtlety an English boy might have given it. 'Sexy girls,' he said, putting an arm round me and leading me down the precarious icy slope towards a purring car. Well, sputtering car. There were already five boys in it, all of them smoking, and the thing itself had obviously been made some twenty or so years earlier. Actually, looking back, it was probably brand new, but a 1985 Lada. The seats were covered in filthy acrylic fur and the interior reeked of Soviet petrol.

'Let's go back, Alice. Seriously,' said Flo, getting into the car and finding herself hoisted on to the knee of someone who introduced himself as Vlad.

An hour earlier I would have been terrified. We had no idea where we were going, it was all probably illegal and these people were blackmarketeers and therefore technically criminals. But I wasn't scared. I was Alice the brave, beautiful, invincible. Nothing bad was going to happen to us tonight. Not to me and my first friend. My best friend. Nothing.

'Beatles? Like?' asked the driver, sticking a cassette into a clunking tape machine. The pale streetlamps became one as the car chugged along the empty roads. The heat and smoke in the car were asphyxiating, but not so much as to interfere with the mad uncontrolled singing of 'Twist and Shout'. '"Come on come on come on come on come on baby now, come on baby . . ."' we yelled, stopping outside a dark and solitary tower block in what looked like a bomb site.

Not a single light was on in the whole twenty-storey building and nothing but snow was visible for miles around.

'Oh shit,' Flo said, laughing hysterically.

Looking up as the boys scrambled out of the car, serious now and vaguely worried, I saw a sign above the shop window that dominated the bottom floor of the monstrous edifice. It said 'Shoes'. Sergei knocked on the door. Silence. He knocked again. A voice came from the other side.

'Who is it?' a young man shouted, the edge of aggression in his voice seemingly sending a shiver through our crowd outside.

'Seriozha. Dima's friend,' Sergei said, his face pressed against the door. It opened.

Flo and I held hands as the boys jostled us down some very dark stairs that smelt of cabbage, cat piss and stale ashtrays.

'I blame you,' hissed Flo, digging me in the ribs with her elbow.

Whoever was in front shoved open another door and an explosion of light and noise burst out on to the staircase. Two hundred people were packed into a tiny cellar. Some of them sat at little tables and drank out of china teacups, but most were locked into couples, gyrating under red and blue lights to a song that Flo recognised as being by Samantha Fox.

'My God!' Flo laughed, but I was already being dragged on to the dance floor by an eager Sergei, who threw his coat, scarf and gloves to Vlad as he tugged at me. He pressed his body hard against me, pulling me tight into his groin, my breasts against his chest and my face to his neck. He smelt of cheap soap and sweat. Thirty seconds or so into what he was passing off as a dance he shoved his hot tongue into my ear. Beaming, and barely able to control my glee, I tried to explain that I wasn't that sort of girl.

'I don't occupy myself with intercourse!' I shouted over the music.

He was pretty good-humoured about the whole

thing and when we had woven our way back through the drunks to the little plastic table where the others waited he held out my chair for me and then poured me a cup of thick sweet syrup from the teapot.

'Cognac,' he said.

Flo flashed me a smirk. 'I think it's port,' she mouthed through the din.

For hours we sat huddled round the table, shouting idiotically at each other about the weather in London.

'Fog?' Sergei asked.

'Rain,' I answered.

When we had got through a teapot each of the sickly alcoholic stuff Sergei and Flo disappeared into the throng. In their absence I conducted an illuminating conversation with Vlad about the popularity of different brands of cigarette worldwide and the reason for the secrecy and the teapots – Mikhail Gorbachev's new prohibition.

When Flo and Sergei returned they were wrapped obscenely around each other, chewing each other's earlobes and sucking each other's fingers lasciviously. Flo got my attention with a drunken wave and pointed proudly at a huge stain on her neck. 'LOVE BITE!' she shouted, collapsing in giggles. I loved her.

On the way back to the hotel, crammed into the hot stinking car, mascara running and lipstick rubbed off, we both had to get out and throw up into the endless piles of snow by the sides of the road. We arrived at the prohibitive revolving doors at six fifteen by Flo's Swatch but it was still completely dark. The whole city was quiet and frozen. This time there was no problem with the passes. We showed ours and Sergei marched straight in behind us, slapping an unopened packet of Flo's Silk Cut into the doorman's hand. Nobody said a word. We could hear the dough woman's snores from the lift door and we crept past her on tiptoes, grabbing our key from behind her lolling head.

Splashing icy water on to my face I checked again in the mirror. I was afraid I might have changed back. Back into a frightened, mousy girl whose crippling lack of confidence made her own beauty dowdy. I hadn't. I came out of the loo talking.

'Hey, can I borrow this when we get back?' I asked, waving the lacy top I had worn before me with a flourish. I wished I had stayed where I was. Flo was lying back naked on her bed with her eyes shut, moaning softly. Seriozha, still fully clothed down to his woolly scarf, had his head between her legs and his ravenous hands on her breasts. Neither of them noticed me.

'I'll just erm . . .' I muttered, grabbing the pillow off my bed and hurrying back to the bathroom. Lying down on the floor, my head underneath the sink's grimy U-bend, I felt for my wand inside the pillow case and smiled. This is the best day of my life, I thought, drifting off to sleep in the alcoholic haze of Flo and Sergei's cries and the glare of the flickering fluorescent light above the sink.

Somebody seemed to be punching me in the temples. Over and over again. Pound. Pound. Thump. Thump. The pain was unbearable. It was minutes before I came round and went to see who was knocking on the door.

'Flo! Flo! Are you in there? Has she hippified you or what?' Tara was yelling. I peered out at her. 'Hey, Janice, is Flo there? It's time for the Gorky Park trip. You can commune with nature,' she laughed, arrogant, unaware that I, Alice, was no longer the person she thought I was. Ignorant of the fact that I was beautiful Alice the Brave.

'Fuck off, Tara,' I heard myself say, before I shut the door in her face. 'Once and for all, fuck off,' I continued, creeping in to see if Flo had surfaced.

'I feel awful,' she moaned when she saw me.

'You should. You are,' I said, loud enough to wake Sergei, whose peach-coloured thermal long johns I was standing on.

Later, the freezing air blowing our hangovers into the ether, me and my friend held woolly gloved hands and skated around the paths of Gorky Park. We swooshed under the Ferris wheel, past the boulevards of trees and on to the boating lake, laughing and screaming. I stamped my blades up and down while Flo lit a cigarette and I thought how lovely she looked with flushed cheeks and tiny icicles on her lashes.

Tara, meanwhile, appeared to be in agony. This made my new-found composure all the more satisfying. Imperceptibly at first, Tara's entourage had begun to gravitate towards Flo's lack of virginity and my miraculous beauty and confidence. The more Tara struggled the tighter the net around her became. She stumbled over to Flo on the ice to ask for a light.

'So, I hear you've become an easy lay,' she sneered, hoping to humiliate Flo into renewed submission.

'Listen, virgin, there's nothing easy about it. You'll find out when you grow up,' Flo laughed, taking me by the arm and skating away. 'You know her title's fake,' she whispered to me loudly. 'Her mum's an aristo, but her dad nicked the title and made one up for Tara,' she screeched, spinning round to skate backwards and pull me along towards her across the pale blue lake. 'They say he's a barrow boy from South London,' she shouted to the stars.

We became inseparable as the week progressed. We snuck out of the Bolshoi Theatre together so Flo could have a cigarette in the interval. Somehow when everything out on the streets is so bleak the awe-inspiring splendour of a colonnaded marble hallway and a red and gold, chandeliered interior is all the more amazing.

We were enthralled by the seriousness with which everyone seemed to take the performance, the reverence of the quiet teenagers sitting bolt upright on their sprayed gold wooden chairs with red velvet upholstery. I didn't hear a single snigger throughout and the applause was rapturous. When a favourite ballerina appeared people stood up and threw roses on to the stage, chanting, clapping and screaming as though they were at a football match.

Although the crowed was dressed very neatly, most of them seemed not to have bathed and their clothes looked like ones I had seen in Mum's photos of her childhood – funny short-sleeved shirts and stubby ties for the men, with pressed trousers that only reached to the ankle, and woollen dresses for the girls, darned in places, with white socks and solid shoes. All the women and the girls over about fifteen had their hair set on their heads, and most of the boys had Brylcreem in theirs. In the interval everyone drank squash and ate stale fairy cakes. I said I wanted a dress made from the spectacular red and gold curtains emblazoned with hammers, sickles and the letters CCCP. 'After the collapse of Communism maybe,' muttered Flo.

We wandered around Moscow, slipping away from Miss Tarlton's not terribly watchful eye, skulking into surreal basement cafés with Sergei and his friends, where nobody removed their fur hats and the air was thick with smoke and steam. The floors were a mess of grimy slush and you had to pick up a tray from a metal counter and make do with what was on it. What was usually on it was a glass of sickly sweet coffee (mostly hot condensed milk) and a bowl of *kasha*, a buckwheat slop with salt and butter. We were surprised at the lack of choice and at the prison-like regime in what was presumably supposed to be a place people might actively want to come. It wasn't, though. It was somewhere you came if you were hungry and left when you weren't any more – functional and fast. Personally I'd still rather have a bowl of *kasha* than a Big Mac.

We rode the metro proudly, pretending as hard as we could to be Russian, keeping our eyes down and contributing enthusiastically to the total silence within the crowded carriages. We gawped at the glittering stations, adorned with statues, mosaics, enormous chandeliers and mottled marble columns. Every stop was as pristine, advertless and graffitiless as the last, an underground museum built by Stalin at great cost (human life-wise).

One night, after walking up Gorky Street arm in arm, we found ourselves standing beneath a vast statue of a handsome man in Laurence Olivier turn-ups, holding a book in his outstretched arm. 'Bit of all right,' smirked Flo. We read the inscription.

'Vla . . . dim . . . ir . . . Mayakov . . . sky. Vladimir Mayakovsky!' I squealed, hugging Flo and bursting into hysterical tears. 'I'm here, Dad,' I whispered, looking up through clouded eyes to the sharp stars.

When Sergei saw us off by the hotel door under the pale glow of a snowy Moscow dawn, his eyes too filled with tears.

'Not forget me,' he mumbled into Flo's collar.

'Not forget you,' she smiled, holding his frozen red hands and kissing him fondly on the cheek.

When he came to hug me he pulled me roughly

against him, squeezed my bum and whispered urgently into my ear, 'It was you I wanted.'

On the plane home we made up for an almost entirely sleepless week. Flo and I slumped on to our tray tables and slept all the way, dead to the drinks and meals, to Miss Tarlton's useless entreaties, to Tara's increasingly desperate commands and to the terrible turbulence that brought bags and coats cascading down from the flimsy and ancient overhead lockers.

Mum was waiting for her meek little girl to run eagerly into her arms in the bright yellow and noise of Heathrow airport. Instead a tall, confident nearly-woman in lip gloss and a lace top sauntered up to her smiling.

'I brought you some vodka,' I said. 'This is Flo. I'm going to stay at her house next week.'

As Mum registered my startling presence with a slightly bemused, 'Fizzy love . . .' a very thin rich woman tapped her on the shoulder. 'I can see her coming now,' she said with a wan smile. 'It was lovely to meet you, darling.' She kissed Mum and clacked off in her heels towards the morose figure of the not remotely honourable Tara Sinclair. It was Lady Hermione. Before the breakdown. Before the final separation from Zander. Before everything.

# Six

I kept quiet in the car. It seemed odd that someone who could obviously afford a Rolls-Royce should be rattling round the countryside in this ancient Volvo estate, full of dog hairs, covered in stains and barely capable of doing fifty miles an hour. I gazed out of the window at the fields of sheep, feeling that I had a lot to learn about the ways of the rich. Flo sat in the front with Stella, her mum, and they argued all the way back to Little Farford.

'Flossy, sweetheart, I see no reason why I should let you out anywhere to engage in what would doubtless be repulsive activities behind my back,' Stella was saying, rapping her filthy nails on the steering wheel.

'Why do you always assume everything I do is repulsive?' Flo whined.

'Isn't it?'

'Not especially.'

'Yes. You see, yes it is.' Stella swerved off the motorway.

Flossy? Part of me mocked the idea of such a screamingly aristocratic nickname. Another part longed for one of my own. I wondered if Fizz – which was what my mum had always called me – would work just as well, and decided to try it out some time.

I pushed a pair of gardening gloves further away from me across the back seat and smiled to myself. Now I was getting somewhere. Bees and butterflies hovered above the unkempt verges by the side of the roads, and the air was thick with pollen and dust. Horses in the fields we passed bowed their heads to eat, and the world inside the car, with Flo and her Mum bickering and Radio Four complaining, seemed loud and intrusive as the April heatwave swept its stifling mugginess through the windows. Gradually, though, the voices faded into the back of my mind and I fell into a melancholy reverie.

I don't fit in, I thought, knowing suddenly that the smart clothes I had brought with me would be stupidly inappropriate. These people wore jeans, sweat shirts and filthy old plimsolls. Only the aspiring, I realised, dressed up for a week in the country.

The roads got smaller and smaller, the cars fewer and fewer, and the light dimmed to a pink glow across the sky as we crunched down the lane to The Old Vicarage.

'Oh God, I left the door wide open,' Stella groaned, looking up at the mass of her imposing house.

'Spastic,' muttered Flossy, sticking her tongue out at her mother.

The place looked like a location for a costume drama. It had in fact *been* a location for a costume drama. 'Absolute nightmare. Frightened the bees away,' Stella said. One day, I decided, I am going to have a house whose name begins with 'The'.

This one, however, seemed to be falling down. The garden, which stretched away towards a stream, was all overgrown and brambly, and the golden stone of the house itself was visibly crumbling. The slates on the roof looked ready to hurtle down into the cherry trees below. I could just make out what I assumed to be the beehives at the end of the garden, and was thinking I had never been anywhere so beautiful, when I was attacked by a pack of dogs.

'Down, Bizzy! Go on, Otty!' Stella laughed, guiding me on to the cold flagstones of the downstairs hall. The dogs snarled disappointedly. I was breathless with fear.

It was freezing inside and very dark. All I could make out was the musty smell of history and a looming cavernous space surrounding me. Nobody switched the lights on and nobody commented on the cold.

'Come on,' said Flossy, dashing off up the wooden stairs, flying round the corner with one hand on the thick shiny banister and both feet flailing through the air.

Holding my overnight bag meekly in one hand I walked up after her, reaching out to stroke dusty velvet curtains and desperately trying to keep my footing in the gloom. The smell of roast beef wafted warmly up from somewhere downstairs.

Flossy's bedroom was big and bare with creaking

floorboards and dim mirrors in gilt frames. A vast four-poster bed was plonked in its centre and Flossy leapt up on to it and crossed her legs like a Buddha.

'Like it?' she asked, rummaging around in her pockets for some cigarettes.

I loved it so much I didn't know what to say. I recognised here that atmosphere, that safety in longevity, the beautiful peace of self-assured continuity I had always longed for. I had never known it would look quite like this, though. I was going to go straight back home and persuade Mum to rip up all the carpets and burn the net curtains.

'It's nice,' I said, looking out of the window and trying to seem at least a little bit unimpressed. Someone was smoking over near the stream. A ghostly figure, barely visible in the twilight, sad and thoughtful.

'There's somebody out there,' I said, partly to make sure it wasn't someone who shouldn't have been there – a poacher, or whatever kinds of intruders you might get in the country.

'It's Cass. I told you about him. Brother? Smelly socks? Porn mags under the bed? I hate him,' said Flossy, rolling her eyes. 'Hey, rat features,' she shouted over the buzz of night insects and the babbling of the fast-running water. 'Throw us a light.'

Cass strolled languidly over to the window, his white shirt flapping in the breeze, and looked up. He ran his ringed fingers through dark floppy hair and put one hand into the pocket of his black jeans.

'What's in it for me, sexy?' he laughed, teeth flashing.

'Oh, fuck off. Chuck us a light or I won't introduce you to Alice,' Flossy giggled, catching the matches in her outstretched hand.

'I'll be heartbroken,' mumbled Cass, and went inside.

Lying in the bath before dinner I looked up at the cobwebs on the ceiling and tried to decide what to wear. The bath was deep and long and had feet like a bear's. My head and the tips of my toes, the only bits of me sticking out of the water, were unbearably cold. Did they not have central heating? I was aware now that my black dress would look ridiculous and I hadn't brought any jeans. It would have to be short black skirt and white blouse, the only things I had taken to Russia that Flossy had deemed acceptable. I had once thought they looked sort of glamorous and Parisian but now I knew I would look like a waitress.

'Friend looks like a waitress,' Cass said to the company at large when I walked into the dining room. I could feel the kind of devastation Tara Sinclair used to inspire heating up behind my eyes until my Flossy winked at me. A dusty and slightly disappointing chandelier hung over the large oak table and the black smoke from the candles tangled itself around the crystal teardrops. Everyone's face was golden and glowing in the flickering light and the portraits on the walls looked gravely down at us through the shifting shadows. One of them was a modern thing of Flossy's father, some sort of a banker who was based in Hong Kong and rarely came home. It was by Lucian Freud – a family friend.

'Ignore Cassian, sweetheart,' said Stella, who had changed out of her gardening clothes into a black woollen dress and sensible shoes. She threw Cass a smirk and patted me on the arm. 'Sit here where he can't get at you,' she said, pulling out a heavy and lavishly upholstered chair.

The windows were open on to the garden and the birds were working themselves up into a bedtime frenzy outside. Stella poured us all wine without even asking and then made me help myself to the bowls of potatoes and salad and the plate of steaming, bleeding beef. Nobody touched the jug of tepid tap water – something I noticed was a key feature of every meal.

Cassian had just got back from a school trip to Venice. He was at Westminster which, according to Flossy, explained his surly manner and his jewellery.

'Which churches did you like best, poppet?' his mother asked him above the glimmer of the candles. I held my breath, waiting for his growling insult.

'Santa Maria Formosa was all right, if you like that sort of thing,' he said, staring at his food.

'Oh, have they finished the restoration?'

'Not quite, but you're allowed in,' he replied. 'I bought you a postcard of it.'

I was baffled. I had misjudged everyone. Even the least cultured seeming of them knew everything.

'Have you been to Venice?' Stella asked me, forking another slab of beef on to her plate.

'No. But I saw *Don't Look Now* with my mum,' I heard myself saying, and I curled my toes into my shoes and blushed deeply into my glass of wine. In fact, Russia had been my first time abroad.

Stella smiled and changed the subject and Flossy made a moron face at me.

Despite Stella's sighs and tuts Cassian disappeared the moment he had finished his food, and Flossy and I went upstairs to smoke out of the window, eventually curling up in the warmth of her huge bed to talk about sex.

'But did you actually see it?' I whispered.

'Of course I saw it,' sniggered Flossy. 'I sucked it!'

'Your mum is right. You are disgusting . . . What did it taste like?'

'Like the sea.'

Lying under the giant white duvet with her arms round my neck, Flossy fell asleep, laughing about her virginity. 'I wouldn't say I lost anything,' she would declare at every opportunity.

I couldn't sleep, though. I was too excited. The floorboards creaked, the dogs growled, my nose was cold and there was an owl or something hooting out there. After an hour or so of lying still and pretending it was my house and my life and I would never have to go back to Clapham, I decided to get up and find the kitchen.

I crept creakily out of the room, my feet stinging with the cold beneath them and my whole body shivering under my thin cotton nightie. It was long and white and from M&S, and I had been ecstatic when Flossy dragged a similar one out of a huge coffin of a moth-eaten drawer and pulled it over her head. Hers was actually Victorian but in the dark they looked nearly the same.

The moonlight shimmering through the windows lit me down to the basement and the first door I tried was the kitchen. It looked like something out of a Jane Austen novel. There was nothing under a hundred years old in there: a deep white bath of a sink with brass taps, a hot Aga rumbling in the corner and a stone-flagged floor that looked as if it had just been mopped. It almost made me miss kettles and sandwich makers and my soda stream. There was some kind of medieval torture instrument lying on the Aga, or it could have been an eighth-century tennis racket. I picked it up and batted an imaginary ball. Next morning I discovered it was for making toast in. No electric toasters in this kitchen. Oh, no.

I poured myself a glass of water from the terracotta jug on the table and peered out of the low window. Something was moving. A thing the size of a rat was scuttling across the bit of lawn in my view. A hedgehog.

Lifting up the heavy iron catch on the back door I went out into the garden and stood over the spiky creature, basking in the warmth of the spring night.

night. The moon made the grass and the bizarre beast look as though they were made of silver and, kneeling over it, I expected to feel cool metal when I touched its spines.

'Don't! They've got fleas,' said Cassian, squatting down next to me.

I gasped stupidly and looked over at him. 'Jesus Christ. What are you doing here? I found a hedgehog,' I sputtered, standing up, trying to quell my fear.

'He lives here. He's called Bill. Hello, Bill,' he said, fiddling with a thick lock of hair in front of his face and blinking furiously. 'I thought you'd come out – can't resist me? I was waiting for . . .' he mumbled. He had a silver ring on each finger and an unlit joint in his hand. 'I'm sorry about the waitress thing. I'm an arsehole. I'm . . . crap. You looked . . . and Flossy would have been deeply suspicious if I hadn't insulted you. OK?' His lazy manner, the dark and the balmy heat made me oddly calm and unselfconscious. 'Anyway, you did look like a waitress . . .' he whispered, essentially to himself.

He didn't seem to be judging me or scouring me for giveaway signs of working classness, and somehow I didn't care if he was.

I sat down on the grass and leant back on my arms, my legs stretched out in front of me. I tickled the blades of grass with my toes. 'Why is it so cold in your house?' I asked.

'We only have fires in winter,' Cass stated, as if I

had wanted to know why cold water comes out of the cold tap. 'Character building,' he smirked.

He lit the tip of the joint and watched as the little twist of Rizla glowed, turned to ash and dropped off. He handed it to me. I told him, feeling stupid now, that I didn't really know how and he took it from me gently, and put it between my lips. I wished for the first and last time that I had watched Mum and Lorry more closely. Snapping his heavy brass Zippo open with a clunk he held the fat flame up and nodded at me to breathe in. I lay back on the lawn, looked up at the stars in the blue velvet sky and blew a delicious stream of smoke out at them. Cassian Vinci lay next to me, silent, examining my face in the dark.

Slowly, he drew himself up on to his elbows. 'Open your mouth,' he said.

'?' I raised my eyebrows.

'Open your mouth,' he said, smiling and bringing his face closer to mine. I opened my mouth and he blew his hot exhaled smoke down my throat, pressing his lips to mine and resting his hand on my shoulder. Laughing, I drew the fumes into my lungs and, suddenly serious, looked up into his face, at his black sparkling eyes, his glowering eyebrows and his naughty smile.

'Again,' I commanded.

Flicking the burning joint far away now into the bushes, he lowered his mouth on to mine and kissed me hard, first slowly, then urgently, driving his tongue into me and covering my face with kisses. I wasn't thinking about anything now, but I knew we were going to do it and that it was not the same 'it' as Flossy had done or that Mum must do with her raggedy blokes. This was ours and it was going to be ours for ever. He pulled my nightdress up over my hips and moved my legs apart. Gently and then not so gently he stroked a finger in and out of me until I thought I might lose consciousness or scream. One finger, then two fingers, then three. I could feel his hard-on straining against me.

'God, you're beautiful,' he breathed, suddenly pressing his weight down on top of me, driving himself deep inside me so that I cried out and arched my back up towards him in pain and pleasure. I melted into the lawn, I smothered my screams in his neck and I bit my lip as he pulled at the thin white cotton that covered my aching body. I barely had time to register that I was in ecstasy.

Silent under the moon I could feel the marks of his kisses on my skin and I hugged Cassian tightly to me and kissed his ear.

'I'd never . . .' I began.

'Me neither but don't tell the press,' Cass giggled, rolling on to his back and pulling my nightie gently down over my knees. I was amazed at myself. I had wanted Cassian more than I had ever wanted anything and I now knew, I thought with a stupid self-satisfied sigh, what it was like to be madly, wildly, incapacitatingly in love. Lying there chatting inconsequentially about the real world that seemed barely to concern us, I knew I would be with him for ever. I felt that I already had been. When we kissed each other good night outside his bedroom door, blinking in the unexpected dawn light, I knew I would always look back on this night as the beginning of my life.

Cassian wasn't up when Flossy and I left the next morning. I wanted to tell her, I really did, but there didn't seem to be a decent way to broach the subject. 'Um, I slept with your brother last night.' Actually, that would have done fine. Far better than nothing. But the moment didn't come and I kept quiet. As soon as she woke up she was bouncing on top of me, hitting me with her pillow, scrabbling under the bed for her fags.

Then there was breakfast. We ran down in our nightdresses and found, to my surprise and Flossy's utter indifference, that a lady called Mrs Bridge had put a pot of coffee on the stove and was making toast in the antique tennis racket on the Aga. There was hot milk with skin on it in a jug on the table and various pots of home-made jam labelled in Biro with a date and contents – 'June '85 Damson' and so on. The dogs were noisily wolfing down enormous bowls of biscuits and milk from which they looked up briefly to snarl when I walked in, milk dribbling down their chops, backs bristling in anticipation of my snatching their bowls away for myself. I didn't bother.

'How's the back, Mrs B?' Flossy asked, pouring coffee and hot milk into a big bowl and wrapping her hands around it. Where were the mugs?

'Not so bad, thank you, Miss Florence. Just the odd twinge now and then,' Mrs B told her, putting both hands to the small of her back and arching to show just how much it could hurt should the need arise.

I was longing for Cassian to come down. Dreading Cassian coming down. Would we speak to each other? Would we smile? I kept hearing footsteps on the stairs and freezing in terror, only to be confronted by Stella, her face and hands already covered with mud, or Mr Bridge, who appeared to be some kind of odd-job man. At least, he carried a hammer and looked sort of dusty.

'Any chance of a tea, petal?' he asked his wife. She shooed him away, wiping her hands on her apron in disgust at his presumptiousness.

It was glaringly sunny outside and you could feel the heat seeping into the kitchen from a low latticed window that opened on to a herb garden.

'What mischief will you girls be up to today?' Mrs B asked, watching Flossy stuff a whole slice of toast into her mouth in one go. I couldn't eat.

'Moin inoo Moxford,' Flossy told her, nodding at me to check that I was happy with the plan. I would have been happy with anything Flossy wanted. 'Got to do something about what you look like,' she told me, wiping the crumbs and jam away from her mouth.

I saluted her obediently and we were off.

The plan was definitely to be naughty. We smoked on the no smoking bus and nobody dared tell us to stop. Well, Flossy smoked and I held a cigarette and occasionally sucked the end of it reluctantly. We sang Madonna songs at the top of our voices all the way, leaping up to dance and getting thrown violently back into our seats every time the bus stopped.

'I hope your mothers know you smoke,' was the most the driver could venture when we fell off in central Oxford, laughing and shouting. Flossy put two fingers up at him as he pulled away and we linked arms and pushed our way into the Saturday crowds.

The covered market was packed with people bustling about for their weekly shopping. Butchers pulled whole rabbits down from hooks and skinned them, fishmongers slapped gleaming wet trout on to their counters and slit their stomachs open, and florists tied vast bouquets up with pink shiny ribbon for people to take to weddings and christenings.

Flossy and I were only concerned with the jewellery stalls, though. We tried on silver rings shaped like snakes and dolphins, earrings that were big silver crosses or hoops down to our shoulders, and chunky Indian bracelets with Karma Sutra drawings carved into them.

'God, I don't think I'm supple enough for that,' Flossy giggled, cramming the bracelet on to her arm to jangle with all her others.

The very idea of sex made my cheeks flush and my eyes close with desire. I could smell him on my skin. I had had only about three hours' sleep and I had honestly never felt so energetic nor so wonderful. 'Worth a try, though,' I laughed and we walked away. When we turned the corner into the next aisle Flossy held up her arm to show me that she was still wearing the bracelet. And a snake ring. I instinctively glanced behind me to see if we were being followed by an irate stallholder or the police, but was immediately embarrassed by my lack of cool in this situation, and smiled at Flossy admiringly.

'Here,' she said, pushing the ring on to my finger. 'That's better already.'

By noon she had stolen me a tight white T-shirt with newsprint on it that barely came down below my breasts, some three-quarter-length black leggings, a heavy belt to hang over the top of them and a silver cross for my ear. Except I didn't have pierced ears.

'Oh, for God's sake . . .' she sighed, taking my hand and leading me down a side street.

Marcy had tattoos all over her face and neck. Her head was shaven apart from an orange strip down the middle, and she had thigh-high patent leather boots on. Not that any of this could be seen clearly in the gothic gloom of her tiny cellar shop.

'Two in this one, one in this one,' Flossy told her, sitting me down on a high stool. 'And one in the . . . left nostril?'

'Fuck off. No way,' I beamed.

'No, you're right. The right nostril,' Flossy nodded, as Marcy cleaned her vicious-looking instruments.

I don't know what came over me. I was doing something my mum would approve of even if Stella wouldn't. Unthinkable. On the other hand it was sunny and I was insanely in love. I was also still fifteen, just about. I suppose the piercings might have hurt if I hadn't been thinking about Cassian's hands.

So when we climbed the steps out of the darkness I was wearing four new silver studs, one of which was immediately torn out of my ear and replaced by my new cross.

We sat on the pavement outside a pub and drank Southern Comfort and lemonade, and ate bags of Bovril crisps. Flossy occasionally nodded to middle-aged women who were presumably friends of Stella's. Certainly they looked at us disapprovingly as though our punishment were only a phone call away.

'Her daughter didn't get into Queensbury . . . Her husband's fucking the au pair . . . She's just had her tits enlarged in LA . . . She shagged my dad when he'd already started going out with Mum,' Flossy informed me as they passed.

It was hot and my mouth was sticky from the drink so we walked down to the river and jumped in. The first tourists of the spring punted by under the willows while we wallowed like hippos, ducking our heads under and splashing about, reluctant to get out and swelter again, waiting for our clothes to dry. My hair was still wet, my new outfit clinging to every inch of me that it touched when we went into a newsagent's to buy cigarettes.

'Twenty Consulate,' Flossy told the man before adding: 'Don't you think those magazines up there are degrading to women?' She was standing in front of the ice-cream freezer and next to a shelf full of boxes of Tampax, jars of instant coffee and Pot Noodles. Student stuff.

He slapped the cigarettes down on top of his pile of *Oxford Mails* and glared at her.

'Because I do,' she said, and walked over to the racks, swiping porn mag after porn mag on to the floor in a flurry of pink tits and arses, glossy parted lips, surprised expressions and sucked fingers. Pushing me in front of her, she then hurried out of the shop, grabbing her unpaid-for cigarettes as she went and leaving the man squatting on the floor picking up his wares in bundles, shame-faced at the sight of all the exposed flesh and lurid colour.

Hand in hand, parading down the street, smiles of teenage immortality on our faces, even I had to concede that the men were all looking at me. 'See, it doesn't take much,' Flossy laughed, slapping my bum. 'If only you knew,' she said. But she wasn't jealous. It was hardly as if she wasn't good-looking anyway, and her self-confidence made her far more attractive than I could ever imagine being. As far as I was concerned, she was the beautiful one.

'Oh my God. You're a human sieve,' Stella said when we walked back into the kitchen that evening. 'I won't be held accountable for this young lady. You tell your mother that I completely abdicate responsibility.'

'Don't worry. Mum will love it,' I told her. It was true.

Cassian, who was slouched at the kitchen table with a kitten on his shoulder and a bowl of cereal in front of him, winked at me. I gasped and looked away.

After that my stay at The Old Vicarage became an agony of longing. Walking the dogs through hazy fields, over stiles, beside streams, picking the fat fruit from heavy trees, playing croquet out on the lawn and eating meal after endless meal with a silent and disdainful Cassian, I thought I might die. He barely glanced at me when others were there, ostentatiously ignoring me, hurling muttered insults at Flossy on the stairs. I breathed him in as he passed, my heart pounding, my mind spinning and my body weak with desire.

We were only together at night, but all day his name would whirl round my head – Cassian Vinci – over and over again, the ecstasy of the words stopping my throat and closing my eyes without my willing it. I couldn't believe nobody else noticed.

At dinner that second night over home-made rhubarb fool – I was beginning to get used to the initially shocking absence of Angel Delight – he sat darkly, looking as though the world offended him, and I stared at my plate, scraping food around it and trying to control the bright flush in my cheeks. I thought we must surely smell of each other, be covered in visible kisses. Our desire ought to have been a tangible thing, stretching across the table, writhing obscenely above the candlelight.

Creeping out again once Flossy was asleep, I was terrified he might not be there. I peered hopefully out of the kitchen window, feeling ridiculous in my bare feet and nightie, wondering how I could ever have imagined he might want me again. Lifting the catch on the door I started telling myself one night would have to be enough. I would go back upstairs and go to sleep, content in the knowledge that I had had my fair share of happiness. What more could I possibly expect?

He grabbed me round the waist and buried his face in my hair.

'Hey, gorgeous,' he whispered, grinning, and he tripped me up to pull me down on to the grass, laughing. We stayed outside, sharing joints, sipping horrible whisky from a silver hip flask, giggling and playing until the sky began to lighten. We never moved more than a centimetre away from each other and I started to think that sex eight times a night was normal. No, in fact, not normal. Not enough. I hated the separation afterwards – being pressed together but not inside each other was too far away. 'Again,' I would say, tapping him on the shoulder, nuzzling my face into his neck when our skin was still sticky, our breath still quick from the last time. I felt that we were two halves of the same person, that without him I was someone who had had an arm lopped off – coping but incomplete.

Was Flossy really so sound asleep every night when I slipped in and out of bed? Can it honestly have been so hot for that whole week in April? Could I seriously have survived on less than two hours' sleep a night? It seems so unlikely now, but I think so.

He called me Alisochka, Russifying my name in honour of the reason for our meeting, and he noticed everything about me as though studying me for an exam. He asked why one of my eyelashes was a billionth of a milli-metre higher than the others and how I had got the barely visible chip in my front tooth. Every night he chose a new favourite bit of me and left a love bite there – in the dimples in the small of my back, inside my right wrist, at the bottom of my throat, on the curve of my left breast and in the dip of my hip bone.

I suppose I knew Flossy would hate it, knew this was the kind of betrayal she would not forgive. And I adored her so much, was so grateful to her, owed what I already saw was a different self to her. I mean, here I was with people who laid the table for each meal as a matter of course, instead of either fending for themselves or chucking an approximate number of knives and forks into the middle of the take-away boxes.

I should have told her straight away. As it was I let her go on and on about Sergei without letting her know that I had already matched her. She didn't even seem to see how tired I was, how much coffee I was drinking, how wired and semi-hysterical with joy and fatigue I was.

The night before I left for home, Cassian told me

he loved me. 'Of course you do,' I whispered to him. 'I am you.' I told him about the bit in *Tess of the D'Urbervilles* when Angel and Tess have their fingers interlinked and can't tell which are hers and which are his. 'They are all yours,' Tess tells him, and that's how I felt. Without Cassian my fingers, my lips, my heart – none of them were any good to me. 'I will love you for ever,' I told him, lying there in the grass, watching him leaning on one elbow smoking a joint, smiling into the night.

In the morning he didn't look up from his cereal and Flossy stuck her tongue out at him over her croissant. 'Alice is going. Perhaps you'd like to say goodbye?' she asked him loudly.

'Bye,' he said, leaning deeper into his bowl and not raising his eyes.

'Bye,' I replied, making a face at Flossy. Sniggering and jostling each other out of the way, we crunched across the gravel to Stella's car, holding hands.

'See you Monday,' Flossy beamed through the sunlight.

'Monday,' I nodded and Stella started the engine.

It might as well have been a different school, such was the transformation. A different me. A different life. Even my mum noticed the difference. She was always telling me how beautiful I looked and how radiant – and I was right about the nose stud. She loved it.

Flossy and I disappeared into our own secret world. We got stoned together in the woods, turning up for lessons in fits of uncontrollable laughter, brambles stuck into our uniforms. I got cautioned about my stud but wore it anyway, a mark of my devotion to my friend. We sneaked into town together nearly every day to drink strong tea at the greasy spoon, to pinch the bums of the boys at our brother school, Kingsbury, as they queued for cigarettes in the newsagent's, and to steal make-up from Boots.

I meandered around the corridors now, always arm in arm with Flossy, as though I belonged there. I slouched over to the Formica table, holding my orange tray of steaming food as if it pained me to make more effort. I slumped into my seat and immediately began a whispering conference with Flossy, screaming with laughter, choking with derision, whooping with glee. I was now officially a teenager – exhausted by the slightest (non-sexual) exertion, irritated to the point of complete exasperation by anyone over eighteen and completely intolerant of the mildest weakness in others. Especially Tara.

Tara and Ursula still stuck together but nobody noticed them much. All Tara's once overwhelming power seemed to have vanished in a puff of smoke. Suddenly she was an ordinary schoolgirl, keen not to be belittled, anxious to build herself up just in case anyone tried to knock her down. It was obvious to me now that she had always considered me a possible rival in beauty and intelligence and had decided the moment she saw me that the worst should never happen. But it had.

# Seven

The first exeat we had I was back at Little Farford, rescued from school and Clapham by the wonderful sight of Stella's Volvo parked in between the Range Rovers in the school drive.

'No you can't,' Stella said as soon as we got into the car and before either of us had spoken.

'Owwwwwww,' Flossy whined. She had been going to ask if we could go to a party in Oxford that night.

'Daddy's home and so will you be,' Stella declared, winding down her window and letting the heat in. 'I've made profiteroles.'

Flossy retched noisily and leant against me in ostentatious resignation.

Giardino was indeed home, looming angrily behind his newspaper and rapping his fingers on the nearest available piece of furniture. Cassian, however, was not. He was on a school climbing expedition in the Lake District. For weeks before exeat I had burnt to see him, scratching his name almost invisibly into my hand with my compass, falling asleep thinking of him, waking up and expecting to see him beside me. I should have been devastated by his absence but somehow I wasn't. After all, I thought, we had the rest of our lives to see each other. It made no difference that we didn't dare speak on the phone, that I might not see him now until the summer holidays – what was the odd weekend in an eternity of perfect togetherness?

So instead of lolling about on the lawn with Cassian I lolled with Flossy instead, suggesting we take our joint outside just so that I could be there, in the exact spot that marked my happiness. Flossy had already forgotten all about Sergei and was involved in an extremely passionate romance with a bloke called Minnow from Kingsbury. She had slapped him on the bum one day in town and rather than blush and cower like the others did he had spun round and grabbed her wrists, glared into her face and asked her what kind of a slag she thought she was. She had laughed and asked him out for a drink that night. The pair of them had been sneaking about all term, having sex in the children's playground of the park near Kingsbury and writing each other dramatic letters full of jealousy and bitterness – each was convinced of the other's betrayal.

'He's shagged Tara, I know he has,' Flossy moaned, opening up the roach in our joint with a matchstick.

'You know perfectly well he's never clapped eyes on the girl,' I told her, laughing.

'Pah. That's what he would say,' she spat, staring angrily into the darkness.

We could see Giardino inside the house, pacing about in his dressing gown, switching the lights on and off, looking lost and angular.

'Jet lag,' Flossy said, turning away from the sight of him, hoping this would stop him noticing us.

Later, when Flossy had gone to sleep, I made my way through the night gloom to Cassian's room, pulling back the sheets on his bed and lying down where he had lain, pushing my face into his pillow to breathe him in better. I must have been in there for an hour, luxuriating in his proximity, watching the red glow of his clock radio telling me to go back to Flossy. Before I left I tore a piece of paper out of a scraggy pad on his desk and wrote him a note by moonlight with a chewed black Biro. I left it under his pillow. 'I love you more than words can wield the matter. More than eyesight, strength and liberty.'

Well, I did.

The end of term seemed a lifetime away. Hundreds of afternoons bunking off and sunbathing on the high grass, thousands of letters from Minnow to analyse and reanalyse, millions of teachers' reprimands to be endured: 'Alice Reynolds, I don't know what's happened to you lately, I really don't,' and similar. The interminable four weeks stretched on and on into the distance as the summer got hotter and hotter and hotter. The chapel was full of bright pink faces glowing in the early morning heat, and sports were a barely endurable nightmare of sunburn and heat exhaustion. The only thing on which my boiling brain could concentrate was my imminent week with Cassian.

'Cass will be there, unfortunately, but at least we can steal his hash,' Flossy told me with an apologetic smirk.

'Don't worry. I like him,' I said, the nearest I ever came to honesty. Not that near, it has to be said.

'Don't be stupid. Nobody in their right mind could like him,' she replied, and she was right. Who could do anything but love him? I thought.

Stella was in a flap about a painting of one of her ancestors that someone was supposed to be delivering the evening Flossy and I were celebrating the end of term so Cassian brought the dinner in himself. I hadn't seen him for nearly eight weeks and I kept my eyes doggedly on my napkin as he lurched into the room with a big bowl of steaming stew and a ladle.

'All right?' he asked us both in as uninterested a way as was humanly possible, plonking the dinner down and nonchalantly collapsing into his chair.

'Was till I saw you,' Flossy snapped back happily, slopping some food on to her plate and shouting for Stella to bring some salt up.

'I have thought of you every second of every day,' he whispered into my ear, still lying on top of me, still hard inside me on the back lawn under our tree only a few hours later. I shut my eyes blissfully and held him tight.

This time, though, it wasn't only the nights we spent together. I made excuses to go into Little Farford, enthusiastically volunteering to fetch whatever Stella needed, especially if Flossy was in the bath or shouting down the phone line at Minnow (who, it transpired, had in fact slept with Tara at her cousin's house one weekend – she losing her virginity, he lashing out at Flossy, whom he suspected of getting off with his friend Darcus at a party in Windsor. She had). Cassian waited for me outside the front gate, leaning back conspicuously into the ivy and shading his face from the sun with a brown braceleted arm. Boys were allowed to wear silver bracelets and eyeliner in those days. It was the eighties. He put his arm proudly round my waist and we paraded into the village, young, beautiful and in love.

'We ought to have a banner,' said Cass. '"Not Married. Just Wicked."' One was also allowed to describe things as 'wicked' back then, but only if you were under twenty. I couldn't see how anyone could miss our imaginary banner, red and billowing above our heads, declaring us the happiest people alive. We sat outside the pub, unable to stop smiling into each other's eyes, barely capable of sipping our drinks since it involved unclasping our hands. Cassian spent half an hour trying to decide whether my eyes were more of a sea or an emerald green. I felt mad with love and the incredible heat.

'I hope I die first,' Cass said, stroking my cheek.

'You're not allowed to. We'll do it together when we're ninety-seven,' I told him.

'Deal,' he agreed, and leant forward to kiss me.

I think it was that very afternoon that me and

Flossy overdid it. I had stolen the grass from Mum's little box before I came down to Little Farford and I had no idea what kind or how strong it was. We had never smoked more than one joint in a day – it had always been something a bit rebellious to do rather than an exercise in total inebriation and it didn't seem like a big deal.

I suppose the trouble was that Flossy had run out of fags, so we rolled all the grass into one enormous joint and smoked it neat out by the river in the field with the dogs dashing around us, leaping in and out of the water, bringing us wet sticks and barking at the passers-by. I was lying on my front topless and Flossy was sitting on my bum rubbing sun cream into my back when Cassian found us. We were giggling insanely (Flossy thought one of the ducks looked a bit like Minnow) and couldn't stop however much Cassian snarled at us.

'Oh my God, Cass, I think Alice just made me smoke opium or something. I've never been so off my face. You should try some. Alice, do the business for my illustrious elder brother,' Flossy said, collapsing on top of me and almost rolling us both into the water. I beamed up at him full of love but he wouldn't catch my eye.

'Listen, you stupid tart, you shouldn't be smoking anything, let alone God knows what. And you,' he said, throwing a hand out at me, 'shouldn't be giving my sister stuff that she very obviously can't handle.'

Suddenly I wasn't stoned any more. My heart

sank and my stomach lurched as I sat up, pulling my top back on and not daring to look at him. He had never spoken to me like that before, never used that awful censorious tone as though he didn't love me at all. I was mortified.

'You have no idea, brother, what I can and can't bloody well handle. I've handled a lot more than you in my time, I can tell you that much. Right, Alice?' she tittered, oblivious to my change of mood.

Cassian had already turned away in disgust and was stomping off back to the house, his head bowed. Just before he got to the stile he turned round.

'I'm supposed to tell you to come back for tea – Dad's just arrived. I'll say I couldn't find you,' he shouted, and jumped over in one leap, making me want him desperately.

'I happen to know that Mr Cassian Vinci is a virgin,' Flossy chortled when he had gone. I looked away.

She was in the shower, trying to sober up, and I had come in from the field and was squinting into the darkness, finding my way by the banister, when he leapt out at me from behind the curtain.

'I need you,' he whispered, biting my neck and dragging me against him. As soon as he touched me the rest of the world blurred out of focus and the strength seeped out of me, melting into an ache of lust and submission.

'I thought you hated me,' I murmured, shutting my eyes and leaning against him, tears of relief welling in me as I slowly accepted the fact that things were still OK. I was beginning to register how stupidly vulnerable love makes a person.

'Oh God, I'm sorry,' he told me, holding my face in his hands and looking into it. 'I just hate Flo doing drugs. I mean, dope's one thing, but I'm really not going to have her even fucking touching anything else,' he said. 'And you,' he added, kissing my nose, 'mustn't either.'

I sighed dreamily. 'Cass, Flossy and I are both old enough to decide whether—' I began, but I felt him tense in my arms and spun round, pulling away from him. Flossy was standing naked on the landing with a white towel turbanned on top of her head.

'Oh, gross,' she said.

I thought my heart would break when she told me we couldn't be friends any more. 'The last thing I want to think about is where my bloody brother puts his body parts. How could you?'

I tried to tell her I loved him but that seemed to make it worse. 'You can't love someone who collects *Spiderman* comics,' she spat, and I packed up my stuff and skulked out of the house, shattered and alone. Crushed. I couldn't find Cass to say goodbye and, leaving The Old Vicarage, the place that was the embodiment of all my childhood dreams, with no word to anyone, I tried to freeze myself into invulnerability as I had once done at school. I told myself that nothing could hurt me. But now I knew it was no longer true.

# Eight

Hill Place is not easy to find. 'Do you have a Lady Hermione Sinclair staying with you?' I had asked the receptionist a week earlier. Moments later Hermione was on the line herself.

'Hi, um, it's Alice Reynolds, Tara's friend . . .' I began, worried she might hang up or not know who I was, or be in such a state that she would not even understand what I was talking about. But no.

'Fizzy, darling, how *are* you?' she cried, full of genuine warmth and enthusiasm. 'Goodness, it's been an age. How absolutely lovely to hear from you. How is your adorable mother? I've not seen her since we travelled up to meet you from Russia, centuries ago. Charming young lady, and such fun!'

She didn't seem to find it in any way odd when I invited myself along for a visit, and she insisted she would pop into the nearest village to fetch some things for tea. She sounded neither mad, drunk nor drug-crazed and I began to look forward to seeing her, the Zander nightmare notwithstanding.

Winding through tiny places called Upper and Lower this that and the other, almost killing a lost cow, and asking directions in at least four thatched pubs, I eventually pulled my car into the gravel drive of what I had thought would be some sort of loony bin. Though it was only the end of April it was hot and sunny and I had the roof down and my shades on. Zander had called me six times since I set off about various projects he wanted me to undertake (more subterfuge – this time in Togliatti). I had never managed to broach the subject of the Chechens and we seemed to have slipped easily back into the intoxicating everyday combat of our relationship. The train felt like ages ago and I was now feeling guilt-stricken about betraying him in his, let's face it, possible innocence. And also, of course, about betraying Hermione by sleeping with her ex-husband without her knowledge. I was not proud of myself, but it was a lovely day and somehow I felt all optimistic for a change.

I think it was down to Dolores. Dolores, a South American beautician at an exclusive hairdresser's on Conduit Street, always made me feel as though, at twenty-eight, my life had barely begun. She had this Latin thing of putting the past behind her and looking ahead. 'You get through the troubles of life,' she would say in a very heavy accent, tearing a million or so hairs from my inner thigh, 'and if you are a woman you carry on. Men, you know, they have the nervous breakdown, they just collapse. But a woman need money she take a job cleaning houses, if we need to feed the children we feed the children, no?' Not that I had any children or anything, but I liked the idea of all this feminine strength in adversity.

She was on her third husband and she was

looking superb. Her first had been an eighteen-year-old football player back home, the second had got her to England and the third, a Serb, was new. She was fifty-seven years old and was having the best sex of her life. 'He like a bull!' she said. 'I thought I just not interested in sex, but Milovan . . . He watching the rugby and I cuddle up to him and he switch the TV off. Straight upstairs,' she rolled her eyes orgasmically.

Dolores was the only woman in London offering 'the full Brazilian'. If you kept your knickers on for a bikini wax she just laughed. 'I have a client, she sixty-five years of age, she always have the full Brazilian. She say it's the only thing still turns her husband on.' Not a dignified procedure but Zander was very much of the same opinion as her old client's husband and I always felt sexy the moment I stepped out of the salon. Like wearing new underwear but better.

The lawns leading up to the gorgeous sixteenth-century manor house that appeared to be Hill Place were on fire with yellow daffodils and people were dotted about amongst them, some reading by the duck pond and some just soaking up the sunshine.

It looked like a stately home, serene but slightly crumbling, and there was no suggestion of security or incarceration.

The hallway was full of cut flowers, and a young woman in a crisp blouse sat behind a valuable-looking desk, talking on the telephone.

'Miss Reynolds?' she whispered to me, her hand

over the receiver. I nodded and she pointed to a door just down the corridor.

I crept along the soft carpet and entered a large light, drawing room, furnished with pink and white flowery sofas and some antique chairs. A small table had been laid for tea, with sandwiches, a fruit cake and some toast and peperium. Lady Hermione was holding an ornate teapot in one hand and a strainer in the other.

'Darling!' she exclaimed, and put everything down to rush across the room and take me in her arms. Although still extremely slim, she was fatter and altogether healthier-looking than she used to be. Her hair had greyed but she looked elegant and imposing, a handsome woman who showed no signs of addiction or illness, mental or otherwise. It was an astonishing transformation considering the last time I had seen her.

'Fizzy, sweetheart, it is gorgeous to see you. Goodness, what happened to your face? You look tired. Sit down and tell me everything. Is your mother as unconventional as ever?'

She clasped both my hands in hers and her blue eyes glittered with affection and joy. I was immediately comforted and thought her, as ever, the perfect representative of the upper classes, a people I had so wanted to become one of and in whom I had been so bitterly disappointed. The money, the houses, the complacency – none of it had turned out to be worth anything. The balls had quite definitely not lived up to a little girl's dream. I thought of the posh louts in black tie vomiting, the couples shagging in the loos; the drugs and poor Flossy. The fairy tale I had hoped could be mine if only I could transform myself into one of them did not exist. I knew that now. But Lady Hermione made it all seem real again.

'I found some cream,' said Stella, pushing open the door to the drawing room with her loafered right foot. 'Ah, Alice, you're here,' she smiled, coming over to give me a kiss.

'You don't mind, do you, darling?' asked Hermione. 'It was Stella's day for coming and I thought it would be delicious for us all to get together. It was awful of me not to have told you.'

I didn't even know they knew each other but it now seemed obvious that they should. I wondered now if Stella knew why I had left Little Farford that day twelve years ago.

'You haven't changed a bit, dear,' Stella said, kissing me fondly. 'You always were so pretty. I wondered if Cassy wasn't sweet on you the time you came down with darling Flossy.' Obviously she hadn't the faintest idea. She tinkled with sad laughter and picked up her teacup with the same old grimy gardener's fingers. Her grey hair was back in a ponytail and she was wearing black jeans and a huge white shirt with the sleeves rolled up. 'Cassy and Tara are coming over next week, actually. You ought to pop down for tea,' she told me. 'You two were both such close friends of Flossy's,' she added, clouding.

There was some general chat about arrangements for Tara and Cassian's impending arrival in Little Farford – it must be odd for Stella and Hermione, I thought, having children who were going out with each other. It was certainly agonising to hear about them.

'Any . . . news?' Hermione wanted to know, looking meaningfully at Stella.

'Oh God, don't,' Stella replied, rolling her eyes to the ceiling. 'I don't think that boy's ever going to propose. We will probably die without grand-children,' she laughed miserably.

'Darling, couldn't you have a word with Tara?' Hermione asked me with a playful smile. 'It really is about time. I have had the pair of them in here sipping tea for over seven years and I have never once even seen them hold hands, let alone start sending out invitations,' she sighed.

Well, that was some comfort, I supposed. Not that I wanted Cassian to be unhappy, but I didn't think I could stand it if he actually married Tara. I hadn't managed to harden up quite that successfully.

Stella, who obviously despaired of them as much as Hermione, looked horribly like her daughter – Flossy's combination of composure and a sparkle of naughtiness. And Hermione was being so kind with her tea and her cake that I felt my defences beginning to crumble as the past crept up on me. For years now I had been totally at ease in this kind of situation – having tea with middle-aged ladies. I found myself genuinely wanting tea around fourish these days and no longer saw it as the sort of thing only Barbara Cartland and the Queen Mother actually did. You couldn't surprise me with a home-made fruit cake and a pot of peperium any more. I had even been known to take buyers for tea at the Waldorf where you can watch old people ballroom dancing over a warm scone with jam and clotted cream. But now I remembered the me I had been when I had first known these ladies – naïve, hopeful, anxious to be accepted.

I couldn't rustle up the energy to do what I had planned and ask Hermione about Zander, at least not without confessing everything and crying a lot. I didn't want to think about him today while the sun was out and I had a slab of cake in my hand.

'So tell us what happened to your poor lovely face,' Hermione said, eager not to dwell on Tara's spinsterhood. She picked up a cake from the silver stand and said 'Thank you' to herself. Her manners were so impeccable that she was unconsciously incapable of receiving anything even from her own hands without expressing gratitude.

'Well actually, I was attacked on a train to Moscow by some blokes who said they um . . . knew . . . Zander,' I offered, overcome with lassitude. I had become too weak to lie and too weak to tell the truth.

'Let's hope they find him, shall we?' she said, suddenly pursing her lips in distaste. 'I assume they want to kill him,' she laughed mirthlessly. 'Keep away from that man, dear girl,' she told me, glaring into my face now. 'Oh, I know he's charming and I know how he can . . .' she paused to be sure she expressed herself tactfully, '. . . how he can . . . hold sway over a woman, believe me – I lost everything to him. I think he only pays for this to keep me quiet,' she added, throwing her arm out at the room in demonstration of what Zander had left her with.

I knew all this, but I devoted a great deal of time and effort to not thinking about it. I suppose a bit of me hoped that Hermione's collapse had had nothing really to do with him.

'But don't be sucked in. He is sad and he will make you sad for him, but don't mistake that for love, Fizzy,' she concluded, softer now, but shining with certitude.

By this stage I had blushed down to my fingertips and my eyes were blurred with tears of shame. God knows how on earth she knew. I think she just guessed I must be shagging Zander because she had heard I was working with him. Did he really have this effect on every woman that ever clapped eyes on him? Seemingly so.

'What is he sad about, Hermione?' I asked meekly, unable to meet her eyes. Might as well plunge in and get an answer now it had begun. I counted the roses on my teacup. Nine. My phone was ringing in my handbag but none of us registered it.

'Darling, it is the most terrible thing imaginable, but it is no excuse for his behaviour. No excuse for his treatment of those who have loved him. None.'

Hermione was shaking with a dull rage that had plainly been her companion here for years. So he had done it, I thought. Whatever it was. In her quiet misery her heavy rings looked too big for her delicate fingers and the cardigan thrown jauntily round her shoulders seemed pathetic in its lime-green optimism.

Stella got up and walked over to the French windows, not embarrassed but exasperated with her friend. 'Mini, you are too soft on that bastard,' she said to the daffodils out on the lawn. She had obviously said this a great many times before. She was used to cataloguing Zander's crimes, to telling Hermione exactly what slime she had managed to marry. 'He barely sees his own bloody daughter, he has stolen your whole life from you, ruined countless others, and as for that poor girl he married . . .' she spat quietly.

Hermione sighed and began to cut another slice of cake. 'Oksana,' she said softly. It dawned on me in the flash of a tea strainer in the sunlight that this must be the Chechen boys' sister.

'I mean, quite frankly I don't know why you don't arrange a little accident for him yourself,' Stella went on, warming to her well-worn rant.

'That's enough, darling,' Hermione smiled weakly, no less used to this routine than her friend. 'Cake?' she asked, though we all had some already.

This whole nightmare meeting was now veering towards the side of the extremely intense. I had never felt more awkward, cowering there, waiting for some new revelation to send the world spinning.

The women chatted on but I was barely listening to them. I was nestled now into an armchair of complete humiliation and confusion, not knowing whether I should pretend we were all friends having tea again or just leave.

I was horrified that everyone knew about me and Zander. I think while it was still a secret I didn't feel so crap about it. Now, though, my total moral disintegration was out in the open. Somehow, without there being any convincingly concrete reason for it, my visit had made me shake off some of my habitual denial and see the cruel truth of Zander's guilt. It wasn't that Hermione had openly accused him of murder, or even joined in with Stella's attack on him, but she had been so open and kind, so much the opposite of what he was, that I felt her to be in the right and him to be in the wrong whatever the issue.

Before I left I found myself promising Hermione tea with my mother in Hampstead, although how I was going to lure Mum to North London I had no idea. I kissed the ladies, barely holding back from bursting into years' worth of tears, begging their forgiveness and pleading for their help and protection. Hugging Stella was probably as close as I would ever be to Cassian or Flossy again.

But I held it together, put my sunglasses back on, dragged my hair back into its ponytail, checked the messages on my mobile and clunked the car alarm off from a distance, simultaneously bringing the roof down. I was not going to fall apart over this, I just wasn't. I would have to force Zander to speak to me properly. Maybe there was some explanation. Maybe he hadn't meant to do it. Maybe I could help him deal with it. Tonight.

I was nauseated by the prospect of facing him with this horror – we both hated emotional outpouring – but I was sicker at the thought of just leaving things as they were. I couldn't carry on sleeping in this man's bed, living in a flat he had bought for me, smuggling his stupid antiques, feeling so wrapped up in him if he was a . . . something so melodramatic-sounding and unlikely that I couldn't quite bring myself even to voice it. I put my foot down and overtook an old man in a Bentley. The wind in my hair and Celine Dion reaching a heartbreaking crescendo in my ears (and, obviously, my soul) I squinted into my rear-view mirror and hoped for the best.

Unfortunately, though, Zander turned up at the flat, wily as a snake, before I was ready for him. He had a soft black Armani shirt on, the same colour as his eyes, beige baggy turn-ups and gleaming chestnut brogues. He sparkled with energy as he strode into the room, glancing around for changes, pacing the floor and tapping his fingers on any pieces of furniture he passed. His powerful magnetism squashed all my thoughts of rebellion – as ever.

'Pleased to see me?' he grinned, slapping my bum

hard enough to turn me on. God, he was irritating. The most idle, the most demeaning, the most arrogant gesture and I was already helpless, though he couldn't see it. Yet.

'No,' I said, ignoring his assault and putting the coffee on the stove, getting the milk out of the fridge and smelling it. It looked suspiciously old in there, alone with only a bottle of Sancerre for company.

'Listen,' he began importantly, moving into work mode, 'about this Togliatti deal. I need you to get going. Check it out, you know? They're not going to wait for ever and the thing is fucking valuable. Know what I mean? I mean *fucking* valuable, OK?'

The way he always talked about this kind of stuff reminded me of the first time Mum met him. She had liked him. She had really liked him. To an annoying extent. I mean, plainly she didn't know he was Tara's dad, and she'd thought he was flash and right wing and dreadful. But she hadn't been able to help it. He had turned up to get me from hers once, lurching his enormous car up on to the kerb by the pub where it shone its beetly blackness all inappropriate for the area. He'd ignored the crappiness of the grim little flat completely and walked into it as if he was walking into a casino in Monte Carlo. He'd had three-dozen pale pink roses for Mum in his arms and he'd told her he wanted to buy the sculptures in the hall. Of course, they were by her: her pregnant stick people. He did buy them as well, and she has loved him ever since, tittering girlishly at the very mention of him. Not a peep from her about him being too old for me. She'd never even asked if he'd been married before or had children or anything.

Actually her sculptures look sort of proper and reputable on his drinks cabinet. People always comment on them.

Anyway, a week later she'd announced her verdict: 'He's the kind of guy who likes to tell you what kind of guy he is.' I hadn't been able to stop laughing. That was exactly the kind of guy he was. I could hear him now telling some client how he didn't take any shit, how he wouldn't compromise on his first price and all the sort of stuff he was forever saying. He was like this now. Kind of guy.

'The thing' was an icon of the Rublev School, almost certainly by Andrei Rublev himself, painted in the late fourteenth century. It was a Hodigitria Virgin, the Mother of God of Smolensk, ingeniously removed from a church in the Moscow Kremlin when Marx was saying that religion was the opiate of the masses. People started losing respect for all things ecclesiastical fairly immediately, but there were always collectors.

This curator, aware that his days in a job were numbered, had got someone to make a shoddy copy of the Virgin and had swapped them round on his night shift. It had moved through four or five owners since then and now these thugs in Togliatti were flogging it, having presumably stolen it themselves. They had no clue as to its actual value but they had managed to work out that Zander was keen.

'It's not the Old Testament Trinity unfortunately, but it should be good for a quid or two, what do you think, Fizzles?' Zander said, raising his eyebrows. The idea of actually holding a lost Rublev in our arms was one of the things that bound us so tightly to each other. And I was flattered, stupid really, that an expert like Zander always consulted a novice like me. If it really was by Rublev I thought it could be good for at least a few hundred thousand quid.

He started to describe the icon. Hodigitria is Greek for 'leading the way' and Greek legend has it that such an icon restored sight to two blind men. Others think she was a talisman for Greek emperors on military campaigns or that she was originally found in a port where sailors prayed to her before going to sea.

The Greek Tsar Konstantin Monomakh, at any rate, blessed his daughter Anna with it when she married a certain Russian Prince Vsevolod. Then Anna bequeathed it to her son Vladimir, who put it in Smolensk Cathedral in 1097. Since then the Virgin has been one of the most popular figures for Russian icon painters and she turns up a lot in one form or another.

I was the only person Zander trusted to get it out and I beat down my uncertainty – refusing not to be excited. I loved all this – the thrill of finding something no one had seen for years, the feeling of elation when I came back to London with my treasure, Zander's arousal at a job well done and the ecstatic sex of success. I pushed the Oksana question as far as possible out of my active consciousness and thought about the job. I had to believe in his innocence – I had no other life to fall back on any more. Anyway, he had paid good money for me.

'No flying internally on this one. It's too big, too conspicuous. Too dicey. You're getting a boat up the Volga and back. It will take just over a week but it will be worth waiting for,' he said, leaning out of my open window on to the high street to check his car wasn't being ticketed. 'We need to get it back here by the end of September at the latest, OK?' he shouted to the street at large.

'And my commission is?' I shouted back out to him.

He came in, squinting from the sun, adjusting his eyes. 'Your commission is the usual plus a fantastic weekend in the Russian countryside with me when you get in. I've got to sort something with a bloke in Brick Factory.'

'You're joking.'

'Nope. Brick Factory. That's what it's called. Anyway, he's got a big dacha near it – *shashliks*, *banya*.'

'Oh, great. Kebabs. Can't wait.'

'Shut up. You'll love it. Anyway, it's a long project, so we don't have to think about it this very moment,' he said, his tone changing. Business over.

I heard him coming up behind me and I shivered as he bit my neck. Anticipating the rest, I had the vague thought that I had failed to confront him about anything at all. Then the lust choked me. Oksana or no Oksana.

'Close the curtains,' he whispered, running his big hands hard over my breasts. 'Unless you want those wankers over there to call the police,' he added, pulling my head back, squeezing my face roughly and ripping my shirt off my shoulders, his knee rammed between my legs. Sex with Zander was an expensive business.

# Nine

Mum was lying on the cushions on the floor when I got home from Little Farford. There was a burning fag in the ashtray by her side and a can of beer in the grate.

'You're disgusting,' I said, throwing my suitcase down and kicking my shoes under the table.

'Fizzy Fizz, don't be like that,' she slurred. 'I didn't think you were coming back till morning. I'd have tidied up . . .'

A bloke I'd never seen before walked into the room followed by the sound of a flushing toilet. 'Hey man,' he said to me and lay down next to Mum, gnarled toenails poking out of the end of his sandals.

Compared in my mind to Flossy's, as every home inevitably would be from now on, the place was repulsive. I hated the filthy net curtains, the burnt grey carpets, the forever flickering telly, the foul purple drape slung over a brown sofa and the hippie bloody cushions. Ejected from heaven I had become very aware that I was now in hell. I snapped.

'Get out,' I said to Gnarly.

'Cool it, baby,' he moaned, looking as surprised as his drug-petrified features would allow.

'I mean it,' I insisted, grabbing him by the hand and pulling him upright. I hustled him to the door as he tried to pick up a brown cardigan that belonged to him. 'Go on. Fuck off,' I said, shoving my hands into his horrible skinny T-shirted back to get him out on to the landing. 'And you,' I said firmly, going back into the sitting room, 'go to bed.'

Mum was too inebriated to argue and she shuffled off compliantly, leaving me to vent my despair in tidying up.

Enraged by my situation and my total impotence as far as making up with Flossy or seeing Cassian were concerned, I decided I would at least take control of this revolting flat. I tore down the curtains and threw them out of the window on to the Tarmac of the dustbin area below. I ripped at the edges of the carpet and found it was barely held down. Heaving furniture out of the way I tore the evil-smelling stuff up off the floor in the cheap squares in which it had been so shoddily laid and I chucked them out on top of the curtains. The boards weren't as awful as they could have been, and once some of the nails had been pulled out they would probably look OK. I was going to buy some material to make curtains, sand the stupid floors and paint these disgusting nicotine-yellow walls white first thing in the morning. I scrubbed the kitchen and bathroom, threw out the thing over the sofa in preparation for re-covering it, hurled the cushions to a better fate than they deserved and followed them with all the copies of *Time Out* and the

*Morning Star*, letters, fag packets, ashtrays and other useless stuff that cluttered the room. I would put bright bulbs in the lamps (to my total embarrassment Mum had green and red-tinted forty-watt bulbs all over the house), vases of fresh flowers everywhere, and I might even try to revarnish the table.

By the time I had done what I could it was four o'clock in the morning and I fell asleep on the sofa under the open windows to a nightmare about Cassian looking for me in the garden but not being able to see me however much I shouted and tugged at his arms.

Mum was very cross when she woke me up at eleven the next day, wrapped in her old black and red kimono. 'Fizzy love, what on earth do you think you're doing?' she complained – about as angry as she gets, which explained her hopelessness as a teacher.

'I am trying,' I said, opening my eyes, 'to make this shithole habitable.'

'I don't know what's happened to you since Russia but it's not very nice,' she said, pottering off to the kitchen to make herself a cup of Nescafé.

'You can't drink instant coffee, Mum,' I told her. 'People only drink real these days.' Tolerantly, she rolled her eyes and made me a cup of instant which I drank, pretending to half gag at every swallow.

'Well, as long as you don't think I'm going to be doing any decorating,' she said, and trundled back to sit on the vanished cushions. 'Bloody hell,' I heard her mutter, perching on the edge of the table in the wreckage of her flat. At this point I took all the cups and glasses out of the cupboards and smashed them on the floor. Then I ground them under my cheap shoes, sobbing loudly and hitting my head against the sharp metal corners of the open cupboard doors.

When my face was covered in tears, snot, saliva and scratches I found myself in Mum's arms on the sofa, biting at the shoulder of her dressing gown and snivelling helplessly.

'What happened there, Princess?' she asked.

'Nothing,' I cried, 'absolutely fucking nothing,' and I chewed the inside of my cheeks until they bled.

Far from redecorating the flat I retired to my room and refused to get out of bed for nearly a week. Mum brought me hot Ribena, boxes of Cheeselets and packets of Wagon Wheels. She hadn't smoked a single cigarette since the night I got back and no blokes had so much as knocked on the door. Whenever she went out she came home with bunches of daffodils or tulips and I could hear her humming to herself like she only did when she was sculpting. Well, one of us was alive.

I tried to force myself to sleep as much as possible. When I was awake my whole body was in an agony of loss, dying for Cassian. It already seemed unlikely that he had ever kissed me, that I had ever smelt of him, that he had ever thought I looked like Belinda Carlisle, even if he did temper it with 'but your tits are smaller'. I no longer believed he existed. If he did he would surely have phoned. I lay there, telling a God I didn't believe in that if he would make Cassian call I would go to church every Sunday for the rest of my life. Obviously God wasn't about to fall for this. Nothing happened.

Nothing except my stupid sixteenth birthday.

'Surprise!' Mum announced the day before it. Five days, seven hours and fifteen minutes since I had last kissed Cassian. She threw a white envelope on to my pillow, triumphant. I sat up, wondering how to pretend to be pleased. There was nothing I wanted that she could give me. Especially not tickets to see some nightmare band of American male strippers on the opening night of their first UK tour.

'Kris designed their costumes!' said Mum, hooting with laughter. 'It'll be a riot.'

'Mum, there is no way I am going to this,' I told her.

'You can bring a friend. What about Florence?' she said, and I burst into tears.

The whole place was pounding with strip-club music, and hundreds of women in shoulder-padded blouses and short skirts were drinking themselves into an anticipatory frenzy. The air was thick with smoke and booze and the little round tables were weighed down with brightly coloured cocktails, palm trees and umbrellas poking jauntily out of them. The terrified barman was selling Orgasms and Slow

Comfortable Screws as though the drinks really delivered what they promised. The light in the club seemed to be uniformly red, and the hormones were raging such that every woman in there was flushed and open-mouthed in eagerness for what they seemed to think would be imminent sex.

I was so miserable I thought it only fair that I faint or die or something. I should start wearing corsets.

I thought I had got out. I thought I had made a friend. I thought I was loved by the most beautiful boy in the world, but it was a joke far crueller than Tara's Valentine's card. I had seen what might have been mine and then the God who hadn't let Cassian phone and rescue me had laughed in my face. Here I was at a strip joint with my hippie mum and her loser friend.

'Check out the red leather pouches!' shouted Kris, winking at me lewdly.

The men were vile, their show grotesque. The light, the smoke, the screaming, the writhing, the thrusting. The men shoved their orange oily bodies in the faces of the eager wailing crowd, throwing their long hair about, rolling their arses into the spotlight, rubbing their cocks through the barely existent costumes Kris had supplied them with and pretending to sodomise the women who ran breathless, pissed and drooling on to the stage.

'Happy birthday, darling,' Mum said to me, handing me a huge strawberry daiquiri.

In the nauseating swill of the loos I could hear

some women sniggering over their make-up bags. 'Someone's had one orgasm too many,' laughed one, presumably blotting her lipstick or making a silly face at her mascara brush. I flushed away my vomit and wiped my mouth.

'Oh my God, I'd let that blond one lick me out any day,' said another with a sigh.

'You'd let anyone lick you out, Angela,' replied her friend.

I emerged from my cubicle and they fell silent, quickly finishing their faces and rushing back to the show.

The finale, involving Christ knows what, was yet to come. I looked at myself in the mirror. I was horribly pale and my hair hung lankly around my face. I had circles under my eyes. I appeared to be dressed in black sacks (some of the few items I hadn't thrown away before I went to Little Farford) and it was no wonder Cassian hadn't phoned me. I didn't think I could bear it any more.

I got a 10p piece out of my see-through purse with the red zip and went out to the front of the theatre to find a phone.

'Little Farford six two eight seven. Flossy? Flossy, is that you, sweetie?' Stella said, and I hung up.

When we got home there was more hell to come. It was probably one o'clock in the morning and I was leaning over the loo when the phone rang. 'Baby, it's your friend in some call-box in Oxford,' Mum shouted, so I staggered out to talk to Flossy, to make things all right.

'You fucking cow,' she slurred when I put the receiver to my ear. 'You fucking stupid cow. I trusted you and you fucked my big brother,' she shouted. She sounded very drunk. 'Just because I got a shag before you, you jealous bitch, you've got to use my fucking family to fuck me over. Fuck you!'

'Where are you?' I asked, more worried about her than anything.

'Ben's squat,' she spat, and hung up. I briefly considered phoning Stella who had sounded worried when I'd got through to her earlier from the club, but I decided I had probably interfered in their lives enough. Plus which I was dying.

I carried on throwing up all night. Mum brought a bucket to the edge of my bed so I wouldn't have to run to the loo and she stayed up doing her sculptures in the transformed sitting room until the sun rose and I fell into a weak and defeated sleep.

We never did sand the floors, but Mum had painted the walls white on my birthday and there were flowers everywhere. She had found a beautiful embroidered quilt to put over the sofa, there was a white lace tablecloth on the wreck of a table and swathes of butter muslin hanging from the curtain rails. Whatever had snapped in me the night I got home from Little Farford seemed to have woken Mum from her stupor, and strange stick-like women with pregnant tummies and serene faces were emerging from her fingertips.

Nine on a Sunday morning seemed a bit early for

the phone but Mum was fast asleep under her duvet and my empty stomach was requiring some dry toast so I got up and answered it. I had stopped hoping for Cassian by then – a week or two is an eternity when you are just sixteen – and I croaked a grudging 'Yes?' into the receiver, holding my dressing gown around me. In fact it was Stella. I remember every word of the conversation as though I had just hung up on her now.

'Um, hello. May I speak to Alice Reynolds, please?'

'Speaking,' I said.

'Alice, hello. It's Stella, Florence's mother. I'm afraid I have some bad news.'

I didn't say anything. There was a horrible black abyss of a pause as if to mark the moment for ever.

'Florence died last night. She was taking,' she seemed to choke here, 'heroin with Cassian. I thought you ought to know. I'll phone and let you know when the funeral will be.'

'Yes. Thank you,' I said, words that sounded stupid to me afterwards.

'Goodbye, Alice dear,' she said.

'Goodbye,' I answered.

Then, before I had unlocked my face from its expression of blank horror, Ursula called me up at home for the first and last time in her life. 'Have you heard the news?' she asked. She was crying into the receiver at her big new house near Ascot with the apricot Jacuzzi baths.

'It's her brother's fault,' she sniffed. She told me

that Cassian had rowed with Stella and run away to a squat in Oxford with a bloke who had recently been kicked out of Westminster. Flossy had gone to see him there, apparently. 'Fuck knows why. I always thought she hated him and his crappy drug-addict friends,' Ursula cried.

If only I had phoned Stella. If only I had realised what kind of a state Flossy was in. All too late, of course.

Ursula said the ambulance men had found Flossy naked and lying in her own vomit. I loathed to think of her any way but sparkling and mischievous, about to do something shocking, about to laugh. All at once the trip to Russia and my summer in Little Farford took on a film-like quality, seeming suddenly fictitious but at the same time completely unforgettable in every detail. Already momentous enough to me, these two episodes were now set apart as the most magical in my life, frozen in their perfection.

The sheer staggering horror of someone like Flossy, who had grown up at Little Farford, who had everything anyone could ever want in life, who was clever and beautiful and funny and rich, sitting in a squat injecting herself with heroin, would not lodge itself in my consciousness. God, I had seen enough friends of Mum's sitting about in squalor smoking joints to know that I never wanted to be near anything but beauty and perfection ever again. So how did all the beauty and perfection that had surrounded Flossy not protect her? I was still too stupid to know that money and class are not defence enough.

The funeral amazed me by being more heart-breaking than Dad's. I went down on the train, reading *Just Seventeen* and drinking dark orange tea from beige plastic cups. I tried to concentrate on something about how you didn't have to feel pressured into sex on the first date if it didn't feel right. There were a lot of rabbits in the fields and hundreds of single magpies as if I didn't know this was a day for sorrow.

The service was held at Little Farford parish church, down the lane by the river. Mocking us all, it was a lovely day. There were tiny white clouds dotted about in the turquoise sky and the river babbled and gurgled, sending shards of bright sunlight bouncing off its ripples into the trees that bowed over it. There were yellow fluffy ducklings swimming behind their mothers as we crossed the plank bridge to the church, and insects buzzed above the thick green grass. There seemed to be a bee in every flower and the people walking their dogs took one glance at us in our mourning and looked ashamed of their happiness on this hot and dreamy day. Outside the pub there was a couple snogging. I have a vivid memory of the girl's sunburnt back in a pink cutaway T-shirt and the boy's hands clasped around her waist making white splodges in her flesh.

I was sweating under my black cardigan as I crackled across the gravel to the church, just in time to see the pallbearers heave Flossy out of the back of the hearse. The coffin was covered with pale pink lilies and there was a card on top that said 'Goodbye Darling, Love Mummy'. I put my hand in my mouth and bit it in an effort to remain in some kind of control. Sunlight poured through the stained-glass windows into the church, making a multicoloured kaleidoscope effect, and I stood in a pew near the back as Flossy was carried in to Albinoni's devastating Adagio in G. The girls from school were huddled together in the front, crying audibly, and over to the right were Cassian and Stella. I longed to feel the coarseness of Cassian's thick black hair in my fingers. Giardino had his arm round Stella's shoulders and his face buried in his free hand. He was hunched with grief and all three of them shook with silent sobs.

The vicar welcomed us to his church 'on this sad occasion' and said something trite about Florence having been taken from us too soon, but God moved in mysterious ways. Then Tara stood up and walked towards the pulpit. She had a black linen shift dress on and a big black straw hat. Her blonde curls leapt out from underneath it and she looked gorgeous. She was obviously trying not to cry and she read very quietly. Shakespeare's 30th sonnet. 'When to the sessions of sweet silent thought I summon up remembrance of things past,' she began. By the time she got to the final couplet: 'But if a while I think on thee, dear friend, All losses are restored and sorrows end', tears were streaming down her face. And mine. And everyone else's.

But it was Cassian who made me choke with the kind of loss I had never thought possible. My stomach leapt to see his face when he turned towards the congregation, sitting on a low stool with a guitar in his lap. Brushing his hair out of his eyes, and speaking without looking at any of us, he said: 'I know a lot of you will find this cheesy. It's actually about Van Gogh, Flossy's favourite artist. Anyway, she was my sister and if you don't like it you can all fuck off.' At this he started playing 'Starry Starry Night'. '"I think I understand, what you tried to say to me, how you suffered for your sanity . . ."'

Seeing him there, so shy, so angry, so beautiful, I could only hope he could see me and know that I loved him. '"But I could have told you, Florence, this world was never meant for one as beautiful as you . . ."' he croaked into the emptiness of a world without Flossy.

When he had finished there was total silence in the church for over a minute as he sat there, motionless, waiting to compose himself before going back to join his parents. We sang 'The Lord's my shepherd' and 'I Vow to Thee my country' (presumably in honour of Flossy's adoration for Rupert Everett) and then the pallbearers moved into place again. She was in there. In the box with the lilies on the lid, not smoking a fag on her four-poster bed, not throwing my crappy clothes in my face, not singing a Madonna song.

Then somebody clicked a switch and a loud voice

began: 'I made it through the wilderness! Yeah I made it through-oo-ooo. Never knew how lost I was until I found you-oooo.'

I smiled through my red and stinging eyes as the tape wailed on, and then I ran out ahead of the Vincis, tripping across the lawn to wait outside for Cassian. When he emerged blinking into the sunlight I ran up and threw my arms around him, kissing his neck and stifling my sobs in the smell of his skin.

'Oh God, it's so awful,' I said, hugging him to me, wanting to absorb his grief and take it all upon myself.

Nothing could have prepared me for his shoving me backwards away from him so hard that I smacked my back against the dry-stone wall.

'Get the fuck away from me,' he spat into my face and, turning to his family, he walked away, running both hands through his hair in a gesture of despair. I watched him put his arm round his father, a hundred yards but a million miles away from me.

In the time it took my heart to break I realised he knew I was the last person she had spoken to. He knew I was lower than slime.

I stood where I was, hoping that the pain in my back might obliterate the agony of Cassian's rejection. I closed my eyes and felt the heat of the stone under my hands and the sun on the back of my head.

'He hasn't taken it well,' someone was saying to me, patting me on the arm. It was Tara Sinclair. I smiled at her, our old antipathy evaporating in our shared sorrow. What did all that trivial schoolgirl shit matter now? She had seen Cassian push me away and she had heard what he had said. 'You know he was there?' she added, moving forward to hug me now, unable to stop herself crying.

'I know,' I said, putting my arms around her shoulders.

Walking back through the village I saw families with fat babies having cream teas on the high street, old ladies in flowery sundresses buying antiques and a few public schoolboys in old paisley shirts getting tans and trying to persuade passing pretty girls to let them weave hair wraps of coloured cotton into their plaits. They almost asked me, but my clothes, my order of service and the state of my face told them to stay away.

When I got back to school everything had changed. I had taken out my nose stud and my earrings and abandoned the image that Flossy had created for me. I wanted to keep as low a profile as possible. For ever. The other girls, though, Tara included, treated me with deference. In fact, oddly, Tara was almost the only person I could talk to about Flossy, since she too had spent time at Little Farford, sleeping in that bed, laughing in that garden.

The others said 'Hi' when they saw me and they invited me to their houses at weekends. They asked me if I wanted anything from the tuck shop if they were going. They sat down with me in the refectory, no longer avoiding my table with a sneer, nor backing away in terror from my exclusive relationship with Flossy. They even asked me for help with their prep.

I wished I could be happy about it. I wanted to be friendly to them, but I had miserably disappointed the only friend I had ever had and I didn't feel worthy. I was polite, of course, but I refused their advances and I worked especially hard. The teachers were pleased that their pet was back on track, but personally I didn't ever expect to be pleased about anything ever again.

When Tara's mum came up to take her out for tea one weekend Tara asked me if I would like to come too. It was the first time she had ever offered anything that might amount to a real apology and I was flattered. I didn't go, but I watched Tara get into the Range Rover, smiling at Lady Hermione in the sunshine, and I felt envious and odious. I couldn't tell that Hermione was drunk and wired, that Tara had wanted me to come to help protect her from her wreck of a mother. All I could see was the shiny car and the cashmere cardigans. It was only later, when she actually began to beg me for help with Hermione, that I realised how much she had genuinely wanted me to come.

After that Tara and I verged on being friends. We borrowed each other's books, were faultlessly polite to each other at all times and bought each other Tampax and chocolate when we went into town. She started to moan a bit about her parents, not completely convinced yet that her mum was in the right. She saw a drunken, out-of-control angry woman, railing against a basically serene man and it was hard for her to side with the lunatic, even though she suspected her father of cold sadism.

We occasionally slipped into town together for coffee and she talked about Zander. She had adored him when she was little, she told me, but had felt horribly rejected when he openly brought teenaged girlfriends home. 'Well, you know, pissed off,' she said, smiling weakly. She hated going home to Cairnsham Hall, and would desperately try to wangle invitations to other people's houses for the holidays. She told me how much she missed going to Flo's and in a way I would like to have asked her back to Clapham, but obviously that wasn't possible. In the end, though, it was with Tara that I spent more time than with anyone else, sitting next to her now in Russian lessons, and sharing cigarettes in the toilets. She reprinted a picture of Flossy for me that she had taken when she went to Tuscany with the Vincis a couple of years before, and I stood it on my chest of drawers.

But I was lonely and I did once, in a fit of miserable confusion, try to phone Cassian at school. I hadn't decided what I was going to say, but it was an Indian summer evening and I had been lying by the lake thinking about Flossy. The grass marks on my knees and elbows made the Vincis seem real again and my face was hot and fuzzy from the heat as I stumbled towards the pay phone in the twilight.

It took two calls to get the number of his house and another to get the boys' phone rather than the housemaster's office.

'Grants, can I help you?' someone said ironically.

I asked if I could speak to Cassian Vinci.

'Cassian Vinci? Are you sure?' asked the boy. 'Won't I do? I'm extremely handsome and an excellent sack artist. Huge knob?'

'Cassian, please,' I said.

'Bloody hell. There's no pleasing some people. VINCI! Hey, WOPSY!' he shouted as loud as he could. 'Another slag on the phone for you. Sounds like she's gagging for it.' I knew the boy was joking. If anyone was used to all this kind of thing it was me. I had been the target of enough jokes to be an expert. But I realised when he described me in terms of an eager suitor that that was what I was. I had told myself I was calling to clear up what must, I was sure, be some terrible misunderstanding. I needed to tell him how sorry I was not to have saved Flossy that night on the phone. But I had to acknowledge before Cassian ever got to the receiver that really I wanted to talk to him because I loved him. I was hoping he would ask to see me, ask me how I had been, tell me he had missed me, say he was sorry. I hung up in shame.

For weeks I thought of nothing else but the absolute necessity of seeing him. I spent every lesson copying notes neatly into my files and thinking about Cassian. I would never get over anything if I couldn't confront him somehow.

I had never thought of myself as a stalker. I didn't exactly think of myself as one now. My plan was simply to go and see him. 'Hello, Cassian. I have come to see you' – that type of thing. I didn't mean to lurk around watching him. I thought maybe we could go and have a cup of coffee and I would tell him how sorry I was and he would hold my hand. Or something.

I snuck away from school first thing on a Tuesday morning, getting the six fifteen train to London. It was full of commuters – women in sheer tights and trainers, their high heels in their bags, and men self-importantly reading the most boring section of the paper and looking harassed. I had to stand up all the way and was not feeling at my most alluring by the time I bought a raisin croissant and a cappuccino at the station's Croissant Express when I arrived.

I walked all the way down Victoria Street, getting elbowed in the ribs by hurrying secretaries and helmeted couriers, feeling swept up in the frenzy to get to work. It was strange, being buffeted along while not at all being part of the whole thing. I moved more slowly than everyone else, looked up at the buildings I passed, fiddled with my hair, glanced at myself in shop windows. But they, they couldn't see anything except their watches telling them how many seconds they had left to get there.

When I got near Parliament Square I started seeing the Westminster boys. Black suits, black ties, white shirts, trying to look as shabby as possible. They all had affectedly messy hair and it was clearly obligatory that one's shirt hang out the bottom of one's jacket. A lot of them were smoking frantically, holding their cigarettes inside cupped hands so as not to be seen by a passing teacher. They had their books in old khaki satchels with strange logos Tippexed on to the flaps. I saw groups of them in nearby cafés, sucking down their last fag before Abbey, holding their coffees in trembling fingers – hangovers, too much caffeine already, nervousness, pretension.

Big Ben stood proud over Parliament Square, gleaming in the morning light, a bright blue sky and a few scudding clouds behind it, its enormous hands telling them they were already late. The Houses of Parliament were suitably imposing to the right, shining black taxis pulling up outside to deliver the harried MPs, pigeons flapping round Winston Churchill's head, policemen trying to retain their dignity despite their helmets by standing around muttering into their walkie-talkies.

It wasn't until I followed a small group of slouching boys in through the gate to Dean's Yard that I remembered that Westminster takes girls in the sixth form. In terms of confidence and all-encompassing superiority complex they looked a bit like the Queensbury lot, but in terms of outfits they didn't. These people, striding into the archway that led to their school, were virtually naked. They were all phenomenally tall and wore tight black skirts that barely reached down below their bums. Mostly they seemed to have DM shoes on their feet and tiny weeny white blouses through which you could see their white bras. Their clean, glossy hair was either loose and unkempt or slapped back in a scruffy ponytail tied with an elastic band. And they spent their days with Cassian Vinci.

There was a blue wooden stand by their archway telling tourists in various different languages to bugger off, though it seems it was permitted to gaze through to the cobblestones to the Inigo Jones archway and the blossom trees in the ancient College Garden beyond. I gazed. However, I was attracting a lot of sniggers and stares from the boys and I was beginning to feel ridiculous so I backed away and thought I might wander around the Abbey until break time or whenever it might be that I would see Cassian.

It was not yet nine but there were already Japanese and American tourists scuttling about, taking illegal photos and whispering very loudly to each other in the cool gloom. I wanted to see Poets' Corner, but I realised as I approached that the school was holding its assembly in the front area. I crept past another 'bugger off' barrier and stood behind a cold stone column watching. And there he was. Standing, reciting something at a mutter, his eyes down on his prayer book, his hand periodically in his hair. His face was lit like an angel's in the dark by the tiny red lamp in front of him on the choir stand, one of hundreds all in a row, but only he stood out. Some of the others were spotty or pale or both, fidgety, open-mouthed, drooling or actually asleep. But Cassian looked beautiful, his hair flopping over his face, his clean white shirt almost asking to have some arms clasped round it. The chaplain announced that someone had been killed the previous afternoon in a jet ski accident on the river and the whole Abbey began murmuring – who had known him, what was he like, what year was he in, who looked upset? Then, after 'Immortal, invisible, God only wise', everyone leapt to their feet and rushed out, pushing and shoving into the cloisters where the sunlight caught the dust above their heads, the scholars moving forward in their black robes, the girls keeping together, heads high, acutely conscious of being admired by all around them. I followed them as far as the brass-rubbing stall and then stopped to watch some Taiwanese tourists taking pictures of them – English public school boys, the same for over four hundred years.

Now I supposed they would be having their lessons so I went to the nearest café and ordered a cup of tea. The woman serving me scowled disapprovingly – obviously sick of teenagers spending two hours over a twenty-pence cup of tea and smoking eight cigarettes each as they did so. She might have known by the meek and presumably miserable look on my face that I wasn't one of those though. The four girls behind me, on the other hand, were. They only had three teas between them and they had their fags on the Formica table before the lady had even plonked the tea down with a snarl. To be fair they did have a couple of bags of Skips as well but obviously not enough to be considered worthwhile customers.

I tried to ignore them as I would have ignored Queensbury girls, loud and full of themselves, but in this case I had to make an exception.

'Vinci definitely fancies you,' a pretty blonde girl with freckles said to one of the others.

'I wish,' answered the happy creature with brown curly hair and a Rolex.

'He does. He can hardly look at you in French, and anyway, Cornelius told me,' Freckles went on, tipping her crisp bag up to get the crumbs, sucking her fingers and then lighting a Silk Cut.

'Bollocks. He's celibate, plus which his sister just died.'

'So? All the better. Get him while he's down. He won't have the energy to fight you off.'

They giggled at this and the subject got changed to a friend of theirs who had been rusticated for being out of school during evening prep. He was caught by a teacher watching the news. The boy ran past a BBC correspondent doing a piece to camera on the lawn in front of the Houses of Parliament. His dad owned three major newspapers.

'Can I help you?' Freckles then sneered at me, blowing her smoke out lavishly and raising her eyebrows. My eavesdropping had lacked some essential subtlety.

I blushed furiously and dashed out, pulling at the door where it said 'PUSH' and dropping my purse twice. A tall bald man with veins throbbing angrily in his forehead charged in past me and, as I looked round through the window, I saw him screaming at the girls, his jaw trembling and his whole body thrown into the act of busting them off school premises and, to make his catch all the more impressive, smoking.

Of course, the whole mission was ridiculous, but somehow I felt so desperate to see Cassian, so driven by my ill-conceived desire to sort things out, that I didn't feel ridiculous. I felt feverish and anxious, as though I had stage fright, as though I was on the brink of something enormous. I went back towards the school itself and peered over the barrier at groups of boys milling about, shyly admiring the girls, eating crisps and hoping the hair hanging over their faces made them look aloof and indifferent rather than adolescent and self-conscious. It was more like a university than a school – people holding books under their arms, no bells, none of the prison-like physical restrictions of Queensbury and the other places I'd seen. Here I got the impression you could pretty much do what you liked. Except find Cassian.

When he did eventually walk past me I almost didn't see him. He was in cricket whites, walking along swinging a bat with twenty or so other boys, all shouting and shoving each other, all dressed in this outfit that suggested wealth and green grass and serenity. One of them tossed the red ball up in the air and the bloke behind him caught it – it was so perfect a scene he couldn't have missed. A few of them looked at me and made giggling comments to each other, but Cassian was preoccupied, walking slightly separately, head bowed, rings catching the sunlight.

I followed them through Dickensian cobbled alleyways and through strange red-brick housing estates by the river to Vincent Square. Standing by the black iron railings I watched them play for a bit, hopelessly failing to work out who was winning or what was going on, but managing to see that Cassian was not the best player on his team. The others jeered when he stood up to bat and he held two fingers up to them with a smile of acknowledgement, brushing a fly from in front of his eyes and hitting the ball up into the air straight back into the hands of the bowler. Even I could see this wasn't the idea. Then he wandered round the back of a little green hut for a cigarette and I went away again.

On my way back I saw the girls from the café coming towards me in netball gear and I knew this might be my only chance.

They stopped dead at my 'excuse me', staggered that someone had had the gall to approach them in all their overwhelming height and beauty.

'I really need to see Cassian Vinci. Where do you think he'll be after school so I can talk to him?' I asked, blushing and shuffling my feet, but determined.

'Granny Lee's,' Freckles told me without hesitation. The others nodded. 'Just by Westminster station. Opposite Big Ben. Granny Lee's. He'll be upstairs.' And they walked off. They hadn't in fact found it that weird and they hadn't been particularly rude either. Granny Lee's.

As I stomped away from them I heard Freckles say to the one Cassian fancied 'See. Competition. Got to act quickly. She was gorgeous too.' Well, it was something at least.

St James's Park was almost empty apart from a few tourists who had wandered in to take photos of Buckingham Palace from among the trees, and some office workers sitting in the shade with their sandwiches. I watched an old lady feeding the swans and bought myself a nasty roll at the café and ate it on the swings, almost peaceful now in the knowledge that I would see him in a couple of hours. I fell asleep by the pond listening to a girl chucking her boyfriend over a shared can of Coke.

'You're not into the sex enough. You don't want to do what I want to do,' she said.

'I do! I'll do whatever you like,' he whined, already aware that he was defeated.

'But I don't just want you to do it because I like. I want you to *want* to,' she almost shouted, throwing her head back in exasperation. 'Anyway, I'm seeing someone else,' she finally admitted.

'Ah,' he nodded, and I dropped off, envying her, pitying him.

So at five o'clock I was in the loos at Granny Lee's,

putting a bit of lipstick on, ruffling my hair, checking that I didn't look too meek or too needy. I tried to affect an air of confidence, of straightforwardness. I bought a hot chocolate in a polystyrene cup and walked up to where I could hear noisy adolescents and smell the smoke. David Owen was sitting in a corner, being interviewed by an apprehensive-looking journalist. Cassian was sitting in another corner, surrounded by rowdy friends, their ties loosened, their earrings inserted the moment they had stepped off school premises. I walked towards him but before he saw me the girl from the café appeared behind him, put her hands over his eyes and made a face at the others to shush. Cassian was actually blushing.

'It's her, Wopsy. It's her, for fuck's sake!' one of his cabal hissed, excitedly.

'Rosie?' Cassian asked, and she pulled her hands away and kissed him on the cheek as he smiled up at her.

I put my hot chocolate down on the nearest table, the lid still on, and went back to school, arriving just in time for supper.

'How was your aunt?' Tara asked.

'Oh, much better. Off the ventilator,' I said, and ate my hamburger.

For God's sake, I lived in Clapham and I had failed to stop his sister killing herself. I was not in his class.

It was this last issue of class that I finally resolved when I got to Oxford, although I had never expected to find Cassian there too, leaning against the college bar, moodily ordering a pint of Tennent's Extra.

# Ten

One of the air hostesses recognised me and plonked two extra vodkas down on my tray table with a wink. She seemed pleased to see a familiar face. 'You must like the snow then!' she said. People always say things like that about Russia.

'Actually it's quite hot there at the moment,' I sighed, trying not to sound irritable.

'Is it?' she said, surprised. 'You don't think of it as fine, do you?'

'Most people don't, no,' I answered, dismissing her by raising my book to my face and picking up my drink. Bloody hell, I thought, didn't they notice the weather when they landed. You know, bright sunlight, blue skies and the ground staff in short sleeves? Obviously not.

Billie her name was. If Zander had been with me he would have used it. 'Billie, you couldn't get us another couple of bottles of champagne, could you, darling?' he would say. She would laugh coyly and wiggle off to get them, not seeing his use of her name badge as in any way demeaning. As we disembarked he would slip a twenty-pound note into her hand and tell her to buy herself something nice. Money didn't seem sordid to him like it would to Hermione, or Stella or even me. The barrow boy in him, or maybe his grandmother's influence. She had been Indian and always brought money out for the children from under her sari, he said. Money and sweets. Still his favourite things.

I drank too much and watched *Shakespeare in Love* on the flickering screen. Even now Gwyneth Paltrow's character plunged me immediately into childish fantasy, longing for that life, that passion, that complete freedom from mundane disappointments. Three of my friends had chucked their boyfriends after seeing it and I read a trashy feature by one of them in the *Chronicle* about the phenomenon. I cried all the way through and tried to pretend to my neighbour that it was an allergy by sneezing every now and then, though I noticed he was crying too by the end. Zander would have thought it was bollocks, aside from some comment about whether or not he would kick Paltrow out of bed. Not, one assumes.

The long scratch on my face had faded to almost nothing over the past four months and people had stopped commenting on it ages ago. I hadn't seen much of Zander since my visit to Hill Place – he'd been frantically travelling, calling me to check that things with the icon were going ahead, and sending me postcards with spidery messages on the back. There was an edge of real urgency in his phonecalls about this job, though, a feeling that it had to go right. 'Be a good girl,' he had said and he wasn't joking. I think he knew my loyalty was becoming less reliable, that my obedience could perhaps no longer be taken for granted. Though this wasn't quite true yet. I still believed in him if I didn't think too hard, and I was confused enough not to question him.

But none of this, obviously, had served to stop me feeling uneasy, not to say extremely worried, now that I was heading back, that the brothers might find me again. As far as I knew they had made no more effort to frighten Zander than their assault on me, but they obviously knew who and where I was somehow or other. Still, it was more niggling now than anything – my initial terror had worn off. It had all begun to seem a bit less credible as the weeks had gone by and I now almost believed that it had been some misunderstanding. I mean, of course Hermione would think the worst because of what had happened to her (though as far as I knew Zander had never actually been physically violent towards her) and these Chechens, as any Russian racist will tell you, are an unreliable and murderous bunch. Though, since this last dreadful and ongoing war, even certain Russians had become slightly more sympathetic towards their Caucasian neighbours, largely thanks to the insanely brave Russian radio correspondent Andrei Babitsky. On the other hand, you still got loony politicians parading round Moscow with signs saying 'A good Chechen is a dead Chechen.'

By the time I had checked into the Slavyanskaya, a nasty modern hotel on the river, it was late evening and the sun was dark orange behind

Stalin's vast and terrifying university building up on the hill. I hated this hotel. It was a Radisson, known as the Radisson Chechenskaya by locals because it is run by a Chechen whose American rival was shot dead at the nearby Kievskaya metro station after a long dispute about ownership of the place. The rooms are small and the sounds of sleazy American businessmen fucking the stunning Russian prostitutes is piped through the air vents along with their cigarette smoke. The lobby is always crawling with fat leather-clad gangsters carrying mens' handbags and mobile phones. A lot of them are fairly visibly armed.

Amazingly beautiful teenagers trip along the marble corridors in tight black dresses, heels and pill-box hats wearing red sashes that advertise the hotel's casino. And the prostitutes, who would all be supermodels if they lived in any other country, eat sushi at the foyer's very visible Japanese place and sip cappuccinos at the Amadeus Café. I can't help envying them their clothes, their immaculateness, their height and, basically, their just astonishing beauty. Russian girls are gorgeous in a way that no others are. The racial mix of east and west that produces that perfect skin, green eyes, wide faces and high cheekbones is endlessly fascinating. I always go for a swim and a sauna at the hotel gym and watch them get ready. It takes hours. The same girl who would be standing blow-drying her hair in a black La Perla G-string and bra when I arrived would still be there putting her liquid liner on two hours later when I came back red, sweaty and panting from the steam. These girls would love Dolores.

The trouble is, the Slavyanskaya is very central, not quite as staggeringly expensive as the Metropole, the National and the Kempinski, and it has an American cinema and a business centre. This means that the city's foreigners spend a lot of time there whether they like it or not, luxuriously eating popcorn over a schlocky film in English, meeting contacts for coffee at the Amadeus and running into each other in the gym.

Walking into my grimy little room I found the message light flashing on the phone. I poured myself some champagne from the mini bar and picked up the receiver. My fixer, an eighteen-year-old girl with a bird-like voice, called Varvara, chirped that the boat I was supposed to be taking had sunk that morning while docked in Samara (typical) and the next one wouldn't be leaving for three days. Zander was going to be livid and I was bored at the prospect of three days in Moscow with nothing to do. I hated seeing friends and drinking when I was here on business. I got restless and couldn't relax until the thing was in my hands. Of course, Tara only lived five hundred yards away, I thought, flicking on BBC Prime. *EastEnders*. Tiff was just about to find out that Grant had slept with her mum. I settled in and opened the can of nuts for fifteen dollars.

The next night I found myself making my way

into the foreigners' compound on Kutuzovsky Prospekt. It is just opposite the White House, the government building that burnt so spectacularly during the coup attempt in 1993, giving all the foreign TV stations such a great view. As soon as *EastEnders* had finished I had phoned Tara. To be honest I quite missed her startling frivolity on every subject and I wanted to pretend to myself that the Zander thing was basically peripheral, that I had my own life too, quite apart from him. She'd been idiotically pleased to hear from me and I'd been relieved to have called her, to have something a bit normal going on in my life – going to see an old school friend. Well, an old school enemy whose father I was sleeping with, but you can't have everything.

I had spent the day in the Tretyakov Gallery gazing for ages at the best painting in the world – Repin's Ivan the Terrible killing his son. Miss Tarlton had shown me a print of it years before but the Tretyakov was closed for refurbishment for over a decade so a print was the best you could do. It is a gruesome and enormous painting. The bald and ageing Ivan, without a hat or crown or any of the pomp of his position, is kneeling on the floor holding his son in his arms, pressing his face to him. The son, a young man rather than a child, is plainly dead, bleeding from the temple, limp and pale. The poker or rod or whatever it is that Ivan has killed him with is lying in the foreground, and some furniture is overturned suggesting a struggle. But the amazing thing about the picture is the look on Ivan's face. The horror in his eyes seems to depict exactly how you might feel after killing your son. His anguish and the love he obviously feels for the boy, his fear and loathing, his total disbelief is all there staring at you. How Ilya Repin can have felt such complete empathy with this vile man who died hundreds of years before he was born, I cannot imagine. The first time I saw the real thing, sliding over the newly restored marble floors in the felt slippers they made you wear, I stood in front of it in tears of grief and horror.

Afterwards I walked through the sweltering heat back to the Slavyanskaya, past the Kremlin glittering in the sunlight, and down the Arbat, which is sometimes referred to as the Covent Garden of Moscow but the similarities between the two are lost on me. It is a pedestrianised road lined with eighteenth-century buildings, all painted lime green, eggshell blue and baby pink, and nowadays it is a place where tourists buy antiques. There are cafés selling kebabs and Georgian *khachapuri* (the most delicious food on earth – a kind of naan thing with melted cheese inside), tea and vodka. There are lines of starving artists wanting to do charcoal portraits of you in which they neaten your hair, clear up your skin and put a healthy twinkle in your eye. Old men with one leg wrapped in grey rags (the other blown or hacked off somewhere) play sad songs of the open steppes on the accordion – usually a tear-jerking Russian classic about a coachman dying in the snow and asking his friend to give his wedding ring back to his wife. They rarely sing the words – everyone knows them. Young men in faded denim jackets and red bandannas play Beatles and Rolling Stones classics to small crowds of their dishevelled friends, and posses of Caucasian gangsters with gold teeth and glinting eyes share bottles of eastern cognac at the cafés. There are lace sellers and Russian doll sellers, who these days speak fluent American English and flirt with their tourist customers. They also do army watches, fur hats and other things for which foreigners will fork out. There used to be a preponderance of Lenin busts, and then there wasn't for a bit, and now there is again. Joke value. Under Communism they cost a few kopecks. Now you can spend two hundred dollars on a big one.

I saw a nasty fight between two gangs of shaven-headed Russian boys, then a bedraggled camel from the zoo having its photo taken with a Japanese girl, and three old drunks with no legs (not together) sitting on makeshift skateboards and exposing their stumps to the generous-spirited while picking the scabs on their heads. I also saw the sun set over the river and a stripy yellow and red hot-air balloon rise slowly into the bright sky behind the imposing gloom of the Foreign Ministry.

'The weirdest thing just happened to me,' Tara announced, kissing me on both cheeks as I came through her double steel doors on the tenth floor of one of the foreigners' 'Stalin houses'.

I added my dusty sandals to the pile of shoes by the door and padded barefoot across her parquet into the living room.

'This terrifying-looking Chechen scumbag just came to the door which Natasha bloody well opened,' she said, following me through. Natasha was the maid who had worked for *Chronicle* correspondents through the decades and told agonisingly embarrassing tales about all of them if you only thought to ask her. Few did. 'And this guy – actually he was quite good-looking, you know how they are – said he knew Dad and asked if he could call back some time with his brother.'

'Oh God,' I said, slumping into a big blue velvet-effect sofa ordered from Finland by a previous correspondent in the early 1980s when this sort of thing was deemed acceptable. A shiver ran down my spine and I suddenly felt cold in the appalling heat.

'Well, you know. Too right "oh God". So I told him of course he fucking couldn't and if he wanted to see me he could come into the office and set up a sodding meeting. At least I hope that's what I said.'

'And?'

'And he said he would, thank you very much and now he had to get back to the market because he'd got someone to man his stall, for Christ's sake. I mean, what is that about?' Tara whined, going into the kitchen now and clunking ice into chunky glasses. 'Gin?' she offered. I was doing my best not to seem scared but it wasn't working. I felt pale and shaky, petrified that they might already be waiting for me in my hotel room. I could almost taste the smell of sausage and vodka on their breath.

Natasha was putting her beret on for the journey home and touching up her lipstick. She was having an affair with the office driver and he walked her to the metro every day after work and stole kisses when he was asked up to put in a lightbulb. Tara was apparently the first correspondent to spot this, though it had been going on for eight years she said. Natasha and the driver were both married to other people.

'Good evening,' Natasha nodded. 'Did you meet the Chechen on his way down? Chechens calling now. Whatever next?'

'I didn't. No,' I answered, breathless and dying for a cigarette though I had given up four years earlier. Natasha nodded pointedly at me again and left.

'You are a cow, staying out of touch for so long. I know you've been here. Daddy told me. Not that I'm really speaking to the wanker, but you know, I sort of can't exactly hang up when he calls. Even Mummy manages to be civil to him if he actually rings her. So?'

'So I've got to pick something up for Zander but it's all gone wrong so I'm stuck here sloping about for a bit.'

'Ugh. Still working for Daddy, then? I won't warn you again, you know,' she said, semi-serious. She had got away from him herself and was always keen to warn others to do the same. I think she really had my best interests, rather than her own, at heart.

'I know, I know. It's the pay. Hey! You know Sergei works at customs at Sheremetievo?' I said, anxious to get off the subject of my relationship with her father.

'You're fucking joking?! Flo's shag from the Russia trip?'

'Yup. Vile slimeball that he is.'

And we started to talk about school. How awful she was to me had become a joke now, and these days I was more concerned with how awful I was being to her. I hadn't been able to resist getting in touch though I knew exactly what Zander would have to say about it ('You scheming little bitch'). The thing was, I really wanted to talk about Oksana if there was any way of broaching the subject.

Noise from the traffic on the six-lane road ten floors below was roaring through the open windows, and the room was full of what Russians call 'pukh', a kind of white fluff that comes off the trees in late spring and fills the air for weeks on end. They call Winnie-the-Pooh 'Vinni Pukh', which always seemed fitting since his brain is supposed to be made of it.

'How's Cass?' I asked, not wanting to hear but not wanting to seem too silent on the subject either.

'God, how is he ever? Morose, broody, you know. You were right about him in the first place, actually. Still, he's away a lot, as you know, so . . .' She laughed, tipping her glass up so that the slice of lemon slid into her lips. She licked it off. 'I keep busy.'

'Doesn't he mind?' I asked, pathetically pleased to hear that Tara didn't take him all that seriously, even if it made me sorry for him to be messed about like that.

'What he don't know can't hurt him,' she said in a silly cockney accent, crossing her legs and smiling. 'Eight years has a tendency to put a bit of a dampener on things, you know.'

I went over to the windows wishing she wouldn't say things like 'bit of a dampener'.

When Yeltsin was still in power you could watch him go to work in the Kremlin every day from these windows in his ambulance-chased motorcade. They closed the whole road off for him and there was an eerie silence followed by an almighty roar as he passed. Tara was always including this in her articles.

'You know that first day at school when Zander turned up to give you some money in the dorm?' I began, slurping the last of my gin and tonic out from under the ice. Had to start somewhere.

'Vaguely,' Tara said, darkening a bit under her blonde curls. She was wearing a beige linen suit and brown Nicole Farhi sandals, but she looked a bit creased and hot from her day at work and all the prettier for it.

'Was that girl he was with his Russian wife?' I knew it hadn't been, but I was desperate for some way into it all.

'God, you know I don't remember him being with anyone, but come to think of it, no. It can't have been Oksana. He didn't even meet her until Mum was already totally fucked up. They must have got married in, God, '93, I suppose. Not that I was invited so I don't know. Why?'

'I just wondered what happened to her,' I said disingenuously, looking out at the White House. 'I met someone who knew her.'

'Yeah, a lot of people wonder what happened to Oksana.' Tara laughed mirthlessly. 'She was a tart, I think. Dad met her in some hotel but she helped him out with a few pieces from Grozny – paintings and shit – and was vaguely doing a bit of what you're doing now.'

Yes, I thought.

'Anyway, she died of an overdose about six months after the wedding. Mum thinks he killed her – not that she actually says so, but I mean, of course he didn't. Well, fuck knows. I never even met her but I spoke to her once on the phone,' she said, sauntering back towards the gin bottle.

'How come?' I asked, attempting to look casually interested.

'She was trying to get me to help her sell one of Dad's pictures. She wanted the money to get her brothers out of Grozny. One of them was in a kidnap gang and the other one was some sort of guerrilla so their mum was going spare. Anyway, I guess she thought Dad might help, but you know what he's like when it comes to helping. So I tried to find a buyer but I never did and then she died before I spoke to her again. That's the lot.' She paused. 'You want to go out to eat?'

'Yeah. Let's.' I said, not moving.

'Anyway, who did you meet?' she asked.

'What? Oh, actually, I think I met her brothers on a train about a month ago. To be honest I think that might be . . . I'm sure that was who came here tonight. They were looking for Zander,' I said, and pointed at the remains of my scratch.

'Fuck me,' Tara said, and stood up to get her bag, beginning to look nervous herself now.

Tara drove the *Chronicle*'s conspicuous red Volvo very badly to a restaurant called White Desert Sun. The car had a yellow correspondent's numberplate that began 001, demonstrating that it was owned by someone English. England was, rather surprisingly, the first country to recognise the Soviet Union officially and was therefore rewarded with this numberplate and a spectacular embassy building over the river from the Kremlin – once a sugar merchant's Moscow home.

She pulled up between some menacing-looking Jeeps with blacked-out windows – the required vehicle for anyone who considers their life to be in danger. If they consider it to be in danger this is because it is, and it is in danger because they themselves have put so many others in a similar situation. It was that kind of restaurant – always more bodyguards than diners. I had been there before when it was the Uzbek, in the days when Moscow had one restaurant per Soviet bloc country and very lucky you were as a Soviet citizen to be dining at any of them. I remember the Praga as being especially vile. These days it is still Uzbek cuisine, but that is the only thing that hasn't changed. The place is a theme restaurant centred around a cult comedy film called *White Desert Sun*, beloved of all Russians and known by heart by at least eighty-five per cent of them. The world's most beautiful Uzbek women wait the tables wearing traditional national costume, all multicoloured Ali-Baba trousers, sequinned hats and diaphanous blouses. Most of the restaurant looks like a Soviet battleship and the rest is supposed to be a kind of desert, with ruined Bedouin buildings dotted about in it.

The food is the best I've ever tasted. They make *plov* (a kind of lamb and rice dish with carroway seeds) in a huge iron pan at your table, bring you spicy salads of aubergine and radish, delicious tender kebabs in bitter pomegranate sauce, steaming green tea in huge blue and gold bowl-like cups, ice buckets of vodka (a Russian touch) and, of course, the dessert table. If you can manage not to stuff your face too much before pudding it is definitely the best bit. There are all kinds of baklava with honey and pistachios, different sorts of Uzbek delight (indistinguishable from Turkish) flavoured with rose water, apricot syrup or almonds, little pastries with sweet dates inside, fruit compotes, tiny sugared buns filled with raisins and spices and a kind of Uzbek peanut brittle made of sunflower seeds and walnuts.

We got chatted up by the Governor of some far northern province where the people were starving and freezing to death – good to see he wasn't going to risk his own life being anywhere near them – and we leered at some of the caramel-skinned, green-eyed chefs doing the *plov*.

'I was doing a story about the Chechens in Moscow the other day and how everyone hates them,' Tara said (another piece of intrepid reporting on her part). 'What do you think they want, these brothers?' She was trying to sound cool about it, trying to hold on to her cavalier attitude to everything, but it wasn't going very well. She was scared.

'Dunno. They didn't seem overkeen on Zander, though. I mean, maybe I'm in more shit because I work for him, on the other hand they might think they can get to him better through you. I wouldn't go around opening your door to anyone with a touch of the tar brush at any rate.' I was beginning to think we might both be in trouble.

'Well, have you asked Dad what the deal is?'

'I didn't tell him they were Oksana's brothers, no. Didn't feel like getting that involved. Anyway, I never see Zander really. It's all over the phone,' I lied, uselessly.

Tara ignored me and gestured for the bill. She wasn't insane with joy about my working for her dad, mainly because of the dangers involved in having anything to do with him, but she knew I was into Russia and she knew he could charm anyone into anything, so she had never made any kind of scene about it.

We kissed goodbye outside her compound and I walked in the dark back to the hotel, past the booths of policemen idly protecting the foreigners inside. Or not, as the case may be.

Tara had asked me to dinner the next night with some of the other correspondents she knew, but first, I thought, I had better go to the market.

It was already seething at nine o'clock in the morning, more like Cairo than Moscow. As soon as you walk through the iron gates you are in another world. People make aisles through the dust with their stalls, selling huge heaps of shining oranges, lemons, pomegranates, bananas, tomatoes, peaches and watermelons. The greyness of Moscow is entirely absent here as dark women with gold teeth and multicoloured headscarves call out their prices and, cheerfully cackling, pop strawberries into the mouths of passing babies in pushchairs. Young boys, already dark but deeply tanned from a life outdoors, push huge metal trolleys loaded high with pigs' heads or stinking fish through the crowds, calling a warning to the people ahead in some hissing, whispering language from the east. The older men sit behind their stalls of spinach, courgettes, potatoes and chilies, drinking mint tea, smoking toothlessly, playing chess and arguing. Most Russians can't afford to shop at the market but for those that can there is no shortage of anything.

You can buy hot Middle Eastern bread, bundles of herbs, spices shovelled from their box into a fold of paper in front of your eyes, fresh honey in its comb that the white-coated women hold out on bits of newspaper for you to taste, home-made eastern cheeses oozing on their slabs, live lobsters from mildewy tanks, whole piglets, pale and bloodless on squares of muslin, sturgeon with long spiky noses and bristly backs, vats of the best caviar in the world, smoked fish, dried fish, fresh fish, pickled garlic, stuffed vine leaves, and large plastic bags of spicy coleslaw from metal buckets.

The indoor area smells like a market in Damascus or Palestine. It is packed into a huge high-ceilinged hall with birds flying about in the dusty eaves. The air is thick with steam and spices, and there is an atmosphere of friendly hysteria as everyone laughs, shouts and haggles.

I had meant just to scour the place for my Chechens from the train, but I ended up buying lavash bread, soft cheese and a bunch of coriander to make myself breakfast with, and then I felt I couldn't eat this sort of sandwich without some fruit, so by the time I spun round to answer the hundredth call of '*dyevushka*' and found Aslan Basayev staring at me, I had almost forgotten I was looking for him.

Holding out a large melon and an enormous knife he looked, if anything, slightly more menacing than he had on the train. He recognised me as soon as I turned to face him and he put down his melon slowly.

'I've been looking for you,' I told him. 'Fizz Reynolds,' I said, and held out my shaking hand.

To my embarrassment he took it and kissed it warmly, waving his melon knife in a flourish as he bowed down.

'Fisss?' he asked, slightly baffled. The trouble with men like this is that they are always so nice. No need to be murderous – no murderousness. I think people who actually are capable of terrible things are much less anxious to show it than those that aren't but wish they were. It's like everyone saying how nice the Kray brothers were when they weren't nailing you to the floor.

'Sorry. Alisa,' I helped him, blushing now.

'Aslan Basayev,' he said. 'I too have been looking for you. Sorry my brother on train. Very drunk. Very angry. We find him now. No problem.'

He was speaking bad and accented Russian and his apology was almost more menacing than his threats.

'You've found Zander?' I asked, feeling worried for the man that I found myself forced to admit was my boyfriend, for better or for worse. Not that at fifty-five he was much of a boy any more.

'Yes. We know where he is. We wait for visa in England. Very difficult. Embassy very bad. They don't give.'

Well, thank God for that anyway, I thought. Embassy must be there for something. Squatting down in the dust with Aslan and chewing on a slice of watermelon, wishing he would put his knife away,

I learnt that he and his brother had been fighting the Russians in Grozny since just before I 'met' them (for want of a better description of our first acquaintance) in Ulyanovsk. I asked him if that was how he had got the scars on his face but he laughed and said he'd had those for years. He explained very matter-of-factly and with an awful chill in his voice that he intended to kill Zander but that as an honourable man he was sorry to have involved me in the procedure. He said he had visited Tara the day before in order to warn her of her father's impending fate but that she had been so pretty and so young that he hadn't been able to bring himself to do so. His brother, Sultan, the one who had in fact cut me, had just gone to buy some cigarettes but if I stayed a while he was sure Sultan would love to meet me again. I declined with as much of a smile as I could manage. Aslan was so sinister-seeming, his gold tooth glinting in the sun, pink watermelon dripping at his fingertips, that I felt stupidly compelled to try to normalise him. A bit like chatting to a taxi driver. In Russia foreigners manage their fear of getting into strangers' cars (something you have to do since genuine taxis are hard to come by) in different ways. Some sit in the back with one hand on their rape alarms, the other on the door handle, hoping against hope that no attack will actually happen. Others go for taming the driver. If you can make him like you perhaps he won't want to rob/kill/rape you. This is how I felt with Aslan. I was scared, so perhaps if I could get to know him I could put a lid on my fear. Or perhaps not.

'My sister loved Moscow. I hate it. She wanted city life,' he said, waving his knife at the grey surrounding buildings, the fumes and the bustle. 'I like country.'

He said he was from the mountains a few hundred kilometres from Grozny, but that Oksana had always longed to get out, to go to Moscow and to marry a rich foreigner. He seemed not to know what line of work she had been in here and I was not about to tell him.

'I hate Russia. Police all the time,' he said, nodding towards the militia man by the gate who did indeed look poised to make another round-up of the local Chechens with no Moscow residence permits. However, considering that the Russians had just totally destroyed Aslan's country and presumably killed a large number of his friends and family he was remarkably calm about it. His mother was now in Moscow too, he said, though she had been forced to stay in Grozny throughout the Russian bombardment, at one stage actually eating a dead cat. Tears welled up in his eyes as he said this and he stabbed his knife hard into the dust at his feet. I flinched. It was getting hot now and I was squinting to see clearly.

'Listen, Tara's having some people over to dinner tonight. Why don't you come?' I said, my brain clearly addled by the increasing heat of the sun, or the sweetness of the melon, or the hard look in

Aslan's eye. I didn't know quite what I was doing, but I knew confronting him was better than letting him creep around on the outskirts of our lives, plotting his murders.

He seemed strangely delighted by the impulsive invitation and agreed joyfully, leaping to his feet and clasping my hands in his. He shouted over to a swarthy boy at the flowerstall, who dashed up to us with a large bunch of pink roses, still in bud and dripping with the water they were constantly sprayed with to keep them fresh. Aslan took them from his hands and presented them to me with a bow.

'Until evening,' he said, smiling.

'Until evening,' I replied, already feeling an idiot. Tara was going to go insane. Perhaps, though, my badly formulated plan might work. Perhaps he might become less of a threat if we could stay in the driver's seat of the relationship. So, he was a bit scarred and battle-worn, but it was a different world in Chechnya and one could hardly expect him to be just like an English public schoolboy.

# ELEVEN

'You fucking what?' said Tara when I phoned her from the hotel.

'Well, he seemed sort of . . . and I just . . . I'm really sorry. I'll go back and tell him not to come,' I offered.

'No, no. Christ, just bring him. He's not exactly going to turn up with a Kalashnikov, I suppose. Anyway, it might be good thing.'

I was extremely relieved. Looking over at my flowers standing in a green Narzan mineral water bottle, I knew I would have felt terrible telling Aslan he was uninvited. This was turning into a mess.

I was the first to arrive at Tara's, and Natasha was still there, peering into her vat of carrot and orange soup, checking on the roast beef and cutting up garlic for the salad dressing. Tara was getting dressed, so I went and lay on her bed to keep her company while she pulled herself into her tights and mushed mousse into her curls to keep them bouncy.

'I can't believe you're doing this,' she said, shaking her head at herself in the mirror.

'Nor can I. Listen, I am really, really sorry. But maybe if we make friends with him we can persuade him that Zander didn't touch his stupid sister . . .'

'Yeah, but it's Dad. I mean, you know, what if

he did?' Tara sighed, too used to everyone loathing her father to react with anything but resignation.

'Don't be stupid. If you really thought that you wouldn't be so relaxed about it,' I said.

'Listen, Fizzles, I could believe anything of Dad, really I could, but I try not to think about it too much. I can't handle it.'

'Sorry,' I said, throwing my head back on Tara's pillow and meaning what I said. Sorry, sorry, sorry. I was very sorry about pretty much everything. It was one thing these people finding you but it was another having them peer into your life, gain some kind of insight into you. Could coming over really deter Aslan rather than encourage him? We drank a Scotch each, eyeing each other nervously. Then the doorbell rang.

By the time everyone had assembled in front of Tara's spectacular river view we looked a very odd collection indeed. There was Adrian and Alexandra, a couple in their early forties who had just had their first baby. He was the number two correspondent on one of the English broadsheets and was very angry and bitter about this, claiming his daily humiliation had driven him to drink, though everyone else said it was the other way round. There was Harry, the correspondent from another, who fancied Tara. They had slept together a couple of times in drunken stupors and newsworthy hellholes but she remained unimpressed by his three-piece suits and stiff upper lip. He obviously thought himself very dashing and intrepid whilst being the perfect English gentleman at the same time. There was a bloke from the BBC, who looked familiar in the way that people off the telly do, and Tamsin, an American correspondent just past child-bearing age. Tamsin was very thin, very trendily dressed and very single. She looked as knackered and war-raddled as the men, but obviously felt a great deal of pressure to be even more gung-ho and butch than they were. And, of course, there was Aslan.

He arrived last, clutching a huge bouquet of yellow, red, pink and white roses for Tara, a bottle of vodka, a bottle of Soviet champagne and a large smoked salmon. Tara seemed genuinely overwhelmed by his kindness and, blushing, she leant forward to kiss him on the cheek. He held her hand a little too long and looked at her penetratingly.

This, gift-wise, is how you turn up at a dinner party in Russia – none of your bottles of cheap red and an apology for its scuzziness but it was all the supermarket had. I realised Aslan would be expecting a proper Russian feast – a table laden with starters that someone had spent a week preparing, followed by soup, kebabs, potatoes, ice-cream, coffee and singing and dancing until dawn. He was going to be shocked and disappointed by some people sitting round competing to be the coolest while at the same time the most understated, drinking three glasses of wine and leaving by eleven thirty.

Adrian was telling a story about a correspondent

who had turned up at lunch with the British Ambassador wearing an embarrassing jacket designed by his sister. 'I mean, it was like lots of pieces of shit sewn together,' he said. Everyone guffawed. He then launched into quite a good one about having a sauna in Siberia and his underpants freezing solid.

Aslan looked mystified.

Somebody made a tasteless joke about the Kursk submarine and Alexandra, who was, of all totally unacceptable things in the painstakingly gritty journalistic world, a housewife, was breast-feeding her baby at the table, and Tamsin was making faces of amazed disgust at the blokes. She drank four glasses of wine straight down as the baby sucked, only relaxing a bit when it was safely asleep on the sofa. Since the child was three feet away at this stage she deemed it safe to light her thousandth cigarette of the day.

'So I'm like hiding under the CNN armoured vehicle when I see *him*,' Tamsin screeched, pointing at Harry, 'running towards me holding a briefcase. A briefcase! In Grozny!' she said, while Harry looked mock-abashed, but was obviously, and not very secretly, proud at his utter Britishness in the face of great adversity. Harry had brought Tara a kilo tin of caviar and I had marvelled at his generosity while Tara and I carried the soup in.

'Don't be too impressed,' Tara had hissed under her breath. 'He gets it off a smuggler who charges a hundred bucks a tin and then he flogs it on to his friends at a hundred and ten to pay for his own.' This was the highest paid correspondent in Moscow. It gratified me to see Aslan wince when he tasted the eggs from the tin the next day. 'Shit. Not expensive,' was his verdict.

As the dinner progressed nobody addressed Aslan at all. He stared at his soup, eating it politely and with difficulty all at the last minute. Carrot and orange didn't seem to be his scene. Then he piled his plate high with roast beef and guzzled the lot without salad or potatoes, complimenting Tara on her meat (imported from Finland at phenomenal expense and sold in shops geared exclusively to very wealthy foreigners). He made everyone tense. He looked every bit as though he was on the point of pulling a gun from under his jacket and wiping the lot of us out. Coiled for action – the slightest unexpected movement might send him over the edge.

Eventually Harry, in a fit of English politesse, asked him in Russian what he did for a living. 'I am at the market, sell fruit,' he said, flashing his eyes in challenge at the guests. The table fell silent.

Tamsin paused before wailing with drunken laughter. 'You are like a watermelon guy?' she yelled.

Aslan grinned without an accompanying smile in his eyes. 'Watermelon guy!' he nodded.

'Holy shit,' Tamsin beamed. 'Good for you.'

Nobody could think of anything to say after this and, following a few minutes of diversionary drink pouring and telling Tara how delicious Natasha's cooking was, (many of them had tasted it in previous years under past correspondents, and anyway it wasn't that great) the talk turned back to Chechnya. All the hacks had recently come home from covering the grisly end to the Russian bombardments, concentration camps and all. They felt that this reflected extremely well on them in terms of bravery and ground-breaking news coverage and they were proud to have known a young Russian photographer who had been killed. In fact in life they had ignored him completely and been irritated at his constantly asking them for use of their satellite phones to call Moscow. He had been just another poor Russian who failed to understand how important they were. Now of course he had become one of them, risking life together for the cause.

'When I escaped across the mountains I met the man who shot that Russian. An arsehole. We went to primary school together. He was stupid,' Aslan suddenly said in Russian. He had obviously understood more than we thought. Tara smiled winningly at Aslan in admiration and Aslan almost smiled back.

'You were in Grozny for the bombardment?' asked Adrian, suddenly impressed and humbled. He was the only one whose Russian was half decent. He had been a student in Moscow in the 1970s, drinking and feeling great camaraderie with the underground poets. 'Poet' in those days essentially meant young drunk with long hair who wasn't in the Communist Party.

'My mother was in the cellar. I was fighting,' he said, raising his arms to an imaginary machine gun. The hacks flinched away from it instinctively. Aslan flashed his eyes around the table, resting on each person in turn as he told us about his friend who had been tortured in a Russian concentration camp. Afterwards he had asked Aslan to kill him and Aslan had obliged. 'The Russians had killed him already. I just gave the bullet,' he said. Alexandra coughed and stared at her wine. Tamsin quietly tapped her ash and Harry put his knife and fork down neatly on his plate.

'Gosh. It's still light,' I said chirpily but Tara raised a threatening eyebrow at me.

Later, when the dreadful pause had been broken by the beginnings of a discussion about the Russian camps in Chechnya, I saw something very interesting indeed. Tara leant across and put her hand over Aslan's. 'Can I get you a cognac?' she asked, in her prettiest voice, entirely failing to address any of the other guests.

He smiled in return, baring his gold tooth and softening his black eyes. 'Please,' he answered in a whisper.

Ashamed now at their mock bravado they stopped talking about their own exploits in Grozny and respectfully asked Aslan lots of questions about what was going on there now. The atmosphere had changed completely and Tamsin, who had rather hoped to persuade everyone to come clubbing or whisky-drinking in a strip joint afterwards, eventually teetered towards the bathroom to slap on another layer of make-up before leaving.

Adrian, Alexandra and little Joshua left with her, propping her up while she put her shoes back on. For a while, Tara, Harry, Aslan and I sat around drinking cognac together. Harry was obviously annoyed at Aslan's seeming unwillingness to leave and kept saying things like, 'Well, the hostess will be needing to get her beauty sleep.' When this approach failed he went for a more brutal type of one-upmanship, dropping hints about his wealth and station. 'You girls should come to my chalet in St Moritz next winter,' he said, in the middle of a conversation about something utterly unrelated. Despite his desire to get rid of Aslan, Harry was unable to stop himself attempting to male bond at the same time. He couldn't stand the thought of Aslan, who was obviously very hard indeed, thinking of him as some sort of wuss.

'Working at the market means you're nice and near the Slavyanskaya,' he said to Aslan at one stage, with a conspiratorial wink. 'Fantastic babes.'

Aslan nodded politely, his back straight, his gaze steady, his antipathy towards Harry almost tangible.

I found I was still very frightened of Aslan. Tara, plainly, was not.

At about one, Harry gave up and left, bristling visibly and being overstatedly friendly and polite. I stuck around, hoping to veer the conversation back to Zander and Oksana somehow, but when Tara said she was too hot and unbuttoned her blouse to expose the top of her breasts, I skulked off back to my hotel in sheer amazement.

'Oh my God,' Tara shrieked into the phone at seven the next morning. 'Oh MY GOD!'

'Hello, hello?' I asked.

'He was so fucking incredible, Fizzy. That was so fucking incredible. I mean, INCREDIBLE. He is ENORMOUS. He like tied me to the—' she began.

'No! I don't want to know,' I laughed.

'OK. But he did. He was . . . oh my God. Seriously, he's so . . . I've never felt like this before. Do you think I could be in love with him?'

'No. Where is he now?'

'He's gone to get Sultan to do the stall today, then he's coming back to fuck me completely senseless all day long. Seriously, though, I didn't know you could sort of lose yourself like this. He recited all this Chechen poetry to me and he looked at me like . . . like nobody's ever looked at me before. I feel as if I've known him all my life. I just looked into his eyes . . . I hope I'm pregnant. This is the best thing EVER! God, I wish I didn't have to travel tomorrow.'

She was hysterical, I thought.

I mean, she was all set to be going on some trip for a travel piece and Cassian was supposed to be going with her, doing the same feature for a different paper. He usually did big investigative freelance crime pieces when he wasn't doing his financial stuff, but this time someone had persuaded him into something softer.

'Jesus. What about your dad? I mean, he was going to . . . What about Cassian?' I asked.

'Sod them. Honestly. If you ever, ever, ever actually tried having sex in your life . . . no, not having sex. You know what? I think I was making love. Oh my God! Anyway, if you ever did it you might understand! I mean, sod them. Dad's in England, Cass won't be back until tomorrow and I have never ever been so bloody happy, Fizz!'

At the mention of my never having sex I quickly leapt off the moral highground to which I was not anyway entitled and I agreed to go round to the flat for a lunch of crackers and caviar with the new lovers later on. The idea of Tara thinking of me as celibate was extremely odd.

Of course, as far as she was concerned I was practically a virgin. I had never told her about Cassian and I don't imagine he had mentioned it. And obviously she didn't know about Zander. She must assume that the couple of weirdos at university was my lot over the past decade. I once considered making a few up to sound more convincing, but quickly abandoned the idea on grounds of taste.

When I got to her place Aslan and Tara were spooning salty black eggs orgasmically into each other's mouths so I told them I had to work the next day and left quickly to watch TV in the hotel until I fell asleep, ready for my train to Samara in the morning and the boat to Kazan. Not even the cries of lust coming through the hotel vents could keep me awake.

Though if I'd known how the trip would turn out, I doubt I'd have shut my eyes for a second.

# Twelve

He didn't see me watching him. Catching him like this, not knowing he was observed, reminded me of seeing him for the first time from Flossy's bedroom window. So quiet and so still. It was the beginning of the downward slide of my university experience and it was only the first night.

I suppose in retrospect going up for interview had been the best bit of the whole thing. I took the train from Queensbury with Tara, Ursula and Minty. We had all passed the exams but it was apparently the interview that mattered most. It must have been February and it was freezing cold. The train skittered through the grey English countryside, icy drizzle spattering against the dirty windows. We bought little bottles of nasty wine at the buffet and stood in the carriage dividers smoking and drinking out of thin plastic cups. I had taken up smoking after Flossy died, largely in honour of her, but also in order to bring myself closer to Cassian. I thought if I were performing all the same actions as him I was somehow nearer to him. I had a Zippo and I learnt to flick it open and light it in one action on my jeans. I inhaled deeply and spent a week teaching myself smoke rings. I felt they looked almost natural now.

We were all interviewing at different colleges and when we got off the train we stood in a bleak huddle outside the station having one last fag together before we had to separate. It was the first time I had experienced real camaraderie with anyone since Flossy.

Tara was very depressed because her mum had just gone into Hill Place. According to the papers, Hermione had taken a massive overdose of valium, paracetamol and gin, and had been found by a groom lying in the woods near the Cairnsham Hall stables. Although Tara had told me a lot now about her parents' relationship she hadn't said anything more than that her mum was going in rehab. You had to feel sorry for her. We expressed this, stupidly, by offering her cigarettes and buying her drinks. Nobody knew what else to do.

For the past few holidays I had been waitressing in a pasta place on Clapham Common, so I had made the money to make myself vaguely presentable. I didn't look posh or rich, but I didn't look awful either and, standing there by Oxford station, smoking with some girls from school, I doubted anyone could easily tell I wasn't quite one of them. I talked like them, stood like them, tossed my hair like them, but I didn't have that knowledge: the absolute certainty that things would turn out in my favour and that, if by some appalling twist of fate they didn't, I could go home and be looked after there instead. That, I was just starting to appreciate, was what poshness was about. Not money or style. Complacency.

I had lost the confidence I had had so briefly with Flossy so I never bought anything too outrageous to wear, and I didn't want to draw attention to the looks I was now aware of having, especially considering what had happened last time. But I had Levi's red tag jeans, baggy checked shirts, a decent black coat, woolly tights, slightly pointy flat shoes, some short but not ludicrous skirts and a couple of M&S polo neck jumpers in red and black. I looked OK.

I spent a lot of time at Camden Lock trying to find bargains. I used to get the tube up there early on Sunday mornings and I was already excited by the time I got on the long escalator up towards Camden with all the punks and the psychobillies, drunks and psychopaths. There were always buskers trying to make themselves heard in the undulating crowds, and gaggles of supertrendy girls waiting for their friends up in the seedy filth of the station itself. They all looked as though they must live round there, they fitted in so effortlessly, with their silver rings, partially shaved heads, spiky shoes and long tweedy coats. They were all plastered in make-up though some of them must have been even younger than I was, and they held their fags in fingerless gloves and ate exciting looking things from pitta bread. They were well-spoken though trying hard not to be, and you could tell they were going home for Sunday lunch with a mildly disapproving family in a couple of hours.

I used to join the crowds, shuffling from one little

stall to another, picking up pairs of jeans and antique white shirts, checking the 1950s summer dresses for holes and trying to choose shoes that hadn't been worn out from immense and chaotic piles, faintly reminiscent of concentration camps. It was ironic really, because all the other girls from school spent their whole time trying to ruin their brand-new and expensive clothes in order to make them look as though they were from Camden Lock. I was doing the opposite. Mum always laughed at me for going to the trendiest market in the world and coming home with such conservative stuff. Sometimes she came with me and bought silver rings and dangly earrings from people with chapped fingers who drank dark tea out of polystyrene cups and ought to have been her friends.

The pasta place that financed my trips was new and had cards on all the tables so that the customers could write what they thought. Mostly the blokes wrote that I had a nice bum or tits. Mostly they tried to touch both.

The manageress, Karen, took her job extremely seriously and used to go on about how this was going to be the best Pasta Palace in London. She had come far enough in her career to buy herself a Volvo 340, she told us (presumably this was supposed to make her staff realise that they too might one day rise to such lofty heights), and she was not going to stop at that. It was the salad bar, she insisted, that must be the envy of all other establishments far and wide.

This, she said, was what the customer saw first and it was this that would make or break us. We had to restock it constantly, dragging the aluminium boxes off into the terrifying walk-in fridge downstairs, and refilling them from the huge Tupperware tubs of the house salads that arrived from head office every couple of days – sweetcorn and beetroot, coleslaw, kidney beans with peas, lettuce and tomatoes, that kind of thing. We also had to decorate the salad bar with shiny fruit and vegetables that were not for sale. We wore green shirts with name tags on them and black trousers. Girls had to have their hair back off their faces.

On my first morning Karen made me practise saying 'Hi, my name's Alice and I'll be your waitress this afternoon/this evening. Can I get you some drinks to start with?' Introducing yourself any other way was a sackable offence. When we picked up the phone we had to say 'Pasta Palace, Clapham Common. Alice speaking. How can I help you?' It always made me giggle, and Karen would scowl disapprovingly. We had to know how to work the cappuccino machine and how to sprinkle chocolate powder delicately over the foam. We had to prepare the puddings ourselves, popping perfectly rounded ice-cream balls out of their plastic shells and adorning them with butterscotch sauce and uniformly chopped nuts – all a regulation size, the same at Pasta Palaces throughout Britain.

I found it easy to maximise my tips, judging in advance whether or not people wanted someone flirty or demure, bouncy or stand-offish, highly interactive or expertly discreet. I loved going home at night, my pockets heavy with thirty quids' worth of change.

I often worked the evening shift and spent the hour between midnight and one a.m. pouring all the salt out of the salt shakers, washing and refilling them for the morning. Once I could have absolutely sworn that I saw Zander – or Tara's dad, as I then knew him – lurking about outside as I picked up all the little vases of carnations from the tables, but by the time my shift was over he had gone and I have never quite dared ask him. It seems so unlikely now.

So, my first choice college was right on the High Street not far from Magdalen Bridge, and it looked bleak and grey that day of the interviews in the grim winter weather. The Oxford I had seen with Flossy, so bright and sunny, had disappeared.

The lawns of the main quad shone green in the twilight and the chapel choir was singing hymns somewhere behind the stained-glass windows in the far corner. It was quiet and cold, and the porter who showed me to my room looked like someone who had been kicked out of the police force for brutality. He *was*, in fact, someone who had been kicked out of the police force for brutality. You could see that most of the walls would be covered with purple wisteria in the summer, but at the moment there were only the gnarled branches writhing up around the dripping gargoyles and creeping on to the ancient latticed window ledges.

The room I was shown to was vast and icy. It was very dark and there were no rugs over the shabby blackish floorboards. The high alcoved ceiling was hung with a bare bulb and the window seats that looked out over another small quad were uncushioned and uninviting. There was a gas fire against one wall which even on tacky orange-glowing full made no impact on the chill. The walls were panelled with oak and in one of the panels there was a poster of Bros stuck on with Blu-tack. The bedroom was across a tiny landing, a minuscule triangle of antique floorboards that had to be carefully dealt with if you didn't want to fall down all the narrow winding stairs leading to the nearest toilet, a freezing four floors below. This room was windowless and about the size of the 1950s iron single bed that was in it. The sheets were damp and cold and the blanket over them filthy. There was a kettle and the dirtiest, most stained mug (Manchester United) I had ever seen, but no tea or coffee, so I warmed my hands on a cup of hot water.

A note by the porters' lodge told me I had both my interviews that evening, one after the other (a general one and one related to my subjects). I had ten minutes to drink my water and collect myself. I was still feeling a bit pissed from the train but maybe that was a good thing. Annoyingly, the interviews at my second choice college were in two days' time – two days with nothing to do and hardly any money.

I sat on a four-hundred-year-old dark wooden chair in a gloomy panelled corridor, wriggling my toes to keep warm, and waited for my summons.

A kind-looking Indian girl eventually emerged, sighing in relief. 'That was terrifying. Good luck,' she said in a thick Birmingham accent that she would spend the next four years trying to lose.

'Thanks,' I smiled, and went in.

The French woman asked me in French if I'd ever been to France and the Russian man asked me in Russian if I'd ever been to Russia. They asked me what books I'd read and wondered what I thought the point was of speaking foreign languages. I had spent my whole school career working harder than anyone else I knew and was confident of my academic abilities. I could see they were impressed, but I couldn't bring myself to be pleased.

The general interview was more difficult. A thin bald man in pinstripes asked me why I wanted to come to Oxford and what I thought I would contribute to college life. If I had been honest I would have answered 'so that I can escape from my background' and 'nothing whatsoever'. I don't remember what I actually said but it must have done the trick because when I went back to check what time my other interviews were I saw they had been cancelled. I discussed this at length with the girls and we concluded it must mean my first choice college was going to take me.

Minty's horror was all still to come, but Tara had been asked which character in *War and Peace* she most identified with and had assumed it was a joke. It wasn't. Apparently the bald bloke had scowled and repeated his question, so she'd said Natasha. Poor Ursula had been told to put some stones and fossils on her interviewer's desk in chronological order. She'd picked the first few up to scrutinise them and immediately dropped them on the floor and then burst into tears. She needed cheering up.

We decided to investigate Oxford's nightlife. Or at least Tara decided that we should investigate Oxford's nightlife, and these days I was happy to go along with her. Actually, I liked her. I had begun to think that I would have picked on me too, given the opportunity. I was so serious and pious. So entirely unrebellious. She wasn't Flossy but she had a certain silliness about her that was definitely attractive. That I envied. I never really felt properly frivolous.

We went to three faintly depressing pubs, full of the kind of students who stay in Oxford during the holidays, and then we went back to Minty's grim modern room in Pembroke to drink a cheap bottle of wine we'd bought. We were all completely gloom-laden.

'God this place is a shit hole,' moaned Tara, bringing up a vodka-and-lime burp.

'I think it's lovely,' Ursula said meekly. 'It's the most beautiful place I've ever been.'

The rest of us rolled our eyes and sighed in exasperation. 'Anthony Andrews isn't actually here, you know,' said Tara. 'It's just those acned pissed wankers in rowing sweatshirts doing yards of ale in the pub.'

'I bet there are all kinds of people. You just have

to find them,' Ursula replied, swigging some wine out of the bottle.

'God, Sulie. It's grey, rainy, provincial and vile. Everyone here thinks they're great but actually they are just square and pompous and there is nothing, absolutely bloody nothing, to do,' shouted Minty, leaping up to pace about the room. Minty's mother taught something called Biodanza which was, she claimed 'more a way of life than a dance' and was heavily into tantric sex. Every time Minty got home for the holidays there would be some new beardy weirdy staying with them and teaching her mum a ground-breakingly orgasmic technique. Minty's dad worked in the City and tried to pretend that all this was as harmless as having tennis lessons or whatever the other bored country housewives did. Whenever Minty (Catherine Minton) was irritated she would dance about shouting in what we decided was a faintly tantric way. I was very nearly enjoying myself.

'You know what is obviously going to happen, of course? We'll all get in except Ursula – the only one who stands an outside chance of having a good time,' Tara said, blowing smoke rings above her curly head. None of us laughed because it was true. Ursula wanted it too much. She had worked too hard for it, set her heart on it. She didn't have the confident nonchalance that seemed to be necessary for impressing these people. We were all going to get in except Ursula.

Bored out of our minds by nine thirty we went on

the prowl. We giggled hysterically at the names above some of the college doors and recited 'Shall I compare thee to a summer's day?' outside the entrance to someone called Dr Pogge Von something's lair. Laughing madly, we wondered whether he actually introduced himself as Pogge in public. Minty stole a bottle of wine from Oddbins and I decided to go back to my room.

I couldn't sleep in the icy cell of the bedroom so I dragged the moth-eaten greenish sofa over to the gas fire in the bigger room and lay fully clothed on that, staring wakefully up at the ceiling. I tried to remember what it had felt like lying on the warm grass with Cassian, not being surprised that he wanted me, thinking myself perfectly worthy of him, taking him in my arms and laughing with him under the stars. It was only two years ago, but I felt decades older already. I woke up to find the sleeve of my jumper smouldering in the gas fire.

Too nervous now to go back to sleep, I sat in the window and watched the silent quad. Every now and then a young couple would walk through, drunk, stumbling together like people in a three-legged race, bound by the arms they had draped across each other's shoulders. Even in this state most people were very obedient about keeping off the grass, I noticed. I saw someone be sick in the corner by a wisteria root, sitting down afterwards in the wet, his head in his hands, trying to pull himself together enough to carry on as far as his room. He would probably forget the incident, and would be horrified to think he had been watched. I almost called out to ask him in for a restorative cup of hot water, but he looked so ghostly down there all on his own that I didn't quite dare break the silence with the creak of my window opening, the sound of my voice echoing about in the rain.

By morning I had a temperature and a bad cold. I knew I was sentenced to four years here and I was almost looking forward to the suffering – penance for my failures. When I left, shivering, the next day, I was too fuzzy to see a piece of paper pinned to the college notice board: 'Keasby Travel Bursary awarded to Cassian Vinci'.

# Thirteen

When I got on to the Samara train I found I had been accidentally booked into slime class and was sharing a compartment with three very rowdy Russian women. They had already settled in and were wearing their slippers and tracksuit bottoms, picking at a chicken carcass wrapped in foil and peeling hard-boiled eggs. They had persuaded the carriage lady to give them tea early and they were sucking it in through sugar lumps held between their teeth. There were four bottles of Soviet champagne and a bottle of vodka standing ominously on the fold-down table between the berths, and one of the ladies, better turned out than the others, with bleached blonde hair and long pink nails, was rummaging around in her bag for plastic cups.

I nodded at them nervously and glanced around to see which bunk was mine.

'You're on top of me,' grinned Tanya, an enormous woman with grey hair pinned back by an Alice band, and blue and white plastic flip-flops on her feet. 'Don't worry – you'll get used to the smell,' she grinned, and they all burst out laughing, swinging their feet under their seats and showing their mouthfuls of food.

Tanya, Svyeta and Ira were, amazingly, classical music journalists, heading for Samara and my very boat trip. They were sailing up the Volga with the Rus International Orchestra. Apparently the orchestra, which would be taking up most of the boat, was on tour, visiting various Volga towns on the way to Kazan and playing concerts in each of them. Nikolai Spletnev, the conductor, was said to be travelling with his mother and his boyfriend. 'Don't be so crude,' Ira said at the mention of homosexuality, raising her hand to her mouth. 'Kolya is married to his music.'

They gave me an egg, a chicken leg and a cup of champagne as the train creaked out of the Moscow station, pulling away from relatives in flowery sundresses, children eating ice-cream and men with tattoos on their wrists, grimacing in the sunlight. For at least an hour or so I sat stony-faced on the top bunk with my legs crossed, reading an old university book about Andrei Rublev, and reluctantly chewing the food they had given me. I was irritated by the commotion below and couldn't believe I was going to have to spend all night with these maniacs.

But before long (perhaps it was the bubbles up my nose) their stupid jokes and their constant cajoling brought me down to sit with them, and by the time it was properly dark I was as drunk and babbling as they were.

Ira's husband was a conductor who rivalled Spletnev in fame and she insisted her husband was by far the superior artiste – it was all in the fingertips. She was a radio presenter and she always smiled and laughed with her lips pursed to hide her goofy teeth. She had a great affected delicacy and was slim and pretty, but like all attractive Russian women wore too much make-up and oddly tarty clothes.

Tanya smoked furiously and said she hadn't had sex for so long that she was essentially a virgin. She wrote for a prestigious broadsheet and, as a former card-carrying Communist, she had strong views on the commercialisation of classical music and the Mafiosi that now packed the Moscow concert halls. Svyeta had just married her second husband, a vodka trader from the far north, and spent a lot of time defending him from the others' accusations of barbarism. Svyeta had big glasses and lots of brown curly hair. She was very sexy without being beautiful – and she knew it. As soon as a man approached, even if he was in a blue uniform and bringing bed linen, she pouted, put on a little girly voice and batted her eyelids furiously to great effect.

'It has been hard recently,' said Ira, standing up with difficulty. 'We have lost everything we once knew. We were educated, respected, with a position in society. Now we are poor and insignificant, forced to compromise our values to make ends meet . . . but, ladies,' she went on, raising her plastic cup, 'we are blessed. We exist on a higher plane, and we appreciate that material things are not everything. That there is something higher than all this. There is music.' The others whooped in appreciation and

Svyeta actually cried as we all drank the toast against the noise of the chugging train.

The silver birches were now barely visible in the twilight behind the thin strip of curtain, patterned with fading hammers and sickles and hanging off a loose plastic rail. The corridor outside our compartment was bustling with people getting ready for bed.

I woke up at quarter to six, sweating and breathless after a horrible dream about a hot beach. There were tall palm trees and huts on stilts. Young travellers with tousled hair and bare feet sat on the planked steps, smoking joints and drinking bottles of beer, and the sea was turquoise and far away across the white sand. Dark people fried circles of flat bread for the foreigners on huge black pans suspended over fires in the sand and filled them with a delicious vegetable slop. Lying on a sand dune, his eyes shut and a quiet smile on his face, was Zander, wearing black tie but not looking too hot. In his arms, also asleep, was a young girl, a bit like me but not me, her head on his chest and her arms happily round his neck. She was wrapped in a white sheet. As I walked along through the hot sand I remember thinking almost consciously that this was a dream and that it was a nice one. The thought must have jinxed me because, letting the surf slap on to my feet, I noticed a fight going on just ahead of me. Struggling in the shallow water, waves sploshing over her screaming head, was Flossy in her soaked school uniform and Cassian, kneeling on top of her, stabbing her over and over again with a huge watermelon knife. I ran up the beach back to Zander and wailed at him to help her, but instead he ran towards them into the sea, leaving the girl asleep, and brought out his own knife. The two of them kept on and on stabbing Flossy but she wouldn't die and the sea was staining with blood.

We arrived in Samara the next morning, scrumpled and hungover, and we shared a taxi to our boat. The *Radishchev* was named after an author who made a journey from St Petersburg to Moscow and, spurred on by his social conscience, documented how depressing it all was. He would not be the last person to make similar observations.

We were not setting sail until tonight, after the RIO's first concert, and the boat was completely full because of the unfortunate fate of its sister ship, whose passengers had all now been shunted on to the concert tour.

My cabin was small, early 1971 in style, with cigarette burns on the white plastic side-table and in the damp grey carpet. I had given up smoking years ago. Zander hates girls who smoke. I missed him despite everything. I was weak without him. The bedspread was a bright nylony orange and the fluorescent strip light above the headboard crackled and then went dead when I tried to turn it on. The shower room creaked when you stepped into it and the whole place smelt awful. I left my stuff and went to find the girls in the bar.

There was a glitter ball in the centre of the ceiling,

and curved sofas, upholstered in red polyester, were set around circular white plastic tables, held up on stalks like inverted cones. The bar itself was also curved and had strips of flashing disco lights above and below it. My new friends found this in no way odd and had ordered coffee with a shot of cognac in it.

'It's good for you, Fizzy. Makes you feel better,' Svyeta insisted. They had translated my name literally into Russian – '*Shipushchaya*' – and laughed every time they said it. 'Like bubbles in champagne?' Ira had asked when I tried to explain it. I was pleased at the thought and nodded enthusiastically. For the first time in the past decade I was beginning to feel seen through. These women had no time for appearances and had taken me for what I was at a glance. They didn't know what my earrings, my nickname and my Calvin Klein blue silk scarf like smoke around my neck signified, and nor did they care.

I drank the disgusting coffee out of an orange cup with big white spots on and refused the cognac to a great deal of communal bafflement. There were lots of fattish blokes in the bar drinking beer, smoking and picking their teeth. They all wore dirty, shiny shell suits in purples and navys, and they all had slippers or flip-flops on, exposing their crusty old peasant feet. When we went down to the so-called restaurant they were there too, asking if they could have their porridge with butter in it, slapping the waitresses' bums and leaning right over their bowls, spoons in one hand, shovelling from back to front, and slice of bread in the other to help along the globs that fell off the spoon. At least two tables had half-empty bottles of vodka on them though it was only about nine in the morning.

I was amazed to see the same men emerging that evening from their cabins in immaculate black tie, clean shaven with their hair slicked back and carrying the instruments they had been practising so beautifully from within all afternoon. These were the best musicians in the former Soviet Union, people who had trained at the Moscow Conservatory or the Gneissin Music Academy, who had played in London, New York and Paris and were revered by music lovers all over the world.

I pottered about near the *Radishchev* during the day, looking for things to buy at the dockside market. People had brought all their personal belongings to arrange on squares of tarpaulin in the hope of raking together a few roubles. There were moth-eaten furs, chipped cups, silver knives and forks from before the Revolution, tiny twisted pieces of jewellery and worn-out shoes. Some had made jars of pickles, jams and cheeses to sell to their neighbours.

'I love all this,' I heard a wizened old lady tell a saleswoman. 'Before, we had all that money and nothing to spend it on. Now there's everything and we're all penniless. Still, at least there's something to look at.'

The girls invited me to that evening's concert and

we walked from the boat to Samara's concert hall, meandering along by the vast river, watching people eating kebabs on the beaches and envying the young couples walking hand in hand under the trees in the twilight. Groups of teenaged thugs lounged around plastic barbecue furniture listening to Western pop from antique ghetto blasters. They hunched over their bottles of beers, wishing there was some excuse for a fight. The air was dusty and, as we heaved ourselves up the steep hills along crumbling streets to the centre of town, it began to get dark. Mothers in aprons leant out of the windows of sloping wooden houses to call their children down from the branches of nearby trees, and stray dogs and cats scrabbled urgently in the grey grime.

When we arrived there was not a spare seat in the place and I had to bribe a door lady twenty roubles (under a pound) to let me sit on the steps at the top. The room, presumably built in the 1930s, was shaped like an open clam shell and all the boxes were miniature shells jutting out into the auditorium. At least half the audience were children under ten, little girls with enormous puffy ribbons like great peonies on their heads and boys in neat blue pioneer uniforms with red scarves round their necks. I didn't spot a single fidget from them during the performance, though personally I couldn't sit still for more than a movement at a time and I was dying for the interval. At the end lots of them took flowers up to Spletnev and led the standing ovation.

Culture had not yet deserted the regions, I thought. Lenin told them that art was for everyone and they believed him. He should have mentioned it to the West.

You could hear the river lapping at its beaches as we walked back through the rustling dark, and the promenade smelt of searing meat and sweet tea. The teenagers all looked so 1950s in their funny dresses and ponytails, kissing their beaux in the moonlight so far from anywhere. We arrived back at the boat just in time to see Tara and Cassian dragging their suitcases up the gangplank.

# FOURTEEN

When I actually saw Cassian I thought I might faint. The beer cellar was packed, airless and smelly, with booze swilling around on the floor, extremely drunken rugby players staggering about holding on to each other and all the new people huddled together looking nervous in the bare-bulbed greenish light. In my somewhat biased eyes Cassian didn't seem a part of all this. Admittedly, he was ordering a pint and looked reasonably at home, but there was no bravado about him. He had one elbow on the bar and his head rested on his hand, his fingers fiddling with his thick hair. He wasn't talking to anybody but he didn't look shy either. He still had silver rings on his fingers but the faintly gothic image had gone. He brought a crumpled fiver out of his pocket, paid for his drink, sipped from the giant plastic cup and then lit a cigarette, allowing the smoke to swirl uninhaled out of his mouth before sucking it back in again. All I could think was that I loved him.

It was then that he looked up. I was standing at the bottom of the steps, half in and half out of the seething room. I was wearing a red polo neck, a black skirt and thick tights. My hair was pulled back off my bare face and I had my purse, a pack of

Marlboro and my lighter clutched tightly in my hands. Cassian's eyes widened and he opened his mouth as if to say something, but he never got the chance.

I turned round as slowly and with as much dignity as I possibly could and then I ran up the stairs and back to my room, breathless and tearful.

Earlier that day Mum and Kris had helped me drag my trunk with the metal corners and, of course, my tuck trunk packed full of bars of chocolates and jars of Nutella, up to the room that would be mine for the year. It was much smaller than the one I had had for interview but I liked it better. For a start it was warm, and had a sweet view over a little cobbled street that ran between colleges. I unloaded my few clothes into the wardrobe and chest of drawers, and kicked my trunk under the bed while Mum tried to make a cup of tea with my new travel kettle. Kris had bought a new pair of earrings for the occasion, gigantic lizards that hung down to her shoulders, and she kept shaking them proudly whenever anyone walked past.

'No style, these student types,' she mumbled every now and then. 'Got to show them how it's done, Stephie.'

Mum rolled her eyes. 'Sweetie, how it was done in 1965 is not necessarily of great relevance now,' she said.

So buy a new outfit, Mother, I thought, but I stayed silent. She had deemed an embroidered Indian smock dress, some red Kickers and her antique caftan suitable attire for taking me up to Oxford. Thanks, Mum.

I gave the ladies a cigarette each (a special treat for Mum) and we shared a cup of milkless tea and ate chocolate biscuits until I felt I could ask Mum and Kris to go away. I had spent a long time deciding how many mugs to bring. Mum wanted to buy me a set of six on a tree from the Oxfam shop round the corner but that seemed much too pathetically optimistic to me. Eventually I wrapped my favourite one (pink and labelled 'MINE') in newspaper and put it in my trunk. Then, just before I left I thought I should be more hopeful and stuffed a horrible brown glass thing of Mum's into my satchel just in case I did meet someone to be friends with.

The scene in the beer cellar had not been heartening. The public school crowd had formed in an instant, but the fact that I had spent seven years of my life with people just like them did not make me one of them. They had all had years off in India, Thailand and Africa. They had deep tans and wore beaded bracelets and tatty but expensive clothes. 'Have you been to India?' someone asked. 'No, but I went to Westminster.' Everybody knows it amounts to the same thing. Their names sounded like some kind of stock check at a supermarket, and indeed the supermarket itself – Jasmin Safeway, Matthew Sellotape, Ben Heineken, Angus McVitie, Beatrice Hoover – that kind of thing. Their parents knew each other, they were relaxed and confident that their lives would turn out OK with not too much effort on their part (not that they gave this a moment's thought) and they laughed with the absolute certainty that they were funny, that their view of the world was the right one, that they had nothing to be ashamed of. 'Gay people all have the same chins,' I had heard one of them saying loudly to another. 'I think it is *de rigueur* to be *au fait* with at least four of the world's capital cities,' another brayed.

I perched on the edge of my bed, tears brimming over on to my cheeks, and I held on to the magic wand that was by now just a pair of chopsticks held together with string. Good old Dad. I looked at myself in the institutional mirror that hung above the sink and then I clenched my eyes shut while the metamorphosis took place. I thought back to Flossy and Russia, to how the mist had cleared that evening we had first met Sergei, and I tried to somehow recapture that feeling, to resurrect Beautiful Alice the Brave.

I was going to change. I was going to be one of them and I was going to make Cassian love me. Alice could go and hide under her duvet with a book, but Fizz Reynolds was going to get down to the bar, drink till she could lie with confidence and make a hundred new friends. She was going to be clever, rebellious, popular and gorgeous – now.

I could hear a Joni Mitchell song playing on someone's stereo a few rooms down. 'I could drink a case of you . . . oooooooo . . . and still be on my feet . . . I would still be on my feet.' I opened my eyes and took a deep breath. I took a precious twenty-pound note out of my purse and stuffed it into my fag packet. I opened a little silver box that had been shut since I got back from Little Farford and I took my silver nose stud out of it and forced it back through its original hole, shook my hair out of its ponytail, lit a cigarette and set off again. I didn't need make-up and anyway, everybody knows posh girls don't wear it.

On my way across the quad I picked up a piece of string that must have fallen from someone's box of belongings and I tied it round my wrist. Just the sort of thing I might have being given for friendship by a local in Timbuktu. I ran back downstairs to the beer cellar, marched up to the group of Sloanes standing near the door and introduced myself.

'Hi, I'm Fizz,' I said, muscling my way into their centre. I chose a likely-looking young man with some beads round his neck. 'Didn't I see you at the Queensbury ball last year?' I asked. I hadn't been there myself.

He shook his head, smiling. 'No, not me, unfortunately. I was never in the right set for that sort of thing,' he said, blushing.

'You didn't miss much!' I laughed. 'Can I get you a drink? Drink, anyone?' I took some orders and moved over to the bar.

Smiling flirtatiously at the harassed bloke serving warm sticky drinks in plastic cups, I made my order and then called over to Andy, my new friend, to help me carry everything. Cassian had gone.

I drank six vodka and limes and when I heard a beautiful and affectedly shabby girl called Betsy murmur about rolling a joint I invited her and a couple of her hangers-on up to my room to smoke it. I told myself that I was now officially somebody else and I was not going to slip up. Thankfully, they refused on the grounds that I had no Rizlas, but they asked me instead to come to Betsy's room where we sat on the floor, listened to Bob Dylan and giggled until about two in the morning. Or at least they giggled and I tried to imitate them. Someone made an origami swan out of the silver foil of a cigarette packet.

Betsy was doing English and had come up from London the day before with her boyfriend, Robin, a sullen type in torn jeans. They had been at Bedales together. Her dad was a diplomat who lived in Cairo, so she and Robin had spent the whole summer travelling round Egypt, getting tans and diarrhoea. The latter was the source of many an amusing anecdote. 'So I've got shit running down my leg and on to this poor camel . . .' Betsy began. It reminded me of evenings with my mum and her friends in the old days, and I smiled weakly. The less I said, I had decided, the better. Preferable that they should think I was a bit cool and sulky than that they find out I had never been anywhere or done anything.

As the night wore on someone tried to make some toast, but it got stuck down and caught fire. While the toaster went up in flames everyone lay there tittering and arguing about who ought to get up and deal with it. 'Definitely, Robin, man. He's been boring the crap out of us all evening,' Andy volunteered.

Robin's car had broken down that day and the battery was sitting on top of Betsy's television, looking forlorn. At this insult he arose from his beanbag and went over to the defunct thing, plonking a little sachet of canteen salt down on top of it. 'Assault and battery,' he said, sniggering, and slumped back down. The fire continued to leap out of the sizzling toaster.

The next morning I went shopping. It was going to cost me half my grant for the term but I had no choice. I needed a piece of old gold jewellery, an expensive jumper that was too big for me and a long woolly scarf that looked like something I had stolen from a boyfriend or brother.

In the dusty antiques shop on the High Street I picked the perfect pair of Victorian earrings out from a blue velvet case glinting with dead people's things. They were 18-carat gold hearts, shiny and pinkish with age. They were fat and hinged and opened out to be two tiny lockets. The old lady with a glass eye told me they had had locks of hair in them. One hundred and thirty pounds.

The jumper came eventually from Joseph. They wrapped it in cream tissue paper and treated me as if I could afford to pay for it. A black man with bleached blond hair and a diamond nose stud said it suited me. Then he sighed enviously and said 'Most things would, though.' It was actually an enormous blue-and-white-patterned cardigan that reached almost to my knees. I wrapped it around myself and felt safe, but not conspicuously smart. One hundred and seventy pounds.

The scarf was much easier. I got a great long multicoloured Dr Who thing from Oxfam on Broad Street for a fiver, and when I looked in the little mirror back in my room I knew that these were the perfect accessories for my pretence at being upper class. Once I would have thought I needed designer clothes and a Rolex. Now I knew that was nouvy and, if anything, more embarrassing than poverty itself, which could be cool of course, or 'real' as I had heard Betsy say of the Egyptians living in abandoned tombs outside Cairo.

'Wicked cardy, Alice,' said Tara, arriving breathless and pink in the porter's lodge for our Russian tutorial.

'Cheers. Listen, I know I should have said ages ago, but you should call me Fizz. Everyone else does,' I said, biting my lip and looking away towards the notice board in case she rumbled me. She didn't even flinch.

'Oh. Right,' she said, twiddling a curl. 'Oh my God. It's whatsisface. Flo's brother,' she suddenly hissed.

I turned round to see Cassian walking towards us.

'Hey! Remember us?' Tara said as he

approached. Then she noticed I had slipped into the room with all the pigeonholes and posters offering coach trips to Munich for 'a piss up in a brewery' and auditions for *Grease*. 'Um, remember me?' she corrected herself.

''Fraid not,' Cassian said without smiling. 'Should I?' I didn't believe he could forget someone who had read at his sister's funeral. Especially not someone so pretty.

'I'm Flo's friend, Tara,' she helped.

'Oh. Hi,' he said and, pulling his pile of books closer to his chest, he tossed his hair out of his face and walked on.

I came back out holding a lecture timetable and smiled as though nothing had happened.

'Fucking wanker,' Tara scowled, screwing her eyes up. 'He just totally blanked me.'

'Cassian? Yeah, he's like that,' I said, as though I'd known him for ever.

'I'll tell you what he's like. He's like gorgeous,' she sighed, and we walked off for our lesson – Dostoevsky's *Notes From Underground*. Tara hadn't read it so I briefed her on the way. 'It's about this bloke who's depressed . . .' I began.

It was hard to avoid Cassian, but it would have been harder to confront him. He seemed to be everywhere. In every gloomy alcove of the library, at every table at meal times, in every corner of the beer cellar and behind every shadow on the main quad. Whenever I stepped out on to the High Street he was driving past in his old green Triumph Spitfire. Sometimes there were girls I didn't recognise sitting in the passenger seat, wearing baseball caps, laughing, leaning their slim, tanned arms out over the side of the car.

But usually he was alone, though he never looked self-conscious about it. It was more as though he had rejected company than that he had been rejected. I decided to spare myself the shame of trying to speak to him, so I lowered my eyes if I had to walk past him and talked animatedly to someone else when he was near. It seemed not to be strictly necessary, though, because he was putting as much effort into ignoring me as I was into ignoring him. But I was planning to make myself so attractive he would be clamouring to find some excuse to approach me. Admittedly I hadn't quite finalised the details of my plan yet, but I was nevertheless hoping for the best.

It had been far easier than I had expected, this making friends thing. I suppose everyone was eager to have someone to hang around with and would happily spend time with whatever they could rake up. I slumped on Betsy's sofa drinking Nescafé out of dirty cups, smoking and complaining about having an essay to do. 'It's like being in a gulag,' I moaned. I went to the Kings Arms with Andy and perched on a low stool, talking about Trollope. 'Isn't the warden just so sweeeet?' I said. People knocked on my door to see if I was coming to lunch with them and I would queue up to buy baked potatoes and salads in The Buttery, chatting and laughing as though I too might be on the first flight towards Tuscany when term ended if only I weren't otherwise engaged. 'Bring me back some almond cantuccini,' I begged.

I even had a boyfriend for a bit.

Tara was constantly trying to set me up with people. She was at Christchurch and spent a lot of time hanging around with people who went beagling and hired prostitutes when their clubs met so it was mostly at tutorials that I saw her.

She forced me to go to lunch with Hermione every time they let her out of Hill Place. She would beg and plead until I relented and then I would have to sit through some hellish mother-and-daughter scene with Hermione drunk and abusive, barely capable of sitting on a chair, and Tara tearful and imploring.

She also made me come to meetings of various dining societies at which we all pretended to be in our fifties, passing the port to the left, knowing which knives and forks to use and not smoking until the Queen had been toasted. The rooms were always dark and wood-panelled, with shining floors and austere portraits. The food was served by the poorer students with the regional accents who supplemented their grants by helping out in the kitchens and, surprisingly, nobody seemed to be particularly embarrassed by this.

I kept my relative poverty a secret and worked only in the holidays and only in London. I was in no danger of running into anyone I knew from university in my bit of Clapham. In any case, nobody questioned me for a moment, not even people like Tara, who knew my background. It began to dawn on me that I might always have been the only person conscious of my deficiencies. Could they in fact be less rather than more snobbish than I was? If I said I was one of them I was, apparently, one of them. It was amazingly easy to assimilate. All you had to do was laugh along, but not too meekly – and, of course, pass the port to the left.

Blondish boys with red faces and alcohol-bleary eyes always made clumsy passes at me at these dining events (watercress soup, smoked salmon, beef wellington and raspberry bavarois – invariably), leaning over their bow ties for a wet-lipped kiss, or draping a heavy arm round my bare shoulders.

Once I had my upper arm kissed by a German count who leant over to me during the meal and said, 'I adore offal.'

I was saved from outfit embarrassment by Minty, who had given me a black off-the-shoulder velvet dress that she said made her tits too prominent. That was exactly what I liked about it.

Still, I had become aware that I needed to choose a partner quickly for propriety's sake. I didn't want to look prudish or unwanted, but on the other hand I needed to find someone for whom I felt and could feel nothing. I wanted to make Cassian think I didn't need him, but I didn't want to put myself in the slightest danger of involvement of any kind. Andy, whose girlfriend had left him for his best friend over the summer while they were travelling round Nepal, insisted it was only safe to sleep with people you absolutely didn't give a toss about. He was in no danger of finding anyone for the time being, though, since his idea of proving he no longer cared was to phone his ex up at five in the morning on her birthday 'just to say I hate you'.

It wasn't long, however, before I homed in on Rupert.

He was tall and slim, the son of an admiral, an old Etonian and a member of the Officers' Training Corps. This more than fulfilled my criteria. He was planning on going straight into the army after Oxford and he entirely neglected his study of politics, philosophy and economics in favour of drinking heavily and socialising with other future soldiers – boys with pink cheeks, stripy shirts under V-neck sweaters and old maroon loafers. 'The squaddies, you know, need keeping in line. These people are basically scum,' they would say. He shamelessly copied other people's essays and was then indignant when the tutors noticed. He took every academic assignment as a personal affront and lied as often as possible. If he'd had tea at breakfast he'd tell you he only ever drank coffee. Once he requisitioned a tie of Andy's and continued to deny it for the next two and a half years, wearing the article on a regular basis while Andy seethed. I liked him.

Entirely unintentionally, almost everything he said made me laugh, and when we were alone together he was faultlessly chivalrous and tender. I knew that he would behave the same way with any woman, out of a sense of honour that was really a peculiar kind of sexism, but I appreciated it. The sheer ludicrousness of our knowing each other at all cheered me up.

It was after eights week – a long rowing competition which my college had won for about the thousandth consecutive year – that I met him. The results of previous wins were carved in stone above the stairway entrances dating back centuries. Anyway, this new victory involved a great deal of frenzied celebration, centring around Pimm's, featuring vodka and culminating in the cremation of a boat in the main quad.

It was a warm night and the quad was packed with onlookers who cheered as each member of the rowing team, now in black tie, leapt over the burning boat. Then their girlfriends did the same, holding up the skirts of their summer evening dresses and screaming in the light of the embers as they flew across the now smouldering remains.

Betsy and I had taken refuge in her room with a bottle of wine she had won in a raffle. She was in hiding, having shamed herself beyond belief the night before. She turned up in my room at six thirty in the morning and flicked the kettle on while I'd sat up woozily in bed, wondering what was going on.

'How embarrassing?' she'd asked me.

'I don't know, B. How embarrassing?' I'd asked back.

'So embarrassing,' she'd clarified. She had been at a party in St John's and had had oral sex up on the roof in full view of various revellers in the main quad. It had not been oral sex with Robin. Robin had, however, been able to view the scene from his vantage point below.

Anyway, fortified by the wine (i.e. too pissed to care) she agreed to be drawn outside into the excitement by the prospect of flames and more alcohol.

Rupert, who was in the year above, stumbled after his leap, slipping on the grass in a slightly drunken manner and staggering on until he slammed into me.

'Awfully sorry,' he smiled. 'Can I make it up to you with a brandy?' Betsy answered for me, so we followed him up some winding wooden stairs to his room. He had brought a painting of his grandfather (a thin bloke in a red jacket with a sword) from home to hang above the fireplace and he had all his drinks in decanters on a dark sideboard. He lit candles in silver sticks and flicked on a tape of Bach cello suites before pouring us each a brandy in huge globe-like glasses. Betsy asked if he would balk at killing somebody if he ever saw active service. I got the impression that the idea turned her on.

'Not at all. I would just take aim as you would at a pheasant or a rabbit,' he answered, after a long pause. Betsy sipped her dark amber drink and nodded, impressed. I kept a straight face, just about. The idea of killing a pheasant or a rabbit was as alien to me as killing a person, but Rupert obviously had a Barbour and a pair of green wellies and thought nothing of polishing off several brace of birds in an afternoon. Not that I knew the words 'Barbour' or 'brace' in those days.

When Betsy left I was still smiling warmly to myself on the sofa and it was then that Rupert came over to kiss me. He knelt down on the floor at my knees and took my smudged brandy glass out of my hand, slowly putting it down on the table next to me. He put one hand on either side of my face and his mouth on mine. He felt so entirely foreign that I hardly noticed. I remember his tongue tasting of booze and his lips being cold and dry, and I know I gasped when he slipped his hand inside my shirt, but I wasn't really there. Not only did I not have it in my emotional vocabulary to find him attractive, but he thought he was kissing Fizz Reynolds, someone who might be friends with his sister, someone whom he could easily meet on a hunt.

Still, I suppose I must have responded to his satisfaction because I woke up naked beside him in a single bed, a bird singing loudly from the wisteria outside the latticed window. He smelt of pine forests, something I later tracked down to a bottle of Polo on his sink. He made real coffee in a cafetière and brought it to me in bed in a green and white Wedgwood cup and saucer with ivy round the rim. He sat by me in a maroon silk dressing gown and watched me drink it, telling me what a pretty girl I was. I laughed at how much like a fairytale handsome prince he was and how totally unable I was to take it seriously. Not my handsome prince. Not my fairy tale.

After that he knocked on my door every day, never assuming I would be free and never asking me in advance to make myself free. Every meeting was like a first date. Would I like to go out for dinner with him at Fifteen North Parade? Would I like to go for a walk by the river? Would I come to the Caledonian ball with him that evening? I always accepted and I always walked arm in arm across the quad with him in the hope that Cassian might see me, but now that I wanted him to appear he never did.

I stayed in Rupert's bed a couple of nights a week (he never presumed to sleep in my room) and we had the kind of sex I had never known existed. It was not unpleasant, but I was pleased to note that I felt nothing at all. Not so much as a twinge of passion or love or anything. I was barely present.

Tara naturally thought Rupert was hilarious, which he was. 'I never thought you'd go for anyone so straight,' she said when she first saw us together. Minty said he reminded her of her Uncle George, who had shot himself with his hunting rifle when his wife came out of the closet and ran off with the housekeeper.

After two terms Rupert dumped me for a girl called Adriana – a good horsewoman from Christchurch whose nickname was Moo. She was very, very posh. The first time I met her I asked what she would be doing over the summer.

'I'm going to France to learn Italian,' she drawled.

'Oh,' I answered, slightly taken aback. 'Wouldn't it be better to go to Italy?'

'No, no. Not France, Flawnce,' she said, irritated.

I thought for a second, racking my brains as to what she could possibly mean. 'Oh! Florence!' I nodded enthusiastically.

They were married within a year in our college chapel.

'I'm awfully sorry, Fizzy,' he said when he told me. 'I've just never felt you really loved me.'

'No,' I said, kissing him on the cheek.

We are still friends. He left the army and went into venture capital. He and Moo have two children and live in Chelsea, and I sometimes go to dinner in their dark red dining room and eat duck and boiled cabbage.

# Fifteen

It didn't work, of course. Nothing from Cassian. Not so much as a flicker of interest. I think the first thing that could be considered a proper encounter with him was the slave auction at the beginning of the summer term.

The whole thing was an agonising procedure whereby volunteers stood on a table and were sold for charity, either to perform an advertised task (wash your knickers for a week/take you out for champagne and caviar) or to do whatever you tell them to according to your bid. The background idea, as with all these excruciating occasions, is to raise money for charity, but really it is an exercise in total humiliation.

Andy was the first to hoist himself up on to the Formica table to be inspected by the drunk and sweaty crowd. There were wolf whistles and shouts of 'Gettemoff!' before the auctioneer, standing on an adjacent table, began the bidding. Eventually a postgrad student bought him to give her a baby oil massage that evening. Her friends hooted and her boyfriend stormed out, slopping his pint of Guinness into the general swill on the lino floor.

Tara and Minty had come over at my express invitation to watch the show, and Tara's as yet unlit cigarette fell out of her mouth into her drink when Cassian got up on to the table. Tara hardly ever graced my college so her sightings of Cassian had been kept to a minimum. However, there was only so much beagling a person could do and tonight she had elected to slum it.

'A very rare and unusual lot, lot number seven – Cassian Vinci,' the auctioneer said, sipping fatly at his third pint. 'You don't see them about much, moody and mysterious but well worth it. Look at those pecs,' he went on, while Cassian stood there, glowering at the back wall, his hands in his jeans pockets. It must have been a bet or a dare because he certainly wasn't enjoying himself.

'Oh my God,' said Tara.

'Oh my GOD. It's Flo's brother,' said Minty.

'Oh my God,' I muttered to myself, trying not to look at him.

'Twenty-five quid to punt us down the Cherwell in his underpants and a gondolier's hat!' Tara shouted, standing up and waving her cash. The cellar exploded in laughter.

'Fifty quid to lick toffee ice-cream off my tits,' screamed a third-year historian before passing out in an ashtray.

'Fifty-five pounds and eighteen pence,' said Minty loudly, gathering together all the coins on our table and pointing at the notes between Tara's teeth, 'for the pants and punting.'

The hammer came down and Tara elbowed me hard in the ribs. 'We've got him!' she beamed, flashing a wink at Cassian, who stepped down off the table, bowing his head so his hair flopped over his face.

'See you at the boathouse tomorrow at two,' Minty shouted, and he smiled a big menacing fake smile at her.

'Can't wait,' he growled and slouched over to the bar.

'I'm not going.'

'You've *got* to come, Fizz,' Tara whined. 'You paid for at least two pounds of him.' She kept on and on, buying me drink after drink until I agreed to go with them. We had stopped watching the auction and were only sucked in again by a sudden silence that fell over the beer cellar just as Tara was explaining how easy it would be to give someone a blow job while they were standing up manoeuvring a punt pole. 'It's just a question of balance,' she said, leaning her hands on the table and opening her mouth in demonstration.

There was a girl standing on the slave table with her hands clasped behind her back. She had bad spots and lankish greasy hair tied in an elastic band. She was wearing black leggings and a college sweat-shirt with crossed oars on it. The back declared: 'Rowers go in Hard, Come out Wet.' I didn't recognise her and nobody could think what she was doing up there. She was blushing furiously and her skin was getting shinier and greasier under the hideous light. I saw a small gaggle of girls trying to suppress their laughter, and I realised, through long experience, that they had somehow put her up to it.

'This is the kind of thing you'd have made me do,' I whispered to Tara, who stuck her tongue out.

'You'd have deserved it,' she whispered back, and I kicked her under the table. But I felt awful for the girl.

'What do I hear for lot nineteen, Karen Lawes from Manchester?' the auctioneer dribbled, too drunk now to be coherent. Nobody spoke. Nobody made a bid. 'Nothing? Not a penny? Come on, boys, she's not that bad,' he said, as the room writhed in communal embarrassment. Someone coughed and Karen looked up hopefully. 'You must be joking,' the perpetrator mumbled and punched his friend in the shoulder. More silence. Tears began to run down Karen's cheeks and we all wished we were somewhere else.

'Sixty-five pounds for the lady to accompany me to the Anonymous Society dinner next week,' Cassian said, walking up to the table and putting out his hand to help Karen down. We all cheered in a huge eruption of relief and Cassian led poor Karen out of the beer cellar as she dabbed at her eyes with a tissue and smiled up at him in pathetic gratitude. Her 'friends' who had been choking in glee throughout her ordeal now looked rather put out.

'You are bunch of sad bitches,' Tara told them when we left, as if to make up for years of not entirely dissimilar behaviour on her part. They stared open-mouthed.

I was dreading the next day. It was going to be

hard enough to face Cassian in the first place without having to see him naked, without it being some kind of awful joke.

I spent three hours clouding my room with cigarette smoke, pacing up and down and chewing my nails before deciding that I needed to talk to him alone before the ghastly event. It just seemed so silly to keep up the silence while trapped on a small boat together, and it wasn't as if I didn't know where his room was. I had seen his name plate often enough. In fact, every time I walked past and saw it there – white painted italics on a thin black strip slotted into a wooden frame with the other names – I sighed to myself.

It was a different issue actually going up there, though.

It was suddenly cold on the stairs, the stone steps and the damp dark walls keeping even this kind of weather out. I wore tatty jeans, blue espadrilles and a white T-shirt, hoping for a very effortless I-don't-give-a-shit-about-you look, and stomped up to knock on his door.

'Come in,' he said, or actually he didn't but I thought he had.

I pushed it open with a creak and stepped into the gloom. The curtains were closed and *La Bohème* was playing very loudly from a stereo in the corner. A home-made fruit cake (good old Stella) stood half-eaten in a tin on the table, and there were Soviet propaganda posters on the walls. A large photo of Flossy, laughing, her arms draped happily round

Cassian's tanned neck, stood on the dresser. A bloke in a striped shirt, V-neck jumper, old green cords and purplish loafers was sitting in the corner. It wasn't Cassian. He looked up at me questioningly.

'Cassian around?' I asked casually.

'He's gone to buy cigarettes. Tea?' the unfamiliar bloke asked without moving.

'I won't,' I smiled, fading fast.

My nerve had left me what with all this mock formality and the last thing I wanted was to try to talk to Cassian in front of his poncy friend.

'Listen, can I ask you a favour? I asked.

The bloke raised one eyebrow coquettishly.

'Could you not tell him I was here, OK?'

'No problem,' he beamed. 'Do you fancy a drink some time?'

I shook my head in disbelief and he waved as I walked out and ran breathless down the stairs, keen not to bump into a returning Cassian.

Tara and Minty turned up in the heat of the next day in extremely high spirits, both semi-naked in tiny cotton tops and short skirts and swinging bottles of champagne. Tara had a big straw hat on and held four champagne glasses upturned in her left hand. Minty had bought strawberries at the covered market and neither was making any secret of the fact that she was on the pull.

'You don't think Flo would mind, do you?' Minty laughed. 'I've got some of Mum's new moves to try out on him.'

'Honey, get in line,' Tara scowled, putting on a

black American accent and kissing her teeth. 'That brother's mine.'

In the event the brother was half an hour late and when he arrived we were all slouched on the steps messily eating ice-creams and getting hot and unglamorous by the greenish mildew of the water.

'OK, darling, kit off,' Tara told him, ignoring his seriousness and his vague air of casual menace. 'You remember Fizz?'

Oh God. Oh God. This was it. A confrontation. He was going to have to say something and I was going to have to respond.

'Yes,' he told her without looking at me. It was over before it began. He took his T-shirt off grumpily and the others drew in their breath. He was very tanned and very . . . just beautiful. When he unbuttoned his flies even Tara glanced away, but he was wearing baggy, multicoloured stripy swimming shorts underneath and he told us 'This will have to do. Me in my pants is not for sale.' He had also failed to provide a gondolier's hat so Tara, mumbling about wanting her money back, made him wear her straw effort and we set off.

I sat with my back to him to avoid further dreadfulness, and Minty and Tara faced him, drooling, popping strawberries into each other's mouths, sipping their champagne and whispering loudly. Yellow ducklings paddled frantically after their mothers next to us and we could see couples snogging under the willow trees on the banks.

My neck and face burnt with embarrassment as we

slid beneath the branches and out on to the deep open river. I could hardly breathe, knowing he was so close behind me. I could smell him, hear him move and almost taste the sweat breaking out on him as he propelled us along. It seemed so unimaginable now that those arms had been around me, that he had said all those things with the same voice, the same mouth. Had he not meant them at all?

Tara stood up, leaning over me and rocking the boat to feed Cassian a strawberry and then Minty did the same, slopping some champagne into his face in an attempt to share.

To my horror he started laughing.

'I should be paying you,' he said, and I noticed that you could see Tara's knickers from where I was sitting and therefore from where he was standing. Was the sight of knickers the type of thing that might turn a man on? I wasn't sure, but I was certainly worried. It was very hot and green algae collected on my fingers when I trailed them through the water in an effort to look unruffled.

'Ah, look. Fizzy's missing Rupert,' Minty teased as we passed another punt on to which some students had loaded an old-fashioned wind-up gramophone with a trumpet sticking out of it. They were listening to some crackling jazz and the boy sitting next to it wore a red-and-white-striped jacket and a boater. He had a monocle in one eye. It was a variation on drunken rugby louts pushing each other in and vomiting, I supposed. Not much less irritating though.

I was relieved that someone had brought Rupert up – a chance to look less pathetic in Cassian's eyes perhaps. 'Oh, I've already moved on,' I said stupidly, biting into the red flesh of a strawberry and lying back in my seat.

'Spit it out then. Who?' Tara asked, surprised.

I said it was no one they knew and felt utterly ridiculous. Now Cassian would think I just shagged anything that moved and he would hate me even more than he already must.

Who had told him about that phone call? Had Flossy said she'd just spoken to me and then died in front of him? Every time the funeral flitted into my mind I hurled it out again for fear of caving in to my grief and humiliation.

By the time we floated back to the boathouse Cassian was happy to be teased by the girls, his face sticky with fruit and bubbles. Nobody said a word about my virtual silence and my reluctance to join in with all the splashing and thrusting forward of breasts.

Pleading fatigue I went back to college almost immediately, my head throbbing from the heat and the alcohol. I was dying to get into the cool of my room and feel a white pillow against my stinging cheeks. I drank a pint of Ribena and fell asleep, a cool breeze blowing through my open window, ruffling my vase of daffodils and soothing the horror of my day so far.

I was woken up by Tara banging on the door with her dreadful news. I staggered over, pulling my shirt across my chest, and poked a drowsy head out into the corridor. Tara charged in past me smelling of outside. 'Minty buggered off somewhere to her yoga or whatever and I asked Cass if he wanted to come back to my room and have sex with me,' she said, sitting down on the bed and lighting a cigarette.

My throat closed up in horror. Her hair was messy and her clothes dishevelled.

'I was sort of joking but he said . . . listen . . . he said, "I wouldn't be averse to that" . . . can you believe it? So he did. We did.'

'You had sex?' I asked, feeling my insides being hauled out of my mouth with a fish hook.

'I don't think we even kissed or anything. I just . . . God I must have been pissed . . . I just took my top off and he took his top off and we got on the bed and . . . he, you know. Then left . . . said he might come and see me tomorrow after some lecture . . .' she told me, slightly shocked herself. I prayed she wouldn't notice the tears that I couldn't stop coming to my eyes.

'What an arsehole,' I choked, hoping this pathetic and meaningless statement might put her off him.

'I'm not sure . . .' she mused.

I pretended I didn't feel very well, and after congratulating her, or whatever you do in these circumstances, I made her go away. Actually I wasn't pretending. I didn't feel very well. I felt sick, tearful and completely crushed. It seemed to be the final insult, the last little thing that totally destroyed the tiniest remains of my hope. So that was it. Cassian was now officially someone I'd shagged when I was fifteen. My first boyfriend. No big deal. Just someone I would laughingly tell my future husband about – 'Oh, I lost my virginity to my best friend's brother. I think I actually thought I loved him at the time,' I would guffaw.

I didn't expect him never to sleep with anyone else – of course I didn't – but the fact that I knew her, that I had once told him how mean she had been to me, the fact that I was forced to imagine the whole affair. This was not good. Not good at all. The feel of him, the smell of him, the stubbornness of him; his eyes closed right in front of mine – hers rather – his breathing fast against her cheek. Did he say those things to her? Did he give her love bites on her wrists? Did she lay her head on his chest and listen to his heart. Did they curl round each other afterwards and forget they were separate people?

Very, very bad. When I told him in the garden ten thousand years ago about Tara and the persecution he had laughed, kissed my collar bone and said: 'Isn't she the one whose dad's some psychopath? Flossy says she's got a crush on me – so you win.' And now, I thought, I lose. For ever. Couldn't I just die? Did I have to go through another fifty years without Cassian? Was I really going to live my whole life in this empty shell of a body, pottering about, doing a job, buying a flat, blank and disengaged, lifeless and fake? Apparently so.

It was May night and the whole college was

bursting with parties. There were balls going on all over Oxford and at six the next morning there would be singing from Magdalen Tower, Morris dancers all over the place and lots of drunk people in black tie crowding the High Street.

My enthusiasm for balls had been dampened to say the least by my first experience of one. I had honestly imagined that I might waltz all night with chivalrous young men who were clamouring to mark their names on my dance card. I thought there would be an orchestra, champagne, tables full of delicious things to eat, fireworks and a general magical aura that would sweep me away into another century. I hired a vast pink taffeta dress and spent all day doing my hair and worrying about my make-up. Andy had agreed to be my date and we arrived in a big crowd of others, only to be spat on at the entrance to our college by a crowd of 'class warriors' – mousy people with dreadlocks and dogs on strings who had mostly been kicked out of public school and taken up a cause despised, or at least ignored, by the genuine working classes who couldn't have cared less whether people go to balls or not unless it affects the minimum wage.

When we got inside we found ourselves standing on planks that had been slapped across the grass of the front quad to make a floor for the marquee. There was half a glass of sweet warm champagne substitute each and a depressed string quartet in the corner, drowned out by the shouts of the rugby crowd, already pissed from the pub and determined to have a really good time (i.e. shout and throw up).

There was no orchestra, just three different deafening discos where people writhed about drunkenly in the dark. There was a bouncy castle that quickly became slick with vomit and you had to queue all night for your one free bottle of champagne. The food was served up in a separate marquee by extremely surly waitresses, all of whom came from Oxford and hated students. Most of the blokes spent all night on the row of fruit machines that had been installed in the Fellows' Garden. Going to the loo meant braving corridors full of staggering couples trying to have sex against the walls, their gorgeous dresses hitched up round their waists, their dress-shirts pulled out of their undone trousers.

I went back to my room at about midnight and cried for a bit before deciding that there was no beating them. When I emerged I found the whole front quad packed solid with screaming people standing in front of a stage. A funk band was playing some music which was actually quite good. The lead singer was leaping about the stage, laughing, dancing and loving the attention. He had a beautiful voice and had managed to completely captivate the drunken crowd with a faintly Freddie Mercuryesque approach. I pushed my way to the front for a better view and he winked flirtatiously at me, cheering me up no end.

So I drank until dawn, was sick behind the cherry tree on the back quad and tore my dress getting out of a dodgem car. When I went to look for Andy just before it got light I found him passed out under a Formica table.

Unfortunately he was the only person I really knew in the beer cellar that night too, with all the May festivities going on, and I told him, in a massive understatement, that I was depressed – the old 'someone I fancy has slept with someone else' chestnut. He bought me lots of drinks and went on and on about his ex. After she had ditched him for his friend he had had to fly home with them and they got off with each other for eleven hours solid in the seat next to him.

'Grim,' I agreed.

Sharing our despair we drove round the countryside in his MG all night long, listening to Wham – *The Final* – very loudly as we careered through sleepy villages in the mist, singing 'I Will Survive' outside the gates to Blenheim Palace and swigging a bottle of sweet warm wine in the parked car near Port Meadow. As the sky began to lighten we walked hand in hand towards the dewy bulk of some sleeping horses. White mist hovered over the long grass and the breath of the animals steamed in the dawn light. I leant down and touched my nose to a big shire beast's furry muzzle. 'Boo!' I whispered. He leapt up, stumbling slightly on his sleepy legs, neighed in horror and trotted off into the wet grass towards the stream.

It was cold and Andy put his arm round me, so I rested my head on his shoulder. I wasn't out for revenge but I wanted to feel someone's warmth around me, and when we got back to town we wove our way through the people in last night's taffeta, mascara streaming down their faces, love bites on their necks, wine stains on their shirts, and we went to bed in my room. I could hear the Magdalen choir singing from the tower as he pushed his fingers into me, and the bells were ringing throughout the city when he ripped a condom packet open with his teeth and said, 'I've been in love with you for ages.'

When we woke up around lunchtime Andy was sick in my sink and I spent an hour in the bath hoping he would have left by the time I got back. He hadn't, though, and we sat on my bed with our backs against the wall and smoked cigarettes over cups of hot Ribena. After a while we leant against each other, some support in our mutual despair, perhaps. He didn't mention love again until the next time we had sex.

Later that day I had promised Tara I would go out for tea at Rosie Lee's with her and her mother. It was not an event I was going to face easily – what if Tara brought Cassian with her or something? – but Hermione in those days was unmanageable by just one person, as I had often been reminded. Tara turned up at my room early and started going on about how sweet Cassian had been. She said he had already sent her a note through pigeon post and that he had cried last night when they watched the video of *An Affair to Remember*. I was beginning to hate her again. Hermione was out of Hill Place for the day and had, as ever, used the opportunity to get as drunk as possible. It was a tedious routine and I hated it. I felt sorry for Hermione who was clearly lovely underneath her bleary-eyed dribbling. She remembered my birthday and brought me a silk scarf wrapped in eggshell blue tissue paper, and she often asked after Mum, seeming to remember her out of all proportion to the length of their meeting at Heathrow after the Russia trip. She tried to be kind to Tara but was so angry with Zander that it all got mixed up and inevitably ended in carnage. Tara seemed to think I was the only person she could ask. The only one who shared a bit of her history, what with Flossy and all.

Hermione immediately ordered a bottle of wine with tea and was hiccoughing so much that she spat crumbs all over the table. 'Your father ish a bloody bashtard,' she slurred, slumping her head into her hands. All the grace and composure she had seemed to have at the airport only a few years earlier had completely disappeared. 'Fithy, Fithy, tell my daughter that her father is a bloody bashtard,' she instructed me. 'Being a decent . . . lay . . . doesn't buy you the bloody world. Lord Sinclair my . . . tits,' she said, the mild obscenities sticking in her aristocratic throat even in this state. 'He's a gutter louse . . . and Margaret Thatcher ish a man,' she declared, addressing the parents of a shy boy with spots and glasses at the next table. The mother, in a lilac twinset and thick flesh-coloured tights, bristled and turned away ostentatiously. 'I thaw him hitting the stable girl,' Hermione went on. 'And I was going to step in until I noticed she was enjoying it. Enjoying it! I stood there watching while he . . . he . . . fucked her in the hay loft. Can you imagine? A fifteen-year-old!' She raised her voice to an embarrassed but defiant squeal for the word 'fucked', as though to demonstrate that the awfulness of the situation had degraded her to the extent of swearing loudly in public.

'Jesus Christ, Mum. Shut up,' said Tara tearfully.

'Oh, that's right. Everyone just gang up on me,' Hermione shouted, and fell backwards off her chair, exposing her suspender belt and big knickers, knocking her head against the nearest table so that her coiffed hair fell out of shape over her face, and losing a pearl earring that she immediately started crawling around the floor to look for.

By the time I had helped her to her feet Tara had gone.

It wasn't long afterwards that I made my first trip to Cairnsham Hall, to a party at the home Hermione had lost, and into the arms of the man who had taken it from her.

# Sixteen

It would have been ridiculous to attempt a low profile in this situation, so I skipped up the gang-plank behind Tara and put my hands over her eyes. My heart was pounding but I was going to play it well.

'Guess who?' I asked in Russian.

She wrenched my arms off her and spun round.

'You're joking? Why didn't you say you'd be here?' she asked, almost cross.

'Why didn't you say you would be?' I asked back, laughing.

'I did. Didn't I?'

'Nope. You said, "I have to travel tomorrow". I told you the same thing. Hey Cass,' I added, looking straight at him. The second thing I had said directly to him since Little Farford.

'Alice,' he bowed, still holding on to his suitcases.

'Well, well, Fizzikins,' Tara said, delighted now. 'This is going to be a laugh. Order us some drinks, we'll see you in the bar.'

Tara, it transpired, was writing a travel piece about the orchestra's cruise and Cassian was doing pretty much the same, although his piece was for a far more high-minded publication than the *Chronicle* and would focus on the charisma and skill of Spletnev as a conductor. His other job, some position as a kind of consultant for a big bank, seemed to be extremely flexible and, as far as I could make out from what Tara said, he just flew about the place a couple of times a month telling people why they should be investing in Russia (it struck me that they probably shouldn't) or writing crime features for *Vanity Fair* and the English Saturday and Sunday supplements.

Under the flashing lights of the bar's ceiling we drank a beer each and watched the world's best trumpeter, now back in his shell suit, hitting on the barmaid. 'You should be a hand model,' he told her, kissing the wrist that she was trying not very hard to wrestle away. Tara and I wittered but Cassian didn't say a single word until my girls arrived and I introduced them. I could barely look up from my drink and I certainly didn't dare address him directly. Tara, always oblivious to any kind of social discomfort, entirely failed to notice our awkwardness. I'm not sure she was even aware that we had never actually spoken to each other in her presence throughout all the years they had been together.

'Oooh. He's gorgeous,' said Tanya when she saw him. 'He'd do for you, Fizzy. Better than your old man.' I had told them about Zander. I seemed to have told them about all sorts of things that I never usually mentioned in public. This happens a lot in Russia.

'Taken,' I said, beginning to blush. 'Tanya, this is Tara, an old friend from school.'

The three ladies heaved themselves into the inadequate space on our curvy sofa and shouted to the fluttering barmaid that they needed some champagne. Tanya blew her smoke straight into Cassian's face, slapped him on the back and asked him why he didn't find himself a nice Russian girl instead of wasting his time with these skinny English broads.

Then, opening his mouth properly for the first time since their arrival, he told a joke in perfect Russian that had Tanya and Svyeta crying with laughter but that Ira judged too coarse. 'I'll tell you why,' said Cassian to Tanya, taking a cigarette from her packet and lighting it. He was already working his crowd, looking round at the table, including me, eyes sparkling naughtily like Flossy's used to. He swigged his beer and began. 'There's an old Chechen man dying,' he said. 'He gathers his sons around him and says, "Sons, I am happy to have seen you grow up, but I am only sad that I never saw you married. On that note I have one piece of advice for you." The sons are eager to hear their father's final words. "What is it, Father?" they ask. "Sons," the father says, "whatever you do, never marry a Chechen girl. She will grow old and ugly and may get ill and die before you do." The sons are baffled by this. All their lives they had been taught to respect and preserve the Chechen culture. "Father," they ask, "who should we marry?" The father draws in his breath and says "Sons, marry Russian girls." Now the boys are aghast. They had been raised hating the Russians who had ravaged their country for so long. "But, Father, Russian girls will also get old and ugly and may get ill and die before us," the sons argue. "I know," replies the old man. "But that doesn't matter so much."'

Cassian sat back, exhaling ostentatiously while we all fell about laughing. 'He's one of us,' beamed Svyeta. 'Bring this man a vodka!' The barmaid came over with a large shot of vodka in a thin glass and Cassian downed it in one to prove the point while the Russians cheered. I had never seen him like this before.

'Shall we go for some dinner?' said Tara, looking a bit pale and tired by this stage. There was no way Cassian was going to be let out of the Russian girls' sight now, and we all clambered down the narrow orange stairs towards the restaurant, yelping at our near falls as the boat clumsily set sail down the Volga.

The musicians were on a high from their performance and the atmosphere under the bright ship lights was exuberant. There was a bottle of vodka on each table, and every now and then someone would break into song, baring his bad teeth and throwing his red face up to the ceiling. Each table was laid with thick mayonnaisey salads, black bread and glass jugs of dark red juice, so we chose one with enough seats for our expanding party and plonked our bottles down in the centre.

'To the foggy Albion!' shouted Svyeta, winking at Cassian, who slopped vodka into all our glasses.

'Actually I'm half Italian,' he said, and the Russians looked put out.

'Oh. To Mussolini then!' grinned Tanya, and we drank, spluttering with laughter and getting progressively pinker. Tara's Russian wasn't up to the incessant babble and she remained fairly quiet while we were served greasy cabbage soup in flat bowls, thin strips of unidentifiable meat on yellowish wet mashed potato and bowls of melted ice-cream. I wondered if Cassian's Chechen joke had made her feel guilty. After all it was only yesterday that she and Aslan had presumably gone to bed in the middle of the afternoon and licked caviar off each other. Still, I supposed that she and Cassian didn't have sex much after eight years. The longest I'd ever managed was two – Zander – so I was in no position to judge really.

I was incredulous that it had been more than a decade since the garden, and no amount of vodka could dim the fact that I was now sitting at a table socialising normally with Cassian Vinci. Twelve years and it was still the most important thing that had ever happened to me. Twelve years and it continued to dominate my life. I had failed to have one normal relationship, I had reinvented myself as someone I hardly recognised and I had thought of almost nothing but what things could almost have been like since the day I walked out of The Old Vicarage.

I looked up at him now across the empty bottles, the smeared plates, the bright light and the noise, and I thought I caught him looking back at me with the kind of recognition I wasn't used to any more.

'I'm going to bed,' Tara announced, leaning down to the floor for her handbag. 'There was something really nasty about that meat.' She made a gagging face at me and scraped her seat back, saying good night to the table as Cassian got up too. He raised his eyebrows in secret apology to the Russian girls, said 'Alice' again to me with a nod of his head and left.

Up on deck later I stood under the enormous black velvet Russian sky and watched the tiny clusters of lights twinkling on the distant banks of the river. I wondered who lived in these wooden villages hundreds of miles from the nearest town. Were they in there now, drinking home-made vodka by their stove, chewing bits of salted fish and thinking about their distant childhoods when they had ridden horses through the fields in summer and were snowed into their settlements for months on end in the winter? I leant over the railings and rested my head on my hands, thinking about being on the same boat as Cassian, thinking how impossible everything was.

Then I caught sight of the barmaid and the trumpeter in a dark corner of the deck, and went back inside to bed.

In the morning the river was so wide that it was like being at sea, and we all took our coffee upstairs to stand in the hot breeze and watch the gulls flying in our wake.

Spletnev's young boyfriend, Sholtevsky, was out there wearing reflector shades and listening to his Walkman. He was going to be conducting tonight in Togliatti, much to Ira's horror. 'He's a child,' she wailed, shaking her head.

Breakfast was bread, jam and strong tea, and neither Cassian nor Tara had turned up. Loathsomely, I now found myself waiting for a sight of him, getting breathless whenever I glimpsed some dark hair out of the corner of my eye, feeling my heart trip when a white shirt whooshed past. Of course when he did appear I didn't notice. He crept up behind my deck chair, already talking to Tanya and Svyeta over the back of my head.

'Considering the vastness of the Russian soul?' he grinned at Tanya, who was looking seriously out at the horizon.

'Yes,' she nodded, as I turned to see Cassian squinting into the light, one brown arm raised to his forehead, one hand in his jeans pocket.

'Where's the missus?' I asked, pushing my dark lenses up on to my forehead as though I had spoken to him in this casual way every day for the past ten years.

'Cabin. River-sickness or food poisoning. She's staying in bed for the rest of her life, allegedly. She said would you go in and see her.' He paused, taking in the company on deck. 'She wants us to go and see the sights of Togliatti together later,' he said.

'Me and you?' I asked horrified, easing my sunglasses back down over my eyes and sighing in terrified delight. Tanya coughed loudly.

When I pushed open the cardboardy door to Tara's cabin I could hear and smell her throwing up in the shower room.

'It's me,' I said. 'I'll come back.'

'No, stay. I won't be any better later anyway,' she croaked, emerging pale and wan with a fistful of tissues. 'Oh God, this is awful. Why only me?'

'I suppose you got the portion with the rat in,' I said, smiling in sympathy.

'Ugh. Fizzy, listen. You won't say anything about Aslan to Cass, will you? Seriously. I might tell him myself but not today. Or tomorrow,' she said, imploring me with big eyes and a pallid smirk. I wanted to hate her for not valuing Cassian as I would have done, not treating him as the endlessly precious gift that he was, but I had to admit I was glad. The faintest chink of hope, even if I wasn't quite able to let myself voice it, was always welcome. If I couldn't have him, at least maybe nobody else would.

'Of course I won't. Anyway, how was Aslan after I left?'

'I swear, it was the most . . . I mean, that guy is . . . Ah! It's weird. I didn't know it was supposed to be like that,' she said, sitting, legs crossed, on her bed in blue silk Chinese pyjamas and throwing her head back in ecstasy. 'You will slope about with Cass today, won't you? I know you can't stand him, but he needs someone there to laugh at his stupid jokes. Please?'

'Of course I will,' I said. 'I can put up with him for a day,' and I threw my eyes up to the ceiling in mock irritation.

Togliatti, it transpired, wasn't much of a town for sights. An industrial Stalinist hellhole, there was one factory after another and some bleak apartment buildings to house the workers, most of whom were no longer working. But on this warm day, the *pukh* blowing in the breeze, the dust clouding the horizon and the Volga twinkling from everywhere you stood, it seemed beautiful and romantic. I was blind to the empty shops, the staggering drunks in that Russian state of beyond drunkenness – sort of comatose but with motor functions miraculously working – and the old women shuffling home with half a loaf of black bread that had cost them their monthly pension. All I could see were very blond children hurtling around on rusty bikes, fishermen with their catch hanging from poles over their shoulders, dogs basking in the sun and teenagers licking ice-creams. The Soviet kitsch sold by all Togliatti's shops seemed hilarious and suddenly exotic rather than depressing. I didn't realise at first that my rose-tinted veil was all down to the company.

We tried shopping first, muttering crossly and not once looking each other in the eye. I bought a ceramic decanter shaped like a fish and painted blue, orange and gold, with six matching shot glasses. Cassian bought a pearl-effect ashtray moulded into the form of a fat peasant and his dog.

I hesitated over a red plastic bucket with a hole in the bottom which the shop assistant told us, stony-faced, was an *umyvalka* for washing while you are at the dacha. Apparently you fill it with water and hold it over your head to create a kind of shower. The woman stared in condescending astonishment as I laughed and then Cass held it over his head and laughed as well, our eyes meeting for the first time in a fit of relieved giggles. Eventually she snatched the item back and returned to a surly examination of her nails in the dark of this vast and empty department store. The lack of shoppers notwithstanding, there was no end to the unhelpful staff, all determined to prevent anyone from making a purchase. We queued for fifteen minutes (despite being third in line) to pay for my fish before being told we could only pay at a different counter. We then waited hours for the girl to hand us the fish once we had our 'paid' receipt because she was demonstrating a multicompartmental pencil case to an old woman who was looking for something for her niece.

'No,' the crone eventually said, 'she wants something with rabbits.'

When our salesgirl did direct her attention towards us she wrapped each item as slowly as possible in brown paper and then put all the packages into another piece of brown paper and tied that up with string as reluctantly as she possibly could, sighing and groaning and periodically checking her cuticles as she did it.

To us, though, still smiling, almost beginning to relax, it was all part of the local colour and we loved it.

We ate *pelmeni*, which always gets translated as ravioli but just isn't. They are little dumpling things in flabby white boiled pastry with minced dog inside and they come in filthy greasy bowls with a dollop of very cheap and always off butter on top. Any variation on the above description and they are not authentic *pelmeni*. We went to Togliatti's central *pelmennaya* in which I was the only woman diner. We queued up along an iron tray rack, loading our plastic trays with dim institutional glasses of unidentifiable and vaguely fruit-based 'drink' (the only other Russian word for a nonalcoholic drink is water) and laughing at the sheer Russianness of the women behind the counter – big doughy creatures in garish make-up, once-white coats and hats and scraggy high heels. The other patrons were men who obviously worked or had worked in the factories, who had not shirked their national service and many of whom were stamped with prison tattoos. They had grimy bull necks, massive red ham hands and the enormous curved shoulders of people who had once been unusually muscular. None of them spoke and they all hunched protectively over their food, daring any passing fool to mess with them and their *pelmeni*.

What was startling about the place was that, after you had pushed past the heavy, dirty glass and steel double doors, it was obvious that this room had been a reasonably genteel shop of some kind, or even someone's drawing room. The floor was actually marble under the filth, and the fantastically high ceiling was decorated with blue and green mosaic and had a hole in the middle for a chandelier.

Sitting there, eating my *pelmeni* with a thin aluminium fork that weighed less than a feather and bent when you touched it, I acknowledged to myself that I had not been wrong. My judgement at fifteen had, startlingly, been perfect. This was the man for me. This was the person who made me feel alive, who freed me of the need to apologise for myself, who allowed me to think that I was just right as I was. I blossomed in his presence like a flower at last held up to the sunlight, my head raised, my cheeks flushed. I was jittery and overexcited. I was having lunch with Cassian.

Our conversation took up where it had left off years before. Any awkwardness that there should have been, that there had been all morning, was now entirely absent, and the misery I had felt in the pit of my stomach since he got together with Tara had completely lifted.

'These really are disgusting little fuckers,' he said, polishing his last *pelmen* off with a greasy smile.

'Repulsive,' I agreed, wiping my mouth with the back of my hand. 'Now what?'

'A swim,' he announced, standing up and holding out his hand to help me out of my seat. I raised my eyebrows at him and took it, curtsying at him as I stood and eliciting a look of blank amazement from a big red-faced creature with cauliflower ears and scars all over him.

As we walked across the glinting tramlines, past once blue and white wooden buildings in a dangerous state of dereliction, and alongside grimy little shops selling bits of sausage, pink and yellow plastic hair slides and clothes people would have turned their noses up at during the war, we talked about the past.

'Alice,' Cassian said, staring at his shoes and keeping his hands determinedly in his pockets, 'why did you leave that day? Why didn't you tell me you were going?'

I was so surprised that I didn't say anything. I just sighed. The idea of all this stuff, so long ignored, coming up again to be resolved once and for all was something I wanted so much that I could barely face it.

He turned his head to look at me, to see me gazing out towards the river and biting my lip. 'You could have said something. You should have let me know you were just going to ditch me,' he said, smiling now and bringing a bit of welcome irony back into his tone.

I could feel tears tingling behind my eyes as I swung my carrier bags by my side and tried to speak. 'Oh God, Cass. It's all so long ago now. I don't know what to say. I didn't leave you. I would have done anything to stay. Flossy said . . . You know when she saw us on the stairs? Well, after that she told me to go . . . I thought she'd have said,' I began.

'She did say. She said you'd talked about it and since it was nothing you'd rather get it over with and leave immediately. I didn't really believe her, but then you didn't phone that night and after that –'

'Cassian, I . . . know it's ridiculous, a million years ago, but . . .' Some boys sped past us, kicking up the dust on their bikes. 'She was cross with me for lying to her . . . and quite rightly. I think that's why she . . . I think if only I had called your mum after Flossy phoned me from the squat . . . Cass, I know it's my fault and I've wanted you to forgive me for so long,' I babbled, feeling hot and tired now, slightly hysterical and too emotional for a rational conversation about something that still defined every aspect of my life. I was coping badly.

'Florence called you from the squat?' Cassian said, drawing in his breath, having difficulty talking about it now.

'Yes. I thought you knew. She shouted at me and said she hated me for sleeping with you and . . . I was ill and I didn't think . . .' I whispered. 'What did you think?'

'Fuck,' Cassian answered, and put an arm round my shoulder, shaking his head to himself. He smelt of beaches. 'What did I think? What did I think? God, Alice. After seeing you two by the river when you'd been chasing the dragon . . .'

'After we what?'

'You know. The heroin you were smoking . . .'

'You must be joking. I've never even seen heroin. Nor had Flossy. Who told you . . .?'

I was crying now, but Cass still had his arm around me, his fingers digging into my arm too hard.

'Ben said he thought she'd done it before. And I thought you, well, I thought you had . . . never mind,' he sighed, laughing without a note of joy in his voice, a horrible dry sound, a decade of bitterness and sorrow.

We walked on like this towards the river's edge in silence and then he suddenly let go of me and started to run, pulling his clothes off, hopping along in his socks to drag his trousers off the end of his feet, struggling with his T-shirt and throwing his sunglasses into the dust. He plunged into the sludgy water, ducking his head under and then shaking it wildly like a dog.

'You're insane,' I yelled. 'That's radioactive.'

'Get in here,' he laughed, treading water and beckoning with his whole arm.

I looked out at the ships anchored by the river's edge, almost visibly leaking sewage and toxic chemicals into the water. I could see a waterside factory spewing bluish smoke into the air on the next bend and the stray dogs ambling along in the mud were obviously looking for the ideal spot to have a shit. I took my white linen dress off and ran in, not even thinking about my entirely unmatching bra and knickers, or the fact that I hadn't seen Dolores in a fortnight. With Cassian I was as unselfconscious as I had been the first night in the grass. I was just me, and it was OK.

We got out covered with a thin layer of slime and had to carry our shoes back on to the road because our feet and ankles were sunk in black mud. We laughed as the locals held their string bags of groceries and stared. I think they were mainly intrigued by Cassian's pants – boxer shorts with little Father Christmases on them. A present from Tara he claimed. The most peculiar thing ever seen on a man, the Russians thought.

Walking back, breathless and filthy in the evening sun, Cassian piped up again, this time with something that forced me to readjust myself completely.

'Alice,' he began, drawing in his breath. 'Florence wasn't your fault. I thought it was partly, but I think I wanted to believe that. I wanted to let myself off. If anything . . . I mean, I was there.'

And then he told me. He told me about how enraged he'd been after I had left and how he had stolen money from Stella's purse, told her to fuck herself and got the bus to Oxford.

He went to stay in a squat with this bloke Ben, a druggy friend from school who wore a tasselled suede jacket and cowboy boots, and they sat around doing drugs all night and all the next day. They smoked joints and Ben took acid until eventually someone turned up with heroin. Cassian had never done it before, so Ben, who was still tripping, showed him how to heat it on a piece of foil and use a straw to inhale the fumes from what became a viscous black gunge. Cassian threw up. 'It was lovely, though,' he added, and meant it. The dealer, a drop-out called Dave, was injecting, strapping a rag round the top of his arm while he held the syringe between his teeth.

When Flossy turned up Cassian had passed out on a beanbag and by the time he came to she was already dead. Ben, apparently, hadn't even known she was Cassian's sister since she'd just walked in and introduced herself as Flo. He thought she was something to do with Dave and assumed she had injected before. As Ben fell unconscious Flossy and Dave were getting off with each other on the floor in the corner. Ben woke up before Cassian and found Flossy in the bathroom. Dave had gone but the police easily tracked him down and he got four years for dealing. Cassian had heard that he is now a counsellor for addicts at his own clinic off Harley Street.

'I mean, if we're apportioning blame here, and we are – it was my fault,' he said quietly, looking out across the river towards the factory. He bent down to pick up a stone and threw it in the direction of the water. 'All my fault.'

I wanted to tell him he couldn't have done anything about it, not as much as I could have done. I wanted to put my arms round him and kiss him, I wanted to say how glad I was he didn't hate me. But I just said, 'Mmm' and carried on walking.

'You must hate me,' he suddenly announced as the boat came into view, a huge bulk against the dimming horizon. 'I could never bring myself to talk to you at university, I was so fucked up about it all. At the funeral, when I shouted at you – I think about that a lot. I had told myself you had started her taking heroin. You know, I don't think I can have really believed it even then,' he said, bringing butterflies of grief up in my stomach.

'Cassian . . .' I said. 'Cassian . . .' but by then we were walking up the gangplank and I had an icon to acquire. 'I'll see you at the thing tonight. I hope Tara's better.'

I needed to kiss him. I wanted to be so close to him that I became a part of him. I wanted to hold on to him until I died, never let go.

I handed him his ashtray and watched him walk away from me, running his fingers through his hair. I wanted to call him back, but the words stopped in my throat. If we separated now it might all change. We would meet up that evening with everyone else, my job hopefully done, formal, reserved, adults of twenty-eight and twenty-nine.

Everything I had assumed about myself, about Cassian, about what had happened between us, had been completely wrong. I was swept back years and, sitting in my cabin, biting at my cheek, I could barely pull myself back into the present. I needed to be Fizz – composed and self-assured, closed off and efficient, resigned to my cynical but accurate view of the world. I looked at myself in the mirror and tried to see someone I recognised. But there was Alice Reynolds – frightened, hopeful, uncertain, fifteen.

# Seventeen

The steps were flanked by two elephants. Minty dug me in the ribs and made a drooling face at me from behind her pink chiffon veil when she spotted the elephants' guardians – black male models in white turbans and Persian baggy trousers.

Zander, who was in tasteful black tie, contrary to his own instructions (the dress code was 'Eastern'), shook hands with us at the top of the steps to the Great Ballroom from underneath two flickering candelabras and a lot of expensively familiar-looking artwork. I spotted a very recognisable sunflower and another unmistakable water lily. His wife, Trinny, a girl of about our age, was standing next to him. I remember thinking how handsome he looked, a bit of grey salt-and-peppering his thick black hair, his eyes gleaming in the light of the candles behind him. Trinny was wearing, or sort of not wearing, silver tassels on her nipples and a completely see-through bluish sarong tied in a knot just under her tummy button so that it exposed her silver G-string. Zander, I noticed, had his non-shaking hand clamped on to her essentially bare arse. Even then I thought he looked at me with a bit too much interest, but perhaps I'm exaggerating with the knowledge of hindsight.

Realising that no excuse for not coming would have been good enough, Andy and I had arrived at Minty's house the night before to wallow in her bottom-of-the-garden sauna and to laugh at her mum's karma-of-sex books in preparation for the event. Mrs Minton was in Tibet on a retreat with a beardy weirdy she had met at the Hale Clinic, and Mr Minton was in his London flat with his plump secretary, so we were able to slurp our margaritas down in peace. Minty's fridge had a built-in ice crusher and a magnet on it that said 'Boring women have tidy houses'.

Andy, who had become my boyfriend through no fault of my own, was going to the party as Colonel Gaddafi and had hired a white uniform, black wig, reflector shades and peaked military cap. He put lots of too-dark foundation on and leered menacingly while I helped him get his sash straight.

Minty was doing a sort of belly-dancing, harem-member effort with a pink chiffon skirt, a kind of gold bra and a pink and gold headdress. She looked like someone in a *Carry On* film, which apparently was the idea. 'Ooh, what a lovely pear,' Andy said in a Sid James voice, snatching a pear out of the fruit bowl and staring at her largely exposed tits.

I had been tempted to go in full Islamic hijab, with black cloth covering even my left eye, but everyone told me that was too grim to be funny, so I went instead for a purple and gold sari with purple satin slippers and big silk flowers in my hair. Any jauntiness the outfit offered me was almost certainly cancelled out by the look on my face. I couldn't have been dreading this more.

It was a joint party for Tara's twentieth and Cassian's twenty-first birthday and the whole university seemed to have been talking about nothing else since the huge silver pieces of card had arrived in our pigeon holes in their fat cream envelopes. Only one of the three hundred or so people invited had ever been to Cairnsham Hall before, and that was on the official tour (fifteen pounds – fairground and safari park included).

My crass and embarrassing attempts at putting Tara off Cassian ('He's so pretentious . . . He always looks like he's in a bad mood . . . Why doesn't he get a hair cut?') had failed dramatically, and I had ended up seeing far less of Tara than before because she thought I hated her new boyfriend for no good reason.

At eight fifteen the minicab arrived at Minty's house to fetch us and the driver didn't need directions. In fact Tara's party turned out to be heavily signposted from the motorway. I smiled to myself at the thought of our flat in Clapham being signposted from miles away with one of those brown 'of historic interest' type placards that they have for Cairnsham Hall, Windsor Castle and Hampton Court.

The taxi entered the vast iron gates, went past the empty kiosks where the tourists pay, and on for over a mile up a tree-lined drive until, from a bend in the lane, we could see the estate below us glittering in the night. It was still five minutes away, but it was clear from this distance that it was bigger than Buckingham Palace. 'Must cost a fortune in Windolene,' said Minty, peering out in awe from under her veil.

Tara had always been too ashamed of her father to invite anyone to Cairnsham Hall, and since Hermione had gone into Hill Place she had barely been there herself. Crippled with the humiliation of Zander's affairs with, and marriages to, teenaged floozies, she had sworn she was never going to speak to him again. Until he suggested the party.

Sweeping down the gilt and marble staircase in the hall, a toastmaster shouting our names from his position at the top of the steps – 'Mr Andrew Carstairs, Miss Catherine Minton and Miss Fizz Reynolds' – I had a brief and vile realisation that this was it. Here I was, at a ball, in a stately home, among friends, not out of place, with my boyfriend. There was an orchestra playing waltzes and a twenty-foot high champagne fountain bubbling in the centre of the Elizabethan ballroom. I had made it. And was I happy?

Pah. I was in agony. The boy I loved was currently on horseback being photographed by Tatler with his aristocratic girlfriend – the very person who had single-handedly ruined my school years. Fair enough, she was my friend now, but that wasn't the point. I had heard they were decked out as Ivan the Terrible and his first wife Anastasia.

When people started pouring towards an outer

cloister to get themselves some dinner I spotted the German count from college. He was in full Hussar's uniform happily tucking in to some blini and caviar, despite the fact that he had purported to 'abhor buffet' when he had first received his invitation. 'Well, this is not such an abominable one,' he snapped when confronted.

Andy was extremely annoyed to see a Yasser Arafat, a Sadam Hussein and a King Hussein of Jordan in the room, but the *Hello!* photographer was not annoyed at all and got them together outside, looking menacing with the camels. Although I had not spent long with Andy it was already clear to me why his ex had run off with the nearest available specimen. He was strangely obsessive and clingy in a way that said much more about his own oddness than it did about his actual view of me, or her for that matter. He was constantly claiming to love me madly and then whining at me endlessly when I didn't reciprocate. 'What's wrong with me?' he would ask. Nothing, I told him, I just don't know you well enough to love you. 'Am I a terrible person?' he went on. 'Do I smell?'

I wandered around on my own, smiling vaguely at people and feeling totally incapable of taking in the glorious surroundings or drinking enough to dull my senses. I must have had six glasses of champagne by nine thirty but I was still raw with despair. A fag hanging unattractively from my lips, I went up to another girl who was skulking about on her own and asked her for a light. She got a book of matches out of a pocket in her enormous silk trousers and lit my cigarette for me.

'I don't actually smoke, but I carry these around just in case,' she admitted shyly. 'You're Fizzy, aren't you?'

'Mmm,' I agreed, sucking my smoke in and putting my champagne in my other hand. 'Oh my goodness,' I suddenly smiled. Behind the funny gold headdress thing she had on and underneath the layers of artful make-up I recognised Karen Lawes from Manchester, slave auction victim. 'How are you?' I asked.

'Oh, you know. Out of my depth as usual. Cassian invited me. I don't know anyone,' she said. 'That is, I only know one other person and she's pretending not to recognise me.'

'Bitch. Who?'

'Trinny, Tara's dad's wife. She was at school with me but she left to be a stripper after O levels,' Karen said, giggling slightly.

'No? Bloody hell. Poor Tara,' I laughed.

At this point Moamar, Yasser and Sadam bounced up all excited by their prospective fame, and later that night through a blur of misery I caught sight of Karen and Yasser in a clinch out by the papier-mâché sand dunes.

I felt as though I was being openly mocked by some malign wizard, bent on ruining my life, cackling evilly to himself as he threw another rat's claw into his bubbling cauldron. I knew that this was the culmination of everything I had ever longed for, and yet rather than being a dream come true there was something awful and hell-like about it.

Andy's make-up had begun to run and all the flailing diaphanous skirts, leering painted masks and quietly shuffling shoes had a phantasmagorical air about them, like a colourful whirling scene from a nightmare when everything is spinning out of your control and you are silent and unnoticed in the middle of it. Admittedly, all the champagne wasn't helping, so I kept closing my eyes and hoping that when I opened them again things would be cooler, stiller and more manageable. I tried to picture Alpine lakes and dark rustling forests as I sat on a gilt and velvet chair in a vain effort to keep it together.

But when I flicked my eyes open in readiness for an increased level of sanity I saw Cassian standing in front of me, a fur-rimmed bejewelled hat on his head and a long sable-edged gown embroidered with gold and silver wrapped around him. He had a pearl earring dangling from one ear and wore dark eyeliner and heavy ruby and emerald rings. He was leaning right in towards me, his features distorted by his sudden proximity and his voice echoing and seemingly amplified in the gloom of my corner.

'Alice? Are you OK?' he asked, reaching out to touch my shoulder.

I flinched away from him, folding my arms in defence and pushing myself into the wall behind me.

'Why wouldn't I be?' I said sharply, looking past

him into the room. 'Look, here's Tara.'

She was indeed coming up behind him, all sparkly and opulent, and as he glanced round to see she grabbed him about the neck and bit his ear gently.

'Are you hassling Fizzles? Leave the poor girl alone,' she told him, laughing and dragging him away. 'Don't miss the fireworks, Fizzy! Ten minutes,' she called back.

A feeling of real breathless, chest-constricting panic rose in my throat at the thought of the whole sky ablaze and all these costumed maniacs roaring up at it. Moving against the throng, I made my way back to the buffet to see if I could get a glass of water.

A comforting woman with a huge bosom and rosy cheeks handed me a bottle of cold Evian and suggested I go outside for some fresh air. I nodded and wandered off up some red carpeted stairs, hopefully to find some bit of the house where there was no party going on.

I found myself in a long high-ceilinged corridor, lined with marble and bronze busts of eminent-looking chinless people, gilt-edged fusty mirrors and serious portraits of sad-eyed women, adult-faced children and military men. It was cooler up here and the water seemed to be slightly calming my panic and general lunacy. I sat down on the only chair that didn't have a piece of prohibitive tassel hung around it to stop fat American tourists slumping dangerously down with their camcorders

camcorders and rucksacks, and I listened to my breathing slow down.

I had a mouthful of water and was just about to swallow when Lord Sinclair came out of what I had vaguely assumed was some sort of ornamental door in the wall. It didn't look like something you might use for opening and shutting.

'Hey, Princess. What's up?' he asked.

I was extremely embarrassed to have been caught creeping around his house (well, Hermione's house) and he seemed so normal and friendly, so sober and separate from the horror downstairs that I looked up at him and burst into tears.

'Oh God, sorry,' I sniffed, standing up and catching my sari on the edge of the chair as I did so. The bright silk tore in a jagged gash the length of my thigh and I fumbled to cover myself. 'I must be drunk . . . I . . .'

I didn't even see him come closer but suddenly his big arms were around me, my cheek was pressed into his clean white shirt and he kissed the top of my head. He had one arm round my shoulders and the other in the small of my back, and for a while we just stood there like that.

'Don't cry, sweetheart,' he said, stroking my hair, and straightening one of my flowers. 'Don't cry.'

I looked up to thank him, still squashed against him, weak and peaceful, held up by his strength, and he took my hand and led me into a little room with red leather chairs, high bookshelves and green glass lamps. There was a fat decanter of brandy on a small table and two heavy crystal glasses sitting next to it as if waiting for us. He gestured for me to sit down in one of the chairs and I obeyed, almost paralysed by embarrassment. He poured us out a drink and I stood back up again to receive it, rooted now to the spot. He held out the glass to me but I didn't move. I just stood there shaking. With one finger he gently parted my lips and an electric current seemed to surge through me as I became overtaken by the desire that came out of nowhere, for him to lift me on to the sofa and screw me. But instead he lifted the glass to my mouth and poured a sip of brandy into me, like someone trying to revive a frozen skier on a mountain. A tiny dribble of the golden liquid was left on my lips and, taking my face in one hand he kissed it off. I thought I might faint. At first there was something almost avuncular about it, gentle, concerned and, I thought then, a bit guilty. He smelt deliciously of spices and I couldn't help pressing myself into him, hoping to be engulfed. I had never been held with such certainty before, by someone who must have held hundreds of women in his arms. I felt safe, as though there was no need for me to support myself physically any more – he would do it for me. I looked up again and he stared into my face, surprised and almost angry, searching for something in me which he seemed to find. He kissed me again, hard this time, sending shards of uncontrollable lust searing through me as he pulled my waist up towards him and bent me over backwards, stroking my throat with a strong hand.

And then he pulled away as suddenly as he had come forward, adjusted a cufflink that had come loose in the embrace and cleared his throat, helping me up to standing and, unbelievably, patting me on the shoulder. 'What's your name?' he asked quietly, like a father meeting one of his daughter's friends by accident in the library.

'Fizz,' I told him. 'Fizz Reynolds.'

'Well, Fizzy. How about I get someone to take you home?' he commanded, running his hands through his hair and dismissing me.

I threaded my way, sober and shaken, through the crowds of gold and glitter, trying to find Andy and Minty, hoping that when I did find them I could seem normal, not like the harpy I had now become. I had nearly had sex with Tara's father. Had I? Did I seduce him? Did he kiss me out of politeness and then not know how to get away from me? What had happened was so strange I was running through every possibility in my mind. I tried to blank Tara from these thoughts, but I was glad now that she had Cassian. God knows, I didn't deserve him.

Nobody I needed was anywhere to be found so I gave up and went into the loo to splash my face clean of all this awfulness before going outside to meet the chauffeur.

Pushing back the heavy door I gasped and stopped short. Minty was kneeling on the floor by the basins, her chiffon skirt in a pool of water. She was giving Andy a very enthusiastic blow job. He had his trousers round his ankles and his grotesquely made-up face thrown back in pleasure, his wig and hat slipping from his head. 'I've been in love with you for ages, Minty,' he moaned, grimacing in orgasm. I backed out in horror, but not before Minty saw me. Within seconds she came running out of the door wiping her mouth, bedraggled, frantic, her veil and headdress in one hand, her hair everywhere.

'Oh my God, Fizzy, I'm so, so sorry. I don't know what happened. Oh fuck, listen . . .' she sobbed, holding on to my sari.

'Minty, Minty,' I tried to calm her down. This trivia was almost funny against the background of my evening. 'Honestly, it's really OK. I didn't want to see him any more anyway. Please don't feel bad. I swear, I don't mind at all,' I told her, my hands on her shoulders.

'Really?' she smiled forlornly. 'Really, truly?'

'Really, truly,' I laughed. 'I've got us a lift home. Coming?'

At this Andy emerged from the loos, shamefaced and fiddling with the top button of his trousers.

'Pandy, she doesn't mind!' Minty grinned at him.

'Oh,' he nodded, not looking as pleased as he might and refusing to meet anyone's eye.

Peter, neat, fresh and alcohol-free in his blue uniform and hat, drove us home in silence apart from the expensive purr of the car. Minty leant, blissful and drunk, against a confused and awkward-looking Andy while I rested my face against the window and attempted to make my whole consciousness a complete blank.

# EIGHTEEN

I had an address for the icon but no phone number, so I was assuming that Zander had warned them I would be three days late. I got off the boat and walked over towards the road where I thought I might rustle up a taxi. There were six dusty puppies scampering about their stray and sleepy mum and a few policemen in grey-blue summer uniforms, slumped at their posts, chatting and drinking tea. Some boarded-up wooden kiosks surrounded a tiny patch of fenced-off grass, and by the flaky metal sign that said 'Taxi' Cassian was smoking a cigarette.

He waved when he saw me and I walked over to him, squinting through my glasses and wondering how to play it, not at all certain we could just carry on where we had left off just an hour ago.

'Looking shifty,' he said. 'What you up to?'

I smiled. I felt a bit shifty.

'Yeah. Picking something up for Zander. You?'

'Coming with you to pick something up for Zander,' he beamed.

'No. I don't think so,' I told him, but somehow when the first taxi rolled up we both got in and leant back on the hot sticky seat, smiling quickly to each other at the sight of the plastic nude hanging from the rear-view mirror.

Togliatti had lost its morning allure and it was starting to look as bleak as its reputation described. Depressingly, the taxi stopped miles out of town among the grey high-rises dotted about in their ubiquitous wasteland. Quite a few of the buildings were unfinished and the others looked largely uninhabited, apart from a couple of gloomy cats and an old lady or two. Our entranceway stank of cat piss and cabbage, and most of the blue metal letter boxes with the apartment numbers Tippexed on to them had been prised open and gaped ominously. The bulb was out both in the lift and on the twenty-first floor, so we stood outside apartment 83 in the pitch-dark beginning to feel quite nervous. Not, however, as nervous as we were about to be. Someone opened the door in a balaclava.

'Who the fuck's that?' he said, nodding at Cassian and dragging him by his wrists into the flat.

'Hey! Hey! He's a friend . . . a colleague. He's helping me for Zander . . . Lord Sinclair,' I shouted, running in after them to find three huge blokes, one in a balaclava and the other two with stockings hideously distorting their features, tying Cassian to a chair with some telephone flex and shoving a sock into his mouth.

There were empty vodka bottles on the coffee table and the whole room was obscured by cigarette smoke. There were ornaments and plates in the glass cupboards and a flowery rug on the floor. The flat did not belong to these people, I concluded.

'What are you doing?' I asked, really scared now.

Thank God we hadn't brought any money with us. That, apparently, was already seen to.

'Lord Sinclair said just a girl. Don't want any crap from him,' the main guy told me, slapping Cassian gently round the face with the back of his hand. Cassian's eyes were wide with fear and his breathing was heavy through his nose.

'You fucking call Zander now and let me speak to him. He is not going to be happy about this,' I said, not quite lying. He would not be happy. He would be incensed I had taken his daughter's boyfriend with me on a job and even more angry that I had made trouble about it when I got there.

Amazingly, the beast seemed slightly unnerved by this. He fiddled with the butt of the ill-concealed gun under his jumper and became thoughtful. As thoughtful as someone with hands the size of Frisbees, swollen and red, with bitten nails and two fingers missing on the left can become, that is. I looked at Cassian. The fat silver ring on his wedding finger and the bare ankles above his old trainers made my stomach lurch with pity.

'Boys, untie him,' the leader said, making his decision. 'I hope you won't feel the need to mention this to Lord Sinclair. We just like to be cautious . . .'

The appalling realisation came to me that these people were afraid of Zander. I could imagine it, though. He had the sort of dreadful authority that people like this warmed to, and I certainly knew how hard it was not to do what he said. I had always thought of it as a natural willingness on my part to obey him, just because he sort of sounded convincing. Now I was becoming aware that it was real fear.

I mean, there was no denying that our sex life was a bit s-and-m-ish, but I still tried to consider this something I played along with; something I almost enjoyed – as penance for sleeping with Tara's father, for losing Cassian, for masking myself in constant lies. But what if one day I didn't want to have sex with him? Really didn't want to, and resisted? Clenching my teeth together in acknowledgement of my horrible situation I admitted to myself that he would rape me as violently as was necessary to subdue me.

'I won't mention it,' I said, as Cassian began to cough and choke at the removal of his gag. 'Where's the icon?'

Balaclava nodded over to his thugs and one of them slipped into the bedroom where I spotted a knitted pink bedspread and a painting of Lake Baikal on the wall. There was a cigarette butt and new burn on the carpet in front of me where one of these guys had just stubbed out on the floor. His mother's floor? His grandmother's?

The icon was wrapped in a sheet and they wouldn't let me look at it before taking it. They all seemed to be getting edgy now, as though something was going wrong. Perhaps the thought of Zander's revenge for tying Cass up was getting to them.

One man spat violently into a delicate white and

blue teacup, coughing up twenty years of tar.

'See you again some time,' said the main man, holding open the door as Cassian carried the icon out of it and I followed.

'I do hope so,' Cassian told him.

'Give my best to Lord Sinclair,' Balaclava continued.

'Will do,' I promised, leaping into the lift behind Cassian and falling against him in laughing relief as the doors closed.

'What the hell is this?' he asked as the lift began to plummet.

'An Andrei Rublev,' I answered, as it suddenly jolted to a halt. 'Almost certainly.' For a few seconds we stood there in total darkness waiting for the doors to open, surrounded by silence. They didn't open. I decided we must be somewhere around the sixteenth floor.

'Jesus Christ,' Cassian said, either in astonishment at holding an Andrei Rublev, or in exasperation at being trapped in a lift in a partly deserted building. Or both.

'Oh shit,' I whispered, slumping down to sit on the filthy floor. 'This is somewhat irksome. You claustrophobic?'

'No. But that doesn't mean I'm enjoying myself,' Cassian spat, flicking his lighter open to search for the alarm. He pressed it but nothing discernible happened. In that second, lit by a flame, bending down to scrutinise the buttons, he was more lovely than ever.

Feeling, presumably, that he had explored all the avenues available to us in terms of rescue, he sat down too, knees to his chest, the toes of his shoes touching mine. He was breathless and panicky, shifting around spasmodically as though hoping to discover some immediate way out of our coffin. He asked if I thought there was a vent we could climb out in the ceiling. No, I said.

'I can't breathe,' he panted.

I reached out for him in the dark and put my hands on his shoulders. I told him to hold his breath for eight counts and then breathe out as slowly as possible.

'A bit better,' he said. 'Sorry.' There was a pause in the blackness where he tried to pull some dignity back together and contain his terror.

'This is what you do for Zander? Pilfer Russia's remaining antiques? How the hell do you get them out?' he asked, with a desperate attempt at a resigned tone, as though I were the boring person whom he had been sat next to at a dinner party and whom he had finally, while coffee was being served, felt obliged to turn to and address.

'I doubt Customs would notice in any case, but we have a bloke who helps. I just go up to his booth and he stamps some forms he's already got and gives them to me,' I told him, omitting to mention that Flossy had lost her virginity to the said bloke so many years before. 'Otherwise I go through VIP and skip the whole thing. This one's being delivered to London for us by the big customs guy. He gets ten per cent . . . We could bloody die here. Would you eat me if I died first?' I asked.

'I don't think so, although you do have some delicious-looking bits. Anyway, those oafs are hardly going to walk down twenty-one floors,' Cassian gabbled, hopefully. And he took my hand.

Even if I hadn't known he was there, even in dark like this I would have recognised his touch from all that time ago. With that hand on me I felt complete, as though someone had finally put the last piece of me on and I could function normally.

'Yeah, but are they going to bother rescuing us?' I went on, in my normal voice, as though no contact had been made. He ran his hand up my arm and stroked my cheek, pushing a stray strand of hair behind my ear.

'They can't afford not to. They seem to be shit scared of Tara's dad. Have you any idea how dangerous all this is? I did a story about the antiques Mafia once – they are not people in the usual sense of the word. There are some really, really serious slimeballs doing this stuff. I would imagine that anyone who can get hold of a Rublev for a Western buyer is one of the big guys. If you need to know anything about your unsavoury friends just ask me. I'm an expert . . . Why the fuck do you work for him?' he wondered, holding both my hands and kissing them, forgetting his claustrophobia and our imprisonment.

'He . . . pays me a lot,' I told him, beginning to lose the ability to speak coherently. 'And . . . I get to come here . . . and do . . . things like this.' My heart was pounding.

'Alice,' Cassian Vinci began, taking my face in his hands. As one hand slipped down on to my breast I forgot about the icon and the boat, about Tara, Zander and our current imprisonment.

'I . . .' he went on, and the lift whirred back into action, hurtling down to the ground floor before either of us had a chance to say anything.

When the doors opened into the light the intimacy of darkness and the horror of the thugs above us seemed a million miles away. We coughed, straightened ourselves and started again. 'Oh good! Taxi's still waiting,' I said, practically running towards it, my leather sandals urgently slapping the soles of my feet.

As we passed through the city again I peeped under the sheet to see the virgin. She was perfect. Beautiful. She stared straight at me from the canvas, holding her son in her left hand. Christ was in a bright red tunic highlighted in gold, extending a blessing. The background looked as though it had once been pale green. Zander would be elated to get this on his website www.russart.sinclair.co.uk – authenticity unconditionally guaranteed, discreet representation in public and private sales. For my own part, I could think of nothing more sublime than sitting in a hot taxi in Togliatti with a Cassian Vinci who didn't seem to hate me and an Andrei Rublev icon.

'Tara wanted me to pop back and see how she is

after lunch,' he said, ruining my mood in an instant. Poor Tara. Vile me. I had secret lives now with her father and her boyfriend. Cassian put his hands over his face in a gesture of despair and slapped his jeans pockets for a packet of cigarettes, sniffing and blinking what must have been tears away from his eyes. He draped himself across the back of the passenger seat and grinned at the driver, scrounging a horrible, dry, filtreless monstrosity off him and sucking it down thankfully, sitting back next to me, finally able to relax.

'Not been raped yet this time then, Fizzles?' Zander asked me when the Togliatti Post Office finally connected my cubicle to London. There was a stick with a rusty nib on the end in front of me, jammed into a wooden ink well full of thick, congealed blue gunge. I poked the stick around nervously as I talked and scratched out a telegram form to send to my mum, who I thought might find it funny to get a telegram from Togliatti.

'Not yet, thanks, no. I have, however, got you a rather splendid little something,' I told him.

'No! Already? How was it? How is it? How were the boys?' he went on, delighted.

'The boys? The fucking boys? Those people are murderous psychopaths,' I squeaked. 'It's fine, though. It's beautiful. Have you got a buyer?'

'All under control, Fizzy my love,' he laughed, unwilling to tell me anything. 'Can't go wrong with a murderous psychopath I always say.'

I guffawed over-enthusiastically, a chill of fear creeping down my spine.

'Listen, I'll meet you at the Slavyanskaya. Brick Factory awaits us. Can't wait to get inside you,' he said, and hung up.

I found I had scrawled, 'Mum, I'm scared' on my telegram form. I screwed it up and dropped it on the floor in disgust, readjusting my face to smile sunnily at Cassian, who was waiting outside the cubicle, eating an ice-cream.

I had put the icon under my mattress on the boat while Cassian went off to find Tara, but he was back in seconds, eager to come back out on the town with me.

'She wasn't at her sink, so she must be at large,' he told me, raising his eyebrows quizzically.

Later that evening, I washed my hair and scraped it back off my face. I put a black suit on over a white T-shirt and wore my Dolce and Gabbana high heels. I wanted to feel invulnerable again if I was going to have to spend the evening with Tara and Cassian, being seen through not only by the Russians but now by him as well.

In the event he knotted my stomach and dried my throat by not showing up, and I walked into town with Tanya, Svyeta and Ira, laughing about my fish and the ashtray. Ira didn't see why it was funny. 'My mum's got one of those decanters,' she said.

Maybe Cassian and Tara had gone back to

Moscow? Maybe I would never see him again? I laughed too loudly at Tanya's jokes.

The concert hall in Togliatti was not up to much. In fact it was just the auditorium in the cultural centre – a place where schools put on their end-of-year shows, where big local meetings take place and where the supremely tacky regional beauty contests are held. The orchestra had been due to play in another hall but the Government had switched the electricity off for non-payment. The chances of it being switched back on again in the next couple of decades looked slim.

At home I would have tried to sit quietly while this boy stood in front of his lover's orchestra in his tails, tanned, blond and beautiful, visibly nervous. I would have pretended to have been moved by the music and would have studied the programme carefully to see when to clap and when I would be allowed to a) get an ice-cream and b) go home. Here, though, with my whole façade slipping perilously away, I couldn't be bothered with the effort of pretence.

'I mean, don't you find it boring?' I hissed to Ira as the lights dimmed. We had just been subjected to a huge woman with set hair and a silver dress telling us about how wonderful the administration of Togliatti was and then giving a large bouquet to an equally huge man in a silvery tux.

'I used to before I met my husband,' she answered quietly through the dark as the musicians took their seats. 'You just need memories that go with it. You should share mine. When I met Igor he said I reminded him of the second movement of Rachmaninov's Third. I'll nudge you when it starts. See if it works,' she said, pointing a pink fingernail at the programme to show me where to expect her nudge.

When the lights came up for the interval I had tears streaming down my face and my programme was a crumpled mess in my lap. I felt as though Rhett had just walked out into the mist. I had been picturing a young conductor and his girlfriend walking around Moscow in the dappled light of the trees around Patriarch's Pond, holding hands and wondering if they might spend their future together – him thinking how soft and sad and mysterious she was, like Rachmaninov's Third.

'Ah, the Rach Three. Always gets to you,' Cassian laughed, slapping me heartily on the back from where he stood at the end of our row.

'Bugger off,' I snivelled. 'What are you doing here? How's Tara?'

'Not so great. I've just been sluicing down our vomit-encrusted bathroom. Doctor says it's a bug,' he told me.

'What doctor?'

'Some drunk on the boat. Gave her charcoal.'

'For God's sake. Keep him away from her. Don't you think you should go home?' I suggested, begging him inwardly to say no.

'We'll see how she is tomorrow. Thing is, it would take so long to get back anyway that we kind of might as well stay. How was Sholtevsky?'

'Gorgeous,' I said, and we went to find some beer out in the foyer. Tanya raised her eyebrows at me over her ice-cream spoon and I couldn't help smiling. I had been rumbled and there was nothing I could do about it. I was rather warming to Togliatti.

A concert from a Moscow orchestra is the biggest deal ever in a place like this. The whole town had turned out not just to hear the music but to see the glamorous and cosmopolitan Muscovites. This was the best chance the women had had in years to dress up and up and up, and for a young man to invite his date to this concert was tantamount to asking a girl to come with you to New York on Concorde for dinner at the Rainbow Room. Everyone female had had her hair done that day – in most cases permed and dyed very bright orange to match her lipstick. Their dresses were backless and largely frontless, with sequins and glitter and slits up the side. All had been designed in Moscow in the seventies and knocked up in Kazan out of polyester in the early eighties. They held miniature plastic handbags and smoked nervously, trying not to smudge their lipstick or look in any way inelegant. The men wore black or brown nylon suits with clip-on grey ties and very thin shirts. There were paunches spilling out all over the place but this entirely failed to dent their owners' vanity. Even the blokes spent the whole interval in front of the foyer's thousands of mirrors combing their hair and brushing the dandruff off their shoulders.

The place was sweltering with the sheer excitement and body odour of the audience and the bar sold out of bits of bread and salami almost immediately, leaving the whole of Togliatti drinking vodka without a snack.

Cassian elbowed his way forward, nudging flabby stomachs and tapping naked shoulders until he had procured two melty ice-creams and a bottle of cherry brandy.

'There is no way I'm drinking that,' I said, smelling the lurid contents of my plastic cup.

'Cheers,' Cassian answered, winking at me and knocking his back in one. 'It's all they had left,' he gasped, screwing up his face in disgust.

By the time we sat down again we had drunk half the bottle, and the rest of the performance went by in a daze of baton and bow. All I was conscious of was that my upper arm was grazing Cassian's shirt, and that the tiniest of barely discernible movements would be necessary to reach out and take his hand. I looked down at his hands, one of them resting on the arm of his chair and the other supporting his face, and imagined what it might feel like. Like heaven, I simpered sillily to myself. I let myself remember his fingers inside me on the lawn that first night so long ago and drew my breath in a sudden ache of desire.

'That cellist. Look. It's Christopher Lillicrap,' Cassian whispered, unsettling strands of my hair with his breath, almost brushing my cheek with his, almost touching my ear with his mouth. For over forty minutes we were both biting our lips to stop ourselves giggling hysterically.

Zander would have been sitting there with his hand halfway up my skirt, and an arm round my shoulder, brushing his fingers against the nearest breast, but it wouldn't have felt like this. I was going completely mad with a need to be nearer to Cassian. Much nearer.

We all got a bus back to the boat and I forced myself to sit next to Ira, leaving Cassian to be teased by Tanya about how he had deserted his ailing girlfriend to drink cherry brandy with another woman. 'You can't put all your eggs in one basket,' he told her, laughing. 'What eggs?' she wanted to know. It took the rest of the journey to explain to a cackling Tanya exactly what this expression meant.

Walking back up the gangplank, which clanked its chains as we went, I caught up with Cassian. I would like to say that we stood in a warm breeze and were lit by the moon as the water lapped softly below us. We probably did and we probably were and it probably did, but I didn't notice.

'Sorry,' I said, panting. 'It's just because I'm drunk, but I wanted to say I never blamed anyone but myself. I thought I must remind you of it all, that you must feel sick at the sight of me after everything. I really . . . I loved you,' I told him, standing still and staring into his blank face. The others pushed past us but we didn't notice. Cassian was holding my hands in his and looking at me, trying to see something, to decide something.

'And now?' he asked, still serious and frowning.

'I still love you,' I whispered, looking down at my shoes.

He stared at me questioningly, as though digesting what I had just said, and then he led me silently by the hand on to the boat.

At two o' clock that morning I was lying on my back up on deck, making out the constellations crowding the sky above me and having champagne dribbled inexpertly from the bottle into my mouth.

Tara was in bed, the boat was all but empty, the journalists having gathered enough material, the orchestra continuing their tour on a different boat as the *Radishchev* took us back to civilisation. We were gliding along the black Volga with only the swish of the wake behind us breaking the enormous silence.

'I don't understand what you see in me, Alice Reynolds,' Cassian whispered, smiling into the vastness of the sky.

'Cricket whites,' I told him.

He raised one eyebrow.

'No, really. Cricket whites. I want your life. I want to drink Pimm's, watch you playing cricket in the golden light of a summer afternoon and eat scones,' I confessed, laughing at my own idiocy, quite pleased to have pinned it down and ridiculed it at last.

'Why? Pimm's is disgusting,' he said, baffled. 'And I'm crap at cricket.'

'I know. I hate Pimm's,' I admitted. 'It's those bits of cucumber . . . I just want to be able to ignore the fact that the world's shit, Cass. Just for a bit.'

'So you thought you'd become an antiques smuggler for one of the world's biggest shits?' he laughed, swigging champagne himself now. 'You should stop, you know. Seriously.'

'Sod off. I didn't even start anyway until after I'd given up on ever having a nice life,' I snapped, snatching the bottle off him, irritated. I sat up and pulled my cardigan around my shoulders defensively.

'And now?'

'And now I'm terrified.'

Leaning over me, obscuring my sky, he kissed my eyelids and stroked my hair. 'Don't be,' he said, and took me in his arms. 'Please don't be.' Under the night sky the level of our intimacy increased gradually over what felt like hours but might, I suppose, have been a delicious, seemingly endless, half an hour.

First I appalled myself by having a drag on his cigarette – fingers first touching, then interlinking. Then we argued about whether or not it was out of character for Billy Crystal to have ordered the mixed green salad when he has dinner with Meg Ryan in *When Harry Met Sally* after they've slept together (me – definitely. He would have steak tartare or something. Cassian – not at all. He wants to placate her by having what she has) and we fought playfully. Then we talked about Flossy a while more and how funny she was and I cried so he kissed the tears away from my cheeks. Then we didn't say anything for a bit and he just held me in his arms, kissing my hair and smelling like the sea.

'Do you think we can ask to be buried like this?' he whispered.

Slowly removing my clothes he began to kiss me all over as gently as butterflies landing, taking the thin white material of my T-shirt up over my head and laying it softly aside to kiss the inside of my arms, then my toes, my tummy, my breasts, and, pulling my trousers off the end of my feet, the inside of my thighs. I had never been touched so softly and I lay still with my eyes shut, smiling and feeling myself melt.

When he finally got to the place I was longing for him to go I came almost immediately, my whole body shuddering at the touch of his tongue. I held on to the boat's railings as he moved on top of me and when he pushed up inside me I felt I had merged into him such that to separate now would mean ripping flesh from bone. I could hear the water beneath us and see the stars above us as we moved into perfect togetherness, tearing the core of ourselves each out of the other in painful ecstasy.

I must have fallen asleep safe in Cassian's arms, his shirt draped over me, a smile on my face and my head on his chest. I realised as I sank into oblivion that I hadn't made love since I was fifteen – and never to anyone except Cassian Vinci.

After that all I remember is feeling a hard surface

beneath me and coming fuzzily round to a dream about Zander pinning me to a table. My eyes were still shut when I said it, but I knew my words had been audible and that it was a disaster.

'Zander, leave it out, I'm asleep for Christ's sake,' I moaned, wriggling away. I felt some arms untangle themselves from around me as Cassian leapt to his feet in the cold dewy dawn. The river was covered in mist and its banks were barely visible in the distance under the thin yellow light. Birds were beginning to fill the air, screaming and wailing, and I could hear the stomping of the restaurant staff stirring *kasha* under the deck.

'You disgusting whore,' Cassian said, scrunching up his eyebrows and looking down at me with withering contempt though I was barely awake, pulling his face into the kind of hideousness that he now saw in me. 'Tara's Dad? Jesus.'

'Cass! Cass!' I called sleepily after him as he turned his face away from me.

'Don't even think about it . . . Fizzy,' he said, reaching down to tear his shirt from my back. He had sneered 'Fizzy' with as much derision as he could summon, showing his disgust for my preposterous affectations and toe-curling pretensions. How could I ever have thought to impress him with this crap? I hugged my knees to my chest in humiliation and tears began to roll hotly down my cheeks while I shivered, desperately trying to pull my clothes on.

'Would it be possible to sink any lower than you?'

he spat, pushing his hair off his face, wincing at the thought that he had made love to me only hours earlier.

Tara was wearing some sort of Lycra exercise get up and trainers, all ready to jog round the deck, or do some aerobics or something. She was holding a bottle of mineral water.

'Oh, you must be joking,' she said, emerging from the staircase to find us shouting, dragging our clothes on, crying. Cassian pushed past her and disappeared into the boat to leave us there facing each other.

'Couldn't move fast enough could you? Bet you've been dying to fuck him since university. You do realise this is the man I have been going out with for eight years?' She was screaming at the top of her voice. Devastated, hung over and hysterical I lost control. Standing up to confront her I started shouting too. 'Eight years during which you've fucked everything else you could lay your grotty little hands on – why shouldn't he be getting some too?'

'With you? With some pathetic little working class slag who couldn't even stand up for herself at school? I don't think so. He can do better than that,' she seethed, with which she spat on to the boards in front of me before walking slowly away back towards her cabin.

It wasn't until a boy came out to mop the deck that I finally dragged myself inside to crouch on my bed and watch the world slip by.

# NINETEEN

By the time the brandies were in front of us I was very drunk.

'Anything else for you, madam?' the waiter asked me with a tiny bow. Madam! I grinned at him and shook my head.

'Just the bill,' Zander commanded without looking at him.

'Right away, sir,' the waiter nodded, and, linen napkin over his arm, he moved silently away.

It must have been four or five months after Tara's party that Zander turned up at college one evening out of the blue. I had been in my room, writing an essay, chain-smoking and drinking coffee when he knocked on the door. Seeing him there I thought maybe he had come down to see Tara and that she and Cassian might be standing behind him.

'Hi. I brought you this. A replacement. It was my sister's,' he announced, striding into the room, though it was strictly a one-stride-only sort of place. 'You remind me of her,' he said, peering down at my essay.

'The significance of the Grand Inquisitor chapters in *The Brothers Karamazov*?' he grinned. 'And?'

'And there is no God. Or there is a God. Depends how you look at it,' I muttered, pulling a delicate green and gold sari from out of the folds of some white tissue paper. I laid it across my shoulder. 'It's beautiful. Thanks. The other one was hired actually . . . um . . . won't she mind?' I asked, holding it up against me.

Zander looked at me draped in the silk and then looked away. 'No,' he said. 'Dinner?'

'Yes,' I answered, picking up my cigarettes and grabbing my bag. I flicked off the light and followed him out of the door into a silent quad and through the heavy gate by the porter's lodge to the comfort and apprehension of the shiny car that stood alone on the kerb in the fog, dominating the street, All Souls and Magdalen Tower notwithstanding.

The months since the party had been particularly bad. A crushingly awful holiday serving pasta and getting in the way of Mum's frenzied sculpting – I heard Tara and Cassian had gone to stay on a champagne vineyard near Epernay – and then back to college for more torture.

Steve, one of the waiters at Pasta Palace, had developed a crush on me, so every shift was a battle to fend him off. He made sure we were always working the same hours and he left little presents for me under my tip box. Horribly personal and intrusive things. He found a picture of my dad in the local paper archives from when he had died ten years before and got a friend who worked there to get the original for him. It was a horrible photo and I had a copy anyway. The whole thing really gave me the creeps – a seriously stalker-style thing to do.

I had told him I was into Russia and he got some unheard of shop to send him Russian books for me. Not interesting ones, just anything at all. Old pamphlets on five-year plans, flimsy volumes by obscure (i.e., crap) poets and Soviet children's stuff. I'd rather have had less cloying things – like bunny rabbits won at the fair, or heart-shaped chocolates. Come to think of it he left them too, smiling conspiratorially at me when I found them, or worse, winking.

When I tried to take extra time filling the salt pots I would find him waiting for me outside, hunched in his coat and scarf, his car parked in front of the restaurant. He always wore a ridiculous amount of clothing covering every tiny inch of his body. Polo necks right up to his chin, sleeves pulled over the top of his hands, scarves wrapped up round his face. And it was summer.

Steve was obsessed with his car and whenever I let him give me a lift home he would somehow make sure to point out how well stocked it was. He had the neatest tape collection ever known to man, bottles of water, miniature torches, folded blankets, a flask of coffee, various gadgets for opening this, that or the other, and a tiny tool kit that he plainly never used. He wore a mobile phone round his waist before anyone else had one at all and, to make himself feel big, he used it obsessively to check his home answermachine, pretending something vital was going on – always coming back grim-faced and serious, often swearing to emphasise how key the message or call had been. He did occasional shifts reporting for the *Clapham Gazette* and used this as the nominal reason for his tension and general importance. If, when driving along, he saw a police car with its lights flashing he wanted to follow it to be certain he wasn't missing anything he should be involved in.

In an effort to make himself sound more interesting he pretended his father had beaten him when he was little and that his mother was so crazed that he might soon have to certify her. He made sure everyone thought he was racked by both issues. One day, however, they both came in for lunch and they were perfectly sweet and normal. His dad had a Napoletana and a side salad and his mum had spaghetti carbonara with garlic bread. He tried to ignore them and they asked me if he was always like this at work. I said he was.

Towards the end of the summer he proposed to me in the walk-in fridge, holding my wrist with his clammy hand and staring into my eyes like a puppy that has just shat on the carpet. He said he had been offered a full-time reporting job and would one day be the editor of the *Chronicle*. The idea of a life in Clapham with this twerp was enough to strengthen my resolve to get as far away as possible from my roots and to leave Pasta Palace for ever that very evening.

'Thanks, I'll think about it,' was all I had the strength to say. Not exactly Zander Sinclair, I remember thinking at the time, remembering the kiss at Cairnsham Hall and the strength of the arms that had held me.

When I didn't show up for work he lurked outside our flat for a week, pouncing on me every time I came out, pretending he was having a drink with some friends in the pub. Eventually he started calling me and I told him to fuck off.

'How dare you treat me like this?' I heard him squealing as I hung up. My life sickened me.

I got a postcard from Tara and Cassian, showing a pale beach and a sunset and I imagined them there, happier than any two people had ever been, holding hands, gazing into each other's eyes and kissing tenderly in the moonlight. For all I knew they could be rowing about who was competent enough to read a map, curling up at night on opposite sides of the bed in the solitude of their irritation with each other and wishing they had brought Walkmans. But I doubted it.

And Mum was no help. The whole flat was full of clay dust and she had been given a colossal second-hand kiln that was always firing away in the corner. She barely ever looked up from her work, head bowed, forehead creased, eyes narrowed with fevered concentration. They were quite good really, her funny stick women, but I wasn't about to tell her that.

I hadn't seen Tara at all over the summer and Minty and Andy were avoiding me for obvious reasons. The new term seemed empty without them. Betsy was developing a serious drug problem and shouted at me whenever I tried to talk to her about it. She was doing ecstasy all the time – it had just arrived in Oxford – and she would stay out all night dancing at gloomy clubs on the Cowley Road. She wore T-shirts with yellow smiley faces on and she thought the 'Ebeneezer Goode' song was funny.

When she got in she took a lot of sleeping pills and then when she woke up she needed speed to get her going again. I backed away from her in terror. I didn't want to sound boring and pious going on about Flossy but I couldn't see it all as the good clean fun it was alleged to be.

This left me with nobody to talk to. Now that shame had sunk back into my bones, I felt, as I had felt at school, that friends and intimacy were not for me. I was unworthy of this stuff that other people took for granted. I had now basically shat on the only two proper friends I had ever had and I was beginning to toughen up to this fairly bleak reality. So, when Zander turned up on my doorstep I thought, why not go with him? What bloody difference does it make at this stage?

He put his hand on my knee in the car as we pulled on to the High Street and a shiver of desire unexpectedly shot through me. Every time I thought about the party I did my best not to be turned on by the thought of Zander. But there was little getting away from it. I loved the idea of being completely consumed by someone – totally abdicating responsibility and allowing myself to be engulfed by their strength. Zander's overwhelming strength. I asked about Trinny.

'Kicked her out,' he said, looking straight ahead at the traffic. 'Why? Getting moral on me?' he smiled, squeezing my thigh, a bit too high up for me to pretend it wasn't happening. He heard me gasp and he looked over as I shut my eyes. He laughed quietly to himself and put his hands back on the wheel.

I discovered later that Zander's separation from Trinny had in fact been in all the tabloids – largely because she had done a photospread for the *Sun* in her lingerie and given an interview in which she alleged that Zander had beaten her up and that he had personally fed Hermione the drugs and drink that eventually caused her to disintegrate.

A beautiful French girl my age opened the door to the Elizabeth for us, her shiny brown hair tied back in a black velvet ribbon, her hands clasped over her white apron. 'Lord Sinclair. Madam,' she nodded at us. At that stage, though, I was just glad nobody took me for his daughter. I barely registered the new-found status that seemed to go with being by Zander's side.

She led us through the candlelit dark, wooden panels gleaming in the flickering light, to a table in a corner, laid with gleaming cutlery, sparkling glasses and white napkins. She pulled out a chair for me and I sat down, embarrassed but delighted. I wished I had changed. My shabby jeans and black cardigan were hardly appropriate. Almost all the diners were over fifty apart from a couple of students eating with their wealthy parents.

Did I look like that? We smiled at each other a bit across the candlelit table, aware that people were talking about us. His smile made my heart lurch. I blushed and looked down at my hands. One woman, with a kind of Margaret Thatcher bouffant hairdo, pursed her lips in disapproval and glared at her bald husband as though Zander's lechery was his fault. Perhaps he had once had an affair with a younger woman or, almost worse, wanted to but didn't.

'So, Princess, I've got you all to myself,' Zander whispered, leaning across the table and brushing the back of his hand against my cheek. Oh God, I thought, I am going to have sex with him. I wondered what it would be like. I could see he would be good at it. He looked as though he had spent two of my lifetimes practising.

I couldn't think of anything to say so I excused myself and went to the loo. Even the loo looked expensive. The kind of loo only a date (or a daughter) of Zander Sinclair's might use. I washed my hands next to an old lady in a lilac suit who glanced disapprovingly at me and I wished I had had a bath that evening.

'I ordered for you,' he told me, standing up to pull my chair out for me when I came back in. 'Châteaubriand OK?' I had no idea what it was but nodded energetically. 'Perfect,' I said. Actually the last thing I wanted was bleeding meat, but the wine was heavenly and I was looking forward to an *isle flottante* after it.

I suppose we must have talked about something but what I remember most was the silence. It was not exactly uncomfortable. He ate, drank and stared at me, scrutinising my every move, and I quivered under his glance, got goosepimples when he leant to touch my arm and felt dizzy when he ran a finger across my lips, his eyes sparkling darkly and a half-smile spreading over his face.

'You like that?' he asked and I looked away, feeling ridiculous. He was playing with me and he was going to win.

I stuffed my pudding down as though I hadn't eaten for weeks, wiping the excess inelegantly off my face with my napkin while Zander laughed at me. 'Look at me, Fizzy,' he insisted, calmly, serious now. I looked at him, blushing and feeling my age. Nineteen. 'No,' he said. 'No. You have never really been loved, have you? Such a defensive little thing. There's no need for that with me. No need.' He spoke slowly and thoughtfully, and when he finished I found I was crying. This man could see me.

The waiter poured me steaming black coffee from a silver pot. 'Milk for you, madam?' he asked deferentially, although he must have been my exact contemporary. I nodded and he toddled off for a little silver jug and a dish of big brown sugar cubes with delicate but heavy tongs. Zander stroked my throat and sighed to himself as though he knew he would have to slit it and was sorry to have to mutilate something so lovely. I could feel my chest heaving and my whole body reaching out for him.

The bill was enormous but Zander didn't even look at it, tossing his credit card into the leather envelope with a sigh as though the formality of payment bothered him with its tedious bureaucracy. I was wildly impressed. He asked me what my favourite painting was and when I told him he said he had a Repin above the fireplace of his London flat. We looked at each other as though this fact was of dreadful significance. And in a way it was.

When we pulled back on to Oxford High Street I was breathless with excitement. I tried not to think of the loathsomeness of my imminent actions, or, I hoped, passivities, and I concentrated on exactly what he would do to me, how he would tear my clothes off me and ravish me as a gentleman would a Mills & Boon serving girl. He drove up outside the college gates and leant over to me, taking my face in his hand and kissing me hard on the mouth. I moved over in my seat to receive his kisses better, opening my mouth slightly in anticipation.

'Good night, Fizzy,' he said to me quietly, leaping out of the car to come round and open my door, not even turning the engine off. Suddenly I was idiotic, cold and small, about to slip back into my room alone, away from the warmth of Zander's money and the treatment it afforded me. Zander was completely detached, helping me out as he would any woman in his car with a glazed look in his black eyes, uninterested in me now that I was going and already thinking ahead to whatever it was he was doing next.

Without meeting my gaze he dipped into his purplish wallet and pulled out three fifties. He folded them neatly and pressed them into my hand along with a little leather box. It had started raining while we were in the restaurant, so he kissed me quickly on the cheek, thanked me for my company and roared off into the night.

I burst into tears of utter humiliation, standing there on the pavement in the rain and the dark, shivering in my thin cardigan, a hundred and fifty quid screwed up in my hand. When I got back to my room I opened the box to find a pair of antique diamond studs nestling expensively in some blue velvet. I hurled them angrily across the room and, still snivelling, lit the cigarette I had been absolutely dying for all evening. I promised myself I would confess to Tara and never see her repulsive father again. In the end, though, I didn't quite get round to it. It took me ages to fish one of the butterflies out from under my desk.

# Twenty

'Hiya, sexy,' Zander smiled when I walked into my hotel room, lugging the icon.

'Me or it?' I asked, trying to seem normal although I knew I would never feel normal again. The Cassian thing had demonstrated to me how artificial my allegedly normal life was but had simultaneously deprived me of any other. I was an empty shell of a person, an emotional vacuum.

'Both,' he laughed, putting his newspaper down and getting up to grab my arse.

'Zander, please,' I sighed, lying my treasure on the bed and shaking him off. For the first time ever his gesture had sent a flicker of disgust through me. The smell of his aftershave, the clean slick look of him, the brightness of his eyes, whiteness of his teeth, shininess of his shoes, all seemed menacing. Too well turned out. Too perfect. What was he trying to hide with all this manicured precision? What was so filthy and repulsive that it had to be scrubbed and cleaned to this extent? I shivered.

'Put your glad rags on. Let's go,' he said, sweeping the sheet off his prize and smiling lovingly at the sad faces beneath him. This, at least, was a love we shared. 'Brick Factory beckons.'

'Zander, seriously. I'm knackered. I'll see you

there tomorrow,' I said quietly, wandering into the bathroom and turning a tap on, fully aware that this was the first time I had ever made the faintest suggestion of rebellion. My manner with him might always be sassy, but there had never been any question of anything but my eventual acquiescence – in everything.

I babbled loudly to him about what I'd found out about the Yusupov estate in Archangel. Apparently there is a Kashmiri emerald buried, along with other treasures, forty paces north of the Great Oak. Whoever planned to retrieve it when things died down after 1917 never did. In this mood, though, Zander wasn't interested.

I heard him march over to the grim little bathroom and the bulk of him blocked out the light as he stood in the doorway. 'Listen, my darling girl,' he said, moving in behind me and pulling my skirt roughly up around my waist. 'I've set this up so we can have a nice weekend, and we're leaving in ten minutes,' he went on, biting my neck and pulling my knickers down. He pushed me forward over the sink and held on to my hips as he rammed himself into me, plunging painfully deep, slamming me over and over again into the porcelain until he came. I left my hand under the hot running water so it burnt. I wanted the pain to obliterate everything else.

I stood up to look at myself in the mirror and felt completely vanquished. Game over. I lose. That was that. Zander Sinclair could do what he liked with me. I was past caring whether or not he had killed Oksana, though the fear on the faces of the icon thugs in Togliatti had pretty much persuaded me that he was capable. I almost wished he would kill me.

'Come on, sweetie. You can't be that knackered. What exactly were you up to on that boat?' he leered, zipping himself up and going to get a whisky out of the mini bar. All my sympathy for him had now evaporated and I could see him very clearly through my newfound eyes – he was a nasty piece of work and he was fucking dangerous.

Brick Factory was exactly that. Not many bricks actually got made these days, but the factory was still there, rusting railway lines making their way through the steel gates, piles of crumbling bricks lining the dirt track into the village and smokeless chimneys towering desolately on the skyline, blackened from years of use and wounded, great gaping holes in their sides, from years of disuse. Once a thriving factory community, the village had a House of Leisure and Culture, a blue and white colonnaded building with a creaking sign outside, the word 'Cinema' just discernible in the cracked paint. Youths were now slumped on its steps, smoking spottily, hunched in their teddy-boy leather jackets, angry and bored. There were two shops, which presumably once supplied the people with everything they might need. Now there was only loo roll, some Western chocolate bars, sickly foreign liqueurs and cans of Coke. For anything edible the villagers had to go into New Jerusalem, a few miles away. The place names around here seemed designed to amuse. On the way we had passed through the town of Black Dirt and a small village whose name roughly translates as Cockroachville.

Brick Factory's main street was dominated by a placard on which black-and-white photographs of the factory's most industrious workers were displayed under a big iron hammer and sickle. Svetlana Sakhnova – chief engineer: a bulky brick-like woman with a hard face. Nikolai Ivanchenkov – foreman: a slack-cheeked bloke with a few strands of greasy hair combed over his baldness. I wondered what they were both doing now.

Zander's friends lived in the grandest house in Brick Factory, once the home of the factory manager. Vasily had built a *banya* (a Russian sauna) in the garden, a garage for his BMW and an extension for his mum to live in. Vasily, it seemed, was in trade. Although he had gold chains round his neck, an enormous sound system in his living room and a mobile phone clipped to his shorts, he too was very deferential with Zander. Was there anyone who wasn't scared of him? It appeared not.

He was also extremely courteous to me, pulling my chair in and out for me to sit and stand, refilling my glass after every sip and complimenting Zander persistently on my looks. You could tell he made a lot of money out of the Sinclair art business. In fact it was Vasily who managed to keep the FSB (once called the KGB) off our backs – for a cut.

There was a big dog called Chris on a chain, barking wildly and baring his teeth as we sat on wooden benches in the sun, waiting for the fire to ready itself for kebabs. The table was shuffled around and added to by Irina, Vasily's wife, who had plainly spent weeks baking little assorted pies of mushrooms, cabbage, minced beef and potatoes, and chopping for salads of tomatoes, cucumbers and dill, marinated aubergines with artichokes, spicy red beans with walnuts and green beans with garlic. There was chicken in creamy sauce, tiny blini with black and red caviar, smoked salmon and herring, slices of cured ham and salami, cheese pancakes, bitter coleslaw, whole marinated garlic bulbs and fat pickled tomatoes. These were the starters for the four of us. Women's work.

The kebabs, however, were very much Vasily's territory. They had just got back from a trip to Egypt which had inspired Vasily to try a new marinade for his minced lamb balls – a spicier, more garlicky affair, he claimed. Flashy sunglasses tipped back on to his shaven head, chains swinging over the coals, he poked and prodded his fire, his fag clamped between his lips.

'Hey, you guys should get in the *banya* while you wait. Gonna be a while,' he said, nodding at Irina, who immediately brought out towels, two crystal shot glasses, a frozen bottle of vodka and a string bag of red apples.

It was the last thing I fancied, but Zander grabbed my wrist and dragged me off towards the pine hut, all glittering enthusiasm for the Russian countryside and the native hospitality. My whole body turned cold at his touch. I didn't imagine the *banya* was going to help.

Russian *banyas* are hotter than other saunas, and in winter you come out and roll in the snow, or jump into a lake or river through a specially cut hole in the ice. In summer you have to make do with a cold shower. They have huge brooms of fantastic smelling dried oak leaves with which you beat the dirt out of each other, and strange felt hats to protect your hair.

I lay down naked on the top berth, quite enjoying the scorching heat, my face and knees immediately stinging and the hot air searing down my throat like schnapps. I waited, calmly, to be assaulted, completely detached. I deserved the life I had made for myself. Zander, though, sat on the step below me, slapping his back gently with oak twigs, humming 'Love Me Tender' to himself. He didn't touch me.

My resignation, the heartbreaking loss of Cassian and the prospect of a life with this repulsive figure who trampled everyone he came across into the mud at his feet was making me brave. I was broken anyway, I was worthless in my own and everyone else's eyes, I might as well get the truth out of him and make the best of the results. Now that it no longer mattered I took a deep breath and came down on to his step.

'What can I do for you, Fizzles? Missing me up there?' he smiled, leaning over now to kiss a breast. Bad sign.

'Did you kill Oksana Basayeva?' I asked, looking him directly in the eye, sweat pouring down my face.

I don't know what I expected, but it wasn't silence. He brought his branch down and laid it in front of him. He sighed, staring at his hairy toes which he flexed and unflexed. He clasped his hands over the white towel in his lap and coughed to clear his throat. He spoke very quietly and clearly, spitting his words out in a soft fury.

'No, Fizzy, I did not kill Oksana. Oksana was a whore and a drug addict. I married her out of pity and she died of an overdose in a hotel room. Nobody gave a shit, least of all me, so rather than face an inquest I paid our friend Sergei to get it all covered up and dealt with quickly. I would not have wasted my energy murdering the bitch, who was, incidentally, trying to steal from me to finance a Chechen hostage taker.'

'Her brother,' I whispered.

'You, young lady, know fuck all about it.'

'I know everyone thinks you murdered her,' I said, defiant now.

Zander picked up his oak branch quite slowly and then stood up over me. 'Shut the fuck up,' he shouted, sweating and red-faced. He swung the broom hard at my chest, throwing his full force behind it, nearly falling over in the burning heat, his face contorted with rage. I was knocked flat on to the bench, deep bleeding weals across my throat and breasts. Now that he really was going to kill me I wasn't scared any more.

'I don't believe you,' I choked. 'You killed her, and you destroyed Hermione and you'll do the same to me if I let you.' I was screaming and screaming, trying to get my revenge while I still could. 'I'm not working for you any more, I'm not fucking you any more. You disgust me. You're an evil piece of shit!'

Zander leant over me and pulled me up to standing by my hair. Spitting into my face, his eyes boring into mine, he whispered 'Listen you half-witted, clueless little bitch. Don't presume to meddle in my life or fuck with my family. Nobody cares what you do or do not believe. You have no idea what I'm capable of. You will neither stop working for me nor stop fucking me whatever you may currently believe. Will you?' he asked, both hands round my throat, his knee thrust up in my groin. I stayed silent, staring him in the face. He increased the pressure and blocked my windpipe, pushing my tongue forward out between my teeth with his thumbs at my neck. 'Will you?' he asked.

As best I could I shook my head.

He shoved me back down and walked calmly out of the sauna. I could hear him whistling in the shower while I cowered there, expecting him to come back in and finish me off.

'"For, my darling, I love you, and I always will,"'

he crooned. I coughed and spluttered, my hands to my bruised neck, my eyes stinging with the heat and with belated tears. Perhaps he had somehow jammed the door and I would suffocate in this heat. My skin felt about to blister as I climbed gasping out of the *banya* and into the shower and watched the blood run down my body, between my toes and out through the pale pine slats. I dabbed a towel at my chest and wrapped another around me before I went out into the anteroom where I had left my clothes. I realised that I had meant it. I was going to stop working for him, stop sleeping with him, but I needed to talk to him calmly first, when all this had blown over.

Zander was sitting there, pouring us shots of cold vodka. He had cut an apple up into slices with a penknife and got us tea in thick glasses from the samovar. Towel round his waist, he leant over the table to offer me a drink.

'So – a toast,' he grinned, all affability and charm. 'Forgive and forget?' He winked at me and tipped his shot down his throat. So that was it. All over. Back to normal, give or take a scratch or two. Was that what he thought? 'You do forgive me don't you, angel? Please?' he asked, staring at me as though he cared what I answered.

'Forgive and forget,' I murmured, and drank the vodka, wondering how many more I'd be needing. Ten, I decided. He moved over to me now, pulling my towel off.

'Oh God, sorry, baby,' he mouthed, running his

tongue along my wounds so they stung, sliding his fingers into the wetness between my legs. Defeated, pathetic, I shut my eyes and moaned, falling back into a cushioned chair as he pushed my thighs apart and knelt between them.

Needless to say Vasily and Irina were too polite to mention the stripes across my neck and somehow, now everything seemed to be over and I had lost, I was starving. I tore the meat off the skewers with my teeth, juices dripping down my chin, and piled my plate high with pies and pancakes, swilling huge gulps of sweet tea in between mouthfuls and complimenting the chefs at every bite.

Trains pulled in and out at the remote station across the field and the sky was getting hazy for dusk. Big women in aprons pulled their washing in from crumbling balconies and their husbands, out in the lane in their vests, hauled themselves up with their beers and a sigh to go in and eat.

Zander announced our change of plan casually, saying he needed to get back to London in the morning and wouldn't be staying the night in Brick Factory. Whatever business he had had with Vasily appeared to have been done and the first stars were beginning to gleam above us when we rolled out of the drive in a hired Mercedes, air conditioning blasting the alcohol out of my system, and Schubert compounding my resigned misery. Without mentioning it to me Zander appeared to have moved us to the glamorous Kempinski hotel over the river from Red Square, and when we arrived all our things were already in the room, standing to attention by the luggage rack. The bed was colossal and piled high with bright white duvets and pillows, puffed up like clouds, ready to sink into. The curtains were drawn back, and the gold domes of the Kremlin shone in the moonlight next to the multicoloured floodlit glory of St Basil's cathedral.

There was a silver champagne bucket by the windows, ice almost spilling out under the weight of the green dripping bottle – none of your Soviet stuff here. In the bathroom there were little matt black bottles of exciting potions in a basket on the marble sink, and the bath had a Jacuzzi function and a pile of clean fluffy flannels on one corner. There were thick robes hanging off the back of the door and a kind of dim pink light that made you look serene and already made up.

I went and pressed my nose childishly to the reflecting glass window – designed so that no poor Russians can see in to the opulence – and pushed thoughts of how close I had been to being with Cassian out of my mind. Tears dropping off the edge of my face on to the cream carpet, I turned round to Zander but he was in bed, asleep.

He had never actually hit me before now and the threat that had probably always been there had never seemed real. And, most importantly, I didn't believe a word he said about Oksana. There had been times when I'd hoped he would say exactly what he had said to me in the *banya*, but now his story seemed ridiculous. With Zander you certainly could smell the mendacity – uncannily like Armani aftershave. I could imagine it all now. I pictured her with long black hair that bounced down to the small of her back, caramel skin and huge eyes with long lashes. Her clothes must have been tarty. Zander loved all that – short skirts, high heels, very low-cut tops, breasts straining out of them. And now that I knew how his face could distort with anger, I could see just how he would have looked at her, laying into her with his belt or a shoe, turning himself on as he attacked, hoping she would fight back so he could put more effort into it. Had it been half rape, half murder?

I curled myself into a ball next to him, closing my eyes in horror, trying to dredge a plan of escape up out of myself. There must be a way out that involved my living into my dotage.

In my near sleep a thought of Cassian on the boat crept into the edge of my thoughts – his face in my hair, his arms round my waist. Our burial position.

I was trying not to cry when I felt Zander lurch into life through the darkness, sitting bolt upright in bed, breathless, sweat pouring down his face. He turned to look at me, eyes wide with terror and anguish, begging me to respond. I sat up and pulled my robe tighter to me.

'What is it?' I asked, almost moved to pity by the sight of him.

'Oh God, Fizzy, help me,' he groaned, and collapsed into my lap, wrapping his arms round my legs, burying his face in me and sobbing uncontrollably. 'Please, please, help me,' he cried, choking on his tears.

I couldn't fight it. There was something about this core of agony, ordinarily covered over with so much gloss, that I thought matched my own. The grief he displayed was exactly what I felt at losing Cassian, at being tied to this monster, at having so uselessly reworked myself into a person I hated, at being lonely and ridiculous, frightened and angry. I stroked his hair and lay my head down on him, letting my tears roll down on to his cheeks to mingle with his. But they were not for him.

'I'll help you, Zander. Don't cry,' I whispered. But I was lying. I had run out of sympathy for anyone but myself. I needed to persuade Tara to talk to me. And I had to get away before Zander killed me.

Outside the window the Kremlin twinkled in the night.

# TWENTY-ONE

The drivers were looking at me oddly. I had been standing outside the entrance to Tara's flat for some hours now and was beginning to feel a trifle suspicious. Loafing about by their masters' cars, the chauffeurs who so diligently served the compound's foreigners had started to notice me and were muttering to each other over their cigarettes.

'She the CNN one?' I heard one say.

The CNN driver shook his head and leant back against the huge white armoured vehicle CNN had bought to cover Chechnya. 'Not ours,' he answered.

I had tried the office but Tara's deputy was there, elated to have the power, however briefly. He was ordering the office manager around and sitting at Tara's desk, pretending to himself that he had been chosen instead. 'Called in sick,' he told me. 'Message?'

'No, don't worry,' I said, and withdrew my head from the gap in the door. I had left a thousand messages on her answermachine to which she had presumably listened as I left them, and I had e-mailed her a dozen apologies – all, I imagined, deleted with an irritable flick of a key. I slipped a note under her steel door and even scoured the market for Aslan in the hope of getting to her through him. Now I was left staking out her building, feeling as though I ought to be shoving a microphone in her face when she emerged and asking her whether she was responsible for the Lockerbie bombing.

'Tara,' I ended up saying quietly. I pounced as she swept out from under the porch thing, handbag swinging jauntily, hair bouncing like a shampoo advert.

'Fuck off, sweetie,' she smiled falsely, and pushed past me.

'Tara, please. Give me a chance. We've known each other long enough for a chance. Please?' I whined, not proud of my position but not overwhelmed with choice.

'Ten minutes. Upstairs. I'm having my legs waxed at half-past,' she said, and led me back into her building. We both examined our shoes in the lift and when we got inside Tara sat at her dining table rather than in a sofa, choosing the most formal and least comfortable venue for our conference. Natasha brought us coffee, though Tara would not have offered if it had been left to her.

'So, shall we start with why you were shagging my boyfriend on the boat? Or is that not what you came to talk about?' she demanded, her eyes sparkling with hatred.

'Tara, don't. I wasn't shagging Cassian. I love him. Can you understand that?'

'No, I bloody well can't,' she spat, laughing without her eyes.

'Well, I do. I was going out with him until Flossy died. We got together at her parents' house in Little Farford. She found out just before. She phoned me up from the squat that night to tell me how much she hated me, as it happens,' I explained, keeping all emotion out of my voice for fear that I would collapse on to Tara's Kazakh carpet and sob until I passed out.

'You were fucking Cassian back then? He never told me.' She was genuinely surprised.

'I don't think he was any prouder of it than I am. He has spent the last decade or so thinking that I somehow got her addicted to heroin,' I said, stirring my coffee with a spoon though I don't take anything in it.

'And did you?' Tara asked, eyebrows raised in amazement.

'No, Tara. I didn't,' I told her, cross now myself.

Natasha was unloading the dishwasher and I was somehow taken aback that the world could carry on to the extent of forks being put back into their drawer while my life was being unravelled in front of someone who had once been my worst enemy.

'Do you want the serving plate in the cupboard under the sink?' Natasha shouted, but Tara hadn't understood her and didn't answer.

Concentrating hard on the bookshelves behind her head, I tried to tell Tara how much I had always loved Cassian, how awful it had been for me when she got together with him and how destroyed I had felt by our mutual silence at university – him thinking I had pretty much killed his sister, me thinking I could have saved her after the dreadful phone call.

'Why didn't you just fucking well say so?' Tara wanted to know, things always so simple for her. It was true in a way. She would have marched up to Cassian in my position and shouted her side of things in his face. She would have banned any of her friends from going near him and made sure she reeled him in whatever the obstacles.

'I'm not like you, Tara,' I told her, and she snorted in anger.

'No, you fucking well are not,' she agreed. 'I'm supposed to sit around giving a shit about something I didn't even know about, feeling all accepting about you fucking my boyfriend while I'm ill in bed and it's all OK because you had some fling with him in 1893? I don't think so.'

She stood up and I really thought she might hit me, but she just slapped the table with both hands till it shook. Our coffee slopped over the edges of the cups and Natasha, hearing a noise, rushed in, cloth in fist.

'It wasn't a fling,' I murmured. 'It was the only thing that has ever mattered to me.'

'And me? Did you care what mattered to me? Might I not have loved him too? Maybe he's the love of my life. Maybe I'm just about to marry him and then I find you with your tits in his face,' she roared.

'But, Tara, this isn't fair. You're not just about to marry him.' I paused in utter terror. 'Are you?'

'Well, no. I'm about to marry Aslan,' she said, smiling genuinely now, the warmth back in her face. Much though she despised me now she couldn't help herself grinning, couldn't stop herself telling me about it, about how in love she was and how quickly he had proposed. Apparently he had actually asked her to marry him that first night, saying that he knew the moment he saw her that he had to be with her. She had laughed it off then, but within two weeks she was deadly serious.

'I feel like we're two halves of the same person, Fizz. You know?' she said, beaming madly.

'I do. Yes.'

I followed her into the bedroom and she showed me her parents' wedding photo. There was Hermione, swathed in cream lace, standing on the steps of a grey stone church underneath the yellow roses and white lilies that adorned the archway. There was Zander, tall and proud in his morning suit, squinting into the camera, his arm proprietorially around Hermione's waist, his feet slightly apart. It made me afraid just looking at him now.

'So that's the dress. What do you think? Will it suit me?' she twittered, seeming to have completely forgiven me for Cassian, wallowing now in her elation. Tara wasn't much of a one for dwelling on things.

'Of course it will. Anything would. But do you really want to . . . I mean, you know?' I wondered aloud.

'Well, yeah. So he's a wanker. But Mum's not and it's a gorgeous dress. I don't think these things are cursed,' she giggled. 'He's over the moon I've split up with Cass. Cass has never hated anyone more and as far as I can make out it's mutual. Right?'

'I . . . um. I don't know. We only really talk about the business and stuff,' I tried, peering past the curtains at nothing out in the yard.

'Oh, Fizz. Bollocks. Come on. Everyone knows. Everyone's tried to warn you off him but you're such a blinkered bitch. I mean, it's your business but my father is not a bloke I would recommend anyone hang around with,' Tara babbled, pulling out some earrings and holding them up next to the photograph of the dress. 'I'm sick of pretending not to know, frankly.'

I sat down on the edge of her massive bed and leant my head into my hands, exhausted and uncomprehending. How could Tara have known? How could she not care? How did my life get like this?

'Don't you . . . mind?' I asked her.

'Mind? Why? Fizz, he's done more repulsive things than this and so have you, I shouldn't wonder. I mind for you. I think he's dangerous. Cass thinks he's a murderer. He's always going on about him and the art Mafia but I try not to listen. I do agree he's bad news, though. You don't have to like your dad in life, you know. Not obligatory,' she laughed, sorry for me now. 'I tell you what I do mind, though. I mind Cass being so unhappy.

Seriously. He hates Dad more than you can begin to imagine and the idea that he's slept with someone that Dad's been fucking is enough to tip him over the edge. He coped with Aslan and the wedding and everything really well, but I think this has really pissed him off,' she went on, sitting next to me now and taking my hand.

God. I thought I had come round to stop her being so upset and now she was trying to comfort me.

'He won't be talking to you again, that's for sure,' she sniggered, not without satisfaction.

I snatched my hand away and started to cry.

'Well, what do you expect?' she asked and walked out to answer the phone.

'I love you . . . no, more than that . . . and more than that . . . yes, of course I do. For ever,' she said as I went past her, back into the front room. She kissed the receiver and bounced back in, smiling again.

'All those songs suddenly make sense! . . . "If I had to live my life without you near meeeeee, the days would all be empteeee, the nights would seem so looong,"' she sang, and threw her arms around me, kissing me on the cheek. 'Remember Glen Madeiros?'

I shook her off and sat down, bowled over by our conversation, emotional and shaky as she floated about the room like an angel on its cloud.

'Oh, come on,' she cajoled. 'It's not so bad. Ditch Dad sharpish and come and find yourself a nice

Chechen man. Sultan's up for grabs. Actually, no. A bit psychotic. Aslan says he lost control a lot when he was hostage-taking. Damaged the goods, type of thing. But anyway, there are lots of perfectly affable blokes out there. Lot of them are probably a far better lay than Cassian Vinci, I can tell you.'

I choked back a sob. I couldn't bear her to talk about him like that.

'Anyway, you've got me back for school,' Tara coaxed, gesturing to Natasha to bring me another coffee. 'Right?'

'I don't think I could ever get you back for all that, Tara.' I smiled up at her through my tears and she bent down to kiss me on the cheek.

'You nearly destroyed me. If it hadn't been for Flossy I'd still be that person now,' I said. 'I'd probably have become a nun or something.'

'Leave it out. You were fine. I just teased you a bit. You were such a fucking goody-goody and anyway, I was worried someone might notice you were better-looking than me,' she told me, believing herself. And maybe she was right. Maybe she did see it like that. Maybe she had even seen it like that at the time while I, in my isolation and insecurity, built it up out of all proportion.

I drank the coffee, drained and bewildered, and the doorbell rang.

I could hear little sounds of delight in the hall, the slurp of kisses, the giggles of adoration and I picked up my bag to leave. Aslan bowed and kissed my hand.

'I wanted to thank you, Alisa, for bringing this heavenly being into my life,' he said in Russian. 'For introducing me to my wife.'

Tara, holding on to his hand, glowed in adoration. Aslan seemed to have entirely forgotten that he had actually found her himself because he had been planning to murder her father. I didn't feel especially inclined to raise this as an issue, however, and I nodded in acknowledgement.

'Fizz. Friends?' Tara asked, holding her hands out to me.

'Oh God. Of course friends, Tara. Of course friends,' and I stepped forward to hug her. 'Thanks for agreeing to see me. It has meant a lot,' I said, feeling like someone in an American soap. For a person who balked at sincerity I was doing an awful lot of it lately.

'I think she might be Reuters,' I heard a driver say as I walked past him through the parking lot.

'No. Associated Press,' his friend replied.

# Twenty-Two

I stared up at the Repin Cossack above the fireplace in the hope of gaining strength from it. None was forthcoming. I had one glass of whisky burning inside me and was halfway through another when Zander came out of the shower, rubbing his hair vigorously with an enormous towel, another wrapped around his waist. He grabbed himself a glass and sloshed a drink into it, pouring it delightedly into his mouth and wincing with the strength of it.

'Agh. Great to be home,' he declared, slamming the glass down and shaking his head.

'Zander,' I began, pacing up and down the rug, a Bokhara which I now noticed was largely blood coloured. My aim was to sound casual, yet resolute. 'I was thinking about getting another job, maybe with a gallery. And . . . maybe seeing other people.' I stopped and watched the points of my shoes sink into the dark pile.

'Were you? Were you now?' he laughed. 'And what did my little Fizzikins conclude when she was having these thoughts?' Zander sat down on the sofa – a comic emperor in his towels. But his face was grave.

'Well,' I continued, 'I rather thought I would.' I

couldn't meet his eye and I had made sweat marks on my glass.

'Did you rather?' he asked, the anger rising in his voice. He stood up and stretched his arms out in front of him, linking his hands and cracking his knuckles. He smacked one hand savagely into his own temple. 'Well, I don't think so. I don't think so at all.' He picked up the whisky decanter and raised it above his head. I put my hands up to shield my face, shaking in terror. He threw it hard against the fireplace, smashing it into millions of tiny pieces that tinkled into the hearth. 'Do you?'

'No, Zander,' I muttered, tears stinging my cheeks.

'Go on. Fuck off home for the night, will you? I can't be bothered with this. Be back here by eight tomorrow. We're having dinner with that slag Cara,' he concluded, dismissing me with a flick of his towel. On the way home the taxi driver explained to me why women should be banned from driving.

Mum was delighted with her invitation to tea. She kept phoning me up to check what time she should come and to ask if I needed anything.

'Mother, there is nothing in Clapham that I could possibly need,' I told her. 'Four o'clock. Here. Goodbye.'

She had lost all her old druggy and drinking friends and hadn't made all that many new ones, although there was a gay couple – Martin and Martin – that ran a local gallery where she was now selling her work and they occasionally had her round for drinks, nuts and olives.

They lived in a neat little house near Mum with a front garden full of flowers and a front door painted cornflower blue. The houses surrounding it were all badly kept flats with filthy children spilling out of the front doors, fat mothers leaning angrily out of the windows and a lingering smell of grease pervading everything. Martin and Martin, however, behaved as if they lived at Versailles, steadfastly beautifying their own habitat regardless of the obstacles one might have thought were insuperable. They took turns making dinner for each other from elegant cookbooks and they were extremely 'interested' in wine, going on tasting trips to France at every opportunity and coming back with a bootful of impressive-sounding bottles. Sometimes one of them would have a baking day and turn up, blue-and-white-striped apron all covered in flour, at Mum's door with a little flowered plate of biscuits covered in clingfilm. They called them cookies.

It was difficult to get off the phone from my mother. The date in question was the tea with Hermione that I had so stupidly promised. It had taken me for ever to get round to organising it, and both women were extremely excited.

Hermione, though, had proved rather difficult to track down. When I called her at Hill Place the receptionist told me she had moved out.

Ten years and she had moved out? I wondered what she was using for money. Perhaps Zander had finally let her get her hands on her own cash. It took a call to Stella in Little Farford to discover that Hermione had taken a little flat in Crouch End, North London, lent to her by some ex-Hill Placer who had gone abroad and who had thought to offer Hermione a helping hand – which was more, Stella said guiltily, than any of the rest of us had ever bothered to do. Apparently she had got a job in a health food shop and was having the time of her life.

'Fizzy? Fizzy darling, is that you?' Hermione purred when I eventually located her. 'Listen, my healer is just leaving . . . can I get back to you?' She said she was 'positively dying' to come and have tea with Mum and me and that she would 'adore' to go to Louis on Heath Street – apparently her father had taken her there for treats when she was little.

The window of Louis is heaped with chocolate cakes, sticky buns and fruit tarts and it is always very hard to walk past without getting sucked in to its gloomy Eastern European interior where old Bulgarian men lean over tables of sweet desserts and reminisce.

'Darling, it's a new lease of life,' Hermione enthused, taking a silver fork to her profiterole. 'I'm in a sweet little shop – I tell you I hadn't realised how good you can feel on an Ayurvedic diet with a capful of aloe vera juice for breakfast – and I'm working with the most adorable people.' She told us about Kirk, a German who had had an 'experience' at Glastonbury and become all holistic, and Cally, a single mother who had learnt how to create a positive aura by channelling the reki of the universe. Mum, of course, was captivated by all this, nodding enthusiastically so that her wooden beads bobbed and asking Hermione if she had tried craniosacral therapy. I drank my tea quietly.

Hermione was completely transformed. There wasn't a scrap of cashmere on her, and if you robbed her of her jewellery you probably wouldn't make more than a couple of hundred quid – as opposed to the usual tens of thousands. Under her heavy black coat she was wearing Birkenstock sandals and a long unbleached cotton skirt with a white Gap shirt, looking for all the world as though she had lived in Crouch End all her life and was thinking of starting a post-Cold War anti-nuclear society with all the friends she made at Greenham Common. (Actually I doubted Hermione had even heard of Greenham Common.)

Within half an hour she had invited Mum to a two-day workshop at some healing centre and told her she could stay over at her flat. 'I'm afraid it's absolutely the tiniest little burrow, but I've got a futon and by the time you come I will have had the most angelic Feng Shui lady round to sort it all out,' smiled Hermione, grasping Mum's arm in her enthusiasm.

I had polished off my apricot tart and was considering a Florentine by the time she got round to it. 'Oh my goodness, I had almost forgotten,' Hermione said, rummaging around in her stripy cloth bag. She handed me a postcard of Red Square. I raised my eyebrows and flipped it over. 'Darling Fizzy – Can't wait to see you at the wedding. All love, Tara.'

That was the main topic of conversation then – who was wearing what, who was staying where, how was Cassian coping with the blow.

'You are coming, aren't you, darling?' Hermione asked.

'Oh God, of course I am. I can't wait. I'm so happy for her,' I said, putting the postcard in my bag and knocking my cup off its saucer nervously.

'I know,' Hermione smiled. 'I'm delighted. This thing with Cassian had been going on far too long. No wedding. No babies. He's a darling boy, but really, they never seemed at all suited. He'd do much better for you, dear.' She nodded at me pointedly, presumably thinking about me and Zander. I blushed and said something stupid and too defensive about hardly knowing him.

'I gather you actually found Aslan for her at the market?' Hermione twinkled. I smiled.

'I will let you into a little secret, though,' she whispered loudly, leaning across the table. 'I'm rather thinking of wearing an Egyptian jellabiya to this wedding of Tara's.' She was clearly proud of her idea. 'Don't know what "Lord" Zander Sinclair will think of that,' she declared, plinking her teaspoon down on to her saucer with a flourish.

'I . . . expect he'll um . . .' I mumbled idiotically, incoherently, knowing that I was not, and in any case not wanting to be, in a position to speak for the bloke.

Things were beginning to dawn on Mum, as I suppose I had known they would if she got together with Hermione, and she glowered at me in disbelief. Yes, yes I nodded back at her, smirking my shame with what I hoped might be a dignified, if misplaced, touch of irony. Yes. My boyfriend, Zander, is Hermione's ex-husband.

To make matters a billion times worse Hermione then started trying to persuade Mum to go to the wedding with her. Of course, Mum was immediately gripped and started telling her about Dad's obsession with Mayakovsky and how much she had always wanted to get an insight into the Russian soul.

'It would be the fulfilment of all my dreams,' Mum told her, with utmost sincerity.

'OK, let's go,' I snapped, standing up and waving a twenty-pound note across the teapots and gaudy cake stands at the waitress. Enough, at this stage, was enough in my view.

We pottered along the cobblestones of Flask Walk towards the Heath, and Mum saw a multicoloured wooden caterpillar on wheels in Humla – a baby shop that only sells hand-knitted clothes and Scandinavian wooden toys.

'Oh, Fizzykins. You had one just like that. Do you remember?' she said gooily.

'You must be thinking of someone else, Mum,' I said, and she hit me playfully on the arm. On closer investigation the beast turned out to cost forty-five pounds and we decided mine must have been of humbler origins. 'Who can possibly afford this kind of thing?' Mum wailed.

'Everyone within a two-mile radius of here,' I said proudly.

'Well, I think it's criminal,' she tutted, and Hermione nodded agreement and took her arm. I was beginning to feel like a gooseberry on someone else's date.

We all drooled at the houses on Well Walk, the kind of places that glow a wealthy comforting sort of soft yellowy-orange at night. They have huge brass lion knockers from Venice on their heavy wooden front doors and fat stone steps worn by the feet of all the servants who have lugged deliveries up them over the centuries. There are rows of painted lead soldiers on the ledges of basement kitchen windows and walls full of books in dimly lit studies on the second floors. Sturdy bikes with baskets stand chained to the railings round little ramshackle herb and flower gardens, and happy cut-out shapes are glued haphazardly to top-floor windows.

The Heath was wind-swept and wintry. The ducks were puffing themselves out bravely on the peripheries of the ponds and the willows were curling up against the weather. Perfect for some blustery kite-flying, there were bundled children milling about with their well-dressed parents on top of Kite Hill, ignoring the spectacular grey view of London on one side and the green dome of the Catholic Church in Highgate peeping out of the trees on the other, and staring up, necks craned, at their coloured dots in the sky that hurtled about, tangled round each other and plummeted back down, sticking violently into the hard ground.

While Mum and Hermione twittered, annoyingly now, about marma massage and silent retreats in Reading, I tried to distract myself from thoughts of Zander, Aslan, Tara and, as ever, Cassian, by using the conker-strewn Heath to best advantage.

London's best place for celebrity spotting, I clocked a Julian Barnes, a Boy George (who has a fabulous Gothic horror mansion on the Heath's edge), a Victoria Wood, an Alan Bennett and, unusually, a Boris Berezovsky and wife. The Russian tycoons know exactly where best to house their families. Michael Foot, Melvin Bragg and Nigel Kennedy score no points because you find yourself positively elbowing them out of the way to get into shops on the High Street every day. When we got to the crunchy gravel outside Kenwood House I left the ladies promenading up and down arm in arm while I went to the loo. The house stood creamy and comforting in all its colonnaded loveliness against the sharp wind, reassuring anyone who looks at it that whatever the evidence to the contrary all is actually right with the world.

That evening, when the ladies had left and I was finally in peace in my flat I forced myself to face the fact that there was no avoiding going over to Zander's. No more of the serenity of the afternoon. Only ugliness and lies. I wanted to cry.

Cara never turned up at Olivio, an Italian place

just a quick purr of the Mercedes away from Zander's flat. I ordered risotto but didn't eat it and I couldn't quite stomach the champagne. I couldn't bear to be bullied. I knew I would burst into tears the moment he started.

'Fizz, love,' he said, taking my hand and stroking it in a strangely tender sort of way. The Zander I had first met. 'I know I've been a bit of an ogre about everything.' He cut a piece off his buttery calves' liver and popped it into his mouth. I was amazed. Perhaps I did need a drink after all. The tiny bubbles popped like little needles on the roof of my mouth. I looked up at Zander, too staggered to say anything.

'Sweetheart, it's just that I didn't want to lose you. I know I'm too old for you and this job's too dicey for someone so lovely to do for too long. I shouldn't have got you started with it in the first place,' he said, looking kindly into my face, softened somehow and different. Suddenly older without his energetic glare holding his features together. He looked tired.

We ordered bitter espresso and zabaglione with cats' tongues to share, spooning great dollops of it out of the glass and laughing together.

'The thing is, though, I've found the third crown,' he said, raising his small white cup with his big hand.

'?' I wondered with my eyebrows.

'Nicholas and Alexandra's coronation crowns? There were three. Two in the armoury, one . . . well, one right where I need it. I've been looking for years. My buyer's going upwards of five million. It's at this guy's house near that holiday resort Tara's having her reception at.'

'Zavidovo? "Four days of drinking and dancing in the snow",' I quoted from the invitation. 'Aren't you coming?'

'Not invited, Fizzles. Not invited,' he sighed with a grin. 'I get the elbow after the lunch in Moscow. Mummies only.'

Well, I couldn't help it. It was exciting. I allowed myself a tiny smile. Our eyes met in blissful complicity – this was what we loved.

'Will you do it? The last job? Please? I can't go – they all know me. You're my only hope, love. I promise that's it. I'll let you go. Find yourself a nice boy. Get yourself a decent job. Deal?' He poured out some more champagne and we raised our glasses.

'Deal,' we clinked. I had done it. I was out.

# TWENTY-THREE

We had been standing there in the snow for three hours. That was not so long to queue in Moscow in those days, but my feet were wet and my hands were red and raw, the illusion that smoking makes you warmer long since shattered. It doesn't. It just means your hands get colder.

Tara, who had come up from Leningrad for the week, had managed to persuade me to accompany her on this mad outing. She was doing some sort of art course, which I considered to be cheating since she got to live with a family and go to galleries rather than suffer in some vile flea-bitten institute like the rest of us, and she claimed to have come to Moscow especially to go to McDonald's. It had just opened, glaring the lurid reds and yellows of capitalism into Pushkin Square, obscenely flaunting its gaudy frivolity amid the austere grey buildings and the imposing statues.

'I don't even like this crap,' I moaned, stomping my feet up and down.

'Yeah you do,' Tara told me, slapping me on the back.

'Well, the apple pie's OK,' I admitted, shuffling forwards another inch.

'You're just like Cassy, you are. Down on

everything Western,' Tara laughed, totally unaware of the sinking in my stomach every time she mentioned his name. He had come out to Leningrad to see her for the first month of her stay, allegedly to revise for his finals but really to hang out with these musicians he had met when he had been at the institute there the year before. Now he was with some cousins in Tuscany and kept sending Tara smug postcards of villas and vineyards while she queued for bread off the Nevsky Prospekt. The shortages were bad and unless you sold out and shopped for hard currency (in any case very difficult to do in Leningrad) you were destined to spend at least half your spare time in a queue for something inedibly disgusting. In this case, a Big Mac.

'What will it taste like?' Slava, whose enthusiasm for this expedition was unquashable, wanted to know.

'Like shit,' I told him, sighing.

'You are lying. You capitalists are all the same. Don't want to share it with us,' he laughed, and brushed some snow off my hair.

I had met him at the bar in the Intourist, still one of the few hotels in Moscow where foreigners stayed and one of the only places you could drink in anything like a normal way. They had horrible white metal garden furniture arranged (or not really arranged) in an indoor courtyard surrounded by phone boxes and shops which were absolutely always shut and, had they not been, didn't sell anything a human being might want to buy. The bar had gin, vodka, whisky and beer (quite an array for the time) but there was extremely rarely any tonic and you had to mix the vodka and gin with cans of blackcurrant Sourcy (flavoured fizzy water).

Slava was a minor blackmarketeer. At any rate he had a fake hotel pass and obviously liked practising his English and being in the same space as Westerners. I assume he bought and sold currency as well but I never asked. I was extremely keen not to know. He used to take me swimming at the outdoor pool where the cathedral used to be (and now is again). I swam underwater down the narrow passageway and out into the steam that obscured almost everything from view. The water was hot but anything protruding from it (like my head) immediately became covered in ice as the fat snowflakes melted into the steam from the black starry sky.

He came up to me one evening when I was drinking with some Norwegian girls from the institute and we thought he was an American trying to find himself a prostitute. The prostitutes in the Intourist were astonishing. They weren't terribly well turned out in those days. They all wore cheapish wigs and more make-up than you would imagine was possible to fit on to a face. There was a uniform of heels and fishnets, see-through blouses and black lacy bras and they sat there in little groups, eyeing the men up, crossing and uncrossing their legs and not talking to each other. They smoked those extra thin cigarettes that have a little flower on the packet and they tried to do this as though they were giving someone a blow job. It looked like an incredible effort, but the fat old sweating foreigners seemed to appreciate it after seventeen beers. You would see them ambling over to negotiate with the blank-faced teenagers, supporting themselves on the backs of other people's chairs so as not to fall into a drunken heap on the floor. They were never gone for long. I know because if you settled in for a couple of thousand vodka and fizzy blackcurrants you could keep track of business. Certainly there was sod all else to look at.

'Where are you girls from?' Slava asked, slouching casually in his baseball jacket and jeans, indistinguishable from the American tourists apart from the lack of inanity in his face, the unevenness of his teeth and the despair in his eyes.

'We're not working,' one of the Norwegians told him angrily, puffing her smoke into his face and crossing her Doc Martened feet. Occasionally men not inclined towards the porn star look hoped that some of the slightly more salubrious-seeming girls at the bar might also be on the game. They never were.

'So, you are students?' Slava concluded, sitting down. It quickly transpired that he had no interest in paying to sleep with any of us. He was going to make sure it was free and acquired purely on the basis of merit. This was not going to be difficult. He was fantastically funny and charming and Russian and I had had a call from Tara that very day telling me what a lovely time she was having with Cassian, hanging out with guitarists in Leningrad cellars and getting drunk. They had met Boris Grebinchikov, the lead singer of Aquarium, and he and Cassian had exchanged phone numbers.

I was on my sixth vodka and blackcurrant, and the portions were no sixth of a gil at the Intourist.

We smuggled Slava back into the institute and he slid under the metal barriers beneath the guard's box in such a way as to demonstrate that he had done this before.

Loafing about in the mind-blowingly depressing kitchen at the end of our corridor we proceeded to drink a bottle of kiwi liqueur until the Norwegian girls were too drunk to speak English and lapsed into their native tongue, leaving Slava and me to our own devices. For a while these involved listening to a conversation between an English couple, the male half of which had accused the female half of coming out with a lot of non-sequiturs. The girl, Rachel, was crying. 'I'm not a non-secretary,' she complained, at which point her boyfriend, or presumably ex-boyfriend, walked out laughing.

'Do you want to come back to my room? We could put some music on,' I offered, knowing my smelly-footed roommate to be in her home town of Brussels for the weekend.

The music was Leonard Cohen and the sex was really good fun. Slava was extremely careful to elicit as many sexual compliments as possible from me –

the point of his performance being to engender gratitude. He had lots of requirements. We had to light a candle, he had to remove my clothes as part of the foreplay, I had to lie back and leave him to it and I had to have at least three orgasms before the condom was even out of the packet. This was all fine by me and I didn't think of Cassian once for a whole hour and a half while all this was going on. Slava knew things about women's bodies, about my body, that I hadn't known myself. I never quite worked out where the pleasure was for him, but my thanks seemed to suffice.

He was a language student at Moscow University and so had the kind of strangely prim English accent that is characteristic of the place – so out of keeping with his personality – and he always said 'well' instead of 'um' when pausing.

'That was amazing,' I told him.

'That's wonderfully kind of you, Fissi. My intention is, well, to please,' he said, lying there naked, a fag hanging from his lips, a military dog tag round his neck. If he had been speaking Russian he would have said something that translated more like; 'Glad you liked it, sweetheart.' I giggled and got up for some water. It wasn't until he had fallen asleep snoring that I began, as I had with Rupert and Andy, to feel unfaithful to Cassian. My body belonged to him, and anyone else touching it had to be wrong. I screwed my eyes up tight to block out the awful words Tara used to describe the things she did with my Cassian: 'Huge dick . . . licking me out

. . . doggy-style'. It made me want to vomit, but I had to sit there and smile, trying to sound interested, conspiratorial – just girls talking about their love lives.

By the time we got inside I was actually hungry enough to eat a Big Mac and chips. Slava, who wanted to try everything, ordered a cheeseburger, a Big Mac, an ordinary hamburger, fries, apple pie, cola and coffee. He was positively dizzy with excitement. We could barely find a seat in the enormous 'restaurant' amid the steaming chomping crowds, and when we finally did find three together we had to elbow a family of seven up to the other end of a table and eat around the debris of thousands – few natives had realised you were supposed to clean up yourself, and the staff, anxious to work as hard as possible for their paltry salaries, just couldn't negotiate the crowds to get to the mess.

There was a paper, plastic and lightbulb shortage in Moscow at the time, as well as all the food deficits, so everyone was filling their bags to overflowing with the free straws, napkins and loo rolls (the latter not technically free for the taking, it's true, but readily available) and somebody clever had removed all the toilet lightbulbs to take home to her family. McDonald's soon started rationing napkins and straws over the counter, stopped restocking the loo roll and fixed their bulbs in place with prohibitive-looking glass lampshades.

Tara shut her eyes in bliss as she bit into her Big Mac and I reluctantly admitted that my fries were indeed the most delicious thing I had eaten since I arrived in Russia months earlier – I was getting quite sick of tins of sprats and stale loaves of black bread. Slava threw up in Pushkin Square on the way to the metro. A young couple standing in the queue asked him if he thought they should give up and go home. 'No,' he said. 'It's worth it. I just ate too much.'

'Listen, Fizz, you've got to help me,' Tara hissed while Slava was ridding himself of his meal and the snow was falling thick and fast. Cars skidded about the half-empty roads in the flickering yellow of the streetlamps above our heads.

'Why?' I asked, turning away from the wind to light a cigarette under my coat.

'Dad's here doing some business. He wants to have dinner. Will you come? I can't do it on my own,' she said. She must have noticed that my face fell. I bit my lip and felt totally repulsive. Should I tell her immediately that Zander had kissed me twice. That I had liked it? In short, no.

'Oh, please. Look, I know he's vile but that's why I need you to come. Go on. Don't make me go through it without you,' she whinged.

I couldn't think of a reasonable excuse not to see him, especially since I had already said I'd spend the evening with her. I was none too happy, though, that she had tricked me into this, claiming to have come to Moscow to see me and eat a hamburger. We left Slava chatting to some American girls in the queue ('We just want to see if it tastes the same as at home') and agreed to meet him back at the institute after dinner.

Zander was waiting in the doorway of Kropotkinskaya 36, the first cooperative restaurant in Moscow and the only one that came anywhere close to most foreigners' idea of a restaurant. Upstairs it had a plush dining room with a grand piano, candelabras, a thick soft carpet and round tables with white cloths on them. There were velvet curtains on the windows and an ancient violinist playing sad songs. A few old men sat eating in silence with young girls. Downstairs the walls were red brick and decorated with Soviet propaganda posters. Here the diners were mostly foreign businessmen entertaining their bosses, in from the West for a day or two to check on the progress of their dental floss factory or whatever (usually no progress to report).

I shivered in excitement at the sight of him standing there so imposingly, perfect in a navy pinstriped suit, fitted by the best tailor in the world, a red rose in his buttonhole and a red handkerchief in his breast pocket. He smelt of money and power and a lifetime's total absence from Russia. His eyes shone like burning coal in his head.

'Evening, ladies,' he said, raising one eyebrow in surprise at seeing me. He treated us both like dates, pulling our seats out for us, pouring champagne for us, asking polite questions about our studies and spooning our vegetables on to our plates as a Russian man would. At one point I was sure he brushed my leg with his hand when he adjusted his starched napkin. Tara barely looked him in the face all evening. She answered his questions monosyllabically and hardly ate anything. It was only partly because we'd just stuffed ourselves at McDonald's.

When he noticed I was wearing the earrings he had given me he smiled warmly and looked as if he would like to hug me. I was livid with myself for not throwing them away. I couldn't help wanting him to touch me again, though, and I smiled a bit as I blushed.

'So, when will you girls next be in England?' he asked over some not very nice ice-cream.

'Dunno,' Tara said.

'I'm actually going back next week,' I said, glad to be talking about something normal.

'Perfect,' Zander glittered, handing me a little box wrapped in a piece of black cloth. 'You wouldn't take this back for me, would you? It's a present a client gave me yesterday. I don't want to lose it and I've got a fair bit of travelling around to do before I set off home. I'll get my driver to pick it up off you at Heathrow. Thanks.'

Tara kicked me hard under the table but I already appeared to have accepted. He had a big black Chaika limousine waiting for him outside and he had it drop us at the institute where Slava was waiting.

When the chauffeur drove him away into the snow Tara let her breath out and gave me a hug. 'Thanks so much for that. I'm really sorry it was such a nightmare. And you got lumbered with some fucking errand for him. It's probably illegal.'

Upstairs in my room the three of us gathered round the box while I pulled the cloth off it and flicked open the lid. An enormous emerald the size of a grape sparkled up at us.

'Bloody hell,' I said, and Slava opened a bottle of warm vodka with his penknife.

# Twenty-four

I didn't see Zander again until after finals. I had got my first, shuffled up in mortarboard and gown in the Sheldonian theatre to pick up the proof, and I even had flour and eggs thrown over me by Betsy and her new boyfriend – a dealer called Simion. I got drunk outside the Kings Arms in all my academic glory. Simion was writing a thesis for his psychology degree at Oxford Poly on the effects of hallucinogenic drugs. It involved a lot of practicals.

And now I was cowering at home with Mum and her sculptures, hysterical with the fear of a future of poverty. She thought I ought to do more waitressing for a bit while I thought about my career but I was too scared. I thought if I started I might never stop. One night I'd take a customer up on an offer, go back to his place, get pregnant and end up married to the manager of a photocopying and printing shop, taking the kids out for pizza on their birthdays and reminiscing about how me and Barry had met.

I was lying prostrate and melancholy on the sofa when I heard a car door slam outside. It was hardly an unusual noise on Clapham High Street but I looked out of the window and saw him marching across the pavement to our door in a Ralph Lauren suit, running a hand through his hair and jangling his car keys. He was holding a three-foot-high bouquet of Moyses Stevens pink roses.

'Oh God,' I muttered, smiling to myself, and glancing in the mirror. I was wearing the earrings. I never wore any others.

'Mrs Reynolds,' he grinned, twinkling his eyes and pushing the flowers into Mum's arms, 'I've come to pick Fizzy up. We're going to Sardinia,' he announced, daring me with a raised eyebrowed smirk to refuse him. I had no idea what he was doing here, but I couldn't deny that I was elated to see him. Escape personified. And maybe this time . . .

'Darling, you never mentioned . . . .' Mum muttered, burying her face in her roses, each one the size of a fist.

'Didn't I? Must have forgotten,' I said sharply, running off to my bedroom to pack, stuffing a pair of jeans, a sundress and some sandals into a carrier bag, rummaging around for my barely used passport and crawling under the bed after an old Speedo swimming costume from school. When I came out Mum's eyes were wet with ecstatic tears and Zander was writing a cheque in his Coutts and Co. cheque book with a fat black and gold Mont Blanc pen.

'Just love these things,' he said, poking a finger out at some of Mum's women.

'Fizzles, I thought you were going to see Betsy in hospital tomorrow?' Mum whispered, not caring remotely either way now that her money problems looked solved for months to come.

'Nope,' I announced, putting my fags into my handbag.

'Come on then?' I said to Zander, brazen now with anticipation. 'What time's the flight?'

I would have done pretty much anything to get out of being in Clapham with nothing to do, so going on holiday with Zander Sinclair seemed to be the least of my worries. Tara and Cassian were, as ever, somewhere glamorous, and I wheedled myself out of the potential guilt by telling myself that Zander and I had never done anything that awful and anyway, he always seemed to make the moves, therefore I hardly had a choice. It wasn't watertight but it would have to do.

We drove straight to Heathrow through a London blistering under the July sun. Zander gave a fiver to a pretty girl in a sweaty T-shirt who cleaned his windscreen, and it took us over two hours to get through the rollerbladers, cyclists, tourists and seething drivers in our way. Everything looked hazy out past the air conditioning and everybody seemed to be on the streets, half naked, eating ice-cream, drinking beer and generally not being at work.

The airport was crawling with fat holidaymakers already slightly sunburnt from the back garden and already in their Costa del Sol clothes, too bright and pressed for England. Grabbing me round the waist Zander rushed us straight through to First Class check-in, where the peace, quiet and general air of deference begins as soon as you cross the velvet rope and leave those less fortunate than yourself three yards behind. There were vases of lilies on the check-in desk and people to carry our extremely minimal luggage the couple of centimetres from rope to counter. We were whisked into a huge and empty lounge where women in glossy lipstick brought us glasses of champagne balanced on paper napkins and offered us sandwiches and fruit tarts. I was already silly and excited and even Zander seemed content, though he had hardly addressed a word to me. The luxury began the moment I was in his presence. I was hurtling along willingly in his wake. 'Do you like me, Fizzy?' Zander asked me, knotting a Hermès scarf gently round my neck and slowly stroking my chin. 'Do you?' he asked, holding my face up to his scrutiny.

'I do,' I smiled and he kissed my forehead. 'I understand you, you know,' he told me and held my hand.

By the time the plane actually took off I was on my fourth glass of champagne since my breakfast of an apple and a cup of coffee and I fell asleep leaning against Zander's shoulder and listening to the roar of the engines. I knew he was a virtual stranger and I knew there was nothing admirable in any of my motivations, but I felt quite at home in this life, with this faintly frightening older man.

When I woke up we were shuddering into Cagliari airport and there was a Duty Free bag on my lap containing a pair of Gucci sunglasses.

'I want to see you later with just that scarf round your neck,' Zander whispered tugging at the Hermès silk as the wheels kissed the runway, and he slid his hand up my thigh. I laughed nervously, not knowing whether he meant it or not. Hoping he did.

'Sure,' I said.

There was a car waiting outside the boiling chaos of the airport to take us to the hotel. The driver wore a vest and a gold chain and his hair was slicked back with Brylcreem. A crucifix hung from his rear-view mirror. He craned his neck to look at every girl we passed as they meandered by the roadside in flimsy dresses, holding baskets of fruit and tossing their thick dark curls over their brown shoulders. From the dusty windows I craned to look at their counterparts – boys my age with golden tanned backs riding mopeds in their shorts, fags hanging out of their mouths. There were olive groves and miles of grapevines, low golden crumbling buildings and every now and then a flash of turquoise sea.

I smiled to myself and didn't bother to tell Zander that I had only been abroad three times before. Most of my holidays had been spent on the beach in Norfolk where chilly seagulls hop about on the vast expanse of greyish sand and bob uneasily in the surf. I had been twice to Russia and once to Paris for a weekend with Mum – spent mostly in this bloke called Fabrice's hippyish sitting room while the two of them went to bars. But this was abroad like on telly.

The hotel was deep in a grove of palm trees,

down an endless winding path between two vineyards. The glorious sun made everything a pinkish gold colour. Apparently this had once been the castle that went with the vines and it had huge stucco balconies over a flagged courtyard where three horses wandered aimlessly about. Out to the back was the sea.

The receptionist recognised Zander and smiled coquettishly when he beamed, '*Buongiorno Carlotta, va bene*?'

'*Bene, bene*,' she blushed, looking down at the computer and then jealously up at me with an admiring smile. '*Cente otto*,' she said, handing Massimiliano, the bell boy, a large brass key attached to some kind of wooden sculpture. He led the way, swaggering idly across marble floors to a sweeping staircase that loomed darkly over one end of what might once have been a ballroom.

Our room seemed to be all sea. The furniture, the terracotta floor, the watercolours and the bowls of fruit were overwhelmed by floor-to-ceiling French windows out to our balcony, and to the blue, blue sea glittering everywhere beyond it. I ran out and leant over the edge, peering down to a grand-piano-shaped pool where a couple of people lounged with cocktails, too lazy to walk down the steps on to the white sand and into the water.

'Oh, Zander, quick, let's go down,' I squealed, pulling my clothes off before the bell boy had even pocketed his tip, and tearing my swimming costume out of my crumpled bag.

'You can't wear that,' Zander laughed while I was grabbing a towel from the bathroom and tying it round my waist. 'You need a little bikini. Show off your body,' he said, giving me a look that slid the straps off my shoulders and exposed my breasts to his gaze. Defiantly I ducked under his arm and out of the door before he could stop me.

When he finally ran, not too shabby for forty-nine, into the sea to join me, I had swum out as far as I could, diving under the tiny waves and spinning somersaults in ecstasy. The last time I had swum in the sea was just before my grandfather's funeral in Bognor Regis. It had not been much like this.

I trod water near Zander, dripping, excited and breathless beside the exploding sunset. I expected him to kiss me, but he just stared at me as though he were already inside me, already making me moan in ecstasy. Then he swam back into shore.

A beautiful boy with a deep tan and a white uniform, whose name tag said 'Gianni', put a silver champagne bucket out by one of the pool-side tables and brought us glasses glistening with condensation. I sat there in my towel all covered with sand, bubbles fizzing up my nose, and I watched the sky stain pink and orange over the horizon while Zander looked at me, his thoughts inscrutable, his white polo shirt freshly ironed.

When I got bored of being the object of such close examination I scuttled upstairs to shower and change, only to be interrupted by Zander banging on the bathroom door to insist I hurry up, it was time for dinner. We walked a long way in almost total darkness, crickets singing in the bushes and mopeds occasionally whipping past us on the dirt track and kicking up the dust. I could see little lights through the pine trees – restaurants or houses nestling in the woods.

Effizio's place was almost empty when we got there. There were enormous red flowers hanging heavily from the bushes out on his porch and a very old lady in black was knitting on the steps, surrounded by a litter of mewling kittens. Effizio himself, a tiny man with a medallion and a whitish nylon shirt, came rushing out to welcome us. He was missing two or three important teeth and had a lot of keys chained to his black and gold belt. Sitting us down at a little table out in the garden he presented us with shot glasses of a repulsive lemon liqueur which was apparently a speciality of the region. A bottle of olive oil with herbs and garlic floating in it rested on a starched linen tablecloth. He brought us hot crusty bread and Zander immediately poured oil on to his plate and smeared the bread around in it, stuffing it with relish into his mouth and closing his eyes happily.

'I used to come here with Hermione,' he suddenly announced, snapping his fingers for some water. He had confided in me and I felt grown up and responsible.

Then he grinned, tearing off another hunk of bread while the insects wailed in the heat. I helped myself to wine from the jug that had appeared between us. Raising his glass to clink it with mine, he moved back to let the waiter put a plate of multicoloured seafood salad in front of us – crab, lobster, squid and lumps of fish all just out of the sea and dripping with a heavenly dressing.

'Still, fuck her,' he laughed. 'To us!' and he flourished his glass again, leaning forward to look down my dress with a proprietorial smile. 'Don't be shy, Fizzy. Me and you – we're different,' he said. And we were.

It was here, in the Ristorante Urru, that he offered me a job. 'Want to work for me?' he asked, mid-mouthful, completely out of the blue.

'Depends,' I said. 'What do I have to do?'

'Go to Russia. Buy stuff,' he said, shrugging. 'Need a pretty girl on the job. Someone unsuspicious type of thing.'

'What stuff?'

'Old stuff.'

'OK,' I agreed, knowing what he meant, dying to see and handle the Russian treasures we loved so much. Beautiful things festering under old ladies' beds until we found them for people who would adore them as we did. 'Yes.' And that was my contract sorted out. I did what he told me and he paid five thousand pounds into my bank account every month. It certainly never crossed my mind to complain.

My first mission was to meet a guy in Petersburg who claimed to be selling the Orlov diamond – a massive stone that Count Grigory Orlov gave to

Catherine the Great. But, of course, the guy was a hustler and there was no diamond. Most of our jobs ended that way, and it could have been disappointing if the successes hadn't more than compensated.

We had got to our sole in butter and parmesan when four young men came to sit at a table near us. I could feel them looking at me lasciviously but since I couldn't understand what they said I happily ignored them, especially since I was wallowing in culinary ecstasy. I felt windswept and salty, my skin all tight and glowing, the sea in my hair – twenty-one and properly on holiday for the first time ever. I was also quite drunk. They must have been as well because one of them fell off his chair and the others laughed and jeered and sloshed the wine around in their glasses. To me they all looked rather handsome – thick dark hair, tans, white teeth and clean shirts, and I was vaguely pleased they had noticed me. But it seemed glaringly insignificant until Zander suddenly stood up, put his napkin slowly down on the table and coughed loudly. The boys stopped talking and stared at him, baffled and still sniggering a bit behind their straight faces. He marched over to them across the deep blue tiles and pulled one of them out of his seat by his shirt collar. Then he punched him hard in the face before letting him slump back into his seat, his hands held up to his bleeding nose. At this point Effizio appeared from inside and ran towards us shouting. Zander said a few words to him quietly and the boys were swiftly ejected, yelling and pointing, kicking their chairs over, outraged and humiliated.

I did my best to pretend nothing was happening, forking lettuce leaves out of a bowl and pouring myself more water.

'Cunts,' Zander said, flicking his napkin back out over his legs.

'What on earth was that in aid of?' I asked, having a lot of trouble enjoying this whole dining experience now.

'One of them made an inappropriate remark about you,' he said. 'Not that I blame him.'

And he twirled a lock of my hair round his fingers. The vile thought that his violence had turned him on occurred to me. The other thing that occurred to me was that it had turned me on too. I smiled at him and parted my lips a bit as he leant across to kiss me roughly.

From that moment on sex was a certainty and I could hardly wait. My heart was pounding and I was no longer able to eat anything.

On the way back to the hotel he kept stopping to kiss me, pulling my body into his, running his hands hard over my breasts, tearing my skirt up to touch my flesh. 'Good girl,' he groaned through the dark, feeling that I had no knickers on. We barely made it back to our room clothed.

When I woke up in the morning, the sea lapping outside the open doors and the flimsy white curtains blowing in the hot wind, I was covered in bruises, and every muscle in my body ached. I felt weak from the orgasms that had shaken my body one after the other all night long as he had rammed himself into me over and over again. Taking me hard from behind over the rail of the balcony and making me scream into the night. Pushing me up against the wall of the shower as the hot water tumbled over us. Kneeling on the floor to tease me to an agonising climax with his head between my legs and making me hold on tight to the balcony door for mercy. Hoisting me on top of him so that he drove into me so huge and hard and deep that I actually blacked out for a second in earth-shattering orgasm.

I had thought that nothing was going to stop him, that I might die if he carried on any longer, but suddenly, just before the sky began to lighten, he drew me into his arms with a strange and unexpected gentleness and fell asleep. 'Stay,' he said, as he drifted off. I was too exhausted to answer.

I wandered down the lane, getting dust in my sandals, squinting against the already blistering sun, and found Zander by a bike-hire place, handing over a fistful of money and reducing the girl serving him to a quivering wreck. She straightened herself out when she saw me and lowered her eyes to her bare feet.

'There you go, Princess,' he said, pushing a bike towards me. 'Sleep well?'

'Mmm,' I grinned happily, lighting a cigarette and getting on.

'You want to give those up,' he shouted to me, meaning he wanted me to give them up.

And I did.

Zander quickly overtook me and clearly had a route in mind, winding through the trees towards the beach and along the glorious turquoise sea front towards some cliffs. We were following a little path but there were no cars in sight and hardly any people – a couple of local families eating an early lunch out of foil and clingfilm in the shade of the trees. The sea shimmered beside us as we trundled along, laughing and shouting to each other, seemingly in a hurry to be somewhere. He stopped when we got to a tiny deserted bay, sheltered by tall cliffs and set away from the path so that you couldn't find it if you didn't know it was there. He took a bottle of wine out of his bike basket, a vast round loaf of bread and some ham and cheese wrapped in waxy paper.

While he messed about with the food I ran gleefully into the sea, dying to feel the cool water around me, soothing my poor pummelled body back to normal. Zander soon plunged in after me, giving chase as though he was trying to save my life. It didn't take him long to catch me. Emerging wet and shaggy as an otter from underneath the water in front of me, he dragged me back into the surf like a drowning person, my head under his arm, the rest of me flailing helplessly against him. He wrenched my costume off me, ducking me under with his arms round my waist, almost scaring me.

'Run away from me, would you?' he whispered into my ear, pulling me up around his waist, naked now, and digging his hands into my back as he pushed me down on to him, driving it into me and groaning, grabbing at my breasts, frenzied in his victory.

He refused to get out and hand me my towel, staying behind in the water instead while I ran naked up on to the beach to where I had left it, yelled at by some local boys on bikes a couple of hundred yards away on the path. 'Bastard,' I muttered uselessly to myself, covering up. Now I did need a new bikini. I lay down in the sand, letting it stick to me all over, embed itself in my hair and behind my nails, and I stared up at the sky, basking in the heat. This was bliss, even with Zander Sinclair.

'Let's eat,' he said, walking past me without a glance, shaking the water out of his hair and tipping his head from side to side to empty his ears.

Sated, I basked in the sun while Zander stared quietly. I even spent an hour or so reading *The English Patient* under his peculiar gaze before he rolled himself distractingly on top of me, grabbing my face in both hands and engulfing me again.

Once he had dropped me back at Mum's, sun-kissed, well-fed, and carrying my stuff in a Louis Vuitton hand-luggage thing that he had bought me at the airport (he was depressed by my Next carrier bag), Zander all but disappeared again. He called with instructions and we met occasionally to finalise details, but he was businesslike and distant. He barely looked at me, let alone touched me. He gave me to understand that the fun was over – more of a job interview than the beginning of anything – and that my main loyalty to him should be a professional one.

I read with indifference about his marriage to Oksana and then with genuine sorrow for him about her ghastly death. When I tried to offer my condolences he changed the subject abruptly and I assumed, ludicrously, that he was grief-stricken. He spent a lot of time abroad collecting, selling, talking to clients, and I spent a lot of time travelling backwards and forwards to Moscow, and sometimes to other places that Zander always referred to as 'Shitsk'. He found this hilarious.

I went to Yekaterinburg (the name had just been changed back from Sverdlovsk) and stood around at a deserted tram stop in the snow for two hours, waiting for an old man with a diamond necklace. He told me that the necklace had been hidden in the bodice of the Grand Duchess Olga when the royal family was executed by the Communists in 1918. Some of the girls had not died immediately when the firing squad laid into them in that dreadful cellar, and they were then bayoneted, but only with great difficulty because their bodices were not only made of bone, they were also stuffed with jewellery. The Romanovs had presumably made plans to escape.

I went to the Hermitage in St Petersburg where some minor official slipped me a Picasso sketch from under his jacket. It had belonged, or arguably still does belong, to Mikhail Baryshnikov, the ballet dancer. The authorities wouldn't return it to him after his defection and it has been sitting, along with two others that he owns, in the Hermitage vaults ever since. Until I took it to London, that is. I also spent a grim week getting dust up my nose in the archives of the Lenin Library trying to find an original letter from Stalin to Beria that Zander had already paid for. It was there, coffee-stained, moth-eaten and neglected, folded in half inside some decree about hydroelectric stations, scrawled in a strange spidery hand – sinister to consider what that scrawl alone had managed to authorise.

And once Tara got posted to Moscow, of course, I used to go and see her when I was there, as long as Cassian was out of the country. Now that I wasn't actually sleeping with her father I thought I could excusably get back in touch and I liked sitting around with her in a horrible restaurant called Santa Fe, drinking margaritas and listening to her stories about work. She often turned up with a shaven-headed photographer called Boris with whom I assumed she was having an affair. Poor Cass.

Boris had bright green, deep-set eyes and the kind of high cheekbones and deathly pallor that you only get in Russia. He was obsessed with fashion and would sometimes appear in a long black skirt (utterly unacceptable in Russia's macho culture) and DMs, or in a kind of luminous yellow plastic cape and combat trousers. He had a deeply odd conversational technique.

Once, when the three of us had already been sitting there for a few hours and Boris had told us how he was the greatest photographer in the world about every fifteen minutes he turned to me and asked me what I usually ate for dinner.

'I don't know – I usually stir-fry some vegetables in a wok and have rice with them and cheese on top if I'm on my own,' I told him after some consideration.

'What vegetables?'

'Um, spinach, broccoli, courgettes, mushrooms . . .' I answered.

'Don't you like cabbage?' he demanded, seemingly offended.

At this point a mariachi band in full costume appeared at our table to deafen us through the dim and smoky atmosphere and across the remains of our sizzling fajitas. Boris glowered at me for the rest of the evening, my treachery over the cabbage somehow unforgivable.

Tara said if you invited him round for dinner, which she presumably did when Cass was out of town, he would complain about everything and tell you how to cook it better next time. Once she'd given him blini out of a packet with the world's best caviar on top and he'd been so disgusted that he had run into the kitchen and whipped up some pancakes of his own, making a terrible mess. In fact his were less nice than the imported Finnish things and he had growled that Tara's flour and butter were inferior.

When I did eventually tell Tara that I was working for her dad she rolled her eyes to the ceiling in exasperation. 'All I can say is I hope he pays you well,' she said. 'He can certainly afford it.'

There was no denying that he paid me well and I loved the money. I drove a Mazda MX-5 and wore clothes that were 'by' people rather than 'from' somewhere. But she was unimpressed. She always came out with something involving the word 'hope': 'I hope you know what you're doing . . . I hope you can look after yourself . . . I hope you can stand up to him.' It wasn't that she minded from the point of view of my getting on with him when she hated him, but she seemed to believe, quite genuinely, that it was a dangerous business being involved with her dad. She told me how Cassian mistrusted him, how the two of them wouldn't go near each other, and she said it was after he'd done a big investigative thing into some Mafia guy who dabbled in antiques that Cassian really got hysterical about it.

But for me, it was sufficient that I had escaped from Clapham and all that that entailed. When Zander eventually bought me the flat my independence from my old life was complete. I didn't have to pretend anything any more – no lies about where I lived, what I did or what I could afford. I lived in Hampstead, dealt in antiques and could afford pretty much anything I wanted (I was not extravagant enough to want a yacht or a villa in the South of France).

But with the flat, of course, came all the rest. I

had thought his designs on me had become purely professional, but Zander was the world's least predictable man.

'Thought we should get you somewhere to live,' he announced one day over the phone from Texas. 'Friend of mine's selling a little place on Hampstead High Street. Yours if you want it, petal,' he said, giving me the address.

I picked the keys up from the woman who owned the shop downstairs and climbed up to have a look. It was tiny and I loved it more than anything. Laughing to myself in joy I lay down in the middle of the floor and beamed up to the ceiling. My flat!

It turned out, typically, that Zander had in fact already bought it, assuming I would obey what was really an ill-disguised command, and he came round the day I moved in with a huge plant and a pair of cream lacy La Perla French knickers for me.

I interpreted the second gift correctly. Standing there amid all my boxes and bags (well, my fifteen boxes and three bags) he raised his eyebrows at me and held out his hands.

'Take your clothes off and come here,' he said, unbuckling his belt with an air of menace that made me gasp. He followed me into the bedroom, lashing at me playfully with his belt, but with enough force to be a threat. 'Now I've got you,' he smiled, and he had.

He had provided the life I thought I wanted and I had proved myself willing to pay for it in whatever way he asked. Don't see Tara, be available to me at all times and do what I tell you. Those were the rules. I stuck to them. I couldn't think of a more alluring option in life than this. The things I really wanted, if I were to admit it properly to myself, were not available so I was making do with the only thing that was actually on offer – Zander Sinclair and all that went with him, including, of course, the antiques. Few people had more charisma than Zander, and almost none of my contemporaries had a job as interesting as mine. I didn't have to go to an office, I didn't have to suck up to my boss or play any corporate games. I got to travel, I was rich, I was treated to frequent and meltingly expert sex as often as . . . well, as often as he wanted, and I used my Russian. The emptiness and soul-crushing insincerity of my life was a side effect I had decided to live with.

Zander had keys to my place and often turned up unannounced, waiting for me on my sofa in the dark, silent and blank-faced. Other times he sent Peter to pick me up and take me to his London flat, but never to Cairnsham Hall. He referred to it as 'the heap' and whenever I suggested we slope off there for a weekend he would bristle and demand to know why I was so interested in it.

'Fizzy, my love, it's not worth your while,' he told me, opening his newspaper, or picking up his mobile phone to make some call he had suddenly remembered. He had a similar reaction to any mention of Cassian. His loathing of him was way beyond an ordinary father's protective urge towards his daughter. In any case, he was hardly an ordinary father and Cassian seemed, to me at any rate, the dream catch, the perfect future son-in-law.

Once, seeing an article Cassian had written in the *Financial Times* about Russia's new stock exchange, Zander positively exploded over his eggs Florentine in the House on the Hill.

'Little prick!' he shouted. 'Killed his fucking sister and had the gall not to kill himself as well. Someone should help him out,' he spat, throwing the paper down and storming out.

I paid the bill, handing my card to a completely bald black woman with bright blue eyes and a figure like Naomi Campbell.

'Dads, eh? You can't keep 'em happy,' she said, and I nodded as though that was exactly what I had been thinking.

I found Zander back in my flat, curled up on the sofa with Elvis blaring out through the speakers. When I tried to touch him he looked up and his eyes filled with tears. He took my hands in his and kissed my palms before getting up to leave. He called me a couple of hours later saying, 'Hey, gorgeous, can you get over here now? I'm dying for a shag.' There was, I sometimes had to acknowledge, something seriously wrong with this bloke.

# Twenty-five

The flight to Russia was an absolute nightmare. Mum turned out to be chronically afraid of flying and spent the whole four and a half hours meditating with Hermione, who kept forcing Rescue Remedy drops into her mouth and saying things like, 'Your fear won't keep the plane in the air, sweetie.'

'What will then?' Mum sobbed, and Hermione was stumped.

I leant over the back of my seat to face them. 'Mum, the engines and the pilot will keep the plane in the air. All you have to do is watch the film and have a drink,' I grinned, waving my vodka miniature at her in demonstration.

'Drinking will interfere with the positive energies I am channelling into her,' Hermione smiled indulgently, and I collapsed back into my seat defeated. I would never have believed there would be a day when I would be trying to persuade my mother to drink more, but here it was.

Not a position that was necessary with Tara's godparents in front of me. They lived in some uncentrally-heated pile in Oxfordshire which tourists occasionally straggled round and they went on countryside marches in full hunting regalia.

They both drank like mad. In the Club Lounge at Heathrow they had mixed themselves enormous gin and tonics despite the fact that it was eight-thirty in the morning and the staff hadn't even finished slicing the lemons for drinks – assuming that most normal people would be on coffee until at least eleven. Not them. Cackling and braying their aristocratic enthusiasm for flying they kept trying to jolly us all into singing a little departure song, or toasting the happy couple in an anticipatory sort of a way.

'Are we all staying at the same hotel?' the wife asked, sloshing some ice on to the blue nylon carpet.

'Not a hotel. A friend has lent us her whole flat,' I reminded her.

'Oh, wonderful! How glorious! So before the ceremony we can all get together and . . . have a drink!' she beamed, delighted at the prospect.

'Yes, we can,' I nodded, that possibility being undeniable.

Now they were buying the entire alcoholic contents of the duty-free trolley and trying to remember in what precise way they were related to the Romanovs.

'I think my great uncle Freddie was married to one of Alexandra's sisters,' Godfather burbled.

'Oh, don't be ludicrous, darling. Your great uncle Freddie was as queer as a nine-pound note and was rogering that Habsburg chappie with the long sword,' Godmother pointed out, and they both hooted with laughter, causing the stewardess to spin round and make sure they were all right. 'You know, the one above the fireplace in the nursery?' she went on.

'Oh him!' shouted her husband. 'God, was he? The old rogue.'

'But I do think,' she then said, 'that my grandmother's cousin Minnie married whatsisface who helped thingummy kill Rasputin.'

'I say, could we have a few more of these?' they shouted, juggling the empty gin bottles.

I put my headphones on.

Tanya and Svyeta were at the airport to meet us and take us back to Tanya's flat. She was the only one with a place big enough to take us since Mum had refused to let me pay for a hotel. The Russian women raised their eyebrows at Hermione's ancient moth-eaten fur, a family heirloom that almost looked grand in England but here nobody could understand why she didn't buy a new one and chuck the bedraggled thing away. It was minus ten, 'not too cold' according to the Russians, who will never admit to it being even mildly nippy until the temperature drops below minus thirty. 'When I was little,' they are forever saying, 'it was forty below all winter long and we played outside till sundown.' Tanya immediately warmed to Mum, despite an insuperable language barrier, and the two talked at each other all the way back, laughing and burbling as though they understood a single word of what was being said.

Tanya was a very frightening driver. Her car, an

old red Lada Zhiguli, was visibly falling apart, and the heating was so hot and localised it was like having a few hair dryers aimed at your face while your feet sat in a bucket of iced water. She weaved about through the Mercedes and Jeeps, skidding in the ice and slush and beeping her horn loudly as we careened past statues and billboards, boulevards and kiosks. A heavy snow had started to fall.

When we eventually got there and had piled in four shifts into the ramshackle lift up to Tanya's place we were pretty much ready for a restorative drink. Which was lucky because there was going to be no stopping Tanya getting a frozen bottle of vodka out of the fridge to toast our arrival. Hermione was allowed some fizzy Narzan mineral water. In Russia the only excuse for not drinking is if you are a recovering alcoholic, so when Hermione shook her head to the vodka Tanya and Svyeta nodded understandingly and rushed off to get her something lighter. The rest of us winced, drank and shoved a gherkin into our mouths.

'I'll share with Mini,' Mum said, enthusiastically picking up her and Hermione's bags and taking them off into one of the bedrooms before any other suggestions could be made. That left the barking godparents on the sofa bed in the front room and me on the floor next to, or actually half under, the piano.

'What happened with the beautiful young man from the summer?' Tanya whispered when she kissed me goodbye to go off to Svyeta's.

'He found out about the ugly old man and chucked me,' I told her.

'Bad luck,' she nodded.

'Isn't it?' I smiled, and she and Svyeta took off, leaving us to sort out our outfits for tomorrow.

I had gone for a flimsy orange Ronit Zilkha thing and some orange and yellow silk flowers in my hair. The trouble with planning any kind of outfit in this country is that interiors are fantastically overheated while it snows outside, so you have to strip down to almost nothing the second you walk through a door. You also have to change shoes since you really need waterproof boots for the street which you can't then stomp over everyone's nice carpets.

'Will there be drinks immediately after the service?' Mum wanted to know.

At this point Zander called me on my mobile to tell me he had just checked into the Kempinski and would I meet him there immediately. Mum, having now discovered what he had done to Hermione, had forbidden me ever to see him again so I was in the preposterous situation of lying to everyone about seeing a man of whom I was increasingly terrified and didn't want to see anyway. I said I was going out to get my hair done and left, leaping into a passing car with a young soldier who was just back from Chechnya.

'This is Mrs Basayeva, Aslan's mother,' Zander told me coldly, presenting a beautiful dark-skinned woman to me in the hotel lobby. She looked like someone who had been a ballet dancer in her youth

– sort of tall and willowy and supple, her hair scraped back into an elegant bun.

'Pleased to meet you,' I said, astounded. Zander, it appeared, had managed to persuadc Aslan and Sultan of his version of the truth about Oksana, backed up by police reports provided by the heavily bribed, compromised and bullied Sergei. He had convinced them he had loved their sister and was as grief-stricken as they were when she died, and the bereaved mother told me Zander had paid for a huge monument to be constructed over Oksana's grave in Novodevichiy Cemetery and that he had bought her a large flat in Moscow to retire in.

'I reckon he did it because he hated Cass so much,' Tara had said. 'He's all over Aslan. It's embarrassing.'

I was pretty sure he was just trying to stop Sultan chopping his fingers off. Well, it wouldn't work in the long run, I thought.

We drank an awkward coffee together and Tasneem told us about the bombardments and how she had seen children blown to pieces by shells, screaming mothers looking for their babies in piles of rubble and the disfigured faces of childhood friends staring out at her from morgue slabs and heaps of still-wallpapered bricks. 'Nobody knows until they see this is what people are capable of,' she said quietly, grim-faced and dignified.

Zander, in a move that staggered me, took her hand and kissed it in a gesture of apparent sympathy and respect. He was up to something and it made my flesh creep.

The flat he had bought her was somewhere in the suburbs so he had checked her into the Kempinski for the wedding and she soon went off to her room, dealing well, I thought, with the contrast between this particularly opulent hotel and the cellar in which she had lived for those dreadful months.

'So, I assume my ex-wife is in tow?' Zander asked, pushing his cup away from him and saying 'ex-wife' with the maximum possible contempt.

'Hermione's staying at my friend Tanya's flat, yes. She seems to have become extremely pally with my mum,' I told him, almost on his side, so annoyed was I that Mum had somehow muscled in on the new life I had made for myself and done it all so much better than me because she wasn't pretending. Zander sneered.

He didn't try to make me go upstairs with him and I got the distinct impression that he had summoned me just so I could meet Mrs Basayeva and see how virtuous, kind and entirely unmurderous he was. I wasn't going to be taken in so easily. There was a definite note of menace about him at the moment – no jokes, no slaps on the bum, no twinkle in his eye. In fact, he was hardly looking at me. His signet ring looked newly polished somehow, his suit better fitting than usual, his rose fresher, his shoes shinier. For the first time since I had first seen him I truly hated him.

'I assume you are a competent rider?' he asked, plonking a cube of sugar into his cup.

'You what?' I asked, thinking for a moment that this was some kind of vile reference to sexual intercourse.

'A horse, Fizzy. Can you ride a horse?' he said, bored at having to rephrase his question.

'Call me Alice. Yes, I can actually,' I told him, half lying. Well, I sort of could but I wouldn't be winning any prizes for it.

'Alice? Really?' he sighed, uninterested. He didn't even know my name.

'So you will ride one from the Zavidovo compound to this dacha here,' he poked a manicured finger at a neat map, drawn out in the black ink of his fat fountain pen.

'Why? That road looks perfectly serviceable,' I said, leaning in to look at his drawing.

'It isn't. In any case, I don't want you coming at the house that way. The owner will be there and doesn't know what we're using it for. Be there at half-three,' he said, folding the map neatly and handing it over to me.

'A.m.?' I asked.

'A.m.,' he confirmed.

'Fucking hell,' I moaned and he flourished his hand in a signature to encourage the waiter to bring the bill.

'Is there anything else?' he asked me irritably.

I got up and left.

Tara looked lovely. She was in the antique cream lace of Hermione's and wore a floor-length lace veil with tiny pink roses somehow fixed into the head-dress. Her face glowed with unadulterated joy and suddenly she looked no older than the day I had first seen her.

She was completely out of place in the House of Weddings where the other brides sat waiting in enormous nylon meringues with sequins and glitter sewn on to the bodices.

Most of the grooms were swinging bottles of vodka in their hands and flicking their fag ash on to the carpet.

Also, our crowd was far bigger than the couple of thugs and their girlfriends that most of the others seemed to have rustled up. And we were a lot weirder. For a start there was Aslan, looking as eastern and manly as ever in a black tux, gold tooth all a-glitter, and his friends, darkly menacing types with shirts that barely stretched across their enormous shoulders.

And, of course, Tara, a vision of beauty in the squalor of the corridor, sweeping about like an angel. Hermione and Mum had a tastefully bohemian thing going, and all the Oxford lot were in very traditional English wedding gear – a few morning suits, though no top hats, lots of brightly coloured woollen skirt suits with beading round the cuffs and collars from Whistles and Karen Millen, and Pied A Terre high heels, mostly ruined by the slush outside.

Minty was there with Andy, and we fell into each other's arms as though nothing had ever happened.

It was, after all, a very forgivably long time ago. Ursula had come over on her own and was standing nervously on the edges of the Oxford people, at least until Harry pounced.

'Well, actually I've just been in Grozny,' I heard him say with a self-deprecating smile.

'Gosh,' said Ursula. 'That must have been terrifying.' The perfect answer.

We stood around noisily in a windowless red-carpeted corridor for over half an hour, sweating in the blistering central heating and getting shiny-faced under the flickering fluorescent lights. The whole place smelt of cheap Soviet cigarettes (not unlike the smell of Gauloises but a bit more acid) and the body odour of the thousands of nervous brides and grooms who had waited here over the years.

It was just before we were ushered in that Cassian turned up, breathlessly late, healthy-looking from the cold. His carnation had wilted and his suit was too big, giving him a shambolic schoolboyish look as he swept his hair out of his eyes and looked round for Tara. He found me instead. Wincing at the very sight of me he straightened his tie and turned round in disgust, destroying all my stupid hopes that I might tell him I had left Zander, that maybe, in the wildest flights of my fantasy, things might be OK. I jutted my chin out and linked arms with Mum.

We eventually walked in to the reedy sound of a violin, scraped by the bow of a very, very old man in a greasy black suit. Tara and Aslan held hands tightly and occasionally glanced up at each other shyly – a look I had never thought might light up Tara's face. These two were actually in love with each other. It was true.

Zander was at the front somewhere on the groom's side of the room, sitting next to Mrs Basayeva. A very fat woman with lurid orange hair piled high above her head asked the happy couple how likely it was that they would be adding to Russia's staggering divorce statistics, or something similar, and we all settled in for the show. The ceremony was incomprehensible to most of the guests and simply tedious for the others, but when Aslan lifted Tara's beautiful veil and kissed her, holding her tightly round the waist and shutting his eyes in disbelieving ecstasy, I couldn't help but cry. I heard Tara's godmother actually sob from somewhere near the back, but that may have been the three gin and tonics she had had for breakfast while the rest of us were banging helplessly on the bathroom door in the hope of hurrying Hermione up.

I'd got ready at the crack of dawn because I'd promised Tara I'd go over to the flat and help her. The snow had been falling thick outside her window and you could barely see the Ukraine Hotel through the blizzard. When I'd arrived Natasha had been making coffee and Tara had been sitting cross-legged on her bed in bra and knickers, painting her toenails pink.

'God, do you think I'm doing the right thing?'

she'd asked helplessly when she saw me poke my head round the door. 'I mean. I met him *yesterday*!'

'Doubt it. Do you usually?' I'd asked, sitting down on the bed.

'Never,' she'd admitted.

'Do you like him?'

'Can't remember. Do I? He's all right.'

'Well, there you go then. Can't go wrong,' I'd affirmed. 'Not many blokes out there who are all right.'

'True,' she'd agreed, perking up and dipping her brush back in the bottle. 'Wedding nerves. Fucking foreign editor's coming. I've sat her next to Sultan. Needs a good shag – the only thing that might sort her out, if you ask me,' she'd sighed. 'She's one of those insecure about her intelligence people – manifests itself mainly as cataclysmic rudeness. Can't write either. Told me my piece should "cascade down" the other day. I ask you . . .'

I'd helped her into the dress and watched her metamorphose into a princess. 'How's Cassian dealing with it?' I'd asked, taking a cup of coffee out of Natasha's hands.

'Good, actually. He's coming,' Tara had told me, pinning her roses into place, making my heart flutter. 'I can't believe we dragged it out so bloody long. I assume you know Dad's here?'

'Yeah. Escorting your rather glamorous mother-in-law,' I said. 'It's over, you know. I ended it.'

'Very wise . . . Bastard,' she'd smiled through a mouthful of pins. 'Don't know why he's smarming up so much to the Basayevs. You didn't tell him about their original plans for him, did you?' she'd asked, almost idly.

'No.'

'So, suddenly Aslan's crazy about him. Can't say a bad word about him. Never mind kill him. Says he's convinced Dad must have a very good reason for being such a shit to Mum and that he obviously loved Oksana to the ends of the earth. Bloody amazing.'

Walking out of the House of Weddings the English guests threw rice over Tara and Aslan, who were clinging tight to each other in the cold, beaming and unable to stop kissing for more than a second at a time.

The snow was relentless and we all stood about in the slush, desperately brushing the flakes off our eyelashes while we waited for the fleet of cars and taxis Zander had ordered.

'I tell you, I thought I was going to take a bullet,' Harry was saying to Ursula as he draped his jacket round her shoulders.

'Goodness,' she beamed, bowing her head against the snow.

'All in the line of duty,' he went on, and I rolled my eyes at Tara, who was also listening in. She stuck her fingers down her throat and grinned.

I tried not to look at the white snow melting on Cassian's thick black hair as he bent forward inside his jacket to light a cigarette. I failed. Drawing in my breath I walked over to where he stood, weaving my way through the excited crowd. I opened my mouth to speak and he looked at me with revulsion.

'Don't bother,' he said, and turned away.

# Twenty-six

It would have been nice if Tara had told me that she had sat me next to Cassian at dinner, though.

Gastronom is the Russian name for a food shop, which is exactly what this particular restaurant used to be. It is on the ground floor of one of Stalin's wedding cake buildings and was designed to be a 'palace for the people'. A few years ago old ladies waded around in the slush on the mosaiced marble floor and waited hours for a couple of rotten apples and a tin of fish, served from a cherry-wood counter under a hundred-foot-high chandeliered ceiling. The mosaics and stained-glass designs were done in a million different colours and there are large slabs of malachite and marble embedded in the walls. There are floor-to-ceiling windows on two sides and vast double doors with shining brass handles. Somehow, when it was a shop, you barely noticed the grandeur amid the squalor of the depressed shop assistants and exhausted shoppers, the poverty of the food on offer and the stench of rotten fish, year-old butter and festering scrags of meat. Now, though, the splendour is breathtaking. The architect himself, a man of at least a hundred and nine, is said to have seen the renovation and cried. All I could think was how much this must be costing

Zander. Lucky the Andrei Rublev thing went OK. There is no way of getting out of Gastronom for less than about seventy pounds for two people, without alcohol. They have live lobster in tanks and do delicious sushi and a wonderful *crème brûlée* with fruit on top.

As it happened we were served a salmon Caesar salad, rack of lamb and then a sort of chocolate mousse cake with strawberries. Aslan opened the festivities by standing on his table, uncorking a bottle of champagne with a ceremonial sword and handing it to his wife to swig. We all cheered and a band struck up in the corner, playing haunting eastern-sounding stuff. Apparently they had come from Ingushetia especially. My cheer was a tiny bit less enthusiastic than it might have been because Cassian was next to me, blowing his smoke murderously out through his nostrils. Evidently he had not been told about the seating plan either.

When he saw his place name next to mine he said, 'Alice,' like someone bringing shards of ice up through his throat.

This was going to be horrific. Fortunately Betsy's boyfriend, Jason, was on the other side of me – a male nurse she had met in rehab. In my efforts not to have to talk to Cassian I forced this bloke to tell me in great detail what heroin withdrawal was like, what the twelve steps really involved and how he had become interested in the recovery of addicts and alcoholics. Eventually, however, my victim had to go to the loo and excused himself politely.

I considered leaning back and talking to Sultan, who was at the table behind me, but he was busy being shouted at by Tara's foreign editor who was giving him a rundown of her career so far, much to his bafflement. 'So I said to her "We're both A-stream people, we ought to have lunch", and we did,' the editor gabbled proudly. I was stuck.

'Where's the boyfriend, then?' Cassian asked with an unpleasant twitch of his mouth. He craned round to look for Zander. 'Oh, not sitting together, I see?' he remarked when he had found him, and he stabbed a cucumber with his fork, crunching the end off it as though it were my head. 'Pity,' he munched.

'Not my boyfriend,' I said quietly.

'Sorry. Your fuck,' Cassian corrected himself and stood up angrily to go and congratulate Tara. I turned to talk to Karen Lawes from Manchester across the empty seat by my side. 'How are you?' I asked her. 'Haven't seen you since the party from hell.'

'Party from heaven, you mean! That's where I first met my husband,' she answered, beaming.

'Not Yasser Arafat?' I laughed, incredulous.

'The very same. Yasser, Peter actually, works at the embassy here,' she said, wiping her mouth with a big linen napkin. 'Have I got salad in my teeth?' she asked me, baring her fangs.

'Not a shred,' I told her. 'So what do you do?'

'Oh, sod all really. I help out in the consular department doing visas and stuff, but mostly I just loaf about at the embassy dacha with the other wives, talking about how much I want to go home.'

Karen had changed a lot since the beer cellar. Even her accent had pretty much disappeared. She patted me conspiratorially on the arm when she said 'home' but pulled back when Jason appeared to reclaim his seat. Later I heard a man introduce himself to her as 'Tara's groom'. She smiled in total bewilderment. The man was, after all, not Aslan. He really was Tara's groom from Cairnsham Hall, a stable boy.

Fortunately, at this point Tara stood up to make a speech. The Chechens all looked a bit taken aback by this, since the bride's role is very much one of adornment at most Chechen weddings, but they cheered anyway, willing to accommodate the strange ways of Westerners.

Tara, pulling her lace up around her, smiled like a queen addressing her subjects and raised her glass. 'In the past, whenever I've thought about spending my life with someone – I mean, let's face it, that's another forty years – I've always shivered in terror. Sorry, Cassian,' she beamed and everyone laughed, especially me. 'But now . . . But now, I consider the forty years I've got left with Aslan and I feel short-changed,' and she drank a toast with the tearful crowds and kissed her new husband happily on the cheek. 'Thank you all for coming!' she beamed.

Moments later Roma, the Tamodar, arrived. The Tamodar is a Georgian tradition and, roughly translated, means toastmaster. The job is very different from that of an English toastmaster and is really that of compèring the wedding (or any other event). Russian toasts are long and lyrical and since it is not really done to drink any alcohol in between them there need to be an awful lot of them. Jokes need to be told, speeches made, glasses lifted. All this is the job of the Tamodar.

He had brought his accordion with him and immediately struck up a Chechen wedding song which got all the swarthier members of the party banging the table with their spoons and glasses and whooping with delight. This was contagious and it wasn't long before Tara's godmother was standing on her chair, slapping her thighs and shouting encouragement to Aslan and Tara, who were required to kiss a lot during the song and then to drink about six shots of vodka at salient points. They obviously couldn't wait to get to bed.

I had completely exhausted the conversational possibilities to my right and was forced to sit in silence, ostentatiously ignored by Cassian and unable to shout across to anyone else in the din. Zander kept looking round at me without a smile and I couldn't remember if he had ever seemed less sinister than this. If he had ever seemed exciting but basically benign. It must have been a very long time ago. I must have been blind.

I went to the loo as often as seemed acceptable and took refuge from everything, staring at myself in the mirror to see if any answers were forthcoming. As I was deciding, for the third time, that they weren't, and touching up my lipstick instead, Betsy came in and snorted two lines of cocaine through a ten thousand rouble note, daring me to comment as she wiped her nose and blinked the tears away from her eyes.

'Chang, Fizzy?' she offered, challenging me to say yes.

'Yes,' I said, feeling aggressive and self-destructive. 'If you've got enough.'

'When the bugle calls, darling, you just have to answer,' she said, laying me out a line on her compact mirror with her American Express gold card. I couldn't be bothered to pretend I'd done it before for Betsy's sake, and she showed me how to roll the note up and put a finger over one nostril while sucking the stuff up through the other one. It seemed to numb the whole inside of my nose and at first I thought it had had no effect at all.

'Thanks,' I said, smiling sheepishly at Betsy in a way that I hoped fully acknowledged my own hypocrisy. She gave me a hug and asked me not to mention it to Jason.

'He's boring as fuck, I know,' she said, 'but that's what I need in life.' She laughed, and we charged out of the door arm in arm, cackling loudly.

I did not immediately attribute the fact that I felt about fifteen foot tall and made entirely of ice to the cocaine, but when I started babbling frenziedly to Betsy about Cassian, I realised I was not completely myself. But I felt proud and beautiful, interesting and mysterious, and suddenly I didn't care about anything.

I winked at Andy and blew a kiss to Sultan, and when Zander took hold of my arm I had almost forgotten I was supposed to be scared of him. I didn't register that he was holding me roughly above the elbow, pressing his fingers hard into my flesh, almost dragging me across the room. He pushed me into the men's loos and I thought he might be about to make me have sex with him. I almost wanted him to.

'Do you want to do this job or not?' he asked me angrily. I recalled that we had agreed to finalise the details after the service.

I hoisted myself up to sit on the sink and grinned at him happily. Knowing I was gorgeous. Knowing he could barely resist me. I licked my lips coyly at him and giggled.

'For you darling, anything,' I laughed, and leant back so he could see more of me.

'Good,' he snapped, but I could see he was turned on. 'So the pick-up is from Nikolai Dyachenkov again. You know the place. The only big dacha in the Zavidovo area,' he went on. 'Don't be late.'

'Again?' I raised my eyebrows. 'Dyachenkov? Who he?'

'The guy with the icon? I gather you didn't take to him,' Zander smiled, moving towards me now.

Briefly, despite the drug rushing through my veins, I had a pang of anxiety. It was true, I had not taken to the icon bloke. I had really felt he could have killed Cassian quite remorselessly.

'Oh, come on, Zander,' I said, worried now. But his eyes went dead at my reticence, and this was, after all, the last job ever ever, ever, ever. He walked towards me with a scary smile and stood between my legs at the sink.

'I think someone's been for a bit of a nose-up,' he said, tapping the end of my nose with one finger.

'There's more if you want it,' I told him, brazen and proud.

'Oh, I want it,' he said, and picked me up off the sink, kissing me so hard I thought my lips might be bruised, and wrapping my legs round his back.

'I'll see you back at the Kempinski when you've got the crown,' he said, dropping me to the floor and patting me on the cheek. He walked out quickly and I looked at myself in the mirror, beautiful, powerful.

Cassian was standing by my left shoulder. He had come out of the cubicle nearest the door.

'I wonder if anyone has ever told you what a fucking disgusting little slut you are?' he said with a kind of chill that made my heart lurch. My euphoria turned quickly to jittery paranoia. My chest was pounding and my left eye kept twitching uncontrollably. Cassian's eyes were full of menace and hatred and my mind was whirring with hideous possibilities. The cacophony of the drunken guests outside verging on hysteria had become sinister and threatening, and I was hyperventilating so much I thought I might actually faint.

I gasped and turned round to face him.

'Well?' he stood firm.

'Cass, please, you've misunderstood . . .'

'You are actually going to try and talk yourself out of this? You are the grimy little whore of a drug addict I always suspected you were. You are enthusiastically getting shafted by one of the most evil men on the planet and you are dealing with the most unpleasant Mafioso Rostov ever produced. And for some completely fucking incomprehensible reason you seemed to find it necessary to make me go where that low-life Sinclair and fuck knows who else has been. I have spent weeks in the shower trying to get you off me, Alice Reynolds.'

I was choking with sobs, holding on to the sink and almost retching into it as he spoke.

I tried to explain but I couldn't get the words out. I wanted to shout: 'I didn't. This is the first time I've even seen cocaine. I've left Zander and I'm not working for him any more. I love you and I always have!' but none of it would come out between my wrenching sobs.

Cassian was still standing there. So unmoved was he, he hadn't even taken his hands out of his pockets or his eyes off me. Striding towards the sink, he rinsed his hands in the basin next to me and dried them on a white linen towel. Smiling hideously at me in the mirror, he spoke again.

'Frankly, my dear, I hope you do go on this job tonight. See if anyone cares. Good luck to you. Give

Dyachenkov my love. Nice knowing you.' At this, he walked away and I threw up.

The Gastronom waiter bowed low in surprise when I asked him for a quadruple shot of vodka in one glass, but he brought it over to me by the huge green fern and asked me if I would like a spoonful of ice from the bucket that had accompanied him. I shook my head, drank the vodka in one go and put my glass back on his silver tray.

'Thanks,' I said. 'Another if you don't mind.'

Both Cassian and Zander had gone.

# Twenty-seven

The traffic out to Zavidovo was terrible. We sat in a smoke-filled car for two hours, occasional gypsy children pressing their tiny filthy hands to the window glass and the odd drunk hassling for money, dribbling through a mucus-encrusted beard, face swollen and chapped with years of home-made vodka and weather.

'Lovely country,' Hermione said, winding her window down to give a few roubles away. Mum was still quite drunk and neither of them seemed to notice that I was pale, shaking and silent.

The driver pulled over at one of the wooden houses by the side of the road. Like most houses in the Russian countryside it was a real fairytale gingerbread house. Wooden, one storey, painted blue, with carved birds and flowers in the roof and around the windows. He jumped out into the thick wet slush and bought a hideous towel decorated with a naked woman, handing his money to an old man who had various of these monstrosities hung on his washing line.

'For my son,' he explained, getting back into the car and throwing the towel into the back.

We weren't far from Zavidovo now. Mum had insisted we stop for a coffee at McDonalds's in Klin, a hellishly depressing little town where the golden arches are the only splash of colour. Tchaikovsky came from here. It is not hard to imagine his motivation for leaving. The girl who leant out into the snow to serve us at the car window was young and pretty, and seemingly perfectly happy to be dishing out fries to drunk drivers every day. This is probably one of Klin's better job opportunities.

I was sharing a dacha with Mum and Hermione, Minty, Andy and Ursula – right next door to Tara and Aslan. I just wanted to get there so I could go to bed and cry. I opened the window and a flurry of snow blew on to my coat and melted there as we arrived at the gates of the compound.

Zavidovo is a holiday centre that was once for foreigners only, but now takes anyone with the money. Behind the barbed wire fences that surround the whole complex people relax in their little wooden dachas or in the main hotel – a big modern thing with a swimming pool and an open-plan bar.

The pool is where you can watch Moscow Mafiosi become human. When you see them outside pulling up in their Jeeps with the windows blacked out you feel you ought to be elsewhere. These are the vehicles hit men pile out of in Moscow to do their contract killing. The murderers are usually KGB-trained and pretty good shots, so there is little danger to the passer-by, but even so. Of the five murders that happen every night in Moscow three of them originate in cars like this (the other two are domestic – drunk men and women taking kitchen knives to each other after seven bottles of vodka each). But at Zavidovo you see the enormous thug get out of the driver's seat – shaven head, medallion, flashy leather jacket, scars – and suddenly the back doors fly open and three children leap out, brought into line by their desperately glamorous mum, far too skinny surely to have children, and too tall to look after them. People have children young in Russia, so she is usually still under twenty-five. 'Daddy, Daddy, can we swim?' they cry and he beams at them, ruffles their hair and pushes them towards the hotel doors. Once in the water they throw the kids off their shoulders, swim underwater to grab at their legs, throw balls to them and rush off to fetch them cans of Coke (well, OK, send the wife off the fetch them). It appears that even these types of Russian do actually love their children too.

There is an indoor tennis court and a gym and you can hire skates to take out on the rink or skis for going into the forest. Out by the lake there are snow mobiles, fishing rods, guns, horses and sledges. The snow mobiles are amazing things, left over from a Red Army expedition to the South Pole in 1950. They pump petrol into the face of the driver and make so much noise you can't even shout audibly to the person riding pillion. They chug and crunch and choke along through the snow, their turning circle bigger than a lorry's.

Tara was standing outside her dacha, an old-fashioned wooden thing, to greet us. Her breath froze in the air and she was framed by the thick warm orange light from an inside that suggested fires, hot food and mugs of tea. 'Hey!' she waved, standing happily on the ice in front of the steps, stomping her furry boots up and down as her husband came up behind her to take her in his arms.

The lights of our car twinkled into the distance and skidded away down the little lane leaving us all to our honeymoon.

I went into my dacha, kicked the snow off my shoes, pulled my gloves off red, chapped fingers and tugged at my coat and scarf as my face began to sting. The others were already sitting round a blazing fire, drinking Georgian red wine they had bought at the bar. The dacha was a hilarious New Russian effort with underfloor heating in the tiled bathrooms and lurid patterned curtains and carpets. The light fittings all involved pink glass globes and gold bits, and the sofa was a four-part suede curved thing that you had to fit together. Still, with the lights off and everyone sitting in front of the fire it had just about been possible to capture something a bit more Chekhovian.

'We'd given you up for dead. Where've you been?' squealed Minty, leaping to her feet and slopping some wine into a mug for me, cheeks glowing with the heat from the fire that was spitting and crackling in the hearth and sending flakes of ash out into the room.

'Buying towels,' I said.

Andy had booked a *banya* for an hour's time and was getting very excited about jumping into the frozen river. He was stuffing his face with sweet cheese pancakes and flexing his arms and legs in preparation for his ordeal. The *banya* was out in a little hut by the river, hard to find in the dark, but equipped with towels, tea, a samovar and a small jetty leading to the ice-hole. Enjoying the experience of getting so hot you can't stand it and having to jump into some ice, and then being so cold you can't stand it and having to run back to the searing heat is a mark of real Russianness. It's like loving the Russian winter. Like vodka, it is said to keep you healthy. Well, either you die doing it or you were already very healthy in the first place. Minty was apprehensive.

'Do you honestly think it's good for you?' she kept asking, only to be reassured it was by people who wouldn't dream of doing it themselves but were amused by the idea of Andy and Minty naked in the ice. Ursula had excused herself from the experience because she was meeting Harry in the bar.

There was a New Russian couple just dismounting when I got to the stables. The woman, slim, tall and acting as though her underwear was extremely expensive and very lacy, was flushed and glittering from the ride and the cold. Her boyfriend held out his hand to help her down as she hopped off her horse. They both wore brand-new jodhpurs and brown leather riding boots with suede spats strapped over them. She had a black mink zip-up jacket on that made her look moody and romantic, and he was in a bright yellow Gore-tex thing under which you could hide your guns and vodka should the urge take you. She kissed her horse on its fuzzy nose and put a sugar lump from her pocket between his big flat teeth before the stable-hand nodded to me to address him, the horse still munching appreciatively. I gave him two hundred dollars to have the horse waiting for me at three a.m. He didn't ask any questions. This, after all, was about three months' pay.

'Name's Fyodr,' the bloke growled at me, patting Fyodr on the rump.

Then I went over to the hotel building to see if I could get a massage. Relaxation didn't seem to be one of the things on offer in our dacha. Elena, a plump woman with twinkly eyes, pummelled and prodded me until I almost fell asleep under her fingers. The chatter she managed to keep up, however, put a stop to that. She had been massaging rich people for ten years, though she qualified as a nurse in her teens. Massage is considered as essential a part of Russian health care as antibiotics and aspirin (and a lot easier to come by), and most nurses are incredibly good at it. She rolled her eyes and took her hands off me in despair at the thought of the billions of reasons why she had given up nursing, cackling madly in demonstration of the crippling lack of funding that leaves doctors and nurses completely unpaid for months on end, electricity periodically turned off in the hospitals, heating sporadic and patients dying of routine complaints because of a lack of anaesthetic, needles, painkillers and X-ray slides.

'This job's easier,' she laughed, and recommended that I go and splay myself out naked on the hot marble slabs of the Turkish bath for half an hour. I did.

When I came out I trudged through the snowy dark to find the others having a barbecue out in front of the dacha. Sultan was spearing chunks of meat on to skewers as though they might have been hostages' toes and Aslan was cheerfully pouring out shots of vodka and shouting to get everyone to drink up. The kebabs sizzled loudly on the fire as the snowflakes fell on to them and Ursula and Harry were now snuggled up happily under his coat. Tara, fantastically drunk by this stage, came over to me, skewer in her hand, fag hanging from her lips.

'Here,' she said, pulling a hot and dripping piece of meat off the end and shoving it into my mouth, the juices dribbling down my chin.

'Ta,' I said, smiling at her, happy for her even in my nightmare.

'What's wrong with you, Fizzles? Look like somebody died,' she cackled, swilling back the drink Aslan had just placed in her hands.

'Oh God. You don't want to know,' I moaned, rolling my eyes.

'Oh, Fizzy, Fizzy, Fizzy, of course I want to know everything,' she slurred, putting her arms round my neck, pressing a freezing cheek to mine, and almost burning my hair with her cigarette.

'Really?'

'Really, reeeeeeally,' she said. So I told her.

'Betsy gave me some coke this afternoon and I'd never taken it before but basically Cassian got the wrong end of the stick and thought I was some kind of drug addict and that I was still sleeping with your . . . with Zander . . . and that I'm mixed up in some sort of Mafia thing and he shouted at me and it was just awful and I don't know what to do,' I gasped, bursting into tears on her shoulder and shaking with the dreadful relief of spewing it all out.

'Oh dear,' Tara said, trying to steady herself. 'Cass is not a big one for drugs, as you can appreciate.' Tara was the type of person who had a secret admiration for the media morons who do lines at dinner parties so she had spent a fair few hours rowing with Cassian on the subject. 'You know. Flossy and that,' she said, stumbling slightly in the firelight.

I wiped my eyes and took a glass from Aslan. Sultan was still busy with the meat. I wasn't sure I had heard him speak since the train. I tried to smile at him a bit but he just glared angrily. Tara assured me he could be sweet really but I wasn't completely convinced.

'You've got to realise, Fizz, that Cass knows all kinds of shit about what Dad gets up to. I just won't let him tell me. I think the brilliant double whammy of drugs and Dad is enough to get shot of him for ever. But listen, we'll try and sort it out tomorrow.

He's staying with some old friends of ours in Moscow so we'll give him a call, OK?' she offered. I was grateful to Tara Sinclair. The only friend I had.

'OK,' I nodded meekly.

'But now,' she said, her face lighting up brighter than the flames beside her, 'I am going to go and fuck my husband.'

'You do that,' I laughed through the remains of my tears, and she and Aslan disappeared inside.

I sat on a blanket on the steps until half-past two, talking to Sultan about the war. He put his arm around me and spoke softly of the horrors, downing his vodkas, smoking one cigarette after the other and making me feel very lucky to be English. When I looked at my watch and announced I had to go to bed he kissed my hand and doused the fire in water. Tara had been right. He could be really sweet.

'Good night, Alice. I'm sorry about the . . .' and he slashed a finger across his face.

'It's OK,' I told him. And it was.

# Twenty-eight

Fyodr was waiting by the stables in the dark, snorting his icy breath into the night and stomping his hoofs on the squeaking snow. He was saddled up and ready, flaring his nostrils in the excitement of being out at such an hour. I could hear the other horses inside, steaming in their hay, shifting about heavily in their sleep.

I buried my face in my fur collar and pulled my hat down over my ears, swinging a boot up into the stirrup to mount. I was glad of Fyodr's comforting warmth as we set off towards the forest, the map crackling in my pocket.

Plodding through the forest in the bright moonlight we clomped under pine trees, nudging great paws of snow from the branches as we went and sending sparkling showers of silver down on to the forest floor. I ducked as we sailed under low trees and hugged Fyodr's steamy neck when I urged him into a gallop on the clear stretches.

When we reached the edge of the woods I could just make out the horizon in the distance, marked by a few trees, thin black skeletons quivering in the night. I remembered Cassian saying that that's what Russia is really – 'a few trees miles and miles away on the horizon'. The snow made everything bright white under the moon as far as I could see and Fyodr stamped his feet in enthusiasm when we paused to check our directions, puffing from his enormous nostrils like a huge black dragon. I had tiny icicles on my lashes but I was warm under my fur with the horse to help me, and I could see the dacha in question, its yellow lights glimmering conspicuously in the emptiness.

I slipped from the saddle at the beginning of the drive and led the horse up towards the house. Fyodr seemed happy enough to chew a sugar lump out by the back door. I tied him to a metal railing glistening with ice and he bowed his head submissively to let me. I tapped nervously on the flimsy plank door and Dyachenkov smiled when he opened it, an expression that seemed to contort his features unnaturally.

If anything Dyachenkov achieved the astonishing feat of being even more frightening-looking without a balaclava on. I had wondered whether or not I would recognise him but I'd have known those massive hands anywhere. You would have thought that missing fingers would make someone seem less able to do harm, but in his case the opposite was true. He looked as though you could lop another few off and he'd hardly notice.

'Hello again,' he said, letting me in with a flourishing sweep of his hand. 'No boyfriend this time?' he laughed.

'No boyfriend that time either,' I told him, and pulled my rabbit fur hat off, shaking my hair out of its confines.

'This is my colleague Sergei Borisov,' he said, and gestured to the corner where Sergei Borisov was indeed sitting. This was a big surprise. I thought he was just the customs guy. He was actually wearing his airport uniform but he was slumped and smoking, obviously a bit drunk and plainly not present in his official capacity. I nodded over to him but he still didn't recognise me.

He had definitely lost his looks. I could see that now that I had time to scrutinise him. His face had gone entirely grey and his beautiful green eyes were dead with years of drudgery and compromise. He ran his fingers through greasy hair and looked up at us in bored expectation, barely acknowledging me. His grey uniform seemed to me to be a symbol of a life of dishonesty and tedium.

'Drink?' Dyachenkov offered, moving over towards a half-empty bottle of vodka on a dusty sideboard. The dacha was old-style – a real writer's retreat with a big green porch, creaking floorboards, an ancient brass samovar bubbling on the oval wooden table and an old ceramic floor-to-ceiling stove heating the room.

'Thanks. No. The crown?' I asked, shuffling my feet about in anticipation of the cold on the ride back. If I rode quickly I could be in bed inside of twenty minutes, I thought.

'Bit of a hold-up on that,' Dyachenkov said, smirking. 'Have a seat.'

'I don't want a seat. I want a crown,' I told him, beginning to feel a bit edgy.

'All in good time,' he smiled, and held out his arm towards the raggedy velvet chaise longue, handing me the glass of vodka I had refused. I drank it and sat back, crossing my legs and becoming aware that I was somehow in vague danger. I just wanted to get back on the sodding horse and into the warmth and safety of Zavidovo.

Then I heard an expensive non-Russian car pull up and a door slam. In a flurry of snowflakes and a blast of icy air Zander Sinclair was with us.

'Aha. Started without me?' he bellowed, marching into the room, his black cashmere coat swinging around him.

'What the fuck are you doing here?' I asked him, jumping to my feet in real fear now. This was not supposed to be happening.

'Come to pick up my coronation crown and have a drink with young Nikolai here. Why? What are you doing here? Ah . . . yes,' he laughed, and threw his coat on to the back of a chair, pouring himself a vodka and slapping Dyachenkov hard on the back.

'Sergei,' he nodded over to the miserable-looking heap in the corner.

'Lord Sinclair,' Sergei replied deferentially.

Zander leant his head in the direction of the door and Sergei stood up and went outside. I moved to follow him, sensing that out was where I would rather be. I should just go now. I didn't need to understand the situation, I just needed not to be in it. I was halfway across the floor when a shot cracked through the air outside, followed by a loud and chaotic thud.

'Jesus. What the fuck . . .?' I spun round to look at Zander.

'Can't have you planning a getaway, sweetie,' Zander grinned back at me. I realised that Sergei had killed the horse.

I sat back down on the sofa and started to shiver though the stove was blazing. I could see that this was bad. Dyachenkov, his eyes flashing through the shifting darkness, handed Zander a cloth bag which Zander immediately opened, pulling out what was in fact the third, the no longer missing, coronation crown, thousands of diamonds shimmering their light into the room, piercing the night with their brilliance.

'You're the best,' Zander smiled at Dyachenkov and Dyachenkov smiled back, before saluting jokily and leaving the room.

'You, however,' Zander continued, placing the crown on the table and turning to me, 'are not.' He took a handful of my hair from behind my head and dragged me to my feet, pulling my face into his and rubbing his other hand hard between my jodhpured legs. I retched.

'Don't like it any more?' he laughed, squeezing a breast through my jacket until I cried out in pain. Then he threw his arm back and hit me in the face, bringing blood dribbling out of my nose and audibly breaking a tooth. I tried to pass out. I wanted to be dead quickly so that he couldn't touch me any more.

He threw me face down on to the sofa and, ripping his belt from his trousers, started whipping me with it, across my arse and thighs, tearing the fabric that covered them, stinging my flesh until I found I was screaming uncontrollably without willing it. This seemed to make him worse and, shouting at me to shut up, he turned me on to my front by my hair and started lashing at my face, badly protected by my now bleeding hands. When I rolled on to the floor he kicked me hard in the stomach and I vomited on to the floorboards at his feet.

As suddenly as he had begun he stopped.

'This,' he panted, breathless from the exertion of beating me, 'is beneath me.'

'Sergei,' I heard him say, and Sergei pulled me up off the floor by one arm and began leading me towards an inside door. I was coughing and choking on blood that was coming from inside my mouth and I was shivering so hard that it felt like involuntary spasms rocking my body.

'Goodbye, Fizzy,' Zander said quietly, beginning to calm himself. 'You know better than to think you can get away from me. It's not much of a secret what happens to the little tarts who want to walk out. Is it now?'

I looked up at him with the eye that was not caked shut with hot blood, but I couldn't speak. Sergei supported me as we descended some wooden steps into some kind of cellar. It was empty and very cold with a fluorescent strip light on the ceiling. When he let go of me I fell on to the floor, my back against the wall.

'You don't remember me, do you?' I slurred through swollen lips.

'Should I?' Sergei asked, uninterested, dragging his Makarov 8mm slowly out of its holster, examining it for dust or flaws.

'Florence's friend, Alice. We were tourists . . . years ago,' I told him and he looked up, staggered. Staring into my face he seemed suddenly to see me there and he almost smiled, resurrecting the once sparkling look of youth and excitement that had seemed to characterise him back then in a different world.

'Alice?' he asked, stunned.

'That's me,' I told him. A chink of hope now seeping into the situation. I kicked my mind into gear. I had to escape and with Sergei to help me it shouldn't be impossible.

Putting his gun away he ran his fingers across his face in astonishment. 'Florence. How is she? You know I think of you both all the time. My life here has been what it has been, but I have always thought of you two on an English lawn with your husbands and children. She is married?'

'Oh, Sergei,' I muttered, truly sorry. 'She's dead. She died quite soon after we got back.'

I thought I saw tears come into his eyes, and he took his head in both hands, rolling it back to the ceiling. I could hear Zander and Dyachenkov talking upstairs.

'Dead,' Sergei said to himself, unnervingly drawing his gun out again. I thought he was going to kill himself and leave me to plan my escape alone. This wouldn't do at all.

'Seriozha. Don't,' I said, trying to scramble to my feet.

'I am what I am, Alice,' he whispered, almost inaudibly. 'If I had lived in the Foggy Albion like you I might have been different. If I had been as privileged as you, if I could have taken everything for granted like you – but I have learnt to do what I'm told. Things are simpler that way.'

As he raised the gun to point it at my head I shut my eyes and tried to black out.

# Twenty-nine

Somewhere in between the quiet squeeze of a trigger and the deafening crack of a bullet whistling into the wall above my head there was a noise from upstairs. People had arrived, things were hitting the floor, I heard a single shot and shouts echoing into the night. Something had shocked Sergei into missing.

I opened my eyes as much as I could to see him quickly taking aim again, frightened and more alert than he had been, but then staggering backwards as Zander jumped down the stairs, dragged me up to near standing and held a gun to my temple. My breathing was laboured and I think he had broken a rib when he kicked me. I couldn't scream any more and I was slipping in and out of consciousness as the pain in my right lung seared through me.

In the flickering of my mind I saw Aslan and Sultan burst into the room, both waving pistols, and with them, I thought I saw Cassian. Zander's gun was held hard to my head and I thought it was actually pressing on my brain, switching something on and off. I tried to adjust my vision and I could see that it was him. It was Cassian.

'OK, arsehole, time to die,' Sultan shouted in Russian, squinting to take aim at Zander. I heard a click by my head.

'I'll kill her,' Zander threatened, sounding afraid and uncertain, his voice quivering. This was a Zander with whom I was not familiar. Sultan laughed.

'Tell me, sir, do I look like someone who gives a shit?' he said and I heard a shot. It must have gone through my skull I thought in a flash, falling to the floor, but landing on top of Zander. I struggled to get up and found my hands in the pool of thick warm blood that was pouring from Zander's chest. Again I retched and collapsed in a heap, my face now lying in the oozing liquid. Nobody came to help me and I knew I must have been shot too. I would feel it any moment.

Sultan walked over towards us and put one foot on Zander's stomach, exerting pressure that caused a hideous cry of pain to pierce the cellar. 'Nobody kills a Chechen man's sister and gets away with it,' he said, and shot Zander again, once in each leg.

'Just finish him off, Sultik,' Aslan snapped, and as I moved my head I saw him on the other side of the room with his knee in Sergei's back, holding him to the wall as Sergei whimpered, his face pressed into the plaster. Quickly, mercifully, Aslan raised a gun to his head and fired, spraying the room with the ghastly matter that had lately been Sergei's brain. Another shot rang out and I felt myself being lifted up gently and hauled up the stairs between two men. They spirited me effortlessly over Dyachenkov's bleeding body near the still crackling stove and I felt the cold air hit me as I was walked out into the silent snowy night.

'Can you lean against me?' Cassian asked, Aslan passing my broken body up into his arms and on to his saddle. I nodded and slumped back, held inside his coat while he negotiated the reins in his other hand. He kissed my bloody forehead gently and I felt a sickening undulation as the horse clomped off into the deep snow. I was aware of cold flakes landing on my face, chilling the swollen mass of my cheeks and freezing the wounds as if to tell me I was still alive, that I was going to be OK. Behind me flames seemed to be leaping into the sky.

We must have been going slowly for my sake, Aslan in front, Sultan behind, for the journey was much longer than it had been on my way out. It seemed endless as we moved, the branches sparkling above my head, the moon huge and yellow in the sky. In half an eternity my breathing eased and I tried to speak.

'Why did you come?' I whispered, and I felt Cassian's warm sigh against my back.

'Oh God, Alice. How could I not?' He spoke gently into my ear, competing only with the whispering trees to be heard. 'A very pissed Mrs Tara Basayeva called me in Moscow around midnight and said I shouldn't be mean to you because you had never done drugs before and because you had split up with Zander. She said you had cried at her barbecue.'

I would like to have laughed but I didn't have the breath.

'There's a big difference . . .' I said with difficulty, 'between this and "not being mean",' I told him.

'Half dead and still cocky,' he laughed for me. 'It's true. But I knew tonight wasn't safe from what I heard Zander say at Gastronom. I did tell you,' he said, turning to check that Sultan hadn't galloped off from behind us to find someone else to kill.

'You know, I thought it was Dyachenkov when we got that icon – the hands?' Cass whispered to me softly. 'He is, he was, a hugely important bloke. They say he gets a kick out of being present at all his own deals – a real power freak. He ran the whole antiques business in Russia, but he hardly ever puts out contracts because he's got this thing for really grisly murders. Remember those blokes with their hands and feet cut off in the boot of that Zhiguli?' I didn't, but I didn't bother to answer. I could see the lights of Zavidovo now and it looked as welcoming as home. 'Zander's been working with Dyachenkov for years. I've tried to tell Tara, and you in fact, but nobody wants to know,' Cassian said, now sounding tetchy that people never took his investigative journalism seriously.

'And Aslan?' I asked, fading fast as the pain surged back through me.

'I've known about Zander killing Oksana for years. I just didn't know until yesterday that she was the Basayevs' sister. It didn't take much to persuade them to come with me, thank God,' he said, leaning round to nod at Sultan in thanks.

We rode into the compound as the sky was beginning to lighten round the edges and Mum and Hermione helped me down from the horse and into the dacha where the fire was blazing and the kettle boiling.

'So you don't hate me,' I asked Cassian, who was supporting me under one arm, his coat engulfing me now.

'I have spent more than a decade wishing I could hate you, Alice,' he smiled, and I fell on to an enormous sofa, just conscious of Elena the masseuse cutting my clothes off me with a huge pair of scissors and sponging me down with hot soapy water from a big metal bowl.

Before I slipped into unconsciousness I reached out a hand for Cassian, my vision blurry now, all the faces merging into one in the firelight. 'Cass,' I murmured.

'He's gone, Princess,' Mum told me, stroking my hair back from my forehead. 'He set off for Moscow a couple of hours ago.'

# Thirty

Tara had a roll of masking tape between her teeth. She was kneeling on the floor in a pair of beige dungarees carefully opening boxes of books, each labelled in her careful hand with a letter of the alphabet. She was currently up to 'E'.

'Goodness me, darling, I don't need them in any sort of order, just put them on the shelves,' Hermione sighed, sipping a cranberry juice and rolling her eyes at Mum who had just walked in with a tray of Sea Breezes for everyone who was allowed one.

Tara sighed and put a handful of paperbacks on the nearest shelf. They looked out of place among all the leather bound classics collected by Hermione's great great grandfather who was staring down at us now, disapproving in his riding breeches. The room looked an awful lot friendlier than it had the night Zander had invited me into it for a brandy that was for sure. Nothing sinister now about the big leather armchairs, the poker hanging on a hook by the fire or the decanter, empty, clean and standing decoratively on its table.

I sat in the same leather armchair I had sat in then, sipping a drink and watching Hermione's funny new friends help her move back into her house. I was not required to help, still being classed as an invalid. My arm was in a cast and I had a few alarming looking stitches in my face but I was basically fine. Mum still kept patting my hand though and asking if I was OK. She had the room next to me up in the Cairnsham Hall attic – Aslan and Tara were in the Karma Sutra room, luridly painted by Hermione's brother just before he died in the 1961 Monaco Grand Prix.

Mum and Hermione had insisted I come and recover at Cairnsham Hall and I had arrived with them a few days after the Zavidovo bloodbath. Sultan set fire to the dacha that night as we left and the bodies inside had apparently been unidentifiable. However, it was no trouble having Zander declared dead and the deeds to Cairnsham Hall were transferred to Tara in the absence of a will. She, obviously, gave it straight back to Hermione, and, it appeared, my Mum.

It seemed strange now that I had thought the upper classes needed infiltrating, that I had once imagined one might have to remake oneself to suit them. Hermione liked Mum because she was nice. No secret. She also didn't seem particularly averse to Kris who had latched on to the two of them for all she was worth, even splashing out on some big silver plates with tassels hanging off the bottom to wear (in her ears) for her first visit to Cairnsham Hall. She too had turned to tofu in an attempt to replace the drink and drugs she had reluctantly abandoned.

*

It had looked different during the day when we all arrived. Somehow more austere and English, less other-worldly. I felt like one of the tourists, wondering what year it was built, when the summer house was added and which bits of it the family still lived in. Except there weren't any tourists. It was windy and pouring with cold grey rain. The trees shivered and shook, and as the drive wound round to give that amazing view, I imagined a mad Mrs Rochester appearing on the battlements or a headless horseman galloping out of the woods at us wielding his sword.

'Someone expecting you?' the taxi driver asked us, blowing a thin stream of acrid smoke at his windscreen.

'I hope so,' Hermione said, getting her purse out, not behaving like someone coming home. The gates had been open but there was nobody in sight when we ground to a halt on the gravel, suddenly surrounded by silence, huddling together by our car in this vast empty palace battered by the wind and the rain. The entrance that had been used for the party all those years before was very obviously locked. Piles of leaves had gathered by the doors and nobody had been up those steps for months at the very least. It took fifteen minutes to walk all the way round, led by Hermione, and I was weak and freezing by the time we made our way through the open door swinging in the wind at the bottom of some narrow steps down to a basement.

'Lady Hermione!' said a doughy lady I

recognised as the woman who had served me a bottle of Evian just before my fateful encounter with Zander in the upstairs corridor. One of the upstairs corridors. A decade older but definitely her. She fell into Hermione's arms, covering her with flour. Hermione and Tara were back where they belonged.

Aslan was helping Tara with the books, kissing her on the head every time he bent down to pick up the next lot.

'What are we doing with these, Mum?' Tara asked, dumping a big box of files and cuttings on to the floor in front of the fireplace.

'Aha!' said Hermione, her face lighting up. 'These can finally go where they belong. In the bin.'

Tara looked up at her questioningly. 'My Zander files. A Hill Place obsession I can at last lay to rest,' she announced, picking up a sheet of typed A4 and symbolically tearing it in half. Mum came forward and kissed her on the cheek, holding both her hands in support and pride.

'Oh, let me,' I asked Hermione, giving her a meaningful look. I dragged myself out of my chair with a wince of pain and scooped up an armful of paper to throw on to the fire. After all, I needed to put him to rest too.

It was only the one file. I don't know why I chose it. I couldn't help it. It just seemed to slip itself into my sling. It was a green battered cardboard folder and it was labelled 'Family/Sara' in Hermione's elegant hand.

While everyone was pottering around helping, drinking Sea Breezes and eating hot buttery toast, I snuck upstairs to my room to have a look at what I had stolen.

The cuttings inside the file were ancient, dating back to the 1960s, and they all showed grainy brownish photographs of a young Zander with a girl, by the look of it slightly younger than him. In fact, as I leafed through them, too taken aback to actually read the headlines – there he was staring at me, so happy, so childish – I realised they were all from the same week in 1969. He had been devastatingly handsome. His face was fatter, his black hair thicker and his eyes more sparkling. But the main thing was his expression. He was smiling with complete joy and innocence, his face looked open and honest, almost sweet – though the word stuck in my mind when applied to Zander.

With butterflies in my stomach I began to read.

*Daily Mail*, April 21st 1969: ENGLISH SCHOOLGIRL MURDERED IN GOA.

An English teenager from South London was brutally raped and murdered yesterday in the Indian coastal resort of Goa when six attackers armed with knives accosted the woman, 17, and her elder brother on Goa's main tourist beach late last night.

The young woman, Sara Sinclair, was stabbed forty-one times in the horrific attack and died at the scene. Her brother, Alexander Sinclair, 19, escaped unscathed. The two had been in India visiting their grandmother, a native of the country.'

I turned frantically to the next cutting, hoping in my horror that it had turned out to be a mistake. That she had survived. That they had got the wrong teenagers in the photograph. But all the articles were the same. Short, to the point, not from the front page. This was not a big story. I read them all, shaking in sudden realisation as one line in a piece from the *Chronicle* struck at me with hideous significance. 'The woman's distraught brother, Mr Alexander Sinclair, told reporters he had been helpless against his assailants. "They said they might let her live if I walked away. They only wanted her. And I did – I walked away," he said, before breaking down in tears outside Goa's main police station yesterday.'

There was a knock at the door and Hermione walked in. Seeing me there crying, looking down at the cuttings in my lap she came over and put her arms round me, kissing me on the head.

'It was no excuse you know,' she whispered.

'I know,' I said.

I was sobbing now, my head in my hands, my heart breaking for Lord Zander Sinclair and his terrible secret. Through the blur of my tears I stared at the photograph in front of me – a young man and his sister – and I could see that Sara Sinclair looked just like me.

*

As the days of reading and eating wore on I got gradually better. I started going for long walks in the rain – the damp green Englishness washing the taint of Zander and Russia out of me, filling me with a sense of permanence. I was going to need all my strength to wait for Cassian. He was fine, said Stella, but he was staying away. Sometimes, my mouth full of rich malt loaf and my hands round a mug of tea, I knew it was over. Sometimes the damage is too great for repair. But other times, usually early in the morning, hope surged up in me and I thought of the Russian girls receiving their invitations to our Tuscan wedding.

My flat was cold and unlived in when I got back to it, healed, fatter, aimless. It felt like a dead person's flat to which I had been sent to collect a memento. Everything was neatly in its place, covered in dust, icy to my nervous touch – the cups, the table, my books. Fizzy's cups, table and books, that is. I, Alice, would have to reclaim them. I turned on a radiator and lit some candles. I moved things from one place to another, ruffled the bedclothes, ran a bath, sprayed a bit of perfume in the air.

I was sad for Zander and all his bluster. I was sad for Cassian and his steadfastness. But mostly I was sad for Fizzy, tough, clever, brave and cold. Gone, but not forgotten. I lay in the deep hot bath for an hour listening to Ella Fitzgerald turned up loud on the stereo in the other room and then I crawled into bed and slept as though I might never wake.

'Jesus Christ,' I muttered to myself hours later, sleepwalking to the window. 'Who the hell is that.' The incessant buzzing of my doorbell had eventually penetrated my black sleep.

I pulled up the sash and leant out on to the empty 3 a.m. High Street.

Empty but for a black Alpha Spider and a Cassian Vinci.

'Hi,' he said, craning his neck up and smiling. To see him there, so ordinary, so mine, so perfect, I couldn't imagine having doubted him. I realised I had long been expecting him and laughed in exhausted delight.

'Methinks I see thee now thou art so low as one dead at the bottom of a tomb,' I said.

'Let me in then for fuck's sake,' he glowered.

He was home at last.

# THIRTY-ONE

A bat fluttered past my face. The night insects were singing and the silhouetted trees were as still as stone in the heat.

'Stop it! Your Mum might come out!' I giggled to Cassian who had wriggled his hands under my T-shirt and was stroking my breasts. I lay back on the dry grass and looked up at the stars.

'God, Alice Reynolds, you've gone very straight over the past fifteen years. You didn't seem to mind last time,' Cassian laughed, rolling over on to his front to light a cigarette.

I think we both saw him at the same time. A fat hedgehog, his spines made silver under the moon, trundling eagerly towards us, rustling in the grass.

'Bill?' I whispered, astonished.

'Must be his great great great great grandson I think,' Cass told me, leaping up to examine Bill Jr. more closely. Bill, naturally, was having none of this, and shuffled off into the bushes away from the intruders on his lawn. 'It's a good omen,' I said, meaning it.

'Bollocks. Who needs an omen? Pull yourself together,' Cassian laughed, coming back to join me under our tree, kneeling over me now, pinning my hands gently behind my head and kissing my eyes, my neck and my mouth so softly it took all my concentration to feel him. It obliterated the rest of the world, everything that wasn't concerned with being kissed by Cassian Vinci. He pulled my T-shirt up over my head and looked at me as though an angel had landed in his garden. I had never been looked at like that before. And I certainly never imagined I might be able to look back with straightforward love and gratitude.

We had come down to Little Farford with the roof off, Stephan Grappelli playing. We had been taking things very slowly and so it was my first trip to an Old Vicarage that didn't contain Flossy. I was nervous. The same horses were grazing in their fields and even the horizon looked familiar, stretching out across the tops of the trees.

When we arrived Stella came out to meet us, drying her hands on a tea towel, squinting into the sunset. She hugged us both and bent down to pick some mint out of the herb garden for a salad. The air was hazy and humming with insects, a goat was tethered to a post out in the nearest field and the dogs lolled heavily under the magnolia tree, their faces pressed into the grass, tongues hanging out. There was no fear in me these days for them to sense. Not of that kind anyway. The chill inside was welcome after the long drive in the sun and the wind, and I kicked off my shoes to put my bare feet on the cold stone.

'I've put you in Flossy's old room. I hope you

don't mind,' Stella told me, holding my hand briefly, and glancing up the stairs to show me where to go. The house even smelt the same. Cassian ran down to the kitchen and left me to climb the wooden stairs alone, reaching out once more for the thick velvet of the curtains, stroking my hand along the banister that Flossy had clung to, wildly propelling herself round the corner. Her bed stood in its place in the centre of the room, reflected in mirrors on every wall. The boards creaked as I entered, holding tight to my bag, and the curtain fluttered in a hot breeze that came through the open window. I threw my stuff on to the bed and went over to the chest of drawers, opening the top one, half hoping that some of her things might be there – some preposterously dated T-shirts like the 'Relax' one she had wanted to give Sergei, or some nylony lacy tops that Madonna would no longer be seen dead in – not at her age.

But the drawers were empty, apart from some paper lining and a sprig of lavender. I went over to the window and drew in my breath. Out at the bottom of the garden I could see the ghostly figure of Cassian smoking a cigarette, his head bowed, his slouch pronounced like a seventeen-year-old's.

He put a finger to my lips now to stop me saying anything and unbuttoned my jeans, kissing my tummy and my hipbones as he did so, pressing his lips to the inside of my ankle. Once I was naked he lay on top of me, hugging me to him as though I might escape at any moment, burying his face in my hair, squeezing me so tight I could barely breathe.

Completely engulfed in him I found I couldn't be still for another second. I wanted him so badly I felt that a moment lost would kill me. Pushing him on to his back, I was alive with a desperation I didn't recognise as lust. I opened his shirt and kissed his shoulders, his chest. I tore at his belt buckle and took him into my mouth. When I knew he was about to come I moved on top of him, driving him deep inside of me, pushing myself on to him as he grabbed my hips and thrust himself high into my body, closing his eyes in ecstasy.

'God I love you,' he told me, pulling me down on top of him, kissing my neck. 'Marry me.'

Still gasping, I lay down by his side, the grass scratching at my back.

He turned to me, smiling blissfully into my face in the moonlight.

'Please marry me. Will you marry me?' he beamed.

I couldn't meet his gaze. I pulled my clothes quickly back on and held my knees, rocking backwards and forwards, staring towards the house.

'Alice? What is it? God, I mean . . . we don't have to. I just thought . . . I didn't mean to hassle you . . .' Cassian said, taking my head in his hands, trying to force me to look up at him, to look up at the face I had loved for so long, had for nearly fifteen years longed to be this close to. I burst into tears.

Wiping my nose on his shirt sleeve, choking and

spluttering, soaking my face with tears I tried to tell him about my stupid life. I just wanted to be happy like the people in books, I began, and I thought if I could go to Queensbury and make people like me, I could escape from Clapham and Mum's hippies and the squalor of cans of beer and Indian take-away cartons full of cigarette butts. When I met Flossy and then him I thought I was going to be happy for ever – it was what I had always dreamed of. But then it was all snatched away and I was left with these pieces, images, memories of what life could be like.

'At Oxford I wanted to make you like me by being self-confident, posh. I thought I wasn't good enough for you like this. I had to be . . . Fizzy,' I snivelled, and Cassian snorted his derision, wiping the tears from my face with a sad smile.

I told him how Zander had given me the trappings of what I had wanted but without the reality of really belonging and I tried to explain how I had lost myself in my assumed identity to such an extent that I didn't know how to feel things properly any more, how to behave.

I was sobbing uncontrollably now, and Cassian had his arms tightly round me in the dark.

'I just . . . I just wanted to be a princess and marry a prince,' I whispered, smiling a little now, beginning to feel silly. 'And look how long it's taken and how much we've been through before even this glimmer of happiness . . .'

'Oh shut up,' Cassian said, and got to his feet, leaving me there and running towards the house.

'Mum!' he shouted at the kitchen window.

'Where the hell have you been? Did you go to an off licence on the moon? Everyone's here,' Stella complained, leaning out into the night.

'We're here. We're here. Can you pass me that box under the thing in the whatsit?' he asked.

'Just hurry up,' she said, passing it out to him.

Cassian ran back over the lawn towards me gleefully. He knelt down and gazed into my face as he handed me the box.

'Will you be Princess Alice Francesco Maria Vinci?' he asked. 'It's only a courtesy title but it's real in Italy. They always call me Il Principe at my cousin's,' he smiled.

'OK,' I agreed, beaming at him through my tears. 'Perhaps I will then.'

I lifted the flaps of the brown cardboard box and found a huge heap of white tissue paper which I removed piece by scrumpled piece, making a pile on the lawn. Underneath, right at the bottom, was the third coronation crown. I opened my mouth and looked up at Cass, beginning to laugh.

'You didn't?!'

'Oh, but I did,' he grinned, pulling it out and plonking it on my head, all the diamonds lighting up his beautiful face as he did so.

'It's heavy,' I said, giggling stupidly.

'Well, you probably won't have to wear it all that often,' he said, taking it back off and laying it down in the grass.

'Now get a grip on yourself. It's most unseemly all

this dribbling. Your Mum's here and everyone,' he said, dragging me to my feet and leading me into the house.

'No, no wait,' I said, pulling him back down to me. 'I've got something for you too,' I told him, producing a pair of chopsticks from inside my handbag.

'Oh thank you my only darling. I'll treasure them for ever. They must be a hundred years old for God's sake,' he said, looking at them, baffled.

'They are nearly twenty years old,' I told him. 'They are the remains of the magic wand my Dad once gave me. I didn't know it at the time, but I wished for you, and now I've got you I want you to have them.' I was feeling a bit tearful again now.

Cassian hugged me, laughing and promised to eat every Chinese takeaway he ever had with them.

'You look radiant, Fizz,' Mum said as soon as she saw me. She was sitting on a sofa in the drawing room drinking a glass of white wine and asking Stella about all the paintings.

I pointed out, with an adolescent slump into an armchair, that now I was nearly thirty it would be nice if she could address me by my real name, but she just made a face at Hermione and laughed. Mum had changed a lot lately. She was sculpting like mad in her new studio up in the Cairnsham Hall roof and she even looked different. Her clothes were all weirdly the same but now they were very expensive. Her long flowing skirts were all from

Ghost and her silver rings had got fatter and weren't the ones that she had bought from those stalls at Camden Lock. Also, she was all glowing and youthful. Hermione had taught her to ride and she went out pretty much every morning at dawn, kicking up the dew on the outskirts of the estate.

All this time I had been trying to escape from Mum's life and in the end she had made a better job of it than I had. It was an odd admission to make. That Mum and, of course, Dad had seen to it that I had always been extraordinarily privileged. You didn't need a cricket bat and a glass of Pimm's to demonstrate that you were lucky. I realised that now.

'God I'm glad I'm not an elephant,' Tara said, clasping her hands over her enormous stomach. 'Nine months is from hell. Two years would be . . . Christ.'

Aslan brushed her on the head from where he stood behind her chair, his gin and tonic raised to his lips. 'Only another month,' he told her, grinning proudly at the rest of us as though he had more than contributed his fair share to the venture.

I slipped down on to the floor, taking the snuffling and snorting dogs under my arms, ruffling their heads as they wagged their tails and taking the paws they held up to be shaken. 'Lie down,' I told them firmly, and they did.

Cassian bounced into the room, popping open a bottle of champagne and making Aslan flinch to the gun that wasn't at his waist.

'Alice and I have a little announcement to make,' he said. Stella walked in behind him carrying a roast chicken on a tray.